Praise for *Code Name Verity*

Longlisted for the 2013
A 2012 Boston Globe-Horn

"The twists will lead readers to fi ____ ___ ___ ___ turn back
to the beginning to see how the pieces slot perfectly, unexpectedly
into place . . . A carefully researched, precisely written tour de
force; unforgettable and wrenching." —*Kirkus Reviews*, Starred

"This intricate tale is not for the faint of heart, and readers will
be left gasping for the finish, desperate to know how it ends.
With a seemingly unreliable narrator, strong friendship, wonderful historical details, and writing that fairly crackles on the page,
this is an excellent book for thoughtful readers."

—*School Library Journal*, Starred

"This novel positively soars . . . It's outstanding in all its features—
its warm, ebullient characterization; its engagement with historical
facts; its ingenious plot and dramatic suspense; and its intelligent,
vivid writing." —*The Horn Book*, Starred

"If you pick up this book, it will be some time before you put your
dog-eared, tear-stained copy back down . . . Both crushingly sad
and hugely inspirational, this plausible, unsentimental novel will
thoroughly move even the most cynical of readers."

—*Booklist*, Starred

"Wein (*The Empty Kingdom*) serves up a riveting and often brutal
tale of WWII action and espionage with a powerful friendship
at its core . . . Queenie's deliberately rambling and unreliable
narration keeps the story engaging, and there are enough action
sequences and well-delivered twists (including a gut-wrenching
climax and late revelations that will have readers returning to
reread the first half of the book) to please readers of all stripes."

—*Publishers Weekly*, Starred

"This innovative spy tale flips the standard progression of the rescue novel to brilliant effect, beginning with a heroine whose doom seems inevitable and then ratcheting up the tension to almost unbearable levels through the sparing introduction of hope . . . This is a dense novel built to be savored, with a vivid friendship at its core and courage and heartbreak infused into every struggle." —*Bulletin of the Center for Children's Books*, Starred

"Wein's story ducks and dodges ingeniously, giving us multiple double-takes and surprises, ratcheting up tension and emotional power as the story moves towards its conclusion. It is superbly plotted, and rereading it only confirms the abundance of Wein's art as a subtle weaver of fiction . . . It is prize-worthy. And a terrific read, to boot." —*Toronto Star*

"*Code Name Verity* . . . is a fiendishly plotted mind game of a novel, the kind you have to read twice. The first time you just devour the story of girl-pilot-and-girl-spy friendship and the thrill of flying a plane and the horrors of Nazi torture and the bravery of French Resistance fighters and you force yourself to slow down, but you don't want to, because you're terrified these beautiful, vibrant characters are doomed. The second time, you read more slowly, proving to yourself that yes, the clues were there all along for you to solve the giant puzzle you weren't even aware was constructed around you." —*The New York Times*

"This heart-in-your-mouth adventure has it all: a complex plot, a vivid sense of place and time, and resonant themes of friendship and courage. Practical Maddie and mischievous Julie are brought to life through their vibrant narrative voices and intriguing backstories . . . In this powerful work of historical fiction, Julie and Maddie need never fear 'flying alone'; the reader will soar with them until the final page." —*The Washington Post*

CODE NAME
VERITY

ELIZABETH WEIN

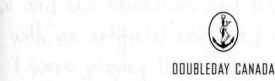

DOUBLEDAY CANADA

Doubleday Canada and colophon are registered trademarks
of Random House of Canada Limited.

Library and Archives Canada Cataloguing in Publication

Wein, Elizabeth

        Code name Verity / Elizabeth Wein.

Includes bibliographical references.
Issued also in an electronic format.
ISBN 978-0-385-67654-0 (bound).--ISBN 978-0-385-67657-1 (pbk.)

        1. World War, 1939-1945--Prisoners and prisons, German--
Juvenile fiction. I. Title.

PZ7.W4358Cp 2012   j823'.92   C2011-908493-7

Published in Canada by Doubleday Canada,
a division of Random House of Canada Limited

www.randomhouse.ca

10 9 8 7 6 5 4 3 2 1

For Amanda
—we make a sensational team—

Passive resisters must
understand that they are
as important as saboteurs.

—*SOE Secret Operations Manual,*
"Methods of Passive Resistance"

PART I
VERITY

I AM A COWARD.

I wanted to be heroic and I pretended I was. I have always been good at pretending. I spent the first twelve years of my life playing at the Battle of Stirling Bridge with my five big brothers—and even though I am a girl, they let me be William Wallace, who is supposed to be one of our ancestors, because I did the most rousing battle speeches. God, I tried hard last week. My God, *I tried.* But now I know I am a coward. After the ridiculous deal I made with SS-Hauptsturmführer von Linden, I know I am a coward. And I'm going to give you anything you ask, everything I can remember. Absolutely *Every Last Detail.*

Here is the deal we made. I'm putting it down to keep it straight in my own mind. "Let's try this," the Hauptsturmführer said to me. "How could you be bribed?" And I said I wanted my clothes back.

It seems petty, now. I am sure he was expecting my answer to be something defiant—"Give me Freedom" or "Victory"—or something generous, like "Stop toying with that wretched French Resistance laddie and give him a dignified and merciful death." Or at least something more directly connected to my present circumstance, like "Please let me go to sleep" or "Feed me" or "Get rid of this sodding iron rail you have kept tied against my spine for the past three days." But I was prepared to go sleepless and starving and upright for a good while yet if only I didn't have to do it in my underwear—rather foul and damp at times, and SO EMBARRASSING. The warmth and dignity of my flannel skirt and woolly sweater are worth far more to me now than patriotism or integrity.

So von Linden sold my clothes back to me piece by piece. Except my scarf and stockings, of course, which were taken away early on to prevent me strangling myself with them (I did try). The pullover cost me *four sets of wireless code*—the full lot of encoding poems, passwords, and frequencies. Von Linden let me have the pullover back on credit right away. It was waiting for me in my cell when they finally untied me at the end of that dreadful three days, though I was incapable of getting the damned thing on at first; but even just dragged over top of me like a shawl it was comforting. Now that I've managed to get into it at last, I don't think I shall ever take it off again. The skirt and blouse cost rather less than the pullover, and it was only one code set apiece for my shoes.

There are eleven sets in all. The last one was supposed to buy my slip. Notice how he's worked it that I get the clothes from the *outside in*, so I have to go through the torment of *undressing* in front of everybody every time another item is given back to me. He's the only one who doesn't watch—he threatened to take it all away from me again when I suggested he was missing a fabulous show. It was the first time the accumulated damage has really been on display, and I wish he would have *looked* at his masterpiece—at my arms particularly—also the first time I have been able to stand in a while, which I wanted to show off to him. Anyway, I have decided to do without my slip, which also saves me the trouble of stripping again to put it on, and in exchange for the last code set I have bought myself a supply of ink and paper—and some time.

Von Linden has said I have two weeks and that I can have as much paper as I need. All I have to do is cough up everything I can remember about the British War Effort. And I'm going to. Von Linden resembles Captain Hook in that he is rather an upright sort of gentleman in spite of his being a brute, and I am quite Pan-like in my naïve confidence that he will play by the rules and keep his word. So far, he *has*. To start off my confession, he gave me this lovely creamy embossed stationery from the Château de Bordeaux, the Bordeaux Castle Hotel, which is what this building used to be. (I would not have believed a French hotel could become so forbiddingly bleak if I had not seen the barred shutters and padlocked doors with my own eyes. But you have also managed to make the whole beautiful city of Ormaie look bleak.)

It is rather a lot to be resting on a single code set, but in addition to my treasonous account I have also promised von Linden my soul, although I do not think he takes this seriously. Anyway, it will be a relief to write *anything* that isn't connected with code. I'm so dreadfully sick of spewing wireless code. Only when we'd put all those lists to paper did I realize what a huge supply of code I do actually have in me.

It's jolly astonishing, really.

YOU STUPID NAZI BASTARDS.

I'm just damned. I am utterly and completely damned. You'll shoot me at the end no matter what I do, because that's what you do to enemy agents. It's what *we* do to enemy agents. After I write this confession, if you *don't* shoot me and I ever make it home, I'll be tried and shot as a collaborator anyway. But I look at all the dark and twisted roads ahead and this is the easy one, the obvious one. What's in my future—a tin of kerosene poured down my throat and a match held to my lips? Scalpel and acid, like the Resistance boy who won't talk? My living skeleton packed up in a cattle wagon with two hundred desperate others, carted off God knows where, to die of thirst before we get there? No. I'm not traveling those roads. This is the easiest. The others are too frightening even to look down.

I am going to write in English. I don't have the vocabulary for a warfare account in French, and I can't write fluently enough in German. Someone will have to translate for Hauptsturmführer von Linden. Fräulein Engel can do it. She speaks English very well. She is the one who explained to me that paraffin and kerosene are the same thing. We call it paraffin at home, but the Americans call it kerosene, and that is more or less what the word sounds like in French and German too.

(About the paraffin, kerosene, whatever it is. I do not really believe you have a liter of kerosene to waste on me. Or do you get it on the black market? How do you claim the expense? *1 lt. highly explosive fuel for execution of British spy.* Anyway, I will do my best to spare you the expense.)

One of the first items on the very long list I have been given to think about including in my confession is Location of British Airfields for Invasion of Europe. Fräulein Engel will confirm that I burst out laughing when I read that. You really think I know a damned thing about where the Allies are planning to launch their invasion of Nazi-occupied Europe? I am in the Special Operations Executive because I can speak French and German and am good at making up stories, and I am a prisoner in the Ormaie Gestapo HQ because I have no sense of direction whatsoever. Bearing in mind that the people who trained me encouraged my blissful ignorance of airfields just so I *couldn't* tell you such a thing if you *did* catch me, and not forgetting that I wasn't even told the name of the airfield we took off from when I came here: let me remind you that I had been in France less than 48 hours before that obliging agent of yours had to stop me being run over by a

French van full of French chickens because I'd looked the wrong way before crossing the street. Which shows how cunning the Gestapo are. "This person I've pulled from beneath the wheels of certain death was expecting traffic to travel on the left side of the road. Therefore she must be British, and is likely to have parachuted into Nazi-occupied France out of an Allied plane. I shall now arrest her as a spy."

So, I have no sense of direction. In some of us it is a TRAGIC FLAW, and there is no point in me trying to direct you to Locations of Any Airfields Anywhere. Not without someone giving me the coordinates. I could make them up, perhaps, and be convincing about it, to buy myself more time, but you would catch on eventually.

Aircraft Types in Operational Use is also on this list of things I am to tell you. God, this is a funny list. If I knew or cared a damned thing about aircraft types I would be flying planes for the Air Transport Auxiliary, like Maddie, the pilot who dropped me here, or working as a fitter or a mechanic. Not cravenly coughing up facts and figures for the Gestapo. (I will not mention my cowardice again because it is beginning to make me feel indecent. Also I do not want you to get bored and take this handsome paper away and go back to holding my face in a basin of ice water until I pass out.)

No, wait, I do know some aircraft types. I will tell you all the aircraft types I know, starting with the Puss Moth. That was the first aircraft my friend Maddie ever flew. In fact it was the first aircraft she ever had a ride in, and even the first one she ever got close to. And the story of how I came to be here starts with Maddie. I don't think I'll ever know how I ended up carrying her National Registration card and pilot's license instead of my own ID when you picked me up, but if I tell you about Maddie you'll understand why we flew here together.

AIRCRAFT TYPES

Maddie is properly Margaret Brodatt. You have her ID, you know her name. Brodatt is not a Northern English name; it is a Russian name, I think, because her grandfather came from Russia. But Maddie is pure Stockport. Unlike me, she has an excellent sense of direction. She can navigate by the stars, and by dead reckoning, but I think she learned to use her sense of direction properly because her granddad gave her a motorbike for her sixteenth birthday. Then Maddie was away out of Stockport and up the unmade lanes on the high moors of the Pennine hills. You can see the Pennines all around the city of Stockport, green and bare with fast-moving stripes of cloud and sunlight gliding overhead like a Technicolor moving picture. I know because I went on leave for a weekend and stayed with Maddie and her grandparents, and she took me on her motorbike up the Dark Peak, one of the most wonderful afternoons of my life. It was winter and the sun came out only for about five minutes and even then the sleet didn't stop falling—it was because the weather was forecast so unflyable that she had the three days off. But for five minutes Cheshire seemed green and sparkling. Maddie's granddad owns a bike shop and he got some black market petrol for her specially when I visited. I am putting this down (even though it's nothing to do with Aircraft Types) because it proves that I know what I'm talking about when I describe what it was like for Maddie to be alone at the top of the world, deafened by the roar of four winds and two cylinders, with all the Cheshire plain and its green fields and red chimneys thrown at her feet like a tartan picnic blanket.

Maddie had a friend called Beryl who had left school, and in the summer of 1938 Beryl was working in the cotton mill at Ladderal, and they liked to take Sunday picnics on

Maddie's motorbike because it was the only time they saw each other anymore. Beryl rode with her arms tight around Maddie's waist, like I did that time. No goggles for Beryl, or for me, though Maddie had her own. On this particular June Sunday they rode up through the lanes between the drystone walls that Beryl's laboring ancestors had built, and over the top of Highdown Rise, with mud up their bare shins. Beryl's best skirt was ruined that day, and her dad made her pay for a new one out of her next week's wages.

"I love your granddad," Beryl shouted in Maddie's ear. "I wish he was mine." (I wished that too.) "Fancy him giving you a Silent Superb for your birthday!"

"It's not so silent," Maddie shouted back over her shoulder. "It wasn't new when I got it, and it's five years old now. I've had to rebuild the engine this year."

"Won't your granddad do it for you?"

"He wouldn't even give it to me until I'd taken the engine apart. I have to do it myself or I can't have it."

"I still love him," Beryl shouted.

They tore along the high green lanes of Highdown Rise, along tractor ruts that nearly bounced them over drystone field walls and into a bed of mire and nettles and sheep. I remember and I know what it must have been like. Every now and then, around a corner or at the crest of a hump in the hill, you can see the bare green chain of the Pennines stretching serenely to the west, or the factory chimneys of south Manchester scrawling the blue north sky with black smoke.

"And you'll have a skill," Beryl yelled.

"A what?"

"A *skill.*"

"Fixing engines!" Maddie howled.

"It's a skill. Better than loading shuttles."

"You're getting paid for loading shuttles," Maddie yelled back. "I don't get paid." The lane ahead was rutted with rain-filled potholes. It looked like a miniature landscape of Highland lochs. Maddie slowed the bike to a putter and finally had to stop. She put her feet down on solid earth, her skirt rucked up to her thighs, still feeling the Superb's reliable and familiar rumble all through her body. "Who'll give a girl a job fixing engines?" Maddie said. "Gran wants me to learn to type. At least you're earning."

They had to get off the bike to walk it along the ditch-filled lane. Then there was another rise, and they came to a farm gate set between field boundaries, and Maddie leaned the motorbike against the stone wall so they could eat their sandwiches. They looked at each other and laughed at the mud.

"What'll your dad say!" Maddie exclaimed.

"What'll your gran!"

"She's used to it."

Beryl's word for picnic was "baggin," Maddie said. Doorstep slices of granary loaf Beryl's auntie baked for three families every Wednesday, and pickled onions as big as apples. Maddie's sandwiches were on rye bread from the baker's in Reddyke, where her grandmother sent her every Friday. The pickled onions stopped Maddie and Beryl having a conversation, because chewing made so much crunching in their heads they couldn't hear each other talk, and they had to be careful swallowing so they wouldn't be asphyxiated by an accidental blast of vinegar. (Perhaps Chief-Storm-Captain von Linden might find pickled onions useful as a persuasive tool. And your prisoners would get fed at the same time.)

(Fräulein Engel instructs me to put down here, for Captain von Linden to know when he reads it, that I have wasted 20 minutes of the time given me because here in my story I laughed at my own stupid joke about the pickled onions and broke the pencil point. We had to wait for someone to bring a knife to sharpen it because Miss Engel is not allowed to leave me by myself. And then I wasted another 5 minutes weeping after I snapped off the new point because Miss E. had sharpened it very close to my face, flicking the shavings into my eyes while SS-Scharführer Thibaut held my head still, and it made me terribly nervous. I am not laughing or crying now and will try not to press so hard after this.)

At any rate, think of Maddie before the war, free and at home with her mouth full of pickled onion—she could only point and choke when a spluttering, smoking aircraft hove into view above their heads and circled the field they were overlooking as they perched on the gate. That aircraft was a Puss Moth.

I can tell you a bit about Puss Moths. They are fast, light monoplanes—you know, only one set of wings—the Tiger Moth is a biplane and has two sets (another type I have just remembered). You can fold the Puss Moth's wings back for trucking the machine around or storing. It has a super view from the cockpit, and can seat two passengers as well as the pilot. I have been a passenger in one a couple of times. I think the upgraded version is called a Leopard Moth (that's three aircraft I have named in one paragraph!).

This Puss Moth circling the field at Highdown Rise, the first Puss Moth Maddie ever came across, was choking to death. Maddie said it was like having a ringside seat at the circus. With the plane at three hundred feet, she and Beryl could see every detail of the machine in miniature: every wire, every strut of its pair of canvas wings, the flicker of the wooden propeller blades as they spun ineffectively in the wind. Great blue clouds of smoke billowed from the exhaust.

"He's on fire!" screamed Beryl, in a fit of delighted panic.

"He's not on fire. He's burning oil," Maddie said, because she knows these things. "If he has any sense, he'll shut everything off and it'll stop. Then he can glide down."

They watched. Maddie's prediction came true: the engine stopped and the smoke drifted away, and now the pilot was clearly planning to put his damaged rig down in the field right in front of them. It was a grazing field, unplowed, unmown, without any livestock in it. The wings above their heads cut out the sun for a second with the sweep and billow of a sailing yacht. The aircraft's final pass pulled all the litter of their lunch out into the field, brown crusts and brown paper fluttering in the blue smoke like the devil's confetti.

Maddie said it would have been a good landing if it had been on an aerodrome. In the field the wounded flying machine bounced haplessly over the unmown grass for thirty yards. Then it tipped up gracefully onto its nose.

Maddie broke into applause. Beryl grabbed her hands and smacked one of them.

"You gormless cow! He might be hurt! Oh, what shall we do?"

Maddie hadn't meant to clap. She had done it without thinking. I can picture her blowing the curling black hair out of her eyes, with her lower lip jutting out before she jumped down from the gate and hopped over the green tussocks to the downed plane.

There were no flames. Maddie scaled her way up the Puss Moth's nose to get at the cockpit, and put one of her hobnailed shoes through the fabric that covered the fuselage (I think that's what the body of the plane is called), and I'll bet she cringed; she hadn't meant to do that either. She was feeling very hot and bothered by the time she unlatched the door, expecting a lecture from the aircraft's owner, and was shamefully relieved to find the pilot hanging upside down in half-undone harness straps and clearly stone-cold unconscious. Maddie glanced over the alien engine controls. No oil pressure (she told me all this). Throttle, out. Off. Good enough. Maddie untangled the harness and let the pilot slither to the ground.

Beryl was there to catch the dragging weight of the pilot's senseless body. It was easier for Maddie to get down off the plane than it had been for her to get up, just a light hop to the ground. She unbuckled the pilot's helmet and goggles; she and Beryl had both done first aid in Girl Guides, for all that's worth, and knew enough to make sure the casualty could breathe.

Beryl began to giggle.

"Who's the gormless cow!" Maddie exclaimed.

"It's a girl!" Beryl laughed. "It's a girl!"

Beryl stayed with the unconscious girl pilot while Maddie rode her Silent Superb to the farm to get help. She found two big strong lads her own age shoveling cow dung, and the farmer's wife sorting first early potatoes and cursing at a cotillion of girls who were doing a huge jigsaw on the old stone kitchen floor (it was Sunday, or they'd have been boiling laundry). A rescue squad was dispatched. Maddie was sent farther down the lane on her bike to the bottom of the hill, where there was a pub and a phone box.

"She'll need an ambulance, tha knows, love," the farmer's wife had said to Maddie kindly. "She'll need to go to hospital if she's been flying an airplane."

The words rattled around in Maddie's head all the way to the telephone. Not "She'll need to go to hospital if she's been injured," but, "She'll need to go to hospital if she's been flying an airplane."

A flying girl! thought Maddie. A girl flying an airplane!

No, she corrected herself; a girl *not* flying a plane. A girl tipping up a plane in a sheep field.

But she flew it first. She had to be able to fly it in order to land it (or crash it).

The leap seemed logical to Maddie.

I've never crashed my motorbike, she thought. I could fly an airplane.

There are a few more types of aircraft that I know, but what comes to mind is the Lysander. That is the plane Maddie was flying when she dropped me here. She was actually supposed to land the plane, not dump me out of it in the air. We got fired at on the way in, and for a while the tail was in flames and she couldn't control it properly, and she made me bail out before she tried to land. I didn't see her come down. But you showed me the photos you took at the site, so I know she *has* crashed an airplane by now. Still, you can hardly blame it on the pilot when her plane gets hit by antiaircraft fire.

SOME BRITISH SUPPORT FOR ANTI-SEMITISM

The Puss Moth crash was on Sunday. Beryl was back to work at the mill in Ladderal the next day. My heart twists up and shrivels with envy so black and painful that I spoiled half this page with tears before I realized they were falling, to think of Beryl's long life of loading shuttles and raising snotty babies with a beery lad in an industrial suburb of Manchester. Of course that was in 1938 and they have all been bombed to bits since, so perhaps Beryl and her kiddies are dead already, in which case my tears of envy are very selfish. I am sorry about the paper. Miss E. is looking over my shoulder as I write, and tells me not to interrupt my story with any more apologies.

Over the next week Maddie pieced together the pilot's story in a storm of newspaper clippings with the mental wolfishness of Lady Macbeth. The pilot's name was Dympna Wythenshawe (I remember her name because it is so silly). She was the spoiled youngest daughter of Sir Somebody-or-other Wythenshawe. On Friday there was a flurry of outrage in the evening paper because as soon as she was released from hospital she started giving joyrides in her other airplane (a Dragon Rapide—how clever am I) while the Puss Moth was being mended. Maddie sat on the floor in her granddad's shed next to her beloved Silent Superb, which needed a lot of tinkering to keep it in a fit state for weekend outings, and fought with the newspaper. There were pages and pages of gloom about the immediate likelihood of war between Japan and China, and the growing likelihood of war in Europe. The nose-down Puss Moth in the farmer's field on Highdown Rise was last week's news, though; there were no pictures of the plane on Friday, only a grinning mug shot of the aviatrix herself, looking happy and windblown and much, much prettier than that idiot Fascist Oswald Mosley, whose sneering face glared out at Maddie from the prime spot at the top of the page. Maddie covered him up with her mug of cocoa and thought about the quickest way to get to Catton Park Aerodrome. It was a good distance, but tomorrow was Saturday again.

Maddie was sorry, the next morning, that she hadn't paid more attention to the Oswald Mosley story. He was there, there in Stockport, speaking in front of St. Mary's on the edge of the Saturday market, and his idiot Fascist followers were having their own march to meet him, starting at the town hall and ending up at St. Mary's, causing traffic and human mayhem. They had by then toned down their anti-Semitism a bit and this rally was supposed to be in the name of Peace, believe it or not, trying to convince everybody that it would be a good idea to keep things cordial with the idiot Fascists in Germany. The Mosleyites were no longer allowed to wear their tastelessly symbolic black shirts—there was now a law in place about public marching in political uniforms, mainly to stop the Mosleyites causing riots like the ones they started with their marches through Jewish neighborhoods in London. But they were going along to cheer for Mosley anyway. There was a happy crowd of his lovers and an angry crowd of his haters. There were women with baskets trying to get their shopping done at the Saturday market. There were policemen. There was livestock—some of the policemen were on horseback, and there was a herd of sheep being shunted through, also on the way to market, and a horse-drawn milk cart stuck in the middle of the sheep. There were dogs. Probably there were cats and rabbits and chickens and ducks too.

Maddie could not get across the Stockport Road (I don't know what it's really called. Perhaps that's its right name because it's the main road in from the south. You should not rely on any of my directions). Maddie waited and waited on the edge of the simmering crowd, looking for a gap. After twenty minutes she began to get annoyed. There were people pressing against her from behind now, as well. She tried to turn her motorbike around, walking it by the handlebars, and ran into someone.

"Oi! Mind where you're pushing that bike!"

"Sorry!" Maddie looked up.

It was a crowd of thugs, black-shirted for the rally even though they could get arrested for it, hair slicked back with

Brylcreem like a bunch of airmen. They looked Maddie up and down gleefully, pretty sure she would be easy bait.

"Nice bike."

"Nice legs!"

One of them giggled through his nose. "Nice ___."

He used an ugly, unspeakable word, and I won't bother to write it because I don't think any of you would know what it means in English, and I certainly do not know the French or German for it. The thuggish lad used it like a goading stick, and it worked. Maddie shoved the front wheel of the bike past the one she had hit in the first place, and knocked into him again, and he grabbed the handlebars with his own big fists between her hands.

Maddie held on. They struggled for a moment over the motorbike. The boy refused to let go, and his mates laughed.

"What's a lass like you need with a big toy like this? Where'd you get it?"

"At the bike shop, where d'you think!"

"Brodatt's," said one of them. There was only one on that side of town.

"Sells bikes to Jews, he does."

"Maybe it's a Jew's bike."

You probably don't know it, but Manchester and its smoky suburbs have got quite a large Jewish population, and nobody minds. Well, obviously some idiot Fascists do mind, but I think you see what I mean. They came from Russia and Poland and later Roumania and Austria, all Eastern Europe, all through the nineteenth century. The bike shop whose customers were in question happened to be Maddie's grand-dad's bike shop that he'd had for the last thirty years. He'd done quite well out of it, well enough to keep Maddie's stylish gran in the manner to which she is accustomed, and they live in a large old house in Grove Green on the edge of the city and have a gardener and a daily girl to do the house-keeping. Anyway, when this lot started slinging venom at Maddie's granddad's shop, Maddie unwisely engaged in battle with them and said, "Does it always take all three of you to complete a thought? Or can you each do it without your mates if you have enough time to think it over first?"

They pushed the bike over. It took Maddie down with it. Because bullying is what idiot Fascists like best.

But there was a swell of noisy outrage from other people in the crowded street, and the little gang of thugs laughed again and moved on. Maddie could hear the one lad's distinctive nasal whinny even after his back had become anonymous.

More people than had knocked her down came to her aid, a laborer and a girl with a pram, and a kiddie and two women with shopping baskets. They hadn't fought or interfered, but they helped Maddie up and dusted her off, and the workman ran loving hands down the Silent Superb's fender. "Tha's not hurt, miss?"

"Nice bike!"

That was the kiddie. His mum said quickly, "Oi, you hush," because it was a perfect echo of the black-shirted youth who had pushed Maddie over.

"'Tis nice," said the man.

"It's getting old," Maddie said modestly, but pleased.

"Ruddy vandals."

"Tha wants to get those knees seen to, love," advised one of the ladies with baskets.

Maddie thought to herself, thinking about airplanes: Just you wait, you idiot Fascists. I am going to get me a bigger toy than this bike.

Maddie's faith in humanity was restored and she pushed her way out of the crowd and set off down the cobbled back lanes of Stockport. There was no one here but kiddies playing street football in screaming bunches, and harassed big sisters with their hair tied up in dustcloths, ungraciously shaking out rugs and scrubbing front doorsteps while their mothers shopped. I swear I shall weep with envy if I keep thinking about them, bombed to bits or otherwise.

Fräulein Engel has been looking over my shoulder once again and has asked me to stop writing "idiot Fascist," because she thinks Hauptsturmführer von Linden will not like it. I think she is a bit scared of Capt. von Linden (who can blame her?), and I think Scharführer Thibaut is scared of him too.

LOCATION OF BRITISH AIRFIELDS

I can't really believe you need me to tell you that Catton Park Aerodrome is in Ilsmere Port, because for the last ten years it has been just about the busiest airfield in the north of England. They build planes there. Before the war it had a posh civil flying club, and it has also been a Royal Air Force base for years. The local Royal Air Force squadron has been flying bombers from that field since 1936. Your guess is as good as mine, and probably a lot better, as to what they are using it for now (I don't doubt it's surrounded with barrage balloons and antiaircraft guns). When Maddie pulled up there that Saturday morning she stood for a moment goggling gormlessly (her word), first at the car park, which contained the biggest collection of expensive cars she'd ever seen in one place, and then at the sky, which contained the biggest collection of airplanes. She leaned against the fence to watch. After a few minutes she worked out that most of the planes seemed to fly in a kind of pattern, taking it in turns to land and roar away again. Half an hour later she was still watching, and could tell that one of the pilots was a beginner and his machine always bounced six feet in the air after touching down before properly connecting with the ground, and another one was practicing absolutely insane aerobatic maneuvers, and another one was giving rides to people—once around the airfield, five minutes in the air, back down, hand over your two shillings and swap your goggles with the next customer, please.

It was a very overwhelming place in that uneasy peacetime when military and civil pilots took it in turns to use the runway, but Maddie was determined, and followed the signs to the flying club. She found the person she was looking for by accident—easily, really, because Dympna Wythenshawe was the only idle aviator on the field, lounging by herself in a long row of faded deck chairs lined up in front of the pilots' clubhouse. Maddie did not recognize the pilot. She looked nothing like either the glamorous mug shot from the papers or the unconscious helmeted casualty she had been when Maddie left her that Sunday past. Dympna didn't recognize Maddie, either, but she called out jovially, "Are you hoping for a spin?"

She spoke in a cultured accent of money and privilege. Rather like mine, without the Scottish burr. Probably not as privileged as mine, but more moneyed. Anyway, it made Maddie instantly feel like a serving girl.

"I'm looking for Dympna Wythenshawe," said Maddie. "I just wanted to see how she's getting on after—after last week."

"She's fine." The elegant creature smiled pleasantly.

"I found her," Maddie blurted.

"She's right as rain," Dympna said, offering a languid lily-white hand that had certainly never changed an oil filter (my lily-white hands *have*, I would like you to know, but only under strict supervision). "She's right as rain. She's me."

Maddie shook hands.

"Take a pew," Dympna drawled (just imagine she's me, raised in a castle and educated at a Swiss boarding school, only a lot taller and not sniveling all the time). She waved to the empty deck chairs. "There's plenty of room."

She was dressed as though she were going on safari, and contrived to be glamorous about it, too. She gave private instruction as well as joyrides. She was the only woman pilot at the aerodrome, certainly the only woman instructor.

"When my darling Puss Moth's mended I'll give you a ride," she offered Maddie; and Maddie, who is nothing if not calculating, asked if she could see the plane.

They had taken it to bits and carted it home from Highdown Rise, and now a team of boys and men in greasy overalls were working at putting it back together in one of a long line of high workshop sheds. The Puss Moth's lovely engine (this is Maddie talking; she is a bit mad) had only HALF THE POWER of Maddie's motorbike. They were cleaning the bits of turf out of it with wire brushes. It lay on a square of oilcloth in a thousand gleaming pieces. Maddie knew instantly she had come to the right place.

"Oh, can I watch?" she said. And Dympna, who never got her hands dirty, could nevertheless name every cylinder and valve that was lying on the floor, and let Maddie have a go painting the new fabric (over the fuselage she'd kicked in) with a mess of plastic goo called "dope," which smelled like pickled onions. After an hour had gone by and Maddie was still there asking what all the parts of the plane were for and what they were called, the mechanics gave her a wire brush and let her help.

Maddie said she always felt very safe, after that, flying

in Dympna's Puss Moth, because she had helped to put its engine back together herself.

"When are you coming back?" Dympna asked her over oily mugs of tea, four hours later.

"It's too far for me to visit very often," Maddie confessed sadly. "I live in Stockport. I help my granddad in his office in the week, and he pays for my petrol, but I can't come here every weekend."

"You are the luckiest girl alive," Dympna said. "As soon as the Puss Moth's flying again I'm moving both my planes to the new airfield at Oakway. It's right by Ladderal Mill, where your friend Beryl works. There's a big gala at Oakway next Saturday, for the airfield's official opening. I'll come and collect you, and you can watch the fun from the pilots' stand. Beryl can come along too."

That's two airfields I've located for you.

I am getting a bit wobbly because no one has let me eat or drink since yesterday and I have been writing for nine hours. So now I am going to risk tossing this pencil across the table and have a good howl

This pen does nt work. Sorry ink blots. Is this test or punishmt
I want my pencil back

*[Note to SS-Hauptsturmführer Amadeus von Linden,
translated from the German]*

The English Flight Officer is telling the truth.
The ink given her was too old/too thick to use
and clotted badly in the pen nib. It has now been
thinned and I am testing it here to affirm that it is
acceptable for writing.

  Heil Hitler!
  SS-Scharführer Etienne Thibaut

You ignorant Quisling *bastard*, SS-Scharführer Etienne
Thibaut, I AM SCOTTISH.

  The comedians Laurel and Hardy, I mean Underling-
Sergeant Thibaut and On-Duty-Female-Guard Engel, have
been very jolly at my expense over the inferior ink Thibaut
found for me to write with. He ruddy well had to thin it with
kerosene, didn't he. He was annoyed when I made a fuss over
the ink, and he didn't seem to believe me about the clogged
pen, so I became *rather upset* when he went away and came

back with a liter of kerosene. When he brought in the tin I knew straight away what it was, and Miss E. had to throw a jug of water in my face to stop my hysterics. Now she is sitting across the table from me lighting and relighting her cigarette and flicking the matches in my direction to make me jump, but she is laughing as she does it.

She was anxious last night because she didn't think I'd coughed up enough facts to count as a proper little Judas yesterday. Again I think that she was worrying about von Linden's reaction, as she is the one who has to translate what I write for him. As it turned out, he said it was an "interesting overview of the situation in Britain over the long term" and a "curious individual perspective" (he was testing my German a bit while we talked about it). Also I think he hopes I will do some ratting on Monsieur Laurel and Mademoiselle Hardy. He does not trust Thibaut because Thibaut is French, and he does not trust Engel because Engel is a woman. I am to be given water throughout the day while I write (to drink, as well as to prevent hysterics) *and* a blanket. For a blanket in my cold little room, SS-Hauptsturmführer Amadeus von Linden, I would without remorse or hesitation rat on my heroic ancestor William Wallace, Guardian of Scotland.

I know your other prisoners despise me. Thibaut took me to . . . I don't know what you call it when you make me watch, is it *instruction*? To remind me how fortunate I am, perhaps? After my tantrum yesterday, when I had stopped writing and before I was allowed to eat, on the way back to my cell, Scharführer Thibaut made me stop and watch while Jacques was being questioned again. (I don't know what his real name is; *Jacques* is what the French citizens all call each other in *A Tale of Two Cities*, and it seems appropriate.) That boy *hates* me. It makes no difference that I, too, am strapped securely to my own chair with piano wire or something, and gasp with sobs on his account and look away the whole time except when Thibaut holds my head in place. Jacques knows, they all know, that I am the collaborator, the only coward among them. No one else has given out a single scrap of code—let alone ELEVEN SETS—not to mention a written confession. He spits at me as they drag him out.

"Little Scottish piece of shit."

It sounds so pretty in French, *p'tit morceau de merde écossaise*. Singlehandedly I have brought down the 700-year-strong Auld Alliance between France and Scotland.

There is another Jacques, a girl, who whistles "Scotland the Brave" if we are taken past each other (my prison is an antechamber to the suite they use for interrogations), or some other battle hymn associated with my heritage, and she spits too. They all detest me. It is not the same as their hatred for Thibaut, the Quisling turncoat, who is their countryman and is working for the enemy. I am your enemy too, I should be one of them. But I am beyond contempt. A wee Scots piece o' shite.

Don't you think it makes them stronger when you give them someone to despise? They look at me sniveling in the corner and think, "*Mon Dieu*. Don't ever let me be like *her*."

THE CIVIL AIR GUARD (SOME FIGURES)

That heading looks terrifically official. I feel better already. Like a proper little Judas.

Suppose you were a girl in Stockport in 1938, raised by loving and indulgent grandparents, and rather obsessed with engines. Suppose you decided you wanted to learn to fly: really *fly*. You wanted to fly airplanes.

A three years' course with Air Service Training would

have cost you over a thousand pounds. I don't know what Maddie's granddad would have earned in a year back then. He did fairly well with his motorbike business, as I have said; not so well during the Depression, but still, by our standards at that time, anyone would have considered his a good living. At any rate it would have cost him most of his year's earnings to buy Maddie one year of flying lessons. She got her first flight free, an hour's excursion in Dympna's restored Puss Moth on a glorious clear summer evening of crisp wind and long light, and saw the Pennines from above for the first time. Beryl got to come along for the ride, since she had been as much involved in Dympna's rescue as Maddie had, but Beryl had to sit in the very back and couldn't see so well and was sick into her handbag. She thanked Dympna but never went for another flight.

And of course, that was a joyride, not a lesson. Maddie couldn't afford lessons. But she made Oakway Aerodrome her own. Oakway came into being in parallel with Maddie's crush on airplanes—I want bigger toys, she'd wished, and hey presto, a week later, there was Oakway. It was only a fifteen-minute motorbike ride from home. The aerodrome was so spanking new that the mechanics there were happy to have an extra pair of capable hands around. Maddie was out every Saturday that summer tinkering with engines and doping fabric wings and making friends. Then, in October, her persistence suddenly, unexpectedly paid off. That is when we started the Civil Air Guard.

I say we—I mean Britain. Just about every flying club in the kingdom joined in, and so many thousands of people applied—free flight training!—that they could only take about a tenth of them. And only one in twenty of those were women. But Maddie got lucky again, because all the engineers and mechanics and instructors at Oakway knew and liked her now, and she got glowing recommendations for being quick and committed and knowing all about oil levels. She wasn't immediately any better than any other pilot who trained at Oakway with the Civil Air Guard. But she wasn't any worse, either. She made her first solo flight in the first week of the new year, between snow flurries.

Look at the timing, though. Maddie started flying in late October 1938 ... Hitler (you will notice that I have thought better of my colorful descriptive terms for the Führer and carefully scratched them all out) invaded Poland on 1 September 1939 and Britain declared war on Germany two days later. Maddie flew the practical test for her "A" license, the basic pilot's license, six months before all civil aircraft were grounded in August. After that, most of those planes were taken into government service. Both of Dympna's planes were requisitioned by the Air Ministry for communications, and she was mad as a cat about it.

Days before Britain declared war on Germany, Maddie flew by herself to the other side of England, skimming the tops of the Pennines and avoiding the barrage balloons like silver ramparts protecting the sky around Newcastle. She followed the coast north to Bamburgh and Holy Island. I know that stretch of the North Sea very well because the train from Edinburgh to London goes that way, and I was up and down all year when I was at school. Then when my school closed just before the war, instead of finishing elsewhere, I went to university a bit suddenly for a term and took the train to get there too, feeling very grown-up.

The Northumbrian coast is the most beautiful length of the whole trip. The sun still sets quite late in the north of England in August, and Maddie on fabric wings flew low over the long sands of Holy Island and saw seals gathered there. She flew over the great castle crags of Lindisfarne and Bamburgh to the north and south, and over the ruins of the twelfth century priory, and over all the fields stretching yellow and green toward the low Cheviot Hills of Scotland. Maddie flew back following the 70-mile 2,000-year-old dragon's back of Hadrian's Wall, to Carlisle and then south through the Lakeland fells, along Lake Windermere. The soaring mountains rose around her, and the poets' waters glittered beneath her in the valleys of memory—hosts of golden daffodils, *Swallows and Amazons*, Peter Rabbit. She came home by way of Blackstone Edge above the old Roman road to avoid the smoke haze over Manchester, and landed back at Oakway, sobbing with anguish and love; *love*, for her island home that she'd seen whole and fragile from the air in the space of an afternoon, from coast to coast, holding its breath in a glass lens of summer and sunlight. All about to be swallowed in nights of flame and blackout. Maddie landed at Oakway before sunset and shut down the engine, then sat in the cockpit weeping.

More than anything else, I think, Maddie went to war on behalf of the Holy Island seals.

She climbed out of Dympna's Puss Moth at last. The late, low sun lit up the other airplanes in the hangar Dympna used, expensive toys about to realize their finest hour (in less than a year, that very same Puss Moth, flown by someone else, would ferry blood deliveries to the gasping British Expeditionary Force in France). Maddie ran all the checks she'd normally run after a flight, and then started again with the ones she'd run before a flight. Dympna found her there half an hour later, still not having put the plane to bed, cleaning midges off the windscreen in the late golden light.

"You don't need to do that."

"Someone does. I won't be flying it again, will I? Not after tomorrow. It's the only thing I *can* do, check the oil, clean the bugs."

Dympna stood smoking calmly in the evening sunlight and watched Maddie for a while. Then she said, "There's going to be air work for girls in this war. You wait. They're going to need all the pilots they can get fighting for the Royal Air Force. That'll be young men, some of them with less training than you've got now, Maddie. And that'll leave the old men, and the women, to deliver new aircraft and carry their messages and taxi their pilots. That'll be us."

"You think?"

"There's a unit forming for civil pilots to help with the War Effort. The ATA—Air Transport Auxiliary—men and women both. It'll happen any day. My name's in the pool; Pauline Gower's heading the women's section." Pauline was a flying friend of Dympna's; Pauline had encouraged Dympna's joyriding business. "You've not the qualifications for it, but I won't forget you, Maddie. When they open up training to girls again I'll send you a telegram. You'll be the first."

Maddie scrubbed at midges and scrubbed at her eyes, too, too miserable to answer.

"And when you're done slaving, I'm going to make you a mug of best Oakway Pilot's Oily Tea, and tomorrow morning I'm going to march you into the nearest WAAF recruitment office."

WAAF is Women's Auxiliary Air Force, auxiliary to the RAF, the Royal Air Force. You don't *fly* in the Women's Auxiliary Air Force, but the way things are now you can do almost any job a man does, all the work associated with flying and fighting: electrician, technician, fitter, barrage balloon operator, driver, cook, hairdresser. . . . You would have thought our Maddie would go for a job in mechanics, wouldn't you? So early in the war, they hadn't yet opened up those jobs to women. It didn't matter that Maddie had a good deal more experience than a lot of boys; there wasn't a place for her. But she'd already learned Morse code and a bit about radio transmission as part of her training for her pilot's "A" license. The Air Ministry was in a panic in August 1939, scrambling for women to do radio work as it dawned on them how many men they'd need to do the flying. Maddie joined the WAAF and eventually became a radio operator.

SOME WAAF TRADES

It was like being at school. I don't know if Maddie thought so too; she didn't go to a Swiss boarding school, she was at a grammar school in Manchester and she certainly never thought about going to university. Even when she was at school she came home every day and never had to share a room with twenty girls, or sleep on a straw mattress made up of three bales like a set of settee cushions. We called them "biscuits." You were always so tired you didn't care; I would cut off my left hand to have one here. That fussy kit inspection they made you do, where you had to lay out all your worldly belongings in random but particular order on the folded blanket, like a jigsaw, and if anything was a millimeter the wrong way, you got points off your score—that was just like being in school. Also all the slang, the "square-bashing" drilling exercises, and the boring meals and the uniforms, though Maddie's group didn't get issued proper uniforms at first. They all wore matching blue cardigans, like Girl Guides (Guides don't wear Air Force blue cardigans, but you see what I mean).

Maddie was stationed at Oakway to begin with, very

convenient to home. This was late 1939, early 1940. The Phoney War. Nothing much happening.

Not in Britain, anyway. We were biting our nails, practicing.

Waiting.

TELEPHONIST

"You! Girl in the blue cardigan!"

Five girls in headsets looked around from their switchboards, pointed to their chests, and mouthed silently, *Me?*

"Yes, you! Aircraftwoman Brodatt! What are you doing here? You're a licensed radio operator!"

Maddie pointed to her headset and the front cord she was about to connect.

"Take the damned thing off and answer me."

Maddie turned back to her switchboard and coolly plugged in the front cord. She toggled the appropriate keys and spoke clearly into the headset. "The Group Captain is through to you now, sir. You may go ahead." She took off the headset and turned back to the troll who was waiting for a reply. It was the chief flight instructor for Oakway's Royal Air Force squadron, the man who had given Maddie her flight test nearly a year ago.

"Sorry, sir. This is where I've been posted, sir." (I did say it was like being at school.)

"Posted! You're not even any of you in uniform!"

Five dutiful Aircraftwomen First Class straightened their Air Force blue cardigans.

"We've not been issued full dress, sir."

"Posted!" the officer repeated. "You'll start in the radio room tomorrow, Aircraftwoman Brodatt. The operator's assistant is down with influenza." And he lifted the headset from her console to perch it precariously over his own large head. "Put me through to the WAAF administration unit," he said. "I want to talk to your section officer."

Maddie flipped the keys and plugged in the cords, and he gave her posting orders over her own telephone.

RADIO OPERATOR

"Tyro to ground, tyro to ground," came the call from the training aircraft. "Position uncertain, overhead triangular body of water to east of corridor."

"Ground to tyro," answered Maddie. "Is it a lake or a reservoir?"

"Say again?"

"Lake or reservoir? Your triangular body of water."

After a short silence, Maddie prompted: "A reservoir has got a dam at one end."

"Tyro to ground. Affirm reservoir."

"Is it Ladyswell? Manchester barrage balloons at ten o'clock and Macclesfield at eight o'clock?"

"Tyro to ground, affirm. Position located. Overhead Ladyswell for return to Oakway."

Maddie sighed. "Ground to tyro, call on final approach."

"Wilco."

Maddie shook her head, swearing unprettily under her breath. "Oh my sainted aunt! Unlimited visibility! Unlimited visibility except for the dirty great city in the northwest! That would be the dirty great city surrounded at 3000 feet by a few hundred silver hydrogen balloons as big as buses! How in the name of mud is he going to find *Berlin* if he can't find *Manchester*?"

There was a bit of quiet in the radio room. Then the chief

radio officer said gently, "Leading Aircraftwoman Brodatt, you're still transmitting."

"Brodatt, stop there."

Maddie and everyone else had been told to go home. Or back to their various barracks and lodgings, anyway, for an afternoon's rest. It was a day of such appallingly evil weather that the streetlamps would have been lit if it weren't for fear of enemy aircraft seeing them, not that enemy aircraft can fly in such murk either. Maddie and the other WAAFs in her barracks still hadn't got proper uniforms, but as it was winter, they had been issued RAF overcoats—men's overcoats. Warm and waterproof, but ridiculous. Like wearing a tent. Maddie clutched hers tight in at the sides when the officer spoke to her, standing upright and hoping she looked smarter than she felt. She stopped so he could catch up with her, waiting on the duckboards laid over the concrete apron because there was so much standing water about that if you stepped in a puddle it came over the tops of your shoes.

"Was it you talked down my lads training in the Wellington bomber this morning?" the officer asked.

Maddie gulped. She had thrown radio protocol to the wind to guide those boys in, bullying them through a ten-minute gap in the low-lying cloud, praying they would follow her instructions without question, and that she wasn't directing them straight into the explosive-rigged steel cables that tethered the barrage balloons meant to deter enemy aircraft. Now she recognized the officer: it was one of the squadron leaders.

"Yes, sir," she admitted hoarsely, her chin held high. The air was so full of moisture it made her hair stick to her forehead. She waited miserably, expecting him to summon her to be court-martialed.

"Those boys jolly well owe you their lives," he said to Maddie. "Not one of them on instruments yet and flying without a map. We shouldn't have let them take off this morning."

"Thank you, sir," Maddie gasped.

"Singing your praises, those lads were. Made me wonder, though; have you any idea what the runway looks like from the air?"

Maddie smiled faintly. "I've a pilot's 'A' license. Still valid. Of course I haven't flown since August."

"Oh, I see!"

The RAF squadron leader set off to walk Maddie to the canteen at the airfield's perimeter. She had to trot a little to match his stride.

"Took your license here at Oakway, did you? Civil Air Guard?"

"Yes, sir."

"Instructor's rating?"

"No, sir. But I've flown at night."

"Now that's unusual! Used the fog line, have you?"

He meant the fierce gas lamps that line the runway at intervals on either side so you can land in bad weather.

"Two or three times. Not often, sir."

"So you *have* seen the runway from the air. And in the dark, too! Well—"

Maddie waited. She really didn't have any idea what this man was going to say next.

"If you're going to talk people down, you'd damn well better know what the forward view from the cockpit of a Wellington bomber looks like in the landing configuration. Fancy a flight in a Wellington?"

"Oh, yes, please, sir!"

(You see—it was just like being in school.)

STOOGE

That is not a WAAF trade. That is what they call it when you go along in an aircraft just for the ride and don't meaningfully contribute to a successful flight. Perhaps Maddie was more of a backseat driver than a stooge.

—"Don't think you've reset the directional gyro."

—"He told you heading 270. You've turned east."

—"Look sharp, lads, northbound aircraft at three o'clock, one thousand feet below."

Once the electric undercarriage failed, and she had to earn her keep by taking her turn at the hand pump so they didn't have to crash land. Once they let her ride in the gun turret. She loved that, like being a goldfish alone in an empty sky.

Once they had to lift her out of the plane after landing because she was shaking so badly she couldn't climb down herself.

Maddie's Wellington joyrides were not exactly clandestine, but they weren't exactly cricket either. She was counted among the S.O.B.—Souls On Board—when the lads took off, but she certainly wasn't authorized to be there coaxing along the novice bombing crews as they practiced low flying over the high moors. So various off- and on-duty concerned people came pelting out of offices and the men's and ladies' tea huts, coatless and white-faced, when they saw Maddie's RAF mates chair-lifting her in their arms across the runway.

A WAAF friend of hers called Joan, and the guilty squadron leader, reached her first.

"What's wrong? What happened? Is she hurt?"

Maddie was not hurt. She was already badgering the Wellington crew who carried her to put her down. "Get off, everyone will see, the girls will never let me forget it—"

"*What happened?*"

Maddie struggled to her feet and stood shivering on the concrete. "We got fired on," she said, and looked away, burning with shame at how much it had taken out of her.

"Fired on!" barked the squadron leader. This was in the spring of 1940—the war was still in Europe. It was before the disastrous May when the Allies fled, retreating to the French beaches, before the siege that was the Battle of Britain, before the thunder and flame-filled nights of the Blitz. In the spring of 1940 our skies were alert and armed and uneasy. But they were still safe.

"Yes, *fired on*," echoed the Wellington pilot in fury. He was white as a sheet too. "By those idiots manning the anti-aircraft guns at the Cattercup barrage balloons. By *our own gunners*. Who the hell's training them? Bloody daft trigger-happy morons! Wasting ammo and scaring the blue bleeding daylights out of everybody! Any school lad can spot the difference between a flying cigar and a flying pencil!"

(We call our jolly Wellingtons "flying cigars," and we call your nasty Dorniers "flying pencils." Have fun translating, Miss E.)

The pilot had been as scared as Maddie, but he was not shaking.

Joan put a comforting arm around Maddie's shoulders and advised her in a whisper to pay no attention to the pilot's language. Maddie gave an uncertain and forced laugh.

"Wasn't even sitting in the gun turret," she muttered. "Thank goodness *I'm* not flying into Europe."

SIGNALS BRANCH

"Flight Lieutenant Mottram has been singing your praises," Maddie's WAAF section officer told her. "He says you've got the sharpest pair of eyes at Oakway"—the section officer rolled her own eyes—"probably a bit of an exaggeration, but he said that in flight you're always the first to spot another aircraft approaching. How do you fancy further training?"

"In what?"

The section officer coughed apologetically. "It's a bit secret. Well: very secret. Say yes, and I'll send you on the course."

"Yes," Maddie said.

To clarify a remark someone made earlier, I confess that I am making up all the proper nouns. Did you think I remembered all the names and ranks of everybody Maddie ever worked with? Or every plane she ever flew in? I think it is more interesting this way.

That is all I can usefully write today, though I would keep on blethering about nothing if I thought that by doing it I could avoid the next few hours' cross-examination—Engel struggling over my handwriting and von Linden picking holes in everything I've said. It must be done … no point in putting it off. I have a blanket to look forward to afterward, I hope, perhaps a tepid dish of kailkenny à la guerre—that is, cabbage and potato mash without the potato and with not very much cabbage. I have not got scurvy yet, anyway, thanks to France's infinite supply of prison cabbage. Heigh-ho—

RAF WAAF RDF Y
S.O.B. S.O.E.
Asst S/O Flt Off
w/op
clk/sd
m'aidez m'aidez mayday

COASTAL DEFENSE

Actually, I am afraid to write this.

I don't know why I think it matters. The Battle of Britain is over. Hitler's planned invasion, Operation Sea Lion, failed three years ago. And soon he will be fighting a desperate war on two fronts, with the Americans behind us and the Russians closing in on Berlin from the east, and organized resistance in all the countries in the middle. I can't believe his advisers don't already know what went on in the makeshift huts of iron and concrete up and down the southeast coast of England in the summer of 1940—in a general sense, at any rate.

Only, I don't really want to go down in history as the one who gave out the details.

RDF is Range and Direction Finding. Same acronym as Radio Direction Finding, to confuse the enemy, but not exactly the same thing. As you know. Well. They call it *Radar* now, an American word, an acronym of *RAdio Detection And Ranging*, which I do not think is easier to remember. In the summer of 1940 it was still so new nobody knew what it was, and so secret that

Buckets of blood—I can't do this.

I have spent a vexing half hour scrapping with Fräulein Engel over the pen nib, which I swear I did not bend on purpose the first time. It is true that it spared me having to continue for a good long while, but it did not move things along for that harpy to straighten it out against my teeth when I could have easily done it myself against the table. It is also true that it was stupid of me to bend it out of shape again, on purpose, the second she handed it back to me. Then she had to show me SEVERAL TIMES how when she was at school the nurse would use a pen nib to make a pinprick for a blood test.

I don't know why I bent the stupid thing again. It is so easy to wind Miss Engel up. She always wins, but only because my ankles are tied to my chair.

Well, and also, because at the end of every argument she reminds me of the deal I made with a certain officer of the Gestapo, and I collapse.

"Hauptsturmführer von Linden is busy, as you know, and will not wish to be interrupted. But I have been told to summon him if necessary. You have been given pen and paper by his judgment of your willingness to cooperate with him, and if you will not write out the confession you have agreed, he will have no choice but to resume your interrogation."

JUST SHUT UP, ANNA ENGEL. I KNOW.

I will do anything: she has only to mention his name and I remember now, I will do anything, *anything*, to avoid him interrogating me again.

So. Range and Direction Finding. Coastal Defense. Do I get my thirty pieces of silver? No, just some more of this hotel stationery. It is very nice to write on.

COASTAL DEFENSE, THE UNABRIDGED VERSION

We saw it coming—someone saw it coming. We were that little bit ahead of you, and you didn't realize it. You didn't realize how advanced the RDF system was already, or how quickly we were training people to use it, or how far we could see with it. You didn't even realize how quickly we were building new planes of our own. It is true we were outnumbered, but with RDF we saw you coming—saw the swarms of Luftwaffe aircraft even as they were leaving their bases in Occupied France, worked out how high they were flying, saw how many of them were making the raid. And that gave us time to rally. We could meet you in the air, beat you back, keep you from landing, distract you till your fuel ran out and you turned tail until the next wave. Our besieged island, alone on the edge of Europe.

Maddie was sworn to secrecy on the life of her unborn children. It's so secret they don't give you a title when you have anything to do with Radar; you're just called a "special duties clerk." Clerk, Special Duties, clk/sd for short, like w/op is for Wireless Operator and Y for wireless. Clk/sd, that's possibly the most useful and damning piece of information I've given you. Now you know.

Maddie spent six weeks in Radar training. She was also given a very nice promotion and made an officer. Then she was posted to RAF Maidsend, an operational base for a squadron of new Spitfire fighter planes, not far from Canterbury, near the Kentish coast. It was the farthest she had ever been from home. Maddie was not actually put to work at a Radar screen in one of the direction finding stations, though Maidsend did have one; she was still in the radio room. In the fire and fury of the summer of 1940, Maddie sat in a tower of iron and concrete taking bearings over the telephone. The other RDF girls did the ID work on the glass screens with the blinking green lights, and wired or telephoned it to Operations; when Operations identified approaching aircraft for her, Maddie answered air-to-ground radio calls as the aircraft came limping home. Or sometimes roaring home in triumph, or newly delivered from the maintenance depot at Swi

SWINLEY   SWINLEY

At *Swinley*. Thibaut has made me finish writing the name. I am so ashamed of myself I want to be sick again.

Engel says impatiently not to bother about the name of the workshop. There have been repeated attempts to bomb it to bits and it's not really a secret. Engel is sure our Hauptsturmführer will be more interested in my sample description of the early Radar network. She is cross with T. now for interrupting.

I hate them both. Hate them all.

I HATE THEM

COASTAL DEFENSE, DAMN IT.

Sniveling idiot.

So. So, on the RDF screen you'd see a green dot for an aircraft, one or two moving across the screen. It might be ours. You'd watch a battle building, the dots multiplying— more joining the first as the pulsing light swept the screen. They'd come together and some of them would go out, like the cinders of sparklers. And every green flash that disappeared was a life finished, one man for a fighter, a whole crew for a bomber. *Out, out, brief candle.* (That is from *Macbeth*. He is said to be another of my unlikely ancestors, and actually did hold court on my family's estate from time to time. He was not, by all contemporary Scottish accounts, the treacherous bastard Shakespeare makes him out to be. Will history remember me for my MBE, my British Empire honor for "chivalry," or for my cooperation with the Gestapo? I don't want to think about it. I expect they can take the MBE away if you stop being chivalrous.)

If they were radio equipped, Maddie could talk to the planes the special duties clerks saw on their screens. She'd tell the pilots more or less what she'd have told them back at Oakway, except she didn't know landmarks so well in Kent. She'd pass bearings to the moving aircraft, along with wind speed and whether or not there were holes in the runway today (sometimes we got raided). Or she'd tell other planes to give priority to the one that had lost its flaps, or whose pilot had a lump of shrapnel lodged in his shoulder, or something like that.

Maddie was listening for incoming stragglers one afternoon following a battle that hadn't involved the Maidsend Squadron. She nearly fell off her chair when she heard the desperate call that came in on her frequency.

"Mayday—mayday—"

Recognizable in English. Or perhaps that was French, "M'aidez," help me. The rest of the transmission was in German.

The voice was a boy's voice, young and scared. He broke off each call with a sob. Maddie swallowed—she had no idea where the anguished cries for help were coming from. Maddie called out, "Listen—listen!" and switched her headset onto the Tannoy speaker so that everyone could hear, and then she grabbed the telephone.

"It's Assistant Section Officer Brodatt in the Tower. Can I get directly through to Jenny in Special Duties? All right, Tessa, then. Anyone with a screen going. I need an ident on a radio call—"

Everyone crowded around the telephone, reading over Maddie's shoulder as she took notes from the direction finding station, then gasping aloud as the meaning of her notes sank in.

"Heading straight for Maidsend!"

"What if it's a bomber?"

"What if it's still loaded?"

"What if it's a hoax?"

"He'd be calling in English if it was a hoax!"

"Anyone speak German?" shouted the officer in charge of the radio room. Silence.

"Christ! Brodatt, stay on the phone. Davenport, you run to the wireless station; perhaps one of those girls can help. Get me a German speaker! *Now!*"

Maddie listened with her heart in her mouth, holding her headset to one ear and the telephone to the other, waiting for the girl at the RDF screen to pass her new information.

"Shhh," warned the radio officer, leaning over Maddie's shoulder and taking hold of the telephone receiver for her so her right hand was freed up for taking notes. "Don't say anything—don't let him know who's listening—"

The door to the radio room banged open, and the subordinate Davenport was back, with one of the WAAF wireless operators hard on his heels. Maddie looked up.

The girl was immaculate—not a blue thread out of place, her chignon of long fair hair coiled in regulation neatness two inches above her uniform collar. Maddie recognized her from the canteen and rare social evenings. Queenie, people called her, though she was not the official WAAF Queen Bee (that's what we call the senior administrative officer on the base), nor was it her name. Maddie did not know her real name. Queenie had acquired a certain reputation for being fast and fearless; she sauced superior officers and got away with it, but equally she wouldn't leave a building during an air raid until she'd made sure everyone else was out. Distantly connected to royalty, she was of some rank herself, of privilege rather than experience, a flight officer; but she was said to work as diligently at her wireless set as any self-made shop girl. She was pretty, petite, and light on her feet, and if there was a Squadron dance on a Saturday night, she was the one the pilots went for.

"Let's have your headset, Brodatt," said the radio officer. Maddie uncurled the gripping earphones and microphone and passed her headset to the pretty little blond wireless operator, who adjusted the phones to fit her head.

After a few seconds Queenie said, "He says he's over the English Channel. He's looking for Calais."

"But Tessa says he's approaching the coast at Whitstable!"

"He's in a Heinkel bomber and his crew's been killed and he's lost an engine and he wants to land at Calais."

They all stared at the wireless operator.

"You sure we're all talking about the same aircraft?" the radio officer asked dubiously.

"Tessa," Maddie said into the telephone, "could the German plane be over the Channel?"

Now the whole room held its breath, waiting for Tessa's disembodied reply as, somewhere underneath the chalk cliffs, she sat staring at the green flashes on her screen. Her answer appeared beneath Maddie's scribbling pencil: *Hostile ident, track 187 Maidsend 25 miles, est height 8,500 ft.*

"Why the hell does he think he's over the English Channel?"

"Oh!" Maddie gave a sudden gasp of understanding and waved at the enormous map of southeast England and northwest France and the Low Countries that covered the wall behind her radio. "Look, look—he's come from Suffolk. He's been bombing the coastal bases there. He crossed the mouth of the Thames at its widest point and he thinks he crossed the *Channel!* He's heading straight for Kent and he thinks it's France!"

The chief radio officer gave the wireless operator a command.

"Answer him."

"You'll have to tell me the protocol, sir."

"Brodatt, give her the correct protocol."

Maddie swallowed. There wasn't really any time to hesitate. She said, "What did he say he's flying? What kind of aircraft? His bomber?"

The wireless operator said the name in German first, and they all looked at her blankly. "He-111?" she translated hesitantly.

"Heinkel He-111— Any other ID?"

"A Heinkel He-111. He didn't say."

"Just repeat back to him the type of his aircraft, Heinkel He-111. That's an open reply. You press this button before you talk; keep it pressed while you're talking or he won't be able to hear you. Then let go when you're done or he won't be able to reply."

The chief radio officer clarified, "'Heinkel He-111, this is Calais-Marck.' Tell him we are Calais-Marck."

Maddie listened as the wireless operator made her first radio call, in German, as cool and crisp as if she'd been giving radio instructions to Luftwaffe bombers all her life. The Luftwaffe boy's voice responded in a gasp of gratitude, practically weeping with relief.

The wireless operator turned to Maddie.

"He wants bearings for landing."

"Tell him this—" Maddie scribbled numbers and distances on her notepad. "Say his ID first, then yours. 'Heinkel He-111, this is Calais.' Then runway, wind speed, visibility—" She scratched notes furiously. The wireless operator stared at the coded abbreviations, then spoke into the headset, giving orders in German with confident calm.

She paused mid-flow and jabbed a perfectly manicured fingernail into the script Maddie had passed to her. She mouthed silently, *R27?*

"Runway two-seven," Maddie said under her breath. "Say 'Cleared straight in, Runway 27.' Tell him to dump his leftover bombs in the sea if he's got any, so he doesn't set them off when he lands."

The whole of the radio room was silent, mesmerized by the sharp, precisely spoken, and incomprehensible instructions that the elegant wireless operator rapped out with the careless authority of a headmistress; and the anguished, equally incomprehensible, gasped answers of the boy in the ruined plane; and Maddie scribbling directions, and the protocol for giving them, on the diminishing notepad.

"Here she comes!" breathed the chief radio officer, and everybody excepting Maddie and the wireless operator—whose heads were tied to the telephone and the radio headset—went running to the long window to watch the Heinkel bomber limping into view.

"When he calls final approach, just pass him the wind speed," Maddie instructed, scribbling furiously. "Eight knots west-south-west, gusting to twelve."

"Tell him the fire service is on its way to meet him," said the radio officer. He clapped one of the other radio operators on the shoulder. "Get the engines out there. And an ambulance."

The black silhouette in the distance grew larger. Then they could hear it coughing and whining on its single belabored engine.

"Christ! He hasn't got the undercarriage down," gasped

the young flying officer called Davenport. "This is going to be one hell of a prang."

But it wasn't. The Heinkel pancaked in neatly on its belly in a shower of grass and turf, and came to rest right in front of the control tower, with the fire engines and pumps and an ambulance screaming up to meet it.

Everyone at the window went pelting down the stairs and out to the runway.

Maddie put her headset back on. The two other radio operators were on their feet at the window. Maddie strained to hear what was going on and heard only sirens. Away from the window she could see sky and the windsock at the end of the runway, but not anything immediately below her. A thin thread of curling black smoke drifted up past the window.

Outside at the edge of the runway, Queenie, or whatever her name was, stood staring at the wreck of the Luftwaffe bomber.

Floundering on its belly, it was like a vast metallic whale spouting smoke instead of seawater. The wireless operator could see, through the shattered Plexiglas of the cockpit, the young pilot desperately trying to free his dead navigator from a torn and bloody helmet. She watched as a swarm of fitters and the fire service team closed in to lift the pilot and his life-less crew out of the plane. And she saw the frank relief on the pilot's face turn to bewilderment and apprehension as he was increasingly surrounded by blue uniforms and the stripes and badges of the Royal Air Force.

The chief radio officer at her shoulder tut-tutted under his breath.

"Poor young Jerry bastard," he intoned. "He won't go home a hero, will he! Must have no sense of direction whatsoever."

He put a kind hand lightly on the German-speaking wireless operator's shoulder.

"If you don't mind," he said apologetically, "we could use your help questioning him."

Maddie was going off duty by the time the ambulance men had finished hurriedly patching up the German pilot and brought him into the ground floor office of the control tower. She caught a glimpse of the dazed young man sipping gingerly at a steaming mug while an orderly lit a cigarette for him. They had wrapped him in a blanket, and it was August, but his teeth were still chattering. The pretty blond wireless operator was perched on the edge of a hard chair at the other side of the room, politely looking away from this shattered and grief-stricken enemy. She was smoking a cigarette of her own as she waited to be given further instruction. She looked just as poised and calm as she had been when she took the headset from Maddie in the radio room, but Maddie could see her casually drilling the back of her chair with one restless, manicured forefinger.

I couldn't have done what she just did, Maddie thought. We'd not have made this catch without her. Never mind speaking German; I couldn't have *faked* it like that, just off the top of my head, no training or anything. Not sure I could manage what she's going to have to do next, either. Thank goodness *I* don't speak German.

That night Maidsend was raided again. It wasn't anything to do with the captured Heinkel bomber; it was just an ordinary air raid, the Luftwaffe doing their worst to try to destroy British defenses. The RAF officers' quarters were blown up (no officers in it at the time), and great big holes gouged out of the runways. The WAAF officers were quartered in the gatehouse lodge at the edge of the estate grounds that the airfield had been built on, and Maddie and her bunk mates were so dead asleep they didn't hear the sirens. They only woke up after the first explosion. They ran through scrub woodland to the nearest shelter in their pajamas and tin hats, clutching gas masks and ID cards. There was no light to see by except the gunfire and the exploding flames—no streetlamps, no cracks of light in any doors or windows, not even the glow of a cigarette end. It was like being in hell, nothing but shadows and jumping flames and fire and stars overhead.

Maddie had grabbed an umbrella. Gas mask, tin hat, ration coupons, and an umbrella. Hellfire raining down on her out of the sky and she held it off with a brolly. No one realized she had it, of course, until she was struggling to get it in the door of the air raid shelter.

"Shut it—shut the damned thing—*leave it!*"

"I'm not leaving it!" Maddie cried, and managed to wrestle the umbrella inside. The girl behind her pushed, and one of the girls ahead of her grabbed her by the arm and pulled, and then they were all trembling in the dark underground with the door shut.

A couple of them had had the sense to grab their cigarettes. They passed them 'round, parsimoniously sharing. There was not a single lad about—the men were quartered half a mile away on the other side of the airfield and used a different shelter—those that weren't scrambling into aircraft to fight back. The girl with the matches found a candle, and they all settled down for the duration.

"Bring us that deck of cards, love, let's have a round of rummy."

"Rummy! Don't be soft. Poker. We'll play for ciggies. For gosh sakes, put that brolly down, Brodatt, are you completely bonkers?"

"No," Maddie said very calmly.

They were all crouched on the dirt floor around the playing cards and glowing tobacco ends. It was cozy in perhaps the way you'd be cozy in hell. Something flying low was peppering the runway with machine gun fire; even buried mostly underground, even a quarter of a mile away, the shelter's iron walls shuddered.

"Glad I'm not on shift right now!"

"Pity the poor souls who are."

"Can I share your umbrella?"

Maddie looked up. Crouched next to her, in the light of the flickering candle and one oil lamp, was the small German-speaking wireless operator. She was a vision of feminine perfection and heroism even in her WAAF regulation-issue men's pajamas, her fair hair tumbling in a loose plait over one shoulder. Everybody else was shedding hairpins; Queenie's hairpins marched in ordered rank on her pajama pocket and would not go back in her hair till she was back in bed. With her slender manicured fingers she offered Maddie her cigarette.

"Wish I'd brought a brolly," she drawled in the plummy, educated tones of the Oxbridge colleges. "Super idea! A portable illusion of shelter and safety. Have you room for two?"

Maddie took the cigarette but did not immediately move over. The fey Queenie, Maddie knew, was given to fits of madness such as stealing malt whisky from the RAF officers' mess, and Maddie was sure that anyone bold enough to impersonate an enemy radio operator on the spur of the moment was entirely capable of mocking someone who burst into tears every time she heard a gun fired. On a military airfield. In a war.

But Queenie didn't seem to be making fun of Maddie— quite the opposite. Maddie budged over a little and made room for another body beneath the umbrella.

"Marvelous!" Queenie cried out happily. "Like being a tortoise. They ought to make these out of steel. Let me hold it up—"

She gently pried the handle out of Maddie's trembling hand and held the ridiculous umbrella up over both their heads inside the bunker. Maddie took a drag on the offered cigarette. After a while of alternately biting her nails and smoking the borrowed cigarette down to a sliver of paper and ash, her hands stopped trembling. Maddie said hoarsely, "Thank you."

"Not a problem," said Queenie. "Why don't you play this round? I'll cover you."

"What were you on Civvie Street, then—" Maddie asked casually. "An actress?"

The little wireless operator dissolved in a fit of gleeful laugher, but still steadfastly held up the umbrella over Maddie's head. "No, I just like pretending," she said. "I do the same thing with our own boys, you know. Flirting's a game. I'm very boring, really. I'd be at university if it weren't for the war. I've not quite finished my first year. I started a year early and a term late."

"Reading what?"

"German. Obviously. They spoke it—well, an odd variant—in the village where I went to school in Switzerland. And I liked it."

Maddie laughed. "You were wizard this afternoon. Really brilliant."

"I couldn't have done it without you telling me what to say. *You* were brilliant too. You were *right there* when I needed you, not a word or call out of place. You made all the decisions. All I had to do was pay attention, and that's what I do all day on the Y sets anyway—Y, wireless, you know—just listen and listen. I never have to *do* anything. And all I had to do this afternoon was read from the script you gave me."

"You had to translate!" Maddie said.

"We did it together," said her friend.

People are complicated. There is so much more to everybody than you realize. You see someone in school every day, or at work, in the canteen, and you share a cigarette or a coffee with them, and you talk about the weather or last night's air raid. But you don't talk so much about what was the nastiest thing you ever said to your mother, or how you pretended to be David Balfour, the hero of *Kidnapped*, for the whole of the year when you were thirteen, or what you imagine yourself doing with the pilot who looks like Leslie Howard if you were alone in his bunk after a dance.

No one slept the night of that air raid, or the next day. We pretty much had to resurface the runway ourselves that morning. We weren't equipped for it, we didn't have the tools or the materials, and we weren't a building crew, but without a runway, RAF Maidsend was defenseless. And Britain too, in the bigger picture. We repaired the runway.

Everyone mucked in, including the captured German—I think he was rather apprehensive about his fate as a prisoner of war and was just as happy to spend the day stripped to the waist shoveling piles of earth with twenty other pilots than to be moved on to some unknown official internment awaiting him inland. I remember we all had to bow our heads in a moment of silence for his dead companions before we set to work. I don't know what happened to him after that.

In the canteen, Queenie was asleep with her head on the table. She must have done up her hair first, before she came in from two hours' stone-picking on the runway, but she'd fallen asleep before she'd even taken the spoon out of her tea.

Maddie sat down across from her with two fresh cups of tea and one iced bun. I don't know where the icing came from. Someone must have been hoarding sugar just in case there was a direct hit on the airfield and everybody needed cheering up. Maddie was quite relieved to see the unflappable wireless operator with her guard down. She pushed the Cup That Cheers close to Queenie's face so that the warmth woke her.

They propped their heads on their elbows, facing each other.

"Are you scared of *anything*?" Maddie asked.

"Lots of things!"

"Name one."

"I can name ten."

"Go on, then."

Queenie looked at her hands. "Breaking my nails," she said critically. After two hours' clearing the runway of rubble and twisted metal, her manicure was in need of repair.

"I'm serious," said Maddie quietly.

"All right, then. Dark."

"I don't believe you."

"It's true," said Queenie. "Now your turn."

"Cold," Maddie answered.

Queenie sipped her tea. "Falling asleep while I'm working."

"Me too." Maddie laughed. "And bombs dropping."

"Too easy."

"All right." It was Maddie's turn to be defensive. She shook tangled dark curls off her collar; her hair was barely short enough to count as regulation, and too short to put up. "Bombs dropping on my gran and granddad."

Queenie nodded in agreement. "Bombs dropping on my favorite brother. Jamie's the youngest of 'em, the nearest me in age. He's a pilot."

"Not having a useful skill," said Maddie. "I don't want to

have to marry right away just so I don't have to work down Ladderal Mill."

"You are joking!"

"When the war's over I *still* won't have a skill. Bet there won't be this desperate need for radio operators when the war ends."

"You think that'll happen soon?"

"The longer the war goes on," Maddie said, carefully cutting her iced bun in half with a tin butter knife, "the older I'll get."

Queenie let out a giddy, tickled laugh. "Getting old!" she cried. "I'm horribly afraid of being old."

Maddie smiled and handed her half the bun. "Me too. Bit like being afraid of dying, though. Not much you can do about it."

"What am I up to?"

"You've done four. Not counting the nails. Six to go."

"All right." Queenie deliberately tore her bun into six equal pieces and arranged them around the rim of her saucer. Then, one by one, she dunked each piece into her tea, named a fear, and ate it.

"Number five, the Newbery College porter. Blimey, he's a troll. I was a year younger than all the other first years and I'd have been scared of him even if he hadn't hated me. It was because I was reading German and he was sure my tutor was a spy! Five down, right? Number six, heights, I'm afraid of heights. That's because my big brothers tied me to a drain spout on the roof of our castle when I was five and forgot about me all afternoon. All five of them got a good birching for it, too. Seven, ghosts—I mean one ghost, not seven, one particular ghost. I don't need to worry about that here. The ghost is probably why I'm scared of the dark too."

Queenie washed back these unlikely confessions with

more tea. Maddie stared at her in growing amazement. They were still eye to eye across from each other with their chins against their hands and their elbows on the table, and Queenie did not seem to be making it up. She was taking her unlikely inventory very seriously.

"Number eight, getting caught stealing grapes from the glasshouse in the kitchen garden. That's another birching. 'Course we're all too old now for birchings *and* for grape-stealing. Number nine, killing someone. By accident or on purpose. Did I save that German laddie's life yesterday, or destroy it? You do it too—you tell the fighters where to find them. You're responsible. Do you think about it?"

Maddie didn't answer. She did think about it.

"Perhaps it gets easier after the first time. Number ten, getting lost."

Queenie glanced up from dipping "getting lost" in her tea and looked Maddie in the eye. "Now, I can see that you are skeptical and disinclined to believe anything I tell you. And perhaps I'm not *really* worried about ghosts. But I *am* afraid of getting lost. I *hate* trying to find my way around this airfield. Every Nissen hut looks the same. My God, there are forty of them! And all the taxiways and aprons seem to change every day. I keep trying to use planes for landmarks and they keep moving them around."

Maddie laughed. "I felt sorry for that lost Jerry pilot yesterday," she said. "I know I shouldn't. But I've seen so many of our own lads get confused, their first flight over the Pennines. Seems it shouldn't be possible to confuse England and France. But who knows what you're thinking when all your mates have been blown to smithereens and you're flying a broken plane. Perhaps it was his first flight to England. I felt dead sorry for him."

"Yes, I did too," said Queenie softly, and swallowed the

last of her tea as if she were throwing back a dram of whisky.

"Was it beastly awful, questioning him?"

Queenie gave her an enigmatic little squint. "'Careless talk costs lives.' I've taken an oath not to tell about it."

"Oh!" Maddie went red. "Of course not. Sorry."

The wireless operator sat up straight. She looked at her ruined nails, shrugged, and patted her hair to make sure it was still in place. Then she stood up and stretched and yawned. "Thanks for sharing your bun," she said, smiling.

"Thanks for sharing your fears!"

"You still owe me a few."

The air raid siren went off.

NOT PART OF THE STORY

I must record last night's debriefing because it was so funny.

Engel flapped down my sheaf of scribbled-on hotel stationery in frustration and said to von Linden, "She must be commanded to write of the meeting between Brodatt and herself. This description of early Radar operations is irrelevant nonsense."

Von Linden made a sound like a very soft puff of air, like blowing out a candle. Engel and I both stared at him as though he'd suddenly sprouted horns. (It was a laugh. He didn't crack a smile—I think his face is made of plaster of paris—but he definitely laughed.)

"Fräulein Engel, you are not a student of literature," he said. "The English flight officer has studied the craft of the novel. She is making use of suspense and foreshadowing."

Golly, Engel stared at him. I, of course, took the opportunity to interpose with pigheaded Wallace pride, "I am not *English*, you ignorant Jerry bastard, I am a SCOT."

Engel dutifully slapped me into silence and said, "She is not writing a novel. She is making a report."

"But she is employing the literary conceits and techniques of a novel. And the meeting you speak of has already occurred—you have been reading it for the past quarter of an hour."

Engel shuffled pages in a frenzy, hunting backward.

"Do you not recognize her in these pages?" von Linden prompted. "Ah, perhaps not; she flatters herself with

57

competence and bravery that you have never witnessed. She is the young woman called Queenie, the wireless operator who takes down the Luftwaffe aircraft. Our captive English agent—"

"*Scottish!*"

Slap.

"Our *prisoner* has not yet elaborated on her own role as a wireless operator at the aerodrome at Maidsend."

Oh, he's good. I would never in a million years have guessed that SS-Hauptsturmführer Amadeus von Linden is a "student of literature." Not in a million years.

He wanted to know, then, why I was choosing to write about myself in the third person. Do you know, I had not even noticed I was doing it until he asked.

The simple answer is because I am telling the story from Maddie's point of view, and it would be awkward to introduce another viewpoint character at this point. It is much easier writing about me in the third person than it would be if I tried to tell the story from my own point of view. I can avoid all my old thoughts and feelings. It's a superficial way to write about myself. I don't have to take myself seriously—or, well, only as seriously as Maddie takes me.

But, as von Linden pointed out, I have not even used my own name, which is what confused Engel.

I suppose the real answer is that I am not Queenie anymore. I just want to *thump my old self in the face* when I think about her, so earnest and self-righteous and flamboyantly heroic. I am sure other people did too.

I am someone else now.

They *did* used to call me Queenie, though. Everybody had stupid nicknames made up for them (like being at school, remember?). I was Scottie, sometimes, but more often Queenie. That was because Mary, Queen of Scots, is another of my illustrious ancestors. She died messily as well. They all died messily.

I am going to run out of stationery today. They have given me a Jewish prescription pad to use until they find something more sensible. I did not know such things existed. The forms have got the doctor's name, Benjamin Zylberberg, at the top, and a yellow star with a warning stamped at the bottom, stating that this Jewish doctor can only legally prescribe medication to other Jews. Presumably he is no longer practicing (presumably he has been shipped off to break rocks in a concentration camp somewhere), which is why his blank prescriptions have fallen into the hands of the Gestapo.

PRESCRIPTION FORMS!

Nom: Anna Engel *Adresse*: Fräulein Engel is the required form. I sometimes use "On Duty Female Guard Mein Führer SIR" to wind her up.	*Date*: Not believed ever to have dated. Does she have a sweetheart? Husband?... She wears no jewelry. (v.L. has a gold signet with a tiny sapphire in it.)

R_x
Needs a damned good shagging. She may choose among the following:

      Maquis guerrilla

      Gestapo

      Résistance

      German army

      French Milice police

      Civilian

Médecin Dr Sigmund Freud (Not Dr. Zylberberg but still appropriately Jewish)	*Rép.* Nightly, 4 or 5 *fois*

I've done her a nicer one, as well.

Nom: Anna Engel *Adresse:*	*Date:* Still looking

R_x

- ✓ 1 cigarette in ivory holder
- ✓ 1 magnum champagne (one normal bottle would not be enough to loosen her up)
- ✓ Chanel cocktail dress ... RED is Engel's color
- ✓ A table at the Hôtel Ritz Paris, if the Nazis ever clear out of it. Why are they so fond of ruining perfectly nice hotels?

Médecin	*Rép.* As needed *fois*

I meant to give her a Night Out, but when I picture this scenario it makes me think of Mata Hari on a mission. Would Engel be happier as a spy, glamorous and deadly? I just can't imagine her in any role other than Beastly Punctilious Official. Also I can't say that the bleak aftermath of a special agent's *unsuccessful* mission has anything to recommend it.

I was going to do prescriptions for William Wallace and Mary, Queen of Scots, and Adolf Hitler, too, but I can't think of anything clever enough to make it worth the reprisals for the waste of paper.

Coffee would be at the top of my own prescription list. Then aspirin. I am running a fever. It won't be tetanus, as they inoculated us, but may be septicemia; I don't think those pins were very clean. There was one I missed for a while after I pulled the others out, and the spot is very sore now (I am a little worried about some of the burns, too, which chafe when my wrist hits the table as I write). Perhaps I will die quietly of blood poisoning and avoid the kerosene treatment.

There's no efficient way to kill yourself with a dress-maker's pin (I wouldn't call contracting gangrene an efficient way to kill yourself)—I puzzled over it for a long time, seeing as they'd left the pins there, but it's just not possible. Useful for picking locks, though. I so loved the burglary lessons we got when we were training. Didn't so much enjoy the bleak aftermath of my unsuccessful attempt to put them to use—very good at picking locks but not so good at getting out of the building. Our prison cells are only hotel bedrooms, but we are guarded like royalty. And also, there are dogs. After that episode with the pins, they had a good go at making sure I wouldn't be able to walk if I did manage to get out—don't know where you pick up the skills for disabling a person without actually breaking her legs, Nazi School of Assault and Battery? Like everything else, it wasn't permanent damage, nothing left this week but the bruises, and they check me carefully now for stray bits of metal. I got caught yesterday trying to hide a pen nib in my hair (I didn't have a plan for it, but you never know).

Oh—often I forget I am not writing this for myself, and then it's too late to scratch it out. The evil Engel always snatches everything away from me and raises an alarm if she sees me trying to retract anything. Yesterday I tried ripping off the bottom of the page and eating it, but she got to it first. (It was when I realized I had thoughtlessly mentioned the factory at Swinley. It is refreshing sometimes to fight with her. She has the advantage of freedom, but I am a lot more imaginative. Also, I am willing to use my teeth, which she is squeamish about.)

Where was I? Hauptsturmführer von Linden has taken away everything I wrote yesterday. It is your own fault, you cold and soulless Jerry bastard, if I repeat myself.

Miss Engel has reminded me. "The air raid siren went." Clever girl, she has been paying attention.

She makes me give her every page to read now as soon as I have finished with it. We had fun doing the prescriptions. Will it get her in trouble if I mention that she burned a few *herself* to get rid of them this time? That'll teach you to try to make a chum of me, On-Duty-Female-Guard Engel.

I have already got her in trouble, without knowing I was doing it, by mentioning her cigarettes. She is not allowed to smoke while she is on duty. Apparently Adolf Hitler has a vendetta against tobacco, finds it filthy and disgusting, and his military police and their assistants are not meant to smoke at work. I don't think this is too strictly enforced except when the place is run by an obsessive martinet like Amadeus von Linden. Shame for him, really, as a lit cigarette is such a convenient accessory if your job happens to be Extracting

Information from Enemy Intelligence Agents.

As long as Engel's crimes are all so minor, they won't get rid of her because her combined talents would be quite difficult to replace (a bit like mine). But her offenses do consistently fall under "insubordination."

ANTIAIRCRAFT GUNNER

The air raid siren went. Every head in the room looked up in dismay and exhaustion at the canteen's pasteboard ceiling, as if they could see through it. Then everybody rocketed from their borrowed church hall wooden folding chairs to meet the next battle.

Maddie stood facing her new friend by the table they had just abandoned, people around her whirling into action. She felt as though she were at the eye of a tropical storm. The still point of the turning world.

"Come on!" Queenie cried, just like the Red Queen in *Through the Looking Glass*, and grabbed Maddie by the arm to pull her outside. "You go on duty at one; what have you got"—she glanced at her watch—"an hour? A quick nap in the shelter before they need you in the radio room—pity you haven't brought your brolly along. Come on, I'll go with you."

The pilots were already racing for the Spitfires, and Maddie tried to fix her mind on the practical problem of how best to take off from the half-mended runway—taxiing would be the hardest, as you wouldn't be able to see the holes in the surface past the high nose of the little fighter planes. She tried not to think about what it would be like running across the airfield to the radio room an hour from now, under fire.

But she did it. Because you do. It is incredible what you do, knowing you have to. A bit less than an hour later—to allow themselves some extra time for dodging bombs—the two girls were outside again, in the moonscape that was now RAF Maidsend.

Queenie steered Maddie at a trot, both of them bent nearly double, hugging the sides of buildings and zigzagging across the open spaces. They'd heard how during the retreat from France the low-flying planes of the Luftwaffe would strafe people on the ground with machine gun fire, just for the hell of it, and right now there were two or three German fighters buzzing low over the runway like wasps with the sun on their wings, drilling holes in windows and parked aircraft.

"Over here! Here!" someone yelled desperately. "Hey, you two, come help here!"

For a few seconds, Maddie, doggedly coping with her own private hell of rational or irrational fear, did not even notice Queenie's change of direction as she headed toward the cry for help. Then sense came back to Maddie for a minute and she realized that Queenie was dragging her to the nearest antiaircraft gun emplacement.

Or what was left of it. Most of the protective concrete barrier and the sandbags surrounding it had been blown to bits, taking with it two of the army gunners who had been valiantly trying to keep the runway fit for the Spitfire squadron that would have to land there after the battle. One of the dead gunners was easily younger than Maddie. A third man who was still standing looked like a butcher without the apron, soaked from neck to thighs in blood. He turned wearily and said, "Thanks for the relief. I'm beat." Then he sat down on the ruined platform and closed his eyes. Maddie cowered next to him, her arms over her head, listening to the hideous rattle of the gunner sucking air into blood-filled lungs. Queenie slapped her.

"Get up, girl!" she ordered. "I won't have this. I'm your

superior officer giving orders now. Get up, Brodatt. If you're scared, *do something*. See if you can make this gun work. Get moving!"

"The shell needs to be loaded first," the gunner whispered, lifting a finger to point. "The Prime Minister don't like girls firing guns."

"Bother the Prime Minister!" exclaimed the superior officer. "Load the damned gun, Brodatt."

Maddie, nothing if not mechanically minded and trained to react positively to orders from people in authority, clawed her way up the gun.

"That slip of a lass'll never shift that shell," croaked the gunner. "Weighs thirty pounds, that does."

Maddie wasn't listening. She was reckoning. After a minute's rational thought, and with strength that she later couldn't explain, she loaded the shell.

Queenie worked frantically over the fallen gunner, trying to plug the holes in his chest and stomach. Maddie did not watch. After some time, Queenie took her by the shoulders and showed her how to aim.

"You've got to anticipate—it's like shooting birds, you have to fire a little ahead of where they'll be next—"

"Shoot a lot of birds, do you?" Maddie gasped, anger and fear making her peevish about the other girl's seemingly limitless talents.

"I was born in the middle of a grouse moor on the opening day of the shooting season! I could fire a gun before I could read! But this poxy thing is just a wee bit bigger than a Diana air rifle, and I don't know how it works, so we have to do it together. Like yesterday, all right?" She gave a sudden gasp and asked anxiously, "That's not one of our planes, is it?"

"Can't you tell?"

"Not really."

Maddie relented.

"It's a Messerschmitt 109."

"Well, clobber it! Point this way—now wait till he comes back, he doesn't know this station's still operational—just wait."

Maddie waited. Queenie was right: doing something, focusing, took away the fear.

"Now go!"

The blast momentarily blinded them both. They did not see what happened. Maddie swore, afterward, that the plane did not go down in a ball of flame until it had made at least two more passes over the runway. But no one else ever claimed to have shot down that Me 109 (oh, how many aircraft I know after all!), and God knows the fighter pilots were a competitive lot of bean counters. So that kill (I expect the Luftwaffe also call it a kill when someone shoots down a plane, like deer) was credited to two off-duty WAAF officers working together at an unmanned gun station.

"I don't think our gun did that," Maddie told her friend, whey-faced, as the black, oily smoke rose from the turnip field where the plane had come down. "It must have been one of our lot, firing from the air. And if it *was* this gun, it wasn't you."

It was bad enough Maddie suspected the reason Queenie was at her side now was because she'd had to give up on the lad whose gun they'd taken over. Bad enough. But there had also been a pilot in that ball of flame, a living young man with not much more training than Maddie herself.

"Stay here," Queenie choked. "Can you load another shell? I'll find someone who knows what they're doing to take over—you'll be needed in the tower now—"

Queenie paused a moment.

"Which way to the northeast air raid shelter from here?"

she asked anxiously. "I get so muddled in the smoke."

Maddie pointed. "Straight line across the grass. Easy peasy if you're brave enough—like finding Neverland, 'Second to the right and then straight on till morning.'"

"What about you? Brave enough?"

"I'll be all right. Now I've got something to do—"

They both ducked instinctively as something exploded at the other end of the runway. Queenie squeezed Maddie around the waist and gave her a quick peck on the cheek. "'Kiss me, Hardy!' Weren't those Nelson's last words at the Battle of Trafalgar? Don't cry. We're still alive and we make a *sensational* team."

Then she hitched up her hair to its two-inch above-the-collar regulation point, swabbed her own tears and the grease and the concrete dust and the gunner's blood from her cheeks with the back of her hand, and she was off running again, like the Red Queen.

It's like being in love, discovering your best friend.

"Get your mac on," Maddie said. "I'm going to teach you to navigate."

Queenie burst out laughing. "Impossible!"

"Not impossible! There's a couple of pilots here who scrapped their way out of Poland after it was invaded. They got here with no maps, no *food*, no language other than Polish. They'll tell you all about it if you let them—bit tricky making sense of their English. Anyway, if a couple of escaped prisoners can find their way across Europe and become RAF pilots, you can—"

"You *talk* to the pilots?" Queenie interrupted with interest.

"There are other things you can do besides dance with them."

"Yes, but *talking*! How unimaginative."

"Some of them won't dance, you know, so you have to talk. That vicar's boy won't dance. Hard to get him to talk, either—but they all like jawing about maps. Or lack of maps. Come on, you don't need a map. We've got the whole day. As long as we don't go anywhere more than five miles away, so I can get back sharpish if the weather clears. But *look* at it—" Maddie waved at the window. It was pouring, rain coming down in sheets, a gale blowing.

"Just like home," Queenie said happily. "You don't get proper Scotch mist in Switzerland."

Maddie snorted. Queenie was devoted to careless name-dropping, scattering the details of her privileged upbringing without the faintest hint of modesty or embarrassment (though, after a while Maddie began to realize she only did it with people she liked or people she detested—those who didn't mind and those she didn't care about—anyone in between, or who might have been offended, she was more cautious with).

"I've got bicycles," Maddie said. "A couple of the mechanics let me borrow them. Rain doesn't stop those lads working."

"Where are we going?"

"The Green Man. Pub at the foot of the cliffs on St. Catherine's Bay, last chance before it shuts down next week. The proprietor's fed up being fired at. Not by the Germans, mind you, it's our own lads drilling the pub sign out there on the edge of the shingle, last thing before they head home after a battle—they do it for luck!"

"Bet they do it to get rid of unused ammunition."

"Well, it's a landmark, and you're the navigator. Find the coast and go south, easy peasy! You can use my compass. If you *can't* find it, I'm afraid it'll be nowt but cold beans straight from the tin for your dinner—"

"That's not fair! I'm back on shift at eleven tonight!"

Maddie rolled her eyes. "Bloomin' 'eck, that leaves us only about fifteen hours for a ten mile push-bike ride! But it'll give me a chance to finish telling you my fears." Maddie had her man's greatcoat on and was tying it up around her shins so it wouldn't catch in the bicycle chain.

"I hope you've got a tin opener," Queenie said ominously, struggling into her own greatcoat. "And a spoon."

It was astonishing, after ten minutes' pedaling away from RAF Maidsend, how peaceful the drenched Kent countryside was. It was true that every now and then you passed a concrete gun emplacement or watchtower, but mostly you were just traveling through rolling, chalky fields, green with turnips and potatoes and mile upon mile of orchards.

"You might have brought your brolly," Queenie said.

"I'm saving it for the next air raid."

They came to a crossroad. There were no road signs, not one; they'd all been taken down or blacked over to confuse the enemy in the event Operation Sea Lion was successful and the German army came swarming inland. "I've no *idea* where we are," Queenie wailed. The mechanic's bike was so big for her that she couldn't sit down on it; she had to stand on the pedals. She seemed in perpetual danger of falling off, or of being devoured by her enormous overcoat. She had the outraged, distraught look of a wet cat.

"Use the compass. Keep going east till you find the sea. Pretend," Maddie told her, inspired. "Pretend you're a *German spy*. You've been dropped here by parachute. You've got to find your contact, who's at this legendary smugglers' pub by the sea, and if anyone catches you—"

Under her dripping plastic rain hat, the kind you get in a tiny cardboard box with a flower on it for a halfpenny, Queenie gave Maddie a strange look. It had challenge in it, and defiance, and excitement. But also *enlightenment*. Queenie leaned forward over the handlebars of her bicycle and was off, pedaling like fury.

At the crest of a low rise, she bounded off her bike in one almighty leap like a roe deer away up the glens, and was halfway up a tree before Maddie realized what she was doing.

"Get down, you daft idiot! You'll be soaked! You're *in uniform!*"

"*Von hier aus kann ich das Meer sehen,*" said Queenie, which is "I can see the sea from here" in German. (Oh—silly me. Of course it is.)

"Shut up! You lunatic!" Maddie scolded furiously. "What are you *doing?*"

"*Ich bin eine Agentin der Nazis.*" Queenie pointed. "*Zum Meer geht es da lang.*"

"*You'll get us both shot!*"

Queenie considered. She looked at the teeming sky, looked at the endless dripping apple orchard, and looked at the empty road. Then she shrugged and said in English, "Don't think so."

"'Careless talk costs lives,'" Maddie quoted.

Queenie laughed so hard she slid gracelessly and painfully from one branch to a lower branch, and tore her coat climbing down. "Now just you be quiet, Maddie Brodatt. You told me to be a Nazi spy and I'm being one. I won't let you get shot."

(I really would like to catapult myself back there in time and kick my own teeth in.)

The outbound route to St. Catherine's Bay was, shall we say, *creative*. It involved Queenie getting off her bicycle at every single crossroad—each one wet, windy, and featureless—and climbing a wall or gate or tree to get her bearings. Then there was always a palaver with the greatcoat as she got going again, and near misses with puddles.

"You know what I'm scared of?" Maddie yelled at the top of her voice, rain and east wind beating in her face as she pedaled energetically to keep up with the small wireless operator. "Cold tinned beans! It's quarter to two. The pub'll be shut by the time we get there."

"You said it doesn't shut till next week."

"For the afternoon, you gormless half-wit! They stop serving till evening!"

"I think that's frightfully unfair of you, blaming it on me," Queenie said. "It's your game. I'm just playing along."

"Another thing I'm scared of," Maddie said.

"That doesn't count. Neither do the tinned beans. What are you most afraid of—what's your number one fear?"

"Court-martial," answered Maddie briefly.

Queenie, uncharacteristically, was silent. And stayed silent for some time, even while she did another of her tree-climbing surveys of the surrounding area. Finally she asked, "Why?"

It had been a good long while since Maddie had given her answer, but Queenie did not need to remind her what the subject had been.

"I keep *doing* things. I make decisions without thinking. Crikey, firing a ruddy antiaircraft gun—no authorization whatsoever, and Messerschmitt 109s circling overhead!"

"The Messerschmitt 109s circling overhead were the reason you were firing it," Queenie pointed out. "I authorized you. I'm a flight officer."

"You're not *my* flight officer and you don't have any gunnery authority."

"What else?" Queenie asked.

"Oh—things like guiding in the German pilot the other

day. I've done something like that before, only in English." She told Queenie about talking down the lads in the Wellington the first time. "No one authorized that either. I didn't get in trouble, but I should have. So stupid. Why did I do it?"

"Charity?"

"I could have killed them, though."

"You *have* to take risks like that. There's a war on. They could have bought it and gone down in flames themselves, without your help. But with your help they made it down safely."

Queenie paused. Then she asked, "Why are you so *damn good* at it?"

"At what?"

"Air navigation."

"I'm a pilot," Maddie said—you know, she was so matter-of-fact, she wasn't proud, she wasn't defensive—just, *I'm a pilot.*

Queenie was outraged.

"You said you didn't have any *skills*, you fibber!"

"I haven't. I'm only a civil pilot. I haven't flown for a year. I haven't got an instructor's rating. I've a good many hours, probably more than most of our lads in the Spitfires; I've even flown at night. But I'm not using it. When they expand the Air Transport Auxiliary I'm going to try to join—if the WAAF'll let me go. I'll have to do a course. There's no flight training on for women at the minute."

Queenie apparently had to turn all this over in her head for a while as she considered the implications of it: Maddie Brodatt, with her unrefined South Manchester accent and her no-nonsense bike mechanic's approach to problems, was a pilot—with more practical experience than most of the young RAF Maidsend Squadron who were daily and sleeplessly hurling themselves toward flame and death against the Luftwaffe.

"You're dead quiet," Maddie said.

"Ich habe einen Platten," Queenie announced.

"Speak English, you lunatic!"

Queenie stopped her bike and climbed off. "I have a puncture. My tire's flat."

Maddie sighed heavily. She propped her own bicycle against the verge and squatted in a puddle to look. Queenie's front tire was nearly completely flat. The puncture must have happened only seconds before—Maddie could still hear the air hissing out of the inner tube.

"We'd better go back," she said. "If we go on we'll have too far to walk. I don't have a repair kit."

"O faithless one," Queenie said, pointing to the entrance to a farm lane about twenty yards farther on. "This is my plan to scrounge a meal before I meet my contact." She sniffed knowingly, nose raised into the wind. "A provincial farmhouse lies less than a hundred yards away, and I smell meat stew and fruit pie—" She took her wounded bicycle by the handlebars and set off up the lane at a determined pace. Land Army girls were hoeing among the cabbages in the adjoining field—no time off for them in the rain, either. They had sacks tied around their legs with string and ground sheets with holes in the middle for rain capes. Maddie and the disguised Nazi spy were well-equipped by comparison in their RAF men's overcoats.

A chorus of vicious dogs began to bark as they approached. Maddie looked around anxiously.

"Don't worry, that's just noise. They'll be tied up or they'd bother the Land Girls. Is the sign up?"

"What sign?"

"A jar of rowan berries in the window—if there's no rowan in the window I won't be welcome."

Maddie burst out laughing.

"You *are* daft!"

"Is there?"

Maddie was taller than her companion. She stood on tip-toe to see over the barnyard wall, and her mouth dropped open.

"There *is*," she said, and turned to gape at Queenie. "How—?"

Queenie leaned her bicycle against the wall, looking very smug. "You can see the trees over the garden wall. They've just been trimmed. It's all very tidy and pretty in a wifely way, but she'll have dug up her geraniums to plant tatties for the War Effort. So if she has something nice to decorate her kitchen with, like fresh cut rowan berries, she's likely to do it, *and*—"

Queenie settled her hair into shape beneath the plastic rain bonnet. "*And* she's the sort of person who will feed us."

She let herself in boldly at the kitchen door of the strange farm.

"Ah've nae wish tae disturb ye, Missus—" Her well-bred, educated accent suddenly developed an irresistible Scottish burr. "We've come frae RAF Maidsend and Ah've had this wee spot o' bother wi' me bike. Ah wondered—"

"Oh, no trouble at all, love!" the farmer's wife said. "I've a couple of Land Girls boarding with me, and I'm sure we've got a puncture repair kit among us. Mavis and Grace'll be in the fields just now, but if you wait a moment I'll check the shed— Oh, and for goodness sake come in and warm your-selves first!"

Queenie produced, as if by magic, a tin of twenty-five Player's from deep in the pockets of her greatcoat. Maddie realized suddenly that this infinite supply of cigarettes was carefully hoarded—realized that she'd scarcely ever seen Queenie smoking, but that she used cigarettes as gifts or as payment in kind in place of cash—for tips and poker chips and, now, bicycle patches and lunch.

Only once, Maddie remembered, had she seen Queenie smoking a cigarette she hadn't lit for someone else—only once, when she'd been waiting to interview the German pilot.

Queenie held out the cigarettes.

"Oh, goodness no, that's *far* too much!"

"Aye, take them, let your lassies share 'em out. A gift o' thanks. But would ye no gie us a loan o' your hob to heat our wee tin o' beans before we go?"

The farmer's wife laughed merrily. "They making WAAF officers take to the roads like gypsies, are they, buying a boil of your tea can in exchange for a smoke? There's shepherd's pie and apple crumble left over from our own dinner, you can help yourselves to that! Just a minute while I find you a patch for your tube—"

They were soon tucking into a steaming hot meal considerably better than any they'd eaten at Maidsend for the past three months, including new cream to pour over the home baking. The only inconvenience was that they had to eat it standing up, as there was so much traffic through the kitchen—the chairs had been removed so as not to clutter up the passage of farmhands and Land Army Girls and dogs (no children; they'd been evacuated, away from the front line of the Battle of Britain).

"You owe me four more fears," Queenie said.

Maddie thought. She thought about most of the fears that Queenie had confessed to—ghosts, dark, getting smacked for naughtiness, the college porter. They were almost childish fears, easily bottled. You could knock them on the head or laugh at them or ignore them.

"Dogs," she said abruptly, remembering the slavering hounds on the way in. "And Not Getting the Uniform Right—my hair's always too long, you're not allowed to alter the coat so it's always too big, things like that. And: Southerners laughing at my accent."

"Och aye," Queenie agreed. It could not be a problem she ever encountered, with her educated upper-crust vowels, but being a Scot, she sympathized with any distrust of the soft Southern English. "You've only one more fear to go—make it good."

Maddie dug deep. She came up honestly, hesitating a little at the simplicity and nakedness of the confession, then admitted: "Letting people down."

Her friend did not roll her eyes or laugh. She listened, stirring the warm cream into the baked apples. She didn't look at Maddie.

"Not doing my job properly," Maddie expanded. "Failing to live up to expectations."

"A bit like my fear of killing someone," Queenie said, "but less specific."

"It could include killing someone," said Maddie.

"It could." Queenie was sober now. "Unless you were doing them a favor by killing them. Then you'd let them down if you *didn't*. If you couldn't make yourself. My great-uncle had horrible cancers in his throat and he'd been to America twice to have the tumors taken out and they kept coming back, and finally he asked his wife to kill him, and she did. She wasn't charged with anything—it was recorded as a shooting accident, believe it or not, but she was my grandmother's sister and we all know the truth."

"How *horrible*," Maddie said, with feeling. "How terrible for her! But—yes. You'd have to live with that selfishness afterward, if you couldn't make yourself do it. Yes, I'm dead afraid of that."

The farmer's wife came in again, with a patch and a bucket to fill with water so they could find the puncture, and

Maddie quickly pulled down the blackout curtains over her bright and vulnerable soul and went off to sort out the tire. Queenie stayed in the kitchen, thoughtfully lapping up the last drops of warm cream with a tin spoon.

Half an hour later, as they walked the bicycles back down the muddy farm lane and out to the road, Queenie commented, "God help us if the invading Germans turn up with Scottish accents. I got her to draw me a map. I *think* I can find the pub now."

"Here's your hairpin back," Maddie said. She held out the thin sliver of steel. "You'll want to get rid of the evidence next time you sabotage someone's tires."

Queenie let out a peal of her giddy, infectious laughter. "*Caught!* I stuck it in too far and couldn't have got it back without you noticing. Don't be cross! It's a *game*."

"You're too good," Maddie said sharply.

"You got a hot meal out of it, didn't you? Come on, pub'll be open again by the time we get there, and we won't be able to stay long—I'm back on duty at eleven and I want a nap. But you deserve a whisky, first. My treat."

"I'm sure that's not what Nazi spies drink."

"This one does."

It was still raining as they coasted along the steep lane that wound down the cliff side to St. Catherine's Bay. The road was slick, and they went cautiously, standing on their brakes. There were a couple of miserable wet soldiers manning the gun emplacements, who waved and shouted as the girls on their bicycles came barreling past, brakes screeching with the steepness of the descent. The Green Man was open. Sitting in its bow window were RAF Maidsend's gaunt and weary squadron leader and a well-turned-out civilian in a tweed suit and spectacles. Everyone else was clustered around the bar.

Queenie walked purposefully to the cheerful coal fire and knelt, rubbing her hands together.

Squadron Leader Creighton rapped out a greeting that couldn't be ignored. "What chance! Come join us, ladies." He stood up and gave a little ceremonious bow, offering chairs. Queenie, comfortable with and indeed accustomed to such attention from superior officers, stood up and let her coat be taken. Maddie hung back.

"This rather small and sodden young person," said the squadron leader to the civilian, "is the heroine I was telling you about—the German speaker. This other is Assistant Section Officer Brodatt, who took the call and guided the aircraft in. Join us, ladies, join us!"

"Assistant Section Officer Brodatt is a pilot," Queenie said.

"A pilot!"

"Not at the moment," said Maddie, blushing and writhing with embarrassment. "I'd like to join the ATA, the Air Transport Auxiliary, when they let more women in. I have a civilian license. My instructor joined in January this year."

"How extraordinary!" said the long-sighted gentleman. He peered at Maddie through lenses half an inch thick. He was older than the squadron leader, old enough he might've been refused if he'd tried to join up. Queenie shook hands with him and said gravely, "You must be my contact."

His eyebrows disappeared into his hairline. "Must I?"

Maddie said furiously, "Pay no attention to her, she's loopy. She's been playing daft games all morning—"

They all sat down.

"Her suggestion," said Queenie. "The daft games."

"It *was* my suggestion, but only because she's so utterly *rubbish* at finding her way anywhere. I told her to pretend to be a—"

"'*Careless talk costs lives,*'" Queenie interrupted.

"—spy." Maddie omitted any damning adjectives. "She was supposed to have been dropped by parachute and had to find her way to this pub."

"Not just any game," exclaimed the gentleman in the tweed suit and thick spectacles. "Not just *any* game, but the Great Game! Have you read *Kim*? Are you fond of Kipling?"

"I don't know, you naughty man, I've never kippled," Queenie responded tartly. The civilian let out a chortle of delight. Queenie said demurely, "Of course Kipling, of course *Kim*, when I was little. I prefer Orwell now."

"Been to university?"

They established that Queenie and the gentleman's wife had been at the same college, albeit nearly twenty years apart, and traded literary quotations in German. They were obviously cut from the same well-read, well-bred, lunatic cloth.

"What's your poison?" the civilian with a penchant for Kipling asked Queenie genially. "The water of life? Do I detect a Scottish burr? Any other languages besides German?"

"Only coffee just now, as I'm on duty later; aye you do; *et oui, je suis courante en français aussi*. My grandmother and my nanny are from Ormaie, near Poitiers. And I can do a fair parody of Aberdeen Doric and tinkers' cant, but the natives aren't fooled."

"The Doric and tinkers' cant!" The poor fellow laughed so hard he had to take off his glasses and give them a wipe with a dotted silk handkerchief. He put them back on and peered at Queenie. The lenses made his blue-green irises seem so large they were startling. "And—how *did* you manage to find your way here today, enemy agent mine?"

"It's Maddie's story," said the enemy agent generously. "And I owe her a whisky."

So Maddie told, to an appreciative audience, how she had

played Watson to her friend's giddy Sherlock Holmes—of the sabotaged tire at the entrance to the well-stocked farm, and the assumptions about the dogs and the food and the flowers there. "And," Maddie finished with a triumphant flourish, "the farm woman drew her a *map*."

The so-called enemy agent glanced up at Maddie sharply. Squadron Leader Creighton held out his hand, palm up, a demand.

"I've burnt it," Queenie said in a low voice. "I popped it in the fire when we first came in. I won't tell you which farm, so don't ask."

"I shouldn't have to go to much trouble to deduce it myself," said the long-sighted civilian, "based on your friend's description."

"I am an officer." Queenie's voice was dead quiet. "I gave the woman a royal ticking off after she'd done it, and I doubt she'll need another warning. But I never lied to her, either, and she might have been more suspicious in the first place if I had. It would be inappropriate to punish anyone—apart from me, of course."

"I wouldn't dream of it. I am agog at your initiative." The man glanced at the silent Creighton. "I do believe your earlier suggestion is spot on," he said, and rather randomly quoted what Maddie reckoned was probably a line from Kipling. "'Only once in a thousand years is a horse born so well fitted for the game as this our colt.'"

"Bear in mind," said Creighton soberly, holding the other man's magnified eyes with his own over the top of his steepled fingers, "these two work well together."

clk/sd & w/op

Bloody Machiavellian English Intelligence Officer playing God.

I never knew his name. Creighton introduced him by an

alias the man sometimes uses. At my interview he jokingly identified himself by a number because that's what the British Empire spies do in *Kim* (though *we* don't; we are told in training that numbers are too dangerous).

I liked him—don't get me wrong—beautiful eyes behind the dreadful specs, and very lithe and powerful beneath the scholarly tweed. It was *wonderful* flirting with him, all that razor-edge literary banter, like Beatrice and Benedick in *Much Ado About Nothing*. A battle of wit, and a test, too. But he *was* playing God. I noticed, I knew it, and I didn't care. It was such a thrill to be one of the archangels, the avengers, the chosen few.

Von Linden is about the same age as the intelligence officer who recruited me. Has von Linden an educated wife, too? (He wears a ring.) Might von Linden's wife have been at university with my German tutor?

The sheer stark raving incredible madness of such a very ordinary possibility makes me want to put my head down on this cold table and sob.

Everything is *all so wrong.*

I have no more paper.

Oh Maddie.

I am lost. I have lost the thread. I was indulging myself in details as if they were wool blankets or alcohol, escaping wholly back into the fire-and-water-filled early days of our friendship. We made a *sensational* team.

I was so sure she'd landed safely.

It has been four days since I last wrote anything, and there is a simple reason why: no paper. When they did not come to get me the first day, I suspected, and spent the whole morning sleeping—just like a holiday. The blanket has changed my life. By the end of the second day I was getting very hungry and a bit tired of sitting in absolute pitch dark. Then those pictures. They'd already shown me the destroyed rear cabin of Maddie's Lysander, but these were new—enlargements from the pilot's cockpit.

Oh Maddie

Maddie

That was the last peaceful moment of my holiday. Also, they have been questioning that French girl again. I was lying with my nose pressed to the crack underneath the door—I'd been crying, and it is the only place I get any light—and recognized her feet as they dragged her by (she has rather pretty feet, and she is always barefoot).

I would not have slept well after those pictures anyway, but have I said before that my room is attached to the suite they use for interviews, etc.? You would have to be stone deaf to sleep through it even in a feather bed.

The following morning a trio of soldiers clapped me into

chains—*chains!*—and hauled me to a subbasement, where I was sure I was going to be dissected. No, it turned out to be the kitchen—literally the *kitchen* of this desecrated hotel, which is where they cook up our delicious gray cabbage soup (they do not bake bread here—when we get bread it is stale ends cast off from someplace else). Apparently the charwoman who scrubbed the pots, swept the floors of sawdust and spread down less moldy sawdust in its place, hauled wood and coal, emptied all the prisoners' waste buckets and slopped them out, peeled potatoes for the Gestapo officers' soup (I like to imagine she did these last two jobs without washing her hands in between)—etc.—has been sacked. More accurately, she has been arrested and sent to prison—not this one, obviously—because she stole a couple of cabbages. Anyway, yesterday and the day before they needed someone else to do all these challenging tasks while they found another drudge to replace her.

Who better suited for such work than an idle Special Operations flight officer? The chains were meant as a reminder that I am a prisoner, not an employee. Chiefly a reminder to the cook and his underlings, I think, but the cook was such a foul and filthy beast he would not have noticed if I'd been in drag as the Führer himself, so long as he could fondle my breasts.

And—*I let him do it.* For food, you might suppose, but no! (Although the old goat *did* very generously let me feast on the scraps when they'd finished peeling the tatties. I did not have to peel anything myself, as they wisely would not give me a knife.) Like an opium addict, I'll do almost anything for more paper.

The basement of the Château de Bordeaux is a warren of strangeness. Rather spooky. There are a few rooms (those with freezers and gas ovens) that they probably use for horrible experiments, but mostly these cellars are empty because they are not secure and are generally just too damn dark for productive activity. All the hotel's catering equipment is still down there—huge coffee urns, copper pans the size of bathtubs, milk cans (empty), empty wine bottles and jam pots stacked everywhere, even a row of dust-covered greasy blue aprons still hanging in a passageway. There are a number of service lifts, dumbwaiters for hauling trays upstairs in addition to the great big one for loading crates and things from the main street, and it was in exploring one of the small ones (with an eye to escaping up it if I could squeeze into it) that I discovered the paper—stacks and stacks of unused recipe cards, shoved in the dumbwaiter to get them out of the way.

I thought about Sara Crewe in *A Little Princess*, pretending she is a prisoner in the Bastille to make her work as a scullery maid more bearable. And you know … I just couldn't do it. What is the point in pretending I am in the Bastille? I have spent the past two days in *chains*, underground, slaving for a monster. Ariadne in the maze of the Minotaur? (I wish I'd thought of that earlier.) But I was too busy slaving to pretend much of anything anyway.

So—I got to take the recipe cards away with me in exchange for being groped, and managed to limit the assault by suggesting I was von Linden's personal Bit of Tartan Fluff and that the Hauptsturmführer would not like it if the cook defiled me.

O Lord! How is one to choose between the Gestapo inquisitor and the prison cook?

Of course I was not allowed to take the paper into my room with me (in case I should tear it into strips and weave it into a rope with which to hang myself, I suppose), so had to wait for a while in the big outer chamber while von Linden was busy with someone else. See me, cowering in the corner in my wrist and leg irons, clutching my armful of blank recipe cards and trying not to notice what they were doing to Jacques's fingers and toes with bits of hot metal and tongs.

After an exhausting hour or so of this melodrama, v.L. took a break and sauntered over to have a chat with me. I told him in my best Landed Gentry voice of frosty disdain how puny an empire the Third Reich must be if it can't afford to supply paper to double-crossing informants like myself, and mentioned that the foul beast in the kitchen and his skivvies are all very demoralized about the way the war is going (Italy has collapsed, German cities and factories bombed to bits, everyone expects an Allied invasion within the year—which is after all why Mssrs. Jacques and I are here, caught trying to hurry said invasion along).

Von Linden wanted to know if I'd read Orwell's *Down and Out in Paris and London*.

I wish I had not gratified him *again* by gaping. Oh! I suppose I did let slip that I like Orwell. What was I thinking?

So then we had a genial argument about Orwellian socialism. He (v.L.) disapproves (obviously, as Orwell spent five months battling the idiot Fascists in Spain in 1937), and I (who don't always agree with Orwell either but for different reasons) said that I didn't think my experience as a scullion *exactly* matched Orwell's, if that was what v.L. was getting at, albeit we may have found ourselves working in similar French hotel basements for similar rates of pay (Orwell's somewhat higher than mine, as I seem to recall he was given an allowance of a couple of bottles of wine in addition to raw potato peelings). Eventually von Linden took possession of my recipe cards, my chains were removed, and I was thrown back into my cell.

It was a very surreal evening.

I dreamed I was back at the beginning and they were

starting on me all over again, a side effect of having to watch them work on someone else. The *anticipation* of what they will do to you is every bit as sickening in a dream as when it is really going to happen.

That week of interrogation—after they'd starved me in the dark for most of a month, when they finally settled down to the more intricate task of picking information out of me— von Linden did not look at me once. He paced, I remember, but it was as though he were doing a very complicated sum in his head. There were a number of gloved assistants on hand to deal with the mess. He never seemed to *tell* them what to do; I suppose he must have nodded or pointed. It was like being turned into a technical project. The horror and humiliation weren't in that you were stripped to your underthings and being slowly taken to pieces, but in that nobody seemed to give a damn. They were not doing it for fun; they were not in it for lust or pleasure or revenge; they were not bullying me, the way Engel does; they were not angry with me. Von Linden's young soldiers were doing their job, as indifferently and accurately as if they were taking apart a wireless set, with von Linden doing his job as their chief engineer, dispassionately directing and testing and cutting off the power supply.

Only, your wireless set does not shiver and weep and curse and beg for water and be sick and wipe its nose in its hair as its wires are short-circuited and cut and fried and knotted back together. It just sits there stoically being a wireless set. It doesn't mind if you leave it tied to a chair for three days sitting in its own effluvium with an iron rail strapped upright against its spine so it can't lean back.

Von Linden was not *any more* human grilling me about Orwell last night than when he was grilling me about those blasted codes two weeks ago. I am still nothing more than a wireless set to him. But now I am a rather *special* wireless set, one he enjoys tinkering with in his spare time—one he can secretly tune in to the BBC.

Well—four days have passed, three of them mentally and/or physically draining, and I have lost the thread. I haven't got my prescription forms to look over, or even Engel to remind me where I was. I suppose she must have other duties besides me, and may even get a day off every so often. Beastly Thibaut is here with another man today, hence I am writing like a demon, any old drivel, so as not to draw attention to myself. I hate Thibaut. I am not exactly afraid of him the way I am afraid of the cook or the Hauptsturmführer, but *buckets of blood*, I despise Thibaut—as I suppose he despises me—turncoat thugs that we are. He is crueler than von Linden, I think, enjoys it more, but has not v.L.'s genius or commitment. As long as I am writing, Thibaut leaves me alone. I just wish he did not fix these cords so savagely tight.

I forget where I had got to, and I am also panicking a bit about Time. It is the 9th day since I started, and v.L. said I could have 2 weeks. I don't know if that includes the past 4 wasted days or not, but at this rate I am not going to reach a conclusion (I think we all know I am never going to look at that stupid List again).

I will beg him for another week, in German, this evening. It puts him in a civil humor when people are formal and polite. I am sure that part of the reason I am treated as such a dangerous lunatic, apart from biting that policeman when I was arrested, is because I am always so foul-mouthed and foul-tempered. They had another British officer in here one time, an English airman, very *I-say tip-top well-bred* chap, and though he was kept under guard he was always allowed to walk about with his hands free. (I'll bet he had not got my amateur escape artist's reputation. And I really can't help my foul temper.)

No, I *will* take a look at that list again after all. Perhaps it will give me some idea of where to pick up the story. Also, Thibaut and his mate will have to scurry about to find it, which will be entertaining.

RANDOM AIRCRAFT

Puss Moth, Tiger Moth, Fox Moth
Lysander, Wellington, Spitfire
Heinkel He 111, Messerschmitt 109
AVRO ANSON!

AIR TAXI WITH THE ATA

How could I forget the Anson!

I don't know how you manage to keep the Luftwaffe supplied with serviceable aircraft. The Air Transport Auxiliary is how we manage with the RAF, ferrying planes and taxiing pilots. A constant and steady supply of broken planes coaxed back to repair sites, new ones delivered from factory to operational base—all flown by civilian pilots, no instruments, no radio, no guns. Navigating by trees and rivers, railway tracks and the long straight scars of Roman roads. Hitchhiking back to base for the next assignment.

Dympna Wythenshawe (remember her?) was one of these ferry pilots. One blustery autumn afternoon when the frantic days of the Battle of Britain had faded and flared into the explosive nights of the London Blitz, Dympna landed at RAF

Maidsend in a twin-engined transport plane, delivering three pilots who were to fly broken Spitfires away for repair. (Three lads. They didn't let lassies fly fighter planes, not even broken ones, till a bit later in the war. Not much later.) Dympna came into the canteen for a hot cup of something, and there was Maddie.

After they'd finished hugging and laughing and exclaiming (Dympna knew where Maddie was stationed, but Maddie hadn't been expecting Dympna), and had consumed cups of Camp Coffee (chicory extract and hot water, *blechhh*), Dympna said, "Maddie, come fly the Anson."

"What?"

"You can have the pilot's seat. I want to see if you remember how to fly."

"I've never flown an Anson!"

"You've flown my Rapide a dozen times. The Annie's got twin engines too, not so different. Well . . . a bit bigger. And quite a lot more powerful. And it's a monoplane, with a retractable undercarriage—"

Maddie gave an incredulous bark of laughter. "Not so different!"

"But I'll take care of the undercarriage. It's a right pig to raise and lower, you have to do it by hand, 150 turns—"

"Done that on a Wellington," Maddie said smugly.

"There you are!" Dympna cried. "No worries, then. Come along, I've got to make a hop to RAF Branston and drop off another ferry pilot."

She looked around the canteen approvingly. "It's *so nice* to land at an airfield where you can get hot buttered toast. So many airfields are strictly Boys Only, with a cold sitting room for the ladies, usually empty. Heaven help you if you can't get off the airfield before blackout—I had to spend the night in the back of a Fox Moth once. I nearly froze to death."

Maddie looked away, her eyes welling with tears of envy at the thought of a frozen lonely night in the back of a Fox Moth. She'd not touched an aircraft's flight controls since before the war started. She'd never flown anything so big or so complicated as an Avro Anson.

Queenie was walking toward them, carrying her own cup of steaming black engine oil. Dympna stood up.

"I've got to get going before I lose the light," she said casually. "Do come, Maddie. I'll drop you here again on my way back. It's only a twenty minute hop each way. Take off, fly straight and level—"

"'Second to the right, and then straight on till morning,'" Queenie said. "Hello! You must be Dympna Wythenshawe."

"And you must be Maidsend's impromptu crack gunner!"

Queenie gave a little bow. "I am a gunner on Tuesday mornings only. Just now I am in Bomb Disposal. See?" She held up her own half-slice of dry toast. "Out of butter already."

"I'm about to take your friend Maddie for a flight lesson," Dympna said. "An hour off base. There's room for one more, if you're free."

Maddie saw no flinch or blanch pass over the fair skin. But Queenie said calmly, putting her cup on the table, "No, I don't think so." Then she repeated every one of Maddie's own objections. "She's not flown this type. She said so. And only as a civilian." She articulated exactly how long since Maddie had piloted a plane, a known fact. "A year ago. More than a year."

Reason had been hammering at Maddie. She'd thought in rapid succession: I shouldn't leave base, I don't know what I'm doing, it's probably illegal, I'll be court-martialed, and so forth. But now she made up her mind. Reminded how long it had been since she had flown a plane, Maddie made up her mind. It had been far too long.

"Now," Maddie said. "Now I wear Air Force blue and already this year I've been fired on in the air and I've shot down an enemy plane myself, or as good as. And Dympna's my instructor and I'm a pilot and *you—*"

Queenie needed twisting. She was still on her feet, still clutching her untouched toast.

"Pretend," Maddie told her, inspired. "Pretend you're Jamie. Your favorite brother, the one you worry about, on a training mission. You're sure and full of yourself. You've done your solo in a Tiger Moth, and now you're going along as a stooge, and all you have to do is raise and lower the undercarriage, which will leave the instructor free to concentrate on the tyro pilot—"

Suddenly Maddie faltered. "You're not really afraid of heights, are you?"

"A Wallace and a Stuart, feart o' *anythin'?*"

Maddie thought it must be like having a little brass peg in your mind, like the hinged switch on an electric hall light, and when you flipped it you turned instantly into another person. Queenie's stance was different, her feet slightly farther apart and flat on the floor, her shoulders squared back. Perhaps more like a drill sergeant than her Eton-educated older brother, but certainly more man than any WAAF flight officer. She cocked her blue cap back at a hellish angle.

"High time they put the RAF in kilts," she remarked, flipping the hem of her uniform skirt disdainfully.

Maddie said a silent, secret thank-you to Adolf Hitler for giving her this utterly daft chameleon for a friend, and chummed Queenie out to the airfield, following Dympna.

The sky was low and gray and wet. "You'll get an hour in your logbook, P1 under training," Dympna told Maddie over her shoulder as they crossed to the Anson. "Taxi, takeoff, and a full flight to RAF Branston. I'll talk you through the landing there, and you can try it yourself when we get back to Maidsend."

There was a lad (a real one) giving the aircraft the once-over when they reached it, and chatting with a couple of ground crew. He turned out to be Dympna's other passenger, the other ferry pilot on her taxi run. He glanced up at Dympna as she approached and gave a laugh, and exclaimed in a broad American accent, "Well, look what we have here—three gorgeous English gals to fly with!"

"Yankee idiot!" cursed the youthful blue-kilted bomber pilot. "I am a *Scotsman*."

Maddie climbed in first. She crawled forward through the fuselage (ex-civil passenger aircraft, impressed by the RAF like Dympna's Puss Moth) and into the left-hand seat, the pilot's seat. Then she sat scanning the collection of gauges and instruments. She was surprised by how many of them were the friendly, familiar faces of dials she knew: rev counter, air-speed indicator, altimeter—and when she took hold of the flight controls and felt the ailerons and elevator responding reliably to her command, for one moment she thought she was going to cry properly. Then she glanced over her shoulder and saw her passengers climbing in behind her. Dympna slid her elegant length into the right-hand seat beside Maddie, and Maddie pulled herself together. On her behalf, a random squall peppered the panes of the cockpit with fat raindrops for about ten seconds. Then the shower stopped suddenly, like a squirt of machine gun fire.

What's a lass like you need with a big toy like this?

Maddie laughed aloud, and said to Dympna, "Run me through the checks."

"What's so funny?"

"This is the biggest toy ever."

"We'll get bigger ones soon," Dympna assured her.

To Maddie it felt like the last day of school, like the summer holidays beginning.

"Two fuel tanks in each wing," said Dympna. "Two oil pressure gauges, two throttle levers. But only one mixture control—set that to normal for start-up. The ground crew takes care of the priming pumps—" (I am making this up. You get the idea.)

Maddie had taxied this familiar airfield and roared down the rutted runway in her head so many times it felt as though she'd done it before; or as though she were dreaming now. The Anson leaped into the air in a gust of headwind. Maddie fought the aircraft for a while, straightened the rudder, felt the speed increase as Dympna's laborious cranking of the undercarriage began to progress and the extra drag fell away. The wings lifted and dipped in the blustering wind like a motorboat riding swells. It was lovely flying a low-winged plane, with its unblocked, endless view of sky—or, on that occasion, low-hanging cloud.

"Hey, Scottie!" Dympna ordered, shouting over the engines. "Stop squeaking and give me a hand."

The whimpering Scot crept toward the cockpit, keeping low to the floor of the aircraft to avoid having to look out. Maddie glanced over her shoulder; she could tell her friend was manfully battling some demon or other.

"If you're scared, *do something*," Maddie shouted, not without irony.

The Scot, whey-faced and determined, reached down alongside the pilot's seat and took hold of the undercarriage crank. "My real fear," Scottie gasped, giving the crank a turn, "is not of heights"—another turn—"but of being sick."

"Doing something should help," yelled the Yank from the back, enjoying the view ahead of him for different reasons than the rest of them.

"Looking at the horizon helps," yelled Maddie, her own farseeing eyes focused on the distant place where the battered gray land met tumultuous gray cloud. Conversation was not really possible. Most of Maddie's being was absorbed in flying the buffeting Anson. But a little corner of her mind was sorrowing that her friend's first flight was not being made through a still summer evening of golden light over the green Pennines.

Maddie landed the Anson into wind with a wallop, and Dympna kept her hands to herself, letting Maddie do it. The Yank said it was a whale of a landing, which he meant as a compliment. Afterward the Scot stood quivering on the runway with gritted teeth while the aircraft was refueled and the Branston ground crew chatted with the ferry pilots. Maddie stood close by, not close enough to touch, not anything so babyish. But offering silent sympathy.

Minus the Yank ferry pilot, the Anson crew set off back to Maidsend. Fitful sunlight, low on the horizon, gleamed through the heavy cloud in the west, and Maddie, rather desperate to improve the experience for her suffering passenger, was able to climb a little higher, where the wind was brisker and not so gusty. (The ferry pilots are not allowed to fly higher than 5000 feet. Engel will have to do the metric conversion—sorry about that.)

Blooming crosswind, Maddie swore to herself as they crawled back toward home.

"Still feeling sick?" Dympna bellowed at the hapless Scot. "Come sit in the front."

The Scot, in weakened state, was easily bullied (as you know). Dympna crawled out of her forward seat and Scottie crawled into it.

Maddie glanced at her friend, grinned, and took hold of the finely manicured hand that gripped the edge of the copilot's seat. She forced the hand around the flight controls.

"Hold this," she bellowed. "See how we're slant against the sun? 'Cause there's a whopper of a crosswind, so we have to crab. Just like sailing. You point the plane sideways. Got it?"

Scottie nodded, face pale, jaw set, eyes alight.

"See?" Maddie held her own empty hands aloft. "You're in control. You're flying the plane. The Flying Scotsman!"

The Flying Scotsman squeaked again.

"Don't cling to it—just hold it gently— Oh, well done."

They beamed at each other for a moment. Then they looked back at the sky.

"Dympna!" cried Maddie. "Look, look at the *sun!*"

It was green.

God's truth—the rim of the lowering sun, all they could see of it, had turned green. It was sandwiched in between a bank of low dark haze and a higher bank of dark cloud, and just along the upper edge of the haze was this bright lozenge of flaming green, like Chartreuse liqueur with light behind it. Maddie had never seen anything like it.

"My God—" Dympna whispered something to this effect, but no one heard her. She laid a hand on each girl's shoulder, gripping them hard.

"Fly the plane, Maddie," she commanded hoarsely, an instructor's reminder.

"I am."

Maddie flew the plane, but she stared at the sun's green edge, too, for a long, wind-buffeted glorious half minute. Thirty seconds it lasted, green sunlight breaking the cloud on the horizon. Then the light winked out below the haze again and all three pilots were left blinded in the dull gloom of a showery autumn afternoon.

"What was it? Dympna, what was it? A test? A new bomb? What—"

Dympna relaxed her grip on their shoulders.

"It's called the green flash," she said. "It's just a mirage, a trick of the light. Nothing to do with the war." She let out a little gasp of delight. "Oh! My father saw it once when he was camping on Kilimanjaro, years ago. Get to work, Scottie; undercarriage needs lowering. And I need the instructor's seat back to make sure Brodatt lands us safely."

Down on earth, Dympna tossed out the two tyros and took off again without herself setting foot on the ground at Maidsend, hurrying back to her own base before it got dark or the weather closed in (ATA pilots are able to authorize their own flights).

Queenie, herself again, took hold of Maddie's hand and squeezed it tightly. She walked all the way back across the airfield without letting it go. Maddie closed her eyes and flew again in the ethereal pale green light. She knew she would never let it go.

I'm sorry. This has got absolutely bugger all to do with Air Taxi.

But it was that flight that shoehorned Maddie into the ATA. She was released to them by the WAAF, not seconded— a somewhat unusual procedure then, though they did more of it later in the war; unusual because the ATA is a civilian organization and the WAAF military. But Maddie had been on the ATA's waiting list since it was drawn up, and having Dympna on her side put her at an advantage over other applicants who might have been equally qualified. The women on the waiting list were all far more qualified than the men, because the qualified men didn't have to wait. Also, Maddie's Oakway night flying and fog line landings made her a bit special (*night and fog*, brrrr, even innocently and in English it makes me shiver). Lads with her experience were flying bombers now. The ATA needed her.

They fly without radio or navigation aids. They do have maps, but they are not allowed to mark balloons or new airfields on them, in case they lose the maps and you lot pick them up. Maddie did a training course when she joined, early in 1941, and she had one instructor who told her, "You don't need a map. Just fly this heading for as long as it takes to smoke two cigarettes. Then turn and fly the next heading for another cigarette." You can fly hands-free and light a cigarette mid-flight pretty easily if the aircraft is set up properly—CDF, Cigarette Direction Finding.

About the same time Maddie joined the Air Transport Auxiliary, her friend the wireless operator was seconded to the SOE, the Special Operations Executive. Maddie did not know this. They'd been swapping letters for a while after Maddie left Maidsend, and then suddenly Queenie's letters started arriving from an undisclosed address and were full of black censor's marks, as though they were coming from a soldier in North Africa. And then Queenie asked her to write to her at home, which had the impressively simple (and palindromic!) address of Craig Castle, Castle Craig (Aberdeenshire). But she was not at home. That was just for forwarding purposes. So they did not see each other most of that year except:

1) When Queenie turned up unexpectedly during a break in the Manchester Blitz, and they spent three wet and stormy days burning black market petrol up and down the Pennines on Maddie's Silent Superb.

2) When one of Queenie's Top Ten Fears materialized and her favorite brother Jamie the bomber pilot (the real Jamie) and his crew got shot down. Jamie spent a night floating in the North Sea and afterward had to have four frozen fingers and all his toes amputated. Maddie went to visit him when he was in hospital. In fact she had never met him before, and perhaps that wasn't the best time to meet him, but Queenie actually sent Maddie a telegram—only the second telegram she'd ever got—asking her to come along to see him, and Maddie did. It was perhaps not the best time to meet Queenie, either.

3) When Queenie was sent up to Oakway for parachute training. And they weren't allowed to talk to each other that time.

That should be a separate section, SOE Parachute Drops. But I have not got to that bit yet, and now von Linden is just arriving, and I will have to translate what I have written today for him myself, since Engel is not here.

I am alone. O God. I have tried to undo Thibaut's knots, but I can't reach them with both hands. I was translating today's writing for von Linden, my elbows on the table and my head between my hands, not daring to look at him. I'd already asked him for more time, and he'd said he would consider it after he'd heard today's material. And I know I have given him nothing today. Nothing but the events of the past two weeks, which he already knows, and the green flash. Almighty Christ. After I'd got to the bit about the cook feeling me up—*so* embarrassing, but if I'd skipped it and v.L. found out later, I'd pay for it in blood—he came over and stood by me. I had to look up. When I did, he took a handful of my hair and held it lightly off the back of my neck for a moment.

He never smiles or frowns or *anything*. I could feel my face flaming. Oh why did I have to put down that coarse, filthy sarcasm about choosing between the cook and the inquisitor? I could not tell what he was thinking. He rubbed my hair gently between his fingers.

Then he said one word. It sounds the same in English and French and German. *Kerosene.*

And he left me here with the door closed.

I would like to write something heroic and inspired before I go up in fireworks, but I am too stupid and sick with dread to think of anything. I can't even think of anyone else's memorable defiance to repeat. I wonder what William Wallace said when they were tying him to the horses that would rip him into quarters. All I can think of is Nelson saying, "Kiss me, Hardy."

They have WASHED MY HAIR. That was what the kerosene was for this time. FLAMING HEAD LICE. Now I stink of explosive but I have not got nits.

Just after the Hauptsturmführer left me last night <u>there was an air raid and everybody scrambled to the shelters as usual.</u> I sat weeping and waiting <u>for two hours,</u> just as I did sometimes during that week of interrogation, begging God and the RAF for a direct hit that they NEVER DELIVER. After it was over, no one came back for another hour. THREE HOURS without anyone telling me what was going on. I expect v.L. was hoping that in my panic I would write something more productive as a last resort, only I struggled so much trying to get my legs free that the chair I was tied to fell over. Needless to say, I could not write in such a state (and did not even consider calling for help). Eventually, a number of people came in and found me doing a frantic imitation of an upside-down tortoise.

I had managed to drag myself and my chair over to the door and prepared an ambush that sent two guards sailing head over heels as they tripped on me when they came in. Von Linden really should know me well enough by now to realize that I am not going to face my execution without a fight. Or with anything remotely resembling dignity.

When they had got me resurrected and pulled up to the table again, von Linden came in and laid a single white pill in front of me. Like Alice, I was suspicious. I still thought I was about to be executed, you see.

"Cyanide?" I asked tearfully. It would be such a humane way to go.

But it was not a suicide tablet, it turns out. It was an aspirin.

Like Engel, he does pay attention.

He has given me another week. But he has doubled my workload. We made a deal. Another one. Truly I thought I couldn't possibly have anything left of my soul to sell to him, but we have managed to strike another bargain. He has a tame American radio announcer who does Nazi propaganda in English aimed at the Yanks—she works from Paris for Berlin's broadcasting service, and she has been badgering the Ormaie Gestapo for an interview. She wants to give her American battleship audiences a sugarcoated inside perspective on Occupied France: how well prisoners are treated, how stupid and dangerous it is that the Allies force innocent girls like me to do dirty work like mine, blah blah blah. Despite her shining legitimate Third Reich radio credentials, the Ormaie Gestapo are reluctant to respond, but von Linden believes he can *use me* to make a good impression. "I would not be here if my own government were not so ruthlessly inhumane," I will tell her for him. "By contrast, see how humanely the Germans deal with captured agents? See how I am doing translation work, neutrally occupying myself while I await trial?" (A joke—they will not give me a trial.)

(After my second escape attempt, while they were waiting for von Linden to turn up and pronounce punishment, a couple of his stupid subordinates casually blabbed a great many administrative secrets in front of me, not realizing I understand German. So I know a lot more about their plans for me than I'm supposed to know. I fall under a sickening policy called *Nacht und Nebel*, Night and Fog, which allows them to do whatever the hell they feel like to people suspected to be "endangering security," and then make them disappear— really disappear. They don't execute them here; they ship them off without leaving a trace, into the "night and fog." Oh, God—I am a Night and Fog prisoner. It is so secret they don't even write it down—just use the initials "NN." If this manuscript survives me, they will probably black out everything I've just written. It is not really *Nacht und Nebel* policy to grant interviews for radio broadcasts, but these Gestapo are opportunists if nothing else. They can always chop me into bits afterward and bury the scraps in the cellar.)

If I cooperate with the propagandist I can have more time. If I tell the bleak truth—then no. And they'll probably make the American broadcaster disappear, too, and I'll have that on my conscience.

The aspirin and kerosene are part of Operation Cinderella, a program designed to transform me from a feverish, nit-infested, mentally unstable prison rat back into a detained flight officer of cool nerve and confidence, suitable for presentation to a radio interviewer. To add credibility to our story, I have been given a sort of translation job copying Hauptsturmführer von Linden's own notes from the past year here, with names (when he knows them) and dates and, ugh, some *methods* used, in addition to information extracted. Oh, mein Hauptsturmführer, *you are an evil Jerry bastard*. A copy is to be made in German for his C.O. (he has a Commanding Officer!) and another made in French for some other official purpose. I am doing the French one. Fräulein Engel is doing the German (she is back today). We are working together and using up all my ill-gotten recipe cards. We are both cross about that.

The job is both horrific and unbelievably tedious. And so deviously *instructional* it makes me want to put the man's eyes out with my pencil. I am made to see into a small methodical corner of von Linden's mind, not anything personal, but *how he works*. And also that he is good at it—unless, of course, it is all fabricated to intimidate me. I don't actually think he is imaginative enough to do that—at least, not in the way I use my imagination, not to pretend anything, not to concoct a fake collection of half a dozen notebooks bound in calfskin and filled with tragic miniature portraits of a hundred and fifty doomed spies and Resistance fighters.

But he is creative in his own scientific way—a technician, an engineer, an analyst. (I'd love to know what his civilian credentials are.) His persuasive techniques are tailored to the individual as he gains understanding into the character of each. Those three weeks I spent starving in the dark, waiting for something to happen—he must have been watching me like a hawk, tallying my silences, my tantrums, my numerous half-successful attempts to clamber out the transom window, the heating duct, the air vent, to pick the lock, garrote and/or emasculate various guards, etc. Observing how I cower and weep and plead whenever the screaming starts in the next room. Observing how I frantically try to put my hair up whenever someone opens the door and sees me (not everyone is questioned in their dreadful undergarments—it is a special torment reserved for the modest and the vain. I am one of the latter).

It is comforting to discover that I am not, after all, the only Judas to have been interned behind these desecrated hotel walls. I suppose von Linden would be sacked if his success rate were that dismal. And now I suspect, as well, that I am exposed to the stubborn ones on purpose to demoralize me, perhaps with the dual effect of humiliating them at their most vulnerable moments with an embarrassing and appreciative audience.

I am still quite presentable. They have always gone easy on my hands and face, so when I'm fully dressed you'd never look at me and think I'd recently been skewered and barbecued—they've packed their partially dismantled wireless set into a smooth and pleasing case. Perhaps it has been v.L.'s intention all along to use me in his little propaganda exercise. And of course—I am *willing to play*. How did he know? How did he know from the start, even before I told him? That I am *always* willing to play, addicted to the Great Game?

Oh, mein Hauptsturmführer, you evil Jerry bastard, I am grateful for the eiderdown they have given me to replace the verminous blanket. Even if it is just part of the temporary scheme to rehabilitate me, it is bliss. Half the stuffing has come out and it smells like a root cellar full of damp; but still, an *eiderdown*—a *silk eiderdown*! It is embroidered "C d B" so it must be spoiling stock from this building's former life as the Château de Bordeaux. I do sometimes wonder what happened to the hotel's furnishings. Someone must have gone to a good deal of effort to empty all the guest rooms of their wardrobes and beds and vanity tables and to bolt bars across the window shutters. What did they do with everything—carpets, curtains, lamps, lightbulbs? Certainly my little room has no Gallic charm to recommend it apart from its rather pretty parquet floor, which I can't see most of the time (as with all the prisoners' rooms, my window has been boarded shut), and which is very cold and hard to sleep on.

I had better get to work—though I have bought my extra week, I now have only half as much time each day for writing. And my day is longer, too.

I am getting tired.

I know, I know. Special Ops Exec. Write—

FERRY PILOT

Maddie went back to Oakway. There was now an Air Transport Auxiliary ferry pool there, and Oakway had also become the biggest parachute training center in Britain. As an ATA pilot Maddie was demoted in rank, and a civilian again, but she was able to live at home, *and* she was given a petrol allowance for her bike so she could get to the airfield, *and* she could trade in a day's completed ferry chit for a two-ounce bar of Cadbury's milk chocolate.

Maddie was in her element at last. No matter that the sky had changed—it was an obstacle course of balloon cables and restrictions and military aircraft and, often, dirty weather. Maddie was in her element, and her element was air.

They throw you through some aerobatics that you'll never use, watch you take off and land something, and hey presto, you're qualified to fly Class 3 aircraft (light twin engines) and all the Class 2s (heavy single engines) without ever having seen most of them. Maddie said they are supposed to do thirty long-distance training flights up and down the country to imprint it on their brains until they can fly without looking at a map, but she got signed off at twelve because it was taking too long to wait for decent weather, and they wanted her working. There is an ATA pilot killed every week. They are not shot down by enemy fire. They fly without radio or navigation aids into weather that the bombers and fighters call "unflyable."

So Maddie, first day on the job, walks into the hut that the Oakway ATA pilots laughingly call their "Mess Hall."

"There's a Lysander chalked up here with your name on it," says her new Operations officer, pointing to the blackboard with its list of aircraft to be moved.

"Is there *really?*"

Everyone laughs at her. But not meanly.

"Never flown one, have you," says the Dutchman, a former KLM pilot who knows the north of England almost as well as Maddie does, having made regular passenger landings at Oakway from the time it opened.

"Well," says Ops, "Tom and Dick are taking the Whitleys over to Newcastle. And Harry is taking the Hurricane. That leaves the taxi Anson and the Lysander for the ladies. And Jane's got the Anson."

"Where's the Lysander going?"

"Elmtree, for repair. Faulty tailplane handwheel. It's flyable, but you have to hold the control column right forward."

"I'll do it," says Maddie.

NOT A SAFE JOB

They gave her a very thorough navigation briefing beforehand, as the aircraft's defect meant she couldn't expect to fly hands-free. She wouldn't be able to juggle maps en route. She sat studying the pilot's notes for an hour (the detailed notes they give the operational pilots who'll only ever fly one type of aircraft), then panicked about losing the weather. Now or never.

The ground crew was aghast at the idea of a girl flying the broken Lysander.

"She won't be strong enough. With the tail set for takeoff yon slip of a lass won't be able to hold the stick hard for'ard enough for landing. Don't know if anyone could."

"Someone landed it here," Maddie pointed out. She'd already been given the chit for the job and wanted to leave while she could still see the Pennines. "Look, I'll just set it neutral by hand before I get in. Easy peasy—"

And she gently pushed the tail into place, stood back, and dusted her hands on her slacks (navy, with an Air Force blue shirt and navy tunic and cap).

The mechanics were still frowning, but they'd stopped shaking their heads.

"It'll be a pig to fly," Maddie said. "I'll just keep the climb-out and landing nice and long and shallow. Come in fast, eighty-five knots, and the automatic flaps'll stay up. It's not too windy. Should be fine."

At last one of the lads gave a slow, reluctant nod.

"Tha'll manage, lass," he said. "I can see tha'll manage."

That first ATA flight Maddie made was hard work. Not frightening; just hard work. It was hard, at first, to look past the gunsight sockets and camera fixing plates and rows and rows of bomb selector switches for bombs she wasn't carrying, a Morsing key for a radio that wasn't connected, etc.

Fly the plane, Maddie.

The six familiar, friendly faces of the flight instrument panel smiled at her behind the control column. One of the ground crew anxiously made sure she knew where to find the forced-landing flare release.

The weather cooperated for her, but the Lysander fought her for nearly two hours. When she tried to land at Elmtree she misjudged the amount of runway she was going to need. Hands and wrists aching with the effort of keeping the control column far enough forward to land, Maddie took off again without touching down, and had to come in over the runway twice more before she got it right. But she landed safely at last.

I sound so authoritative! It must be the immediate effect of the aspirin. Imagine if you gave me Benzedrine. (And I still crave coffee.)

Maddie, also craving coffee, went to scrounge a sandwich from the workshop canteen, and found another ferry pilot there ahead of her—tall, square-faced, with dark brown hair shorter than Maddie's, in uniform navy slacks and tunic with the double gold shoulder stripes of a first officer. For a moment Maddie was confused, thinking that, like Queenie, she was seeing ghosts.

"*Lyons!*" Maddie exclaimed.

The pilot looked up, frowned, and answered tentatively, "Brodatt?"

Then Maddie saw it wasn't the vicar's son who used to fly at Maidsend before being shot down and incinerated in flaming petrol over the South Downs last September, but someone who clearly must be his twin sister. Or an ordinary sister, anyway. They stared at each other in bewilderment for a moment. They had never met.

The other girl beat her to the question. "But how do you know my name?"

"You look exactly like your brother! I was a WAAF at Maidsend with him. We used to talk about maps—he wouldn't ever dance!"

"That was Kim," said the girl, smiling.

"I liked him. I'm sorry."

"My name's Theo." She offered Maddie her hand. "I'm in the women's ferry pool at Stratfield."

"How do you know *my* name?" Maddie asked.

"It's chalked up on the assignment board in the radio room," First Officer Lyons said. "We're the only ATA pilots here today. They usually send girls in the Lysanders—the lads all want something faster. Have a sandwich. You look like you could use one."

"I've never flown a Lysander before," said Maddie, "and I wish I never would again. This one just about killed me."

"Oh, you brought in the faulty tailplane! It's terribly unfair of them to give you a broken Lizzie on your first go. You must have another go *immediately*, flying one that works."

Maddie took the offered half sandwich—bully beef straight from the tin as usual. "Well, I have to, I suppose," she said. "I've got to take one from here down to its normal base this afternoon. It's not top priority but it's got one of those "S" chits, secrecy and a report required. It's my first day on the job, too."

"You lucky thing, that's RAF Special Duties!"

"RAF Special Duties?"

"Your guess is as good as mine. They're sort of embedded in the normal RAF base that you fly in to, but after you've landed there two or three times you start to work it out—a little fleet of Lysanders camouflaged in black and dark green, all equipped with long-range fuel tanks, and the runway laid out with electric lamps. Night landings in short fields—"

She let that hang between them. France, Belgium, Resistance agents, refugees, wireless equipment and explosives smuggled into Nazi-occupied Europe—you didn't dare talk about it. You just didn't.

"It's brilliant fun landing a Lizzie in their training field. They have a mock flare path laid out, little yellow flags, you can play you're a Special Duties pilot. Lysanders are wizard at short landings. You could land one in your granny's garden."

Maddie could scarcely believe that, having just managed to get her first Lizzie down only by using every available inch of runway.

Theo pulled her crust to pieces and arranged three crumbs in an inverted L-shape to imitate torches blazing in a dark French meadow. "Here's what you do—" She glanced quickly over each shoulder to make sure she wasn't overheard.

"They're always a bit boggled when a girl leaps out of the cockpit afterward."

"They were a bit boggled when I got in this morning!"

"How's your navigation? You're not allowed to mark this airfield on your map. Takes a bit of studying before you leave, so you can find it yourself."

"I can manage that," Maddie said confidently and truthfully, having earlier that day done almost exactly the same thing.

"It'll be fun," Theo repeated enthusiastically, encouraging her. "You couldn't get better training if they gave you a course! Flying a broken plane for two hours then landing a fixed one in twenty yards in the same day—we might as well be *operational*."

All right, this airfield, the Special Duties airfield. It is the same one Maddie and I took off from six weeks ago. The pilots who use it are called the Moon Squadron—they fly by moonlight and only by moonlight. The location of their airfield is one of our most closely guarded secrets and I thank God I don't know its name or have any clue where it is. I really don't; though I have been there at least five times, I was always flown there from my own base outside Oxford, in the dark, sometimes via another aerodrome, and I don't even know in which direction we set off to get there. They did that on purpose.

Special Duties planes need a lot of maintenance as they tend to go through them quite rapidly, bashing the undercarriages in the dark and getting bits blown off by antiaircraft guns on their way home. Later Maddie made that run several times, ferrying damaged or mended aircraft in and out of the bigger aerodrome that surrounds them and hides them. More recently she served them as a taxi pilot delivering their rather special passengers. The dozen or so quite suicidally deranged pilots who are stationed there grew familiar with Maddie's increasingly expert dead-stop accurate short-field landings, and by and by they knew when she'd arrived before she got out of the plane.

I am out of time again—hell. I was enjoying myself

Engel thinks I am translating von Linden's horrid notes, but I am sneaking in a few recipe cards of my own because I have got ahead of her.

She can be a perfect fount of information when she's in the mood. It is because of her nattering on at me while I was hard at work that she has fallen behind. She tells me that if I am lucky I will be sent to a place called Ravensbrück when they are finished with me here. It is a concentration camp solely for women, a labor camp and prison. Perhaps it is where the charwoman who stole the cabbages was sent. Basically it is a death sentence—they more or less starve you until you can't work, and then when you become too weak to shift any more rubble for replacing the roads blown up by our Allied bombers, they hang you. (I am ideally suited for shifting rubble, having previous experience on the runway at Maidsend.) If you are not put to work breaking rocks, you get to incinerate the bodies of your companions after they have been hanged.

If I am *not* lucky—in other words, if I do not produce a satisfactory report in the time allotted—I will be sent to a place called Natzweiler-Struthof. This is a smaller and more specialized concentration camp, the vanishing point for *Nacht und Nebel* prisoners, who are mostly men. Occasionally women are sent there as live specimens for medical experiments. I am not a man, but I am designated *Nacht und Nebel*.

God.

If I am *very* lucky—I mean if I am clever about it—I will get myself shot. Here, soon. Engel didn't tell me this; I thought it out myself. I have given up hoping the RAF will blow this place to smithereens.

I want to update my list of "10 Things I Am Afraid Of."

1) Cold. (I've replaced my fear of the dark with Maddie's fear of being cold. I don't mind dark now, especially if it's quiet. Gets boring sometimes.)

2) Falling asleep while I'm working.

3) Bombs dropping on my favorite brother.

4) Kerosene. Just the word on its own is enough to reduce me to jelly, which everybody knows and makes use of to great effect.

5) SS-Hauptsturmführer Amadeus von Linden. Actually he should be at the top of this list (the man blinds me with fear), but I was taking the list in its original order and he has replaced the college porter.

6) Losing my pullover. I suppose that counts under cold. But it is something I worry about separately.

7) Being sent to Natzweiler-Struthof.

8) Being sent back to England and having to file a report on What I Did In France.

9) Not being able to finish my story.

10) Also of finishing it.

I am no longer afraid of getting old. Indeed I can't believe I ever said anything so stupid. So childish. So offensive and *arrogant*.

But mainly, so very, very stupid. I desperately want to grow old.

Everybody is getting excited about the American radio woman's visit. My interview will be held in von Linden's study, office, whatever it is. I was taken to see it earlier today so that I would be forewarned and not fall over in a dead faint of astonishment seeing it for the first time in front of the interviewer (pretend *all* my "interviews" take place beneath the Venetian glass chandelier in this cozy wood-paneled den. Pretend I sit writing at his pretty little eighteenth-century marquetry table every afternoon. Pretend I ask his *pet cockatoo* in its bamboo cage to supply me with unfamiliar German words when I get stuck).

(Or perhaps not. The helpful cockatoo might seem a little too far-fetched.)

I am not writing there now—I am in my usual bare broom cupboard, pulled up to the tubular steel table with my ankles tied to my chair, with SS-Scharführer Thibaut and his mate whose name I haven't been told breathing down my neck.

I am going to write about Scotland. I wasn't ever there with Maddie but I feel as though I was.

I don't know what she was flying the night she got stuck at Deeside, near Aberdeen. It wasn't just Lysanders that she ferried, and she didn't do much taxi work that first year, so it probably wasn't an Anson. Let's say it was a Spitfire, just for fun—the most glamorous and beloved of fighter planes—even the Luftwaffe pilots would let you pull out their back teeth with a pair of pliers if it would buy them an hour in control of a Spitfire. Let's say that late in November of '41 Maddie was delivering a Spitfire to this Scottish airfield where they'd fly out to defend the North Sea shipping, or perhaps to take pictures of Luftwaffe-occupied airfields in Norway.

Our reconnaissance planes are tarted up in a lovely salmony-mauve camouflage to match the clouds. So let's say Maddie was flying a pink Spitfire, but not up to the soaring blue heavens like the fighter pilots. She was flying cautiously, making her way along the coast and up the straths, the wide valleys of Scotland, because the cloud was low. She was 3000 feet above sea level, but between the Tay and the Dee, the Cairngorm Mountains rise higher than that. Maddie flew alone, careful and happy, low over the snow-tipped Highlands on those pretty tapered wings, deafened by the Merlin engine, navigating by dead reckoning.

The glens were full of frost and fog. Fog lay in pillows in the folds of the hills; the distant mountaintops shone dazzling pink and white beneath rays of low sunshine that didn't touch the Spitfire's wings. The haar, the North Sea coastal fog, was closing in. It was so cold that the moist air crystallized inside the Plexiglas hood, so that it seemed to be lightly snowing in the cockpit.

Maddie landed at Deeside just before sunset. But it wasn't sunset; it was twilight gray and turning blue, and she would either have to spend the night in a cheerless, unmade spare bed in the guest room of the officers' billet, or she'd have to find a guest house in Aberdeen. Or she'd have to spend half the night on an unheated and blacked-out train and perhaps arrive back in Manchester at two o'clock in the morning. Unwilling to face the loneliness of the airfield's spartan accommodation, or a dour granite-faced Aberdeen landlady who wouldn't accept her ration coupons for an unarranged evening meal, Maddie opted for the train.

She walked to the branch line station at Deeside. There were no route maps posted on the walls, but a Wonderland-style sign commanding, "If you know where you are, then please tell others." There were no lights in the waiting room because they'd show when you opened the door. The ticket seller had a dim banker's lamp burning behind his wee cage.

Maddie straightened herself out a bit. The girls in the ATA had been given a good splash of publicity in the papers and were expected to live up to certain standards of neatness. But she'd found that people didn't always recognize her navy uniform with its gold ATA pilot's wings, or make sense of them, and Scotland was as foreign a land as France to Maddie.

"Is there a train any time soon?" she asked.

"Aye, there is," agreed the ticket seller, as cryptic as the platform posters.

"When?"

"Ten minutes. Aye, ten minutes."

"Going to Aberdeen?"

"Och, no, not to Aber*deen*. The next train's the branch line to Castle Craig."

To make this easier, I am translating the ticket seller's speech from Aberdeen Doric. Maddie, not being fluent in the Doric herself, wasn't sure she'd heard correctly.

"*Craig Castle?*"

"Castle Craig," this bogle of a railway employee repeated laconically. "Single to Castle Craig, miss?"

"No—no!" Maddie said sensibly, and then in a fit of pure insanity brought on, no doubt, by loneliness and hunger and fatigue, added, "Not a single, I've got to come back. A return, please. Third-class return to Castle Craig."

Half an hour later: Oh, *what* have I done! Maddie thought to herself, as the antique and ice-cold two-coach stopping train lurched and crept past a number of pitch-dark, anonymous station platforms, bearing Maddie farther and farther into the haunted foothills of the Scottish Highlands.

The compartment in the railway carriage was dimly lit by one blue light overhead. The carriage was not heated. There were no other passengers in Maddie's compartment.

"When's the next train back?" she asked the ticket collector.

"Last one in two hours."

"Is there one before that?"

"*Last one* in two hours," he repeated unhelpfully.

(Some of us still have not forgiven the English for the Battle of Culloden, the last battle to be fought on British soil, in 1746. Imagine what we will say about Adolf Hitler in two hundred years.)

Maddie got off the train at Castle Craig. She had no luggage but her gas mask and her flight bag, containing a skirt that she was supposed to wear when she wasn't flying but which she hadn't been able to change into, and her maps and pilot's notes and circular slide rule for wind speed computations. And a toothbrush and her last flight's two-ounce bar of chocolate. She remembered how she'd nearly wept with envy at Dympna's description of having to spend the night in the back of a Fox Moth and nearly freezing to death. Maddie wondered if she'd freeze to death before the train she just got off finally went back to Deeside two hours later.

Here I think I should remind you that my family is long-established in rather the upper echelons of the British aristocracy. Maddie, you will recall, is the granddaughter of an immigrant tradesman. She and I would not ever have met in peacetime. Not *ever*, unless perhaps I'd decided to buy a motorbike in Stockport—perhaps Maddie might have served me. But if she hadn't been such a cracking radio operator and been promoted so quickly, it's not likely we'd have become friends even in wartime, because British officers don't mingle with the Lower Ranks.

(I don't believe it for a minute—that we wouldn't have become friends somehow—that an unexploded bomb wouldn't have gone off and blown us both into the same crater, or that God himself wouldn't have come along and knocked our heads together in a flash of green sunlight. But it wouldn't have been *likely*.)

At any rate, Maddie's growing misgivings on this particular ill-conceived rail journey were mostly based on her certainty that she simply *could not* go knock on the door of a Laird's Castle and ask for accommodation, or even a cup of tea while she waited for the return train. She was only Maddie Brodatt and not a descendant of Mary, Queen of Scots, or Macbeth.

But she had not taken the War into account. I have heard a good many people say that it is leveling the British class system. *Leveling* is perhaps too strong a word, but it is certainly mixing us up a bit.

Maddie was the only passenger to get off at Castle Craig, and after she'd dithered on the platform for five minutes, the stationmaster came out to greet her personally.

"You a mate o' young Jamie up the Big House, are ye?"

For a moment Maddie was too surprised to answer.

"He'll be glad o' sensible company, he will, alone in that castle with them young rascals from Glasgow."

"Alone?" Maddie croaked.

"Aye, the Lady's away to Aberdeen for three days with the Women's Voluntary Service, packing socks and cigarettes to send our lads fighting in the desert. It's young Jamie alone with them evacuees. Eight o' them, the Lady took in, last ones in the queue—no one else would have 'em, the mucky wee lads, wi' their nits an' streamin' noses. Dads all at work on the ships, bombs droppin' night and day, kiddies never been out o' the tenements in their lives. The Lady said she'd raised six weans of her own and five o' them lads, eight o' someone else's lads wouldn't be much different. But she's gone and left young Jamie to make their tea with them puir mangled hands o' his—"

Maddie's heart soared at the idea of helping Jamie make tea for eight Glaswegian evacuees.

"Can I walk there?"

"Aye, half a mile along the main road to the gate, then a mile down the drive."

Maddie thanked him, and he raised his cap to her.

"How'd you know me for a friend of Jamie's?" she asked.

"Yer boots," the stationmaster said. "All you RAF lads wear the same boots. Never seen young Jamie take his off. Wish I had a pair."

Maddie walked through the windy dark to Craig Castle, bubbling over with giddy laughter and relief and anticipation.

I'm an RAF lad! she thought, and laughed aloud in the dark.

Craig Castle is a small castle—I mean, compared to Edinburgh or Stirling Castles; or Balmoral, where the King lives in the summer; or Glamis, where the Queen's family lives. But it is a proper castle, bits of it nearly six hundred years old, with its own well in case of siege, and cellars you can use as dungeons or wine stores, and four different endless spiral stairways so that not all of the rooms on every level actually connect. There is a room lost behind a sealed wall (there is also a window missing on the wall outside, and an extra chimney, so we know the room used to be there). Also, there are gun rooms and trophy rooms, a billiard room

120

and a smoking room, two libraries, innumerable retiring and drawing rooms, etc. At the moment most of these are under dust sheets because everyone is off doing War work, including the staff.

When Maddie arrived, it looked deserted—blackout, of course—but she staunchly rattled the iron ratchet at the main door and eventually a Very Grubby Glaswegian Evacuee with egg smeared from the left corner of his mouth right across to his left ear opened the door. He was carrying a candle in a tin candlestick.

"Jack-be-nimble," Maddie said.

"Me name's *Jock*," retorted the evacuee.

"Have I interrupted your tea?"

Jock responded in a garble of excited Glaswegian syllables. He might as well have spoken German for all Maddie understood.

He wanted to touch her gold wings. He had to point to them to get her to understand.

She let him.

"Come alang through," he said firmly, beaming, as though she'd passed a test. He shut the massive oak-and-iron door behind them, and Maddie followed him into the labyrinth where I was born.

They emerged in the below-stairs kitchen—with four sinks and three ovens and burners enough to cater meals for fifty guests, and a pine table big enough to seat all the staff if there were any. Around this table were seven young lads—properly young, primary-school age, Jock being the eldest at about twelve—all wearing hobnailed boots and short trousers (to save on cloth) and patched-over school pullovers in varying states of grottiness, all their faces smeared with egg, all consuming toast soldiers at an alarming rate. Standing at the great black Victorian stove top, presiding over a bubbling iron cauldron, was the Honorable youngest son of the Laird of Craig Castle—looking every inch the modern Highland hero in a faded kilt of Hunting Stewart tartan, hand-knit woolen kilt hose, and a machine-knit woolen RAF airman's sweater. His boots exactly matched Maddie's.

"Three minutes, who's up?" he announced, upending an extraordinary ormolu-gilt hourglass and displaying a boiled egg with a pair of silver sugar tongs.

His maimed hands, two fingers and thumb remaining on each, were deft and quick. He sniffed the air. "Oi, Tam, you flip that toast before it burns!" he barked, then turned and saw Maddie.

She wouldn't have recognized him as Jamie—tonight he was the picture of rosy health, nothing like the gray-faced, grieving invalid she'd last seen slumping bandaged and unresponsive in a Bath chair. But she'd never have doubted he was her best friend's brother. Same sleek fair hair, same small light build, same quick bewitching features with a faint hint of lunacy behind the bright eyes.

He saluted her. The effect was incredible. All seven young lads (and Jock) joined him smartly, leaping to their feet and scraping back chairs.

"Second Officer Brodatt of the Air Transport Auxiliary," he introduced her. The boys reeled off their names like a row of cadets: Hamish, Angus, Mungo, Rabbie, Tam, Wullie, Ross, and Jock.

"The Craig Castle Irregulars," Jamie said. "Would you like to join us in a boiled egg, Second Officer Brodatt?"

Maddie's egg allocation amounted to one per week. She usually donated it to her gran for baking, or for the Sunday morning fry-up, and she often had to miss that anyway.

"There's hens all over the grounds," Hamish told her as she sat down with the boys. "We get to eat every egg we find."

"Keeps 'em busy, too, lookin' for 'em," said Jamie.

Maddie took the top off her egg with her spoon. The hot, bright yolk was like a summer sun breaking through cloud, the first daffodil in the snow, a gold sovereign wrapped in a white silk handkerchief. She dipped her spoon in it and licked it.

"You lads," she said slowly, looking around at the grubby faces, "have been evacuated to a magic castle."

"It's true, miss," said Jock, forgetting she was an officer. He gabbled at her in Glaswegian.

"Speak *slowly*," Jamie commanded.

Jock spoke loudly instead. Maddie got the gist of it. "There's a ghost that sits at the top of the tower stairs. You go all cold if you walk through him by accident."

"I've *seen* him," said Angus proudly.

"Aw, ye hav'nae," mocked Wullie with deep scorn. "An' ye sleep wi' a teddy. There's nae ghostie."

They broke into an incomprehensible argument about the ghost. Jamie sat down across from Maddie and they beamed at each other.

"I feel dead outnumbered," Maddie said.

"Me too," Jamie agreed.

He was more or less living in the kitchen and the smaller of the two libraries. The Craig Castle Irregulars mostly lived outside. They slept three to a bed in our ancestral four-posters. The laddies were happy to crowd in together, as that's what they were used to at home, and it saved on sheets, leaving Ross and Jock to share on their own (Ross being Jock's wee brother). Jamie had them all wash up and brush their teeth military-style (or school-style) at the four kitchen sinks, two boys per sink, very efficient. Then he literally marched them all up to bed, installed Maddie in his fox's den of a library on

123

the way, and came back to her twenty minutes later carrying a steaming silver coffee pot.

"It's real coffee," he said. "From Jamaica. Mother hoards it for special occasions, but it's starting to lose its flavor now." He sank into one of the cracked leather armchairs in front of the fire grate with a sigh. "How did you ever get here, Maddie Brodatt?"

"'Second to the right, and then straight on till morning,'" she answered promptly—it did feel like Neverland.

"Crikey, am I so obviously Peter Pan?"

Maddie laughed. "The Lost Boys give it away."

Jamie studied his hands. "Mother keeps the windows open in all our bedrooms while we're gone, like Mrs. Darling, just in case we come flying home when she's not expecting us." He poured Maddie a cup of coffee. "My window's closed just now. I'm not flying at the minute."

He spoke without bitterness.

Maddie asked a question she'd wanted to ask him when she'd first met him, only she hadn't had the courage.

"How did you ever manage to save your hands?"

"Popped my fingers in my mouth," Jamie answered readily. "I swapped hands every thirty seconds or so. Couldn't fit any more than three fingers at a time, and thought I'd better concentrate on the ones I'd miss the most. My big brothers and little sister have all started to call me The Pobble Who Has No Toes, which is a very silly poem by Edward Lear." He sipped his own coffee. "Having something to concentrate on probably saved more than just my hands. My navigator, who came down with me, just gave up, only about an hour after we'd been in the water. Just let go. Didn't want to think about it."

"You going back?"

He hesitated a little, but when he spoke, it was with determination, as though he had a puzzle to solve. "My doctor says they might not want me in a bomber crew. But— you've got a chap with one arm flying in the ATA, don't you? I thought they might take me. Ancient and Tattered Airmen, isn't that what they call you?"

"Not me," Maddie said. "I'm one of the Always Terrified Airwomen."

Jamie laughed. "You, terrified! My eye."

"I don't like guns," Maddie said. "Someday I'll be fired on in the air, and I'll go down in flames just because I'm too blooming scared to fly the plane."

Jamie didn't laugh.

"Must be awful," Maddie said quietly. "Have you flown at all—since?"

He shook his head. "I can, though."

From what she'd seen of him that night, she thought he probably could.

"How many hours have you got?"

"Hundreds," he said. "Over half of them at night. Mostly on Blenheims—that's what I was flying all the time I was operational."

"What did you train on?" Maddie asked.

"Ansons. Lysanders at first."

He was watching her intently over his coffee, as though she were conducting an interview and he were waiting to hear if he'd got the job. Of course it was none of her business, and she had no authority. But she'd landed Lysanders herself too many times at that odd RAF Special Duties airfield, you see, even spent a night in the Moon Squadron's private ivy-covered cottage hidden in a small wood at the edge of the normal airfield (there hadn't been any other place to put her, and she'd been very carefully segregated from the other visitors). She had some idea of the difficulties that peculiar squadron had in finding and keeping pilots. Hundreds of hours' night flying required, and fluent French, and though they could only take volunteers, they were such a secret operation that they weren't allowed to actively recruit anyone.

Maddie has a rule about passing on favors, which she calls the Aerodrome Drop-Off Principle. It is very simple. If someone needs to get to an airfield and you can get them there, by taxi Anson or motorbike or pony trap or pig-a-back, you should always take them. Because someday you will need a ride to an airfield too. Someone different will have to take you, so the favor gets passed on instead of paid back.

Now, talking to Jamie, Maddie thought of all the little things Dympna Wythenshawe had done or said on Maddie's behalf, things that had cost Dympna nothing, but had changed Maddie's life. Maddie knew she could never repay Dympna; but now, according to the Aerodrome Drop-Off Principle, Maddie had a chance to pass the life-changing favors on.

"You should ask your C.O. about Special Duties flying," she said to Jamie. "I think you'd have a good chance of getting in with them."

"Special Duties?" Jamie echoed, just as Maddie had echoed Theo Lyons a few months back.

"They fly dead hush-hush missions," Maddie said. "Short field operations, night landings. Lysanders and sometimes Hudsons. It's not a big squadron. Volunteer for RAF Special Duties, and if you need a reference, ask to talk to—"

The name she gave Jamie was the alias of the intelligence officer who recruited me.

It was probably the most daring thing she'd ever done. Maddie could only guess at what he was. But she'd remembered his name—or rather, the name he'd used when he bought her a whisky in the Green Man—and she'd seen him *more than once* on the secret airfield (and he thought he was so clever, too). Plenty of odd civilians came and went from that airfield, but Maddie didn't see many of them, and when she recognized the one she *did* see, it stuck in her head as a most peculiar coincidence.

(Bloody Machiavellian English Intelligence Officer playing God.)

Jamie repeated the name aloud to fix it in his head, and leaned forward to peer at Maddie more closely in the firelight from the library grate.

"Where the devil have you come by *that* sort of information?"

"'Careless talk costs lives,'" Maddie answered sternly, and The Pobble Who Has No Toes laughed, because it sounded so like his little sister. I mean his younger sister. (I mean me.)

How I would love to stay in the library at Craig Castle with them all night. Later, Maddie slept in my bed (Mother always keeps our beds made up, just in case). It was cold with the window open, but, like Mother and Mrs. Darling, Maddie left the window as she found it, also just in case. I wish I could indulge in writing about my bedroom, but I must stop early today so von Linden can prep me for this radio interview tomorrow. Anyway, my bedroom at home in Craig Castle, Castle Craig, has nothing to do with the War.

This bloody radio interview. All lies, lies, and damned lies.

I'm supposed to use this time to make my own notes on the radio interview yesterday—as a kind of backstop in case the actual broadcast doesn't match up with what v.L. remembers of it. I would have written about it anyway but BUCKETS OF BLOOD, WHEN DO I GET TO FINISH MY GREAT DISSERTATION OF TREASON?

They really made an effort to make me presentable, as though I were a debutante to be presented to the King of England all over again. It was decided (not by me) that my beloved pullover makes me look too thin and pale, and is also getting a wee bit ragged, so they washed and pressed my blouse and temporarily gave me back my gray silk scarf. I was flabbergasted to find they still had it—I suppose it must be part of my file and they are still hunting for unrevealed code in the paisley.

They let me put my hair up but made a lot of fuss over how to fix it, because no one trusts me with hairpins. In the end I was allowed to use PENCIL STUBS. MY GOD they are petty. I was also allowed to do it myself because A) Engel could not make it stay, and B) she could not hide the pencils as well as I did. And even after soaking my fingertips in kerosene for an hour (who suspected kerosene has so many uses?) they have failed to get rid of the ink stains beneath my fingernails. But that just adds credibility to the stenographer story, I think. Also, because afterward my hands positively reeked of kerosene, I was then allowed to scrub myself all over with a lovely creamy little bar of curious American soap that *floated* in the basin when you let go of it. Where in the world did *that* come from? (Apart from the obvious, "America.") It looked like hotel soap but the wrapper was in English and it couldn't have been from this hotel.

C d M, *le Château des Mystères*

Engel did my nails. I was not let to do them myself lest I stab someone with the file. She was as vicious as possible without actually drawing blood (she succeeded in making me cry), but otherwise it is a perfect manicure. I feel sure she has fashion sense lurking beneath the Teutonic Mädchen guise she affects for the Gestapo.

They installed me at the marquetry table with some harmless dummy documents to work on—finding the best connections between French rail and bus timetables and making a list of them in German. When they brought in the interviewer I stood up with an artificial smile and crossed the antique Persian carpet to welcome her, feeling exactly as though I were playing the Secretary on the opening night set of Agatha Christie's *Alibi*.

"Georgia Penn," the radio announcer introduced herself, offering me her hand. She is about a foot taller than me and walks with a stick and a prodigious limp. As old as von Linden, big and loud and friendly—well, just *American*. She worked in Spain during the Civil War as a foreign correspondent and got very badly treated by the Republicans, hence her pro-Fascist bent. She is normally based in Paris and does a radio show called "No Place Like Home" full of jive tunes and pie recipes and discouraging hints that if you are stationed on a battleship in the Mediterranean, your girl is probably cheating on you back in the States. This rubbish is broadcast over and over to make the American soldiers homesick. Apparently Yanks will listen to *anything* if it includes decent music. The BBC is too serious for them.

I shook this treacherous woman's hand and said coolly, *en*

français pour que l'Hauptsturmführer, who doesn't speak English, *puisse nous comprendre*, "I'm afraid I can't tell you my name."

She glanced over at von Linden, who stood deferentially at her shoulder.

"*Pourquoi?*" she demanded of him. She is even taller than von Linden, and her French has all the same broad twangy American vowels as her English. "Why can't I know her name?"

She looked back down at me from her colossal height. I adjusted my scarf and assumed the casual pose of a saint stuck full of arrows, hands linked loosely behind my back, one foot turned out before the other with the knee slightly bent, my head cocked to one side.

"It's for my own protection," I said. "I don't want my name publicized."

What TOSH. I suppose I *could* have said "I am supposed to vanish into the Night and the Fog—" Don't know what she'd have made of that. I wasn't even allowed to tell her what branch of the military I am serving with.

Von Linden gave me a chair as well, next to Miss Penn, away from the table where I'd been working. Engel hovered subordinately. Miss Penn offered a cigarette to von Linden, who waved it away in disdain.

"May I?" she said, and when he shrugged politely, she took one herself and offered another to me. Bet Engel wanted one.

I said, "*Merci mille fois.*" He said *nothing.* O *mein Hauptsturmführer!* You *coward!*

She set about lighting the cigarettes and announced in her brisk, straightforward French, "I don't want to waste my time listening to propaganda. It's my job and I'm wise to it. I'll be frank with you—I'm looking for truth. *Je cherche la vérité.*"

"Your accent is frightful," I answered, also in French. "Would you repeat that in English?"

She did—taking no insult, very serious, through a pall of smoke.

"I'm looking for verity."

It's a bloody good thing von Linden let me have that cigarette, because otherwise I don't know how I'd have managed to conceal that every one of us was dealing out her own DAMNED PACK OF LIES.

"Truth," I said at last, in English.

"Truth," she agreed.

Engel came running to my aid with a saucer (there being no ashtrays). I'd sucked the whole cigarette down to the butt, in five or six long drags, composing myself to answer.

"Verity," I said in English, and exhaled every last molecule of nicotine and oxygen I had inside me. Then gasped: "'Truth is the daughter of time, not authority.'" And: "'This above all, to thine own self be true.'" I gibbered a bit, I confess. "Verity! I am the soul of verity." I laughed so wildly, then, that the Hauptsturmführer had to clear his throat to remind me to control myself. "I am the soul of verity," I repeated. *"Je suis l'ésprit de vérité."*

In amongst the tobacco fug, Georgia Penn very kindly handed me what was left of her own cigarette.

"Well, thank goodness for that," she said in a motherly tone. "So I can trust you to give me honest answers—" She glanced up at von Linden. "You know what they call this place?"

I raised my eyebrows, shrugging.

"Le Château des Bourreaux," she said.

I laughed rather too loudly again, crossed my legs, and examined the inside of my wrist.

(It is a pun, you see—*Château de Bordeaux, Château des Bourreaux*—Bordeaux Castle, Castle of Butchers.)

"No, I'd not heard that," I said. And I honestly haven't—perhaps because I am so isolated most of the time. Shows you how distracted I am that I didn't think of it myself. "Well, as you can see I am still in one piece."

She really looked at me hard for a second—just one second. I smoothed my skirt down over my knee. Then she became businesslike and produced a notebook and pen while a pale Gestapo underling who looked about twelve years old poured cognac (COGNAC!) for the three of us (the THREE of us—v.L., G.P., and ME—not Engel) out of a crystal decanter into snifters as big as my head.

At this point I became so deeply suspicious of everyone in the room that I could not remember what I was supposed to say. *Alibi, Alibi,* is all I could think of. This is different, I don't know what's going on, he wants to catch me off guard, it's a new trick. Is the room bugged, why have they lit the fire and not the chandelier, and what does the talking cockatoo have to do with it?

Wait, wait, wait! What else is there to get out of me? I'm GIVING THE GESTAPO EVERYTHING I KNOW. I've been doing it for weeks. Pull yourself together, lassie, you're a Wallace and a Stuart!

At *this* point, I purposefully put out my cigarette against my own palm. Nobody noticed.

To hell with the truth, I told myself fiercely. *I want another week.* I want my week and I'm going to get it.

I asked if we could speak in English for the interview; it felt more natural to talk to the American in English, and with Engel there to translate, the Hauptsturmführer did not mind. So then it was up to me, really, to put on a good show.

He did not want me to tell her about the codes I'd given him—certainly not about the, ah, *stressful* circumstances under which I'd collapsed and coughed them up—nor that the eleven wireless sets in Maddie's Lysander were all destroyed in the fire when she crashed. (They showed me those pictures during my interrogation. The enlargements from the pilot's cockpit came later. I think I mentioned them here but I am not going to describe them.) I don't entirely follow the logic of what I could or couldn't tell the American broadcaster, since if she cared to she could have easily found out from anyone in Ormaie about those destroyed radio sets, but perhaps no one has told British Intelligence yet, and the Gestapo is still playing the radio game—*das Funkspiel*—trying to play back my compromised codes and frequencies on one of their previously captured wireless sets.

(I suppose I *should* have written about those pictures, only I couldn't—literally couldn't—it was during those days when I had run out of paper. But I won't now either.)

I said I was a wireless operator, parachuted here in civilian clothes so I might not attract attention, and that I had been caught because I made a cultural blunder—we chatted a bit about the difficulty of being a foreigner and trying to assimilate yourself into French daily life. Engel nodded sagely in agreement, not while she was listening to me, but as she was repeating it to von Linden.

Oh, how strange this war is, mirabile dictu—the wee Scots wireless set, I mean operator, is still nursing small, hidden, nasty short circuits got during her savagely inhuman interrogation—yet she can keep a straight face as she sits beneath the Venetian chandelier with the American Penn and the Germans Engel and von Linden, sharing cognac and complaining about the French!

It made the right impression, though—finding something we all agreed on.

Penn then remarked that Engel's English must have been picked up in the American Midwest, which left the rest of us speechless for a longish moment. Then Engel confessed that she had been a student at the University of Chicago for a year (where she was training as a CHEMIST. I don't think I've ever met ANYONE with so much wasted talent). Penn tried to make her play the Do-You-Know game, but the only person they had in common was Henry Ford, whom Engel had met at a charity dinner. Engel's American contacts were all very respectably pro-Germany, Penn's less so. They were not in Chicago at the same time—Penn has been based in Europe since the early '30s.

Fräulein Anna Engel, M d M—Mädchen des Mystères

We looked at my translated bus schedule and admired v.L.'s Montblanc fountain pen, which I had been using. Penn asked me if I was worried about my upcoming "trial."

"It's a formality." I could not help being brutal about this. "I will be shot." She asked for honesty, after all. "I am a military emissary caught in enemy territory masquerading as a civilian. I count as a spy. The Geneva Convention doesn't protect me."

She was silent for a moment.

"There's a war on," I added, to remind her.

"Yes." She scribbled some notes on her pad. "Well. You're very brave."

All *TOSH!*

"Can you speak on behalf of other prisoners here?"

"We don't see much of each other." Had to dodge that one. "Or, not to speak to." I do *see* them, too often. "Will you get a tour?"

She nodded. "It looks very nice. Clean linen in all the rooms. A bit spartan."

"Well-heated, too," I said waspishly. "It used to be a hotel. No proper dungeon rooms, no damp, no one suffering arthritis *at all*."

They must have taken her 'round the rooms they use for the orderlies—perhaps even planted a few as dummy prisoners. The Gestapo use the ground floor and two mezzanines for their own accommodation and offices, and it is all kept in beautiful condition. The real prisoners are kept on the uppermost three stories. It is harder to escape when you are at least forty feet above the ground.

Penn seemed satisfied. She heaved a tight smile in von Linden's direction and said, "*Ich danke Ihnen*—I thank you," very grave and formal, then continued in French to tell him how grateful she was for this unique and unusual opportunity. I suppose she'll interview him too, separate from me.

Then she leaned close to me and said in confidential tones, "Can I get you anything? Send you anything—little things? Towels?"

I told her I'd stopped.

Well—I have—and they wouldn't let her anyway. Would they? I don't know. According to the Geneva Convention you're allowed to send useful things to prisoners of war—cigarettes, toothbrushes, fruitcakes with hacksaws inside. But as I'd just pointed out, the Geneva Convention doesn't apply to me. *Nacht und Nebel, night and fog.* Brrr. As far as Georgia Penn knows, I have no name. To whom would she address the package?

She asked, "You're not—?"

It was a rather extraordinary conversation if you think about it—both of us speaking in code. But not military code, not Intelligence or Resistance code—just feminine code.

"You haven't been—?"

I'm sure Engel was able to fill in the blanks:

—Can I send you (sanitary) towels?

—No thanks, I've stopped (bleeding).

—You're not (pregnant)? You haven't been (raped)?

Raped. What was she going to do about it if I had?

Anyway, technically speaking, I've not been raped.

No, I've just stopped.

I've not had a cycle since I left England. I think my body simply shut itself down during those first three weeks. It performs basic functions only now. It knows perfectly well it's never going to be called on for reproductive purposes. I'm a wireless set.

Penn shrugged, nodding, with her mouth twisting skeptically and her eyebrows raised. Her mannerisms are what you'd imagine in a pioneering farmer's wife. "Well, you don't look so healthy," she said to me.

I look like I've just emerged from a sanatorium and am about to lose a long battle with consumption. Starvation and sleep deprivation do leave visible marks, YOU IDIOTS.

"I haven't seen the sun for six weeks," I said. "But sometimes the weather's like that back home, too."

"Well, it's sure nice," she drawled. "It's nice to see they're treating prisoners so well here."

Suddenly, in one great dollop, she sloshed all her cognac—untouched, the entire glass—into my glass.

I slugged the whole lot down like a sailor before anyone could take it away from me, and spent the rest of the afternoon being sick.

Do you know what he did last night—von Linden, I mean. Came and stood in the doorway of my cell after he'd finished work and asked me if I've read Goethe. He has been chewing over this idea that I can "buy" time in exchange for bits of my soul, and he wondered if I likened myself to Faust. Nothing like an arcane literary debate with your tyrannical master while you pass the time leading to your execution.

When he left I said to him, *"Je vous souhaite une bonne*

nuit"—"I wish you a good night"—not because I wished him a good night but because that is what the German officer says to his unyielding passive-resistant French hosts every night in *Le Silence de la Mer*—that tract of Gallic defiance and the literary spirit of the French Resistance. A copy was given me by a Frenchwoman I trained with, just after she was brought back from the field late last year. I thought that von Linden might have read it too, as he is such a Know Your Enemy type (also he is very well-read). But he didn't seem to recognize the quotation.

Engel has told me what he did before the War. He was rector of a rather posh boys' school in Berlin.

A *headmaster*!

Also, he has a daughter.

She is safe at school in Switzerland, neutral Switzerland, where no Allied bombers raid the skies at night. I can safely assert she doesn't go to *my* school. My school shut down just before the War began, when most of the English and French pupils were pulled out, which is why I went off to university a bit early.

Von Linden has a daughter only a little younger than me. I see now why he takes such a clinically distant approach to his work.

Still not sure whether he has a soul, though. Any Jerry bastard with his wedding tackle intact can beget a daughter. And there are a lot of sadistic head teachers about.

Oh my God, why do I do it—again and again? I HAVE THE BRAIN OF A PTARMIGAN HEN. HE WILL SEE ANYTHING I WRITE.

Engel, bless her, skipped over the last few paragraphs I wrote yesterday when she was translating for von Linden last night. I think it was self-preservation on her part rather than any good nature toward me. Someone will eventually discover what a chatterbox she is, but she's growing wise to my efforts to get her in trouble. (She pointed out to von Linden some time ago that I know perfectly well how to do metric conversions and only pretend ignorance to torment her. But it is true that she is better at them than I am.)

In addition to my extra week, I've now been given a fresh supply of paper. Sheet music, surely also the ill-gotten spoils of the Château des Bourreaux—a lot of popular songs from the last decade and some pieces by French composers, scored for flute and piano. The verso of the flute parts are all blank so I have paper in abundance again. I was getting a bit weary of those flipping recipe cards. We are still using them for the other work.

WARTIME ADMINISTRATIVE FORMALITIES

I am condensing now. I can't write fast enough.

Maddie was being groomed by the SOE long before she became aware of it. About the same time Jamie started flying again somewhere in the south of England, back in Manchester, Maddie was put on a course to do night flying. She leaped at the chance. She was so used to being the only girl around, there being no more than two other women in the Manchester ATA ferry pool, that it did not occur to her there was anything unusual going on.

Everyone else on the course was a bomber pilot or navigator. The ferry pilots don't fly at night, in general. In fact Maddie didn't fly at night for a while after she'd clocked the hours and had her logbook stamped, and she had a difficult time keeping in practice because she used it so little. Since 1940 we have not come off daylight-saving at all, and in summer it is double, which means for a whole month it doesn't get dark till nearly midnight. Maddie couldn't have used her night flying anyway in the summer of 1942 unless she'd gone up in the middle of the night, so she didn't wonder about it. She was busy—thirteen days on ferrying and two off, in all kinds of weather, and there were so many ongoing senseless administrative formalities or blunders that a bit of pointless night training was unremarkable.

They gave her parachute training too—an equally random and apparently useless skill. Maddie was trained not as an actual *paratrooper*, but she learned to fly the plane while people were jumping. They use Whitley bombers for the parachute training, a type Maddie hadn't flown before, and they flew from her home airfield—nothing about it seemed strange until she was asked to come along as Pilot 2 when I was making my first jump from a plane over the low hills of Cheshire (at this point I had no choice but to cross "Heights" off my list of fears). Maddie certainly hadn't expected *me* and was too sharp to take it as a coincidence. She recognized me instantly as we climbed on board—despite my hair being uncharacteristically tied back with a ribbon like a pony club competitor (otherwise it wouldn't have fit inside those ducky wee helmets that make you look as though you have stuck your head in a Christmas cake). Maddie knew better than to register surprise or recognition. She'd been told who this group was—or who they *weren't*, anyway—six of them, two of them women, jumping from a plane for the first time.

We weren't allowed to talk to the pilots, either. I made three jumps that week—the women do one less training jump than the men, AND they make us jump first. I don't know if that's because we're considered cannier than men, or braver, or bouncier, or just less likely to survive and therefore aren't worth the extra petrol and parachute packing. At any rate, Maddie saw me twice in the air and never got to say hello.

I got to watch her fly, though.

You know, I envied her. I envied her the simplicity of her work, the spiritual cleanness of it—*Fly the plane, Maddie.* That was all she had to do. There was no guilt, no moral dilemma, no argument or anguish—danger, yes, but she always knew what she was facing. And I envied that she had chosen her work herself and was doing what she wanted to do. I don't suppose I had any idea what I "wanted" and so I was *chosen*, not choosing. There's glory and honor in being *chosen*. But not much room for free will.

Thirteen days' flying and two days off. Never knowing where she'd get her next meal or spend the night. No social life to speak of—but moments, now and then, unexpected and unlooked for, of solitary joy—alone in the sky in the cruise, straight and level at 4000 feet over the Cheviots or the Fens or the Marches, or dipping her wings in salute to a passing vic of Spitfires.

With a pilot assistant as her copilot (she was his senior by a hundred hours' flight time) she delivered a Hudson to RAF Special Duties. You have to take a pilot assistant with you when you ferry a Hudson. The Moon Squadron use them for nighttime parachute drops, the Hudsons being bigger than the Lizzies, not so suitable for short field landings.

They sometimes land them if they have a lot of passengers to pick up. Maddie had flown a few other twin-engined bombers before (like the Whitley), but not a Hudson, and she slammed the tail a bit when she landed. Afterward she spent a long time examining the tailwheel looking for prangs with three of the local ground crew (who decided there was nothing wrong with it). When she and her copilot finally went into Operations to get their ferry chits signed, the radio chap told Maddie politely, "You're to step into the debriefing room in The Cottage for a few minutes, if you don't mind. They're sending a driver. Your second pilot had better wait here."

That was because The Cottage is fairly out-of-bounds, even to people landing at the big airfield on legitimate business. But, of course, Maddie herself had been there before.

She swallowed an anguished sigh. Court-martial? No, it was just a heavy landing; her copilot had supported her loyally when they were talking about it with the ground crew, and the Air Ministry would *laugh* if she tried to file an accident report. She'd be court-martialed for wasting their time. Oh—she thought—what have I done *now*?

The smart and charming First Aid Nursing Yeomanry girl who does the driving for the Moon Squadron didn't ask Maddie any questions. She is trained not to ask her passengers any questions.

No room in The Cottage is so severe and forbidding as the debriefing room (I do know). It was formerly a laundry (about two hundred years ago), I think, all limewashed stone walls and a big drain in the middle of the floor, and only an electric heater to heat it. Waiting in this tiger's lair for Maddie was our dear friend the English intelligence officer with the pseudonym. I suppose you may want to dig his pseudonym out of me, but it's rather pointless—could be anything now.

He wasn't using it anymore when he interviewed Jamie early in 1942, and he certainly wasn't using it when he cornered Maddie in the laundry.

The spectacles are unmistakable, and Maddie recognized him right away and was so immediately suspicious she didn't step through the door. He was leaning casually against the shabby pine desk, which is all the permanent furniture in that room, flexing his bony hands in front of the electric heater.

"Second Officer Brodatt!"

The man is charming.

"Beastly rotten to surprise you like this. But one isn't able to arrange such meetings ahead of time, you know."

Maddie's eyes widened. She felt like Red Riding Hood staring at the wolf in Grandma's bed. *What big eyes you have!*

"Come in," he invited. "Do sit down." There was a chair—there were two chairs—pulled up in front of the heater. Maddie could see that it was all set up as informally and cozily as it was possible to make this bleak little room. She swallowed again and sat down, and found the presence of mind to say something at last.

"Am I in trouble?"

He did not laugh. He sat down next to her, leaning over his knees with concern drawing a line down his forehead. He said sharply, "No. No, not at all. I've a job for you."

Maddie recoiled.

"Only if you're willing."

"I'm not—" She took a deep breath. "I can't do that kind of work."

This time he did laugh, a brief and quiet sympathetic chuckle. "Yes you can. It's air taxi work. No intrigue attached."

She stared at him with tight-lipped skepticism.

"It doesn't mean anything will change for you," he said. "No special missions to the Continent."

Maddie gave him the ghost of a smile.

"You'll have to do some night landings, and you'll have to be available as needed. There won't be any advance notification for these flights."

"What are they *for?*" Maddie asked.

"Some of our people need fast and efficient private transport—travel when and as needed, there and back in one night, no messing about with petrol rationing or limited speed on country lanes or awkward railway schedules. No risk of being recognized on a station platform or through the window of a motorcar at traffic lights. Does that make sense?"

Maddie nodded.

"You're a consistent pilot, a superb navigator, sharp as a tack and exceptionally discreet. There are plenty of men and several women better qualified than you, but none, I think, as appropriately suited for this particular taxi service. You remembered my name. You're well aware of our work here and you keep quiet about it, except when you send us a recruit. If you take the assignments, they'll be given in the most straightforward manner through your ATA ferry pool. 'S' chits, secret, with a report required. You won't be told anything about the men and women you'll be taxiing. You'll already know most of the airfields."

He is really very hard to resist. Or perhaps Maddie just couldn't ever pass up a flying opportunity.

"I'll do it," she said decisively. "I'll do it."

"Tell your assistant pilot you left your clothing ration coupons here on your last flight, and we've kept them for you—"

He thumbed through a file folder, held something up at arm's length, then put it back with a sigh and pushed his heavy spectacles back up his nose. "Getting old," he apologized. "The middle distance is going now too! Here we are."

He pored over the pages again and *produced Maddie's clothing ration coupons.* Her stomach turned over. She never found out how he got them.

He handed them to her. "Explain to your colleague you were called in here today so we could return these and give you a lecture about taking greater care with your personal papers."

"Well, I jolly well will be more careful with them after this," she told him fiercely.

God what a mess. I have to stop here until I stop crying or it will all be illegibly smeared

sorry sorry sorry

ATA "S" CHITS (SECRET)

At first it was much as he'd said—very little in Maddie's life changed. For six weeks she heard nothing. Then twice in a week there were chits marked "S" and bearing her own special code name—just an alert to let her know she was "operational," as it were. But the only way the job really differed from a normal taxi run was that the chaps she picked up obviously weren't pilots.

After that there were special flights that came regularly, but not frequently. Every six weeks or so. They were all prosaically dull. For taxi work Maddie was put back to flying small training and ex-civil aircraft, open cockpit Tiger Moths and a Puss Moth or two. Apart from the occasional night landing, there wasn't much to the actual flying that Maddie found challenging.

There was one Lysander flight that was memorable because her passenger traveled with two guards. There is an armored bulkhead that separates the Lysander pilot from her passengers—you can send her notes or coffee or kisses through an opening the size of a page, which she is able to shut against you if she wants so that you cannot shoot her. Not that shooting your pilot would get you anywhere fast, except down, in a Lysander, as you would not be able to take over the controls.

Maddie was safely separated from her would-be assassin, if he was an assassin. She was never afterward sure whether that passenger had traveled as a prisoner under guard or a liability under protection. At any rate, they must have been very crowded with three grown men in the back of the Lysander.

Then, at last, there was me.

Maddie was interrupted in the middle of a bedtime cocoa, very cozy, at home with her gran and granddad in their house in Stockport. Her Operations officer rang and asked her to make a flight to another airfield that night, collect someone and deliver that someone elsewhere, all to be done ASAP. She'd be told where to go when she got to Oakway, but not over the telephone.

It was September a year ago, a gorgeous, glorious, clear and windless night, some of the best flying weather Maddie had ever known. She scarcely had to fly the little Puss Moth, merely to point it southward along the darkling hills. A great big wonderful waxing bomber's moon was rising as she arrived at the pickup airfield, and Maddie landed just before the local squadron took off. She taxied to the Operations hut as the brand-new Lancasters were leaving. The demure Puss Moth shuddered in the wind of their passing, like a marsh hen among a flock of gray herons—each thrice her wingspan, each with four times as many engines, heavy with the night's fuel and payload of explosive, off to deliver vengeful destruction to Essen's factories and railway yards. Maddie taxied her little plane to the apron in front of the Operations hut and idled the engine, waiting. She'd been told not to shut down.

The Lancasters roared past. Maddie watched with her nose pressed to the windscreen and for a second didn't notice the passenger door being opened. Ground crew, caps pulled low and faces hidden in the wing's shadow, helped the passenger in and fastened her harness. There was no baggage apart from the indispensable gas mask in its haversack, and as usual Maddie wasn't told her special passenger's name. She saw the silhouette of a peaked WAAF cap and could sense that the passenger was hugely keyed up, taut with excitement, but it never occurred to Maddie that she might know this person. Like the SOE drivers, she had been instructed not to ask questions. Over the purr of the engine she shouted emergency exit instructions and the location of the first aid kit.

Once airborne, Maddie didn't initiate conversation—she never did with special passengers. Nor did she point out how splendid the black and occasionally silver landscape was below them in the moonlight, because she knew that part of the reason this person was being flown to her destination at night was so she couldn't guess where she was going. There was a gasp from the passenger when Maddie, all business, unclipped the Verey pistol from the side of her seat. "Don't worry," she shouted. "It's only a flare gun! I haven't got a radio. The flare lets them know we're here, if they don't hear us buzzing them and put the lights on for us."

But Maddie didn't need to let off her firework display because, after circling for a minute or two, the runway lights blazed up, and Maddie put her own landing light on.

It was a very clean landing. But not until the aircraft had come to a full stop and the engine shut down did the passenger startle Maddie by leaning over and giving her a quick kiss on the cheek.

"Thank you. You are wonderful!"

The ground crew had already opened the passenger's door.

"You should have told me it was you!" Maddie cried, as her friend gathered herself to disappear into the night.

"I didn't like to surprise you in the air!" Queenie automatically checked that her hair was still in place, and with one of her gazellelike leaps, vaulted from the plane onto the concrete. "I'm not used to flying and I've never had to go anywhere at night. Sorry!"

She leaned back into the cockpit for a moment—Maddie could see several figures beckoning and conferring behind her. It was nearly two a.m.

"Wish me luck," Queenie begged. "It's my first assignment."

"Good luck!"

"I'll see you when I'm done. You're to take me home."

Queenie vanished across the concrete, surrounded by attendants.

Maddie was given her own little guest room in the increasingly familiar Cottage. It was odd not knowing what was going on. After a while she dozed off, and was almost instantly woken by that night's operational Lysanders returning from France with their booty of shot-down American airmen, hunted French ministers, a crate of champagne, and sixteen bottles of Chanel No. 5.

Maddie would not have known about the perfume except that everybody was extraordinarily punchy the next morning, perhaps due to the champagne breakfast (Maddie, being scheduled to take off again after daybreak, prudently didn't take any champagne). Queenie was smug as a cat and glowing with success. She looked as though she'd just won herself a gold medal at the Olympic Games. The squadron leader gave a bottle of French scent to every woman who happened to be on the airfield, including the Land Girl who turned up on her bicycle with a basket of three dozen unallocated eggs and six pints of milk for the Welcome-to-Freedom breakfast.

Freedom, oh, freedom. Even with the shortages, and the blackout, and the bombs, and the rules, and daily life so drab and dull most of the time—once you cross the English Channel you are free. How simple, and amazing really, that no one in France lives without fear, without suspicion. I don't mean the straightforward fear of fiery death. I mean the insidious, demoralizing fear of betrayal, of treachery, of cruelty, of being silenced. Of not being able to trust your neighbor or the girl who brings you eggs. Only twenty-one miles from Dover. Which would you rather have—an unlimited supply of Chanel No. 5, or freedom?

Stupid question, really.

I have reached the point in this account where, unavoidably, I am going to have to talk about myself *before* Ormaie. And I don't want to.

I just want to go on flying and flying in the moonlight. I dreamed I was flying with Maddie, in the five minutes or however short a time it was when there was a lull next door and I actually fell asleep. In my dream the moon was full but it was green, bright green—I kept thinking, *We're in the limelight!* But of course limelight is white, not green—chemical lime, not citrus. This was like the light in Chartreuse liqueur, like the green flash, and I kept wondering, How did I escape? I couldn't remember how I got out of Ormaie. But it didn't matter; I was on my way home in Maddie's Puss Moth, I was safe and Maddie was alongside me flying confidently, and the sky was quiet and full of the beautiful green moon.

God, I'm tired. I truly shot myself in the foot again and am now being forced to regret it. I have been put back to work till whenever they run out of people to keep an eye on me. Can't decide if this is good news or bad, as I don't mind the infinite supply of paper, but I also forfeited my cabbage soup tonight and I didn't sleep much the past couple of nights, either. (I do wish they'd GIVE UP on that wretched French girl. She is *never* going to tell them *anything*.)

What happened was that when they brought me in this morning, poor Fräulein Engel was sitting at the table with her back to the door, busily numbering my countless recipe cards, and I frightened the living daylights out of her by braying in a deep, stentorian voice of command and discipline, *"Achtung, Anna Engel! Heil Hitler!"* She catapulted to her feet and threw herself into a salute that must have nearly dislocated her shoulder. I've never seen her look so white around the gills. She recovered almost immediately and smacked me so hard she knocked me over. When Thibaut picked me up she smacked me again just for the sheer hell of it. Wow wow wow is my jaw sore. I suppose they are not planning another phony interview.

I can never decide if it is worth it. It was a truly hilarious moment, but all I seem to have achieved this time is a totally unexpected collusion between Engel and Thibaut.

Did I call them Laurel and Hardy? I meant sodding Romeo and Juliet. This is flirting, à la Gestapo underlings:

She: Oh, you are so strong and manly, M'sieur Thibaut. Those knots you tie are so secure.

He: That is nothing. Look, I pull them so tight you cannot undo them. Try.

She: It is true, I cannot! Oh, pull them tighter!

He: *Chérie*, your wish is my command.

It is my ankles, not hers, which he is binding so tightly and with such masculine charm.

She: I shall have to call you in tomorrow morning, as well, to do this task for me.

He: You must cross the cords, so, and knot them behind—

Me: *Squeak! Squeak!*

She: Shut up and write, ya wee skrikin' Scots piece o' shite.

Well, no, she did not use those exact words. But you get the idea.

Something is Up. They have stepped up the pace a bit—not just with me. They are *relentless* with the Resistance prisoners. An inspection due, perhaps? A visit from von Linden's mysterious boss, the dreaded SS-Sturmbannführer Ferber? (I picture Horns and a Forked Tail.) Perhaps he's making an inquiry into von Linden's work here; that would explain why v.L.'s got to get those notes of his in order. Trying to make himself look good.

Desperately trying to marshal my own thoughts in narrative order. I am very tired and (shall I be melodramatic about it?) rather "faint with hunger"—in fact I don't know if it's hunger I am faint with, but I *am* very hungry and feeling quite light-headed (I have not been allowed any more aspirin since the episode with the cognac). Perhaps Engel has given me a concussion. I am going to make some lists to try to get through the next bit.

	Date	Departure	Destination	Return
(night)	Sept. '42	Buscot Aerodrome, Oxford	? Special Duties	Buscot (next day)
	Sept.	Buscot	Branston	Buscot
	Oct.	Buscot	? (northeast)	Newcastle then by train to Oxford
	Oct.	"	Ipswich	train to Oxford
	Nov. '42	"	? (northeast)	same
(night)	Jan. '43	"	? (S.D.)	Buscot
	Jan.	Oakway	Glasgow	Newcastle then train to Manchester
	Jan.	Oakway	Glasgow	train to Oxford

The weather at Glasgow was so dreadful that day that no one would take off and everyone was stuck there. I took the train back, but Maddie had to wait for a gap in the clouds. And sodding Glasgow *still* wasn't finished with me, so I had to go back in

	Feb. '43	Oakway	Glasgow	Who cares?

Mar.—5 flights, various, all in southern England, 2 at night
April—
Oh—

RAF SPECIAL DUTIES, OPERATIONAL CROSS-COUNTRY

I did take the train to assignments, too, more often than I flew. And Maddie taxied other people besides me, who in all likelihood were not doing the same work as me. But those flights I've just listed are the flights that *count*. Fifteen flights in six months. Maddie took the secrecy more seriously than I did—I was never sure how much she guessed. (Turns out, not much. She just genuinely took it seriously. After all, she started as a Clerk/Special Duties.)

On that night last April we had to go back to That Airfield, the secret one, the one the Moon Squadron uses for France. Jamie was stationed there now. Maddie was In the Know with them, and had been for some time—trusted, accepted, invited to supper that night, in fact. No supper for poor Queenie, though, who was instantly whisked away by the usual mob (really my reception committee only consisted of about three people, including my admirer, the RAF police sergeant who doubles as Security Guard and Chief Sausage Fryer for The Cottage, but it feels like a mob when everyone is bigger than you and you don't know where you are being taken). Queenie had a small traveling case, which she left with Maddie, and from experience Maddie knew she wouldn't see her friend again until at least the next morning. Maddie went to supper with the pilots.

It wasn't something she did often, you know—once in a season, perhaps—and it was special because Jamie was there. In fact he was about to go on a drop-off and pickup mission that night, a "double Lysander operation," as they called it, two pilots flying two planes to the same field. There was a third plane taking off with them, taking advantage of the moon, but not technically operational—a new squadron member doing his first cross-country training flight to France. He'd part company with the others over the Channel. He'd fly into France on his own for a bit, then turn back without landing.

This young fellow—let's call him Michael (after the youngest of the Darling children in *Peter Pan*!)—was quite nervous about his navigation skills. Like Jamie, he'd previously been a bomber pilot and had always had a navigator sitting next to him telling him where to go, and also he'd only flown his first Lysander a month ago. His mates were full of sympathy, having all been through it themselves. Maddie was not.

"You've been practicing on Lizzies for a *month*!" she said scornfully. "Crumbs, how long does it *take*? The instruments are the same whether you're flying a Barracuda dive-bomber or a clapped-out old Tiger Moth, and the flaps are automatic! Easy peasy!"

They all gave her Looks.

"You go on and fly to France, then," said Michael.

"I would if you'd let me," she said enviously (not remembering about antiaircraft guns and night fighters).

"Ah ken what t' dooo," drawled Jamie, the Pobble Who Has No Toes, dragging out his vowels to make them exaggeratedly Scots. "Tak' the wee lassie alang."

Maddie felt as though she'd been struck by lightning. She looked up at him and saw the familiar, faint lunacy shining in Jamie's eyes. She knew better than to say anything herself—either the Pobble would win on her behalf, or she couldn't go.

The others laughed and argued briefly. The English SOE agent who was being dropped off that night was disapproving. The Moon Squadron pilots, of necessity a bunch of giddy lunatics, put it to their leader as a proposition. He was clearly torn, but chiefly because Michael was supposed to be solo that night.

"She won't be helping him fly the plane in the back of a Lysander, will she!"

"She could tell him what to do. Keep him straight if he goes off course."

Jamie pushed his empty plate away and leaned back in his chair, his hands behind his head, and gave a low whistle.

"Ooo-ee! Arrre you suggestin' she's a superior pilot to oorrr Michael?"

They all gazed at Maddie, sitting quietly in her civilian uniform, looking very trim and official with her gold wings and gold stripes (she was a First Officer by now). The only person whose eyes she dared to meet were those of the agent who was going to be dropped off that night. He was shaking his head in defeated disapproval as much as to say, *If you must, my lips are sealed.*

"I've no doubt she's a superior pilot," the squadron leader said.

"Well, what in creation is she doing ferrying clapped-out Tiger Moths about, in that case? Give the Bloody Machiavellian English Intelligence Officer a call and get permission," Jamie suggested.

Michael suggested, rather excitedly, "Don't count it as my operational cross-country. I need the practice."

"If it's not an operational flight," said the squadron leader, "there's no need to ring Intelligence. I'll take responsibility."

Maddie had won. She could scarcely believe her luck.

"I don't want this out of this *room*," the squadron leader said, and everybody looked blank, shrugging with innocence and indifference. Maddie walked shoulder to shoulder with the SOE agent when they went out to climb into the waiting aircraft. The ground crew gave her funny looks.

"Michael needing help with his navigation again?" one of them asked kindly, offering her a leg up the ladder into the back of the plane.

Secretly Maddie thought Michael was lucky as a boy with jam smeared all over his face, with his carefully annotated map marked with every single antiaircraft gun and navigation pinpoint all the way into the middle of France and back.

She didn't have her own map, sitting in the back, but she had an absolutely fabulous view out both sides and behind, a view she didn't normally get, and the leisure to enjoy it. She had a job, too, keeping her eyes peeled for night fighters. It wasn't far over the blacked-out villages of southern England before they reached the coast. The great golden moon made the blue lights on the wingtips of the operational Lysanders ahead of them scarcely distinguishable from stars—they bobbed and winked in and out of Maddie's line of sight, but she knew where she was. That river, that chalk quarry, that estuary in the glimmering night—familiar landmarks. Then the unbelievable bright loveliness of the English Channel, a shimmering infinite lamé cloth of silver and blue. Maddie could see the black silhouettes of a convoy of ships below her. She wondered how long it would take the Luftwaffe to find them.

"Oi, Michael," Maddie called out over the intercom. "You're not meant to follow that lot into France! You're supposed to change your heading here, and go farther south on your own, aren't you?"

She heard a lot of cursing from the front before the pilot pulled himself together and reset his course. Then she heard his sheepish "Thanks, mate."

Thanks, mate. Maddie hugged herself with pride and pleasure. *I'm one of them*, she thought. I'm on my way to France. I might as well be *operational*.

Deep in her stomach she nursed two cringing, niggling fears: 1) that they might be fired on, and 2) court-martial. But she knew Michael's route had been carefully plotted to avoid guns and airfields, and that their most dangerous moment had probably been when they crossed the shipping convoy. If they made it home safely, there would be no need for court-martial. If they *didn't* make it home safely, well, presumably court-martial wouldn't be much of a problem in that case either.

Now they were over the ghostly white cliffs of eastern Normandy. The Seine's loops shone like a great unwinding spool of silver mesh off the port wingtip. Maddie gasped at the river's inadvertent loveliness, and all at once she found herself spilling childish tears, not just for her own besieged island, but for all of Europe. How could everything have come so fearfully and thoroughly unraveled?

There were no lights over France; it was as blacked out as Britain. Europe's lamps had all gone out.

"*What's that!*" she gasped into the intercom.

Michael saw it at the same time and banked sharply away. He began to circle, a hair too steeply at first, then with steadier rudder control. Below and ahead of them, lit up like a ghastly funfair, was a rectangle of stark, garish white light desecrating an otherwise blacked-out landscape.

"That's where the last pinpoint is supposed to be!" Michael told her.

"Some pinpoint! Is it an airfield? It's jolly well operational, if it is!"

"No," said the pilot slowly, as he circled back and got another look. "No, I think it's a prison camp. Look—the lighting's around the perimeter fence. To catch anyone trying to get out."

"Are you in the right place?" Maddie asked dubiously.

"You tell me." But he said it with confidence. He stuffed his waymarked map back through the opening in the bulkhead, followed by a pocket-size electric torch. "Keep that under cover," he said. "There's supposed to be an airfield twenty miles to the east. I've been trying to steer clear of it. I damn well don't need an escort."

Maddie studied the map beneath a tent she made of her tunic. Michael was smartly on target as far as she could tell. The glaring prison fence was close to a railway bridge over a river, which should have been the turning-back point. Maddie switched off the torch and stared out the window, her night vision ruined by trying to read the map. But she could tell they had turned back.

"You didn't need my help after all," she said, and passed him back his torch and map.

"I'd have just played follow-my-leader after Jamie all the way to Paris if you hadn't reminded me to turn."

"He's not going to Paris, is he?"

Michael said enviously, "He won't get to buzz the Eiffel Tower, but he's picking up a couple of Parisian agents. He'll have to land well outside the city." Then Michael added in a more sober voice, "I'm still jolly glad you came along. That prison gave me a turn. I was so sure I was in the right place, and then—"

"You were," said Maddie.

"I'm jolly glad you came along," Michael repeated.

He said it a third time when they landed back in England two hours later. The relieved squadron leader grinned and nodded tolerantly as he welcomed them back. "Find your way all right?"

"A piece of cake, apart from the bit at the end where the pinpoint turned out to be next to a ruddy great prison!"

The squadron leader laughed. "I'll say you *did* find your way. That always comes as a surprise the first time. Proves you got there, though. Or did you have help?"

"He found it all himself," Maddie said truthfully. "I can't thank you enough for letting me go along."

"April in Paris, eh?"

"Nearly as good as." Maddie ached for Paris, imprisoned, inaccessible, remote.

"Not this year. Perhaps next!"

Michael went to bed whistling. Maddie found her way through the darkened Cottage with his tune stuck in her head. After a moment she recognized it as "The Last Time I Saw Paris."

DEBRIEFING

It was nearly four o'clock in the morning when, brimming with elation, Maddie crept into the room she was sharing with Queenie. She checked that the blackout blinds were down and then lit a candle, not wanting to put on the lights and wake her friend. But Queenie's bed was empty and unruffled, the counterpane smooth and straight. Queenie's small travel case stood unopened by the foot of the bed, where Maddie herself had set it down earlier. Whatever Queenie was here to do, she was still doing it.

Maddie put on her pajamas and pulled the blankets up to her chin, her mind full of air and moonlight and the silver Seine. She did not sleep.

Queenie came in at half-past five. She didn't think about whether she'd wake Maddie; she didn't even check that the blinds were down. She snapped on the electric light overhead, heaved her travel case onto the bare bureau, and hauled out the regulation WAAF pajamas and a hairbrush. Then she sat down in front of the mirror and stared at herself.

Maddie stared too.

Queenie was different. Her hair was pinned up as usual, but not in the signature French chignon twist she'd been wearing when Maddie had left her last night. Queenie's hair was scraped back severely from her forehead flat against her skull and wound into a tight bun at the nape of her neck. It wasn't flattering. It made her seem plainer, and her face was made up in pale colors that weren't flattering either. There was a harshness to the set of her mouth that Maddie had never seen before.

Maddie watched. Queenie laid down the hairbrush and slowly took off her blue WAAF tunic. After a moment Maddie realized she was being cautious, not slow—moving carefully, as though it were painful to stretch her shoulders. She took off her blouse.

One arm was livid with bruises, red turning purple, the clear, brutal marks of a big hand that had gripped her hard and not let go for some time. Her throat and shoulders were scored with similar ugly marks right the way 'round. Someone had tried to choke her to death a few hours ago.

She touched her throat gently and stretched her neck, examining the damage in the small mirror on the dresser. The room wasn't very warm, and after a minute or two, Queenie sighed and inched herself into the cotton shirt of her men's pajamas, still moving cautiously. Then she stood up, incautiously this time, and wrenched all the steel hairpins from her tightly bound hair. With a vicious scrape of the back of one hand she scrubbed the beige lipstick from her mouth. Suddenly she looked very much more herself, just a bit disheveled, as though she'd pulled off a mask. She turned around and saw Maddie looking at her.

"Hullo," Queenie said with a crooked smile. "I didn't mean to wake you."

"You didn't." Maddie waited. She knew better than to ask what had happened.

"You saw?"

Maddie nodded.

"Doesn't *hurt*," Queenie said fiercely. "Not much. Just—it was hard work tonight. Had to do a bit more improvisation than usual, play it closer to the edge—"

She scrabbled abruptly in her tunic for her cigarettes. Maddie watched quietly. Queenie sat down on the end of Maddie's bed and lit a cigarette with hands that shook a little.

"Guess where I went with the lads tonight," Maddie said.

"To the pub?"

"To France."

Queenie spun around to stare at her, and saw the sky and the moon still lighting up Maddie's eyes.

"France!"

Maddie hugged her knees, reeling with the magic and menace of that stolen flight.

"You're not supposed to tell me that," Queenie said.

"I'm not," Maddie agreed. "I wasn't even supposed to have gone. But we didn't actually land there."

Queenie nodded and examined her cigarette. Maddie had never seen her friend quite so undone.

"You know what you looked like just now," Maddie said, "when you came in, with your hair pulled back in that strict Victorian governess way, you looked like—"

"—*Eine Agentin der Nazis,*" Queenie supplied, taking a long, shaking drag on her cigarette.

"What? Oh. Yes. Like a German spy. Or everyone's idea of a German spy, anyway, fair and scary."

"I think I'm a bit small for the Aryan ideal," Queenie said, observing herself critically. She stretched her neck again, felt the bruised arm cautiously, and raised the cigarette to her lips, more steadily this time.

Maddie did not ask what had happened. She was never so petty. She did not dabble with minnows at the surface when there were thirty-pound salmon swimming deeper down.

"What," Maddie said quietly, "do you actually *do*?"

"'Careless talk costs lives,'" Queenie retorted.

"I don't talk," Maddie said. "*What do you do?*"

"I speak German. *Ich bin eine—*"

"*Be sensible,*" Maddie said. "You translate . . . what? Who do you translate for?"

Queenie turned toward her again with the narrow gaze of a hunted rodent.

"You translate for prisoners of war? You work for Intelligence—you translate at interrogations?"

Queenie hid herself in a cloud of smoke.

"I'm not a translator," she said.

"But you said—"

"No." Queenie was quiet too. "You said that. I told you I speak German. But I'm not a translator. I'm an interrogator."

It is *ridiculous* that you have not already guessed the nature of my Intelligence work, Amadeus von Linden. Like you, I am a wireless operator.

Like you, I am *bloody good at it*.

Our methods differ.

"On the job," as it were, I am called Eva Seiler. That was the name they used for me throughout my training—we were made to live and breathe our alter egos, and I got used to it—Seiler is the name of my school and was easy to remember. We had to discipline people who called me Scottie by accident. In English I can fake an Orkney accent better than a German one, so we went with that when I was operational—obscurely difficult to identify.

That first day—that first assignment, the very first one—remember how giddy everyone was the morning after, when they handed out all the champagne and perfume at The Cottage? I'd caught a double agent. A Nazi agent masquerading as a French Resistance courier. They'd suspected him and they brought me in to be there when they landed him in England—I caught him off guard at the low ebb of his strength and adrenaline (he'd had a long night being hauled out of France; they all did). He was a known womanizer; he didn't have the balls to admit he didn't recognize me when I threw myself at him in that frosty little debriefing room, laughing and weeping and exclaiming in German. The room was bugged and they heard everything we said.

It wasn't always that easy, but it paved my way. Mostly these men were all so desperate or confused by the time I appeared, with my neutral Swiss-accented German and comfortingly official checklist, that they were often gratefully cooperative, if not wholly bewitched. But not this night, not on the night last April when Maddie flew to France. The man I interviewed that night didn't believe in me. He accused me of treachery. Treason against the Fatherland—what was I doing working for the enemy, the English? He called me a collaborator, a backstabber, a filthy English whore.

You know—the stupid man's big mistake was in calling me ENGLISH. It made my fury wholly convincing. A whore—maybe I'll consider that in desperation; filthy, it goes without saying; but whatever else the hell I am, I AM NOT ENGLISH.

"You're the one who's failed the Fatherland, *you're* the

one who's been caught," I snarled at him. "And *you're* the one who will face trial when you're returned to Stuttgart." I recognized his accent, a coincidence and a direct hit. "I am merely here doing my job as Berlin's interpretive liaison"—oh yes, I said that—"and how DARE you call me ENGLISH!"

At which point he launched himself at me—we don't usually bind these men—and took my head beneath his arm in a grip of iron.

"Call for help," he commanded.

I could have escaped. I've been trained to defend myself against an attack like that, as I think I proved during the street brawl when I was arrested.

"Why?" Still sneering at him.

"Call for help. Let your English masters come to your aid, or I will break your neck."

"Calling the English for help *would* be collaboration," I gasped coldly. "I don't depend on the English for *anything*. Go ahead and break my neck."

They were watching, you know—there is a slotted window to the kitchen that they can watch through—and if I had called for help or seemed anything but wholly in control they *would* have come to my aid. But they saw what I was doing, what a tight wire I was walking, and they sat biting their nails and let me win that battle on my own.

And I did win. It ended some time later with him breaking down in tears on the floor, clutching at my leg and begging me to forgive him.

"Tell me your assignment," I commanded. "Tell me your contacts, and I will filter what I pass on to the English. Tell me, and you have confessed to your countrywoman and given nothing to the enemy." (I am shameless.) "Tell me, and perhaps I will forgive you for threatening to murder me."

His behavior then was truly embarrassing, and I actually

kissed him on the top of his head in benediction when he had finished. Miserable, nasty man.

Then I *did* call for help. But with disdain and dismissal, not with fear.

Good show, my dear. My, you've nerves of steel, haven't you! Jolly good show, first rate.

I didn't let on how much he'd hurt me, and they didn't think to check. It was that night's nerves of steel that landed me in France six weeks ago.

I forgot to change my hair back to normal when I changed my clothes—I don't wear my WAAF uniform for interrogations. The hair was a small mistake. They took the nerves of steel into account, but not the small mistake. They didn't notice that he'd hurt me and they didn't notice that I do make fatal small mistakes from time to time.

But Maddie noticed both.

"Come get warm," she said.

Queenie stubbed out her cigarette and turned off the light. She didn't get into her own bed, though; she climbed in next to Maddie. Maddie put careful arms around the bruised shoulders, because her friend was shaking all over now. She hadn't been before.

"It's not a nice job," Queenie whispered. "It's not like your job—blameless."

"I'm not blameless," said Maddie. "Every bomber I deliver goes operational and kills people. Civilians. People like my gran and granddad. Children. Just because I don't do it myself doesn't mean I'm not responsible. I deliver *you*."

"Blond bombshell," Queenie said, and spluttered with laughter at her own joke. Then she began to cry.

Maddie held her lightly, thinking she would let go when her friend stopped crying. But she cried for so long that Maddie fell asleep first. So she didn't ever let go.

my heart is sair, I darena tell
my heart is sair for somebody
O, I could wake a winter's night
a' for the sake o' somebody

ye pow'rs that smile on virtuous love
O sweetly smile on somebody
frae ilka danger keep her free,
and send me safe my somebody

————

We two ha'e paddl'd in the burn
frae morning sun till dine;
but seas between us broad ha'e roar'd
sin' auld lang syne

for auld lang syne, my friend
for auld lang syne
we'll tak' a cup o' kindness yet
for auld lang syne

Oh, God, I am *so tired*. They have kept me at it all night. It is the third night I have had no sleep. Too little, at any rate. I don't recognize any of the people guarding me; Thibaut and Engel are all tucked up in their pensions, and von Linden is busy tormenting that screaming French girl.

I like writing about Maddie. I like remembering. I like constructing it, focusing, crafting the story, pulling together the memories. But I am so tired. I can't craft anything more tonight. Whenever I seem to stop, to stretch, to reach for another sheet of paper, to rub my eyes, this utter *shit* of a bastard who is guarding me touches the back of my neck with his cigarette. I am only writing this because it stops him burning me. He cannot read English (or Scots) and as long as I keep covering page after page with lines from "Tam o'Shanter" he does not hurt me. I can't keep it up forever, but I know an awful lot of Robert Burns by heart.

Burns, ha-ha, Burns to stop the burns.

> *Behead me or hang me, that will never fear me—*
> *I'LL BURN AUCHINDOON ere my life leave me*

Burning burning burning burning

Oh God, those pictures.

burning

Maddie.

Maddie

Von Linden himself put an end to the proceedings last night—came storming in like the Charge of the Light Brigade and swept the pages together while I fell flat on my face on the table in a pool of ink with my eyes closed.

"Lord God Almighty, Weiser, are you an idiot? She will not produce anything worth reading when she's in this state. Look—this is *verse*. English doggerel. Pages and pages of it!" The Jerry philistine proceeded to wad everything I could remember of "Tam o'Shanter" into balls of wastepaper. I think he may read more English than he lets on, if he recognizes Burns as English. "Burn this rubbish. I have more than enough irrelevant nonsense out of her without you encouraging it! Give her water and take her back to her room. And *get rid of that filthy cigarette.* We will talk about that tomorrow."

Which was as emotional an outburst as I have ever heard from him, but I think he is overtired too.

Oh yes, and ENGEL has been CRYING. Her eyes are very red and she keeps scrubbing at her nose, which is red too. I wonder what would make On-Duty-Female-Guard Fräulein Engel blub on the job.

SPECIAL OPERATIONS TRAINING

After that disastrous interview last April (it wasn't disastrous for Intelligence, I suppose, but it left Eva Seiler a bit damaged) Berlin's interpretive liaison was given a week's leave To Think About Her Work and whether she wanted to continue it. In other words, Queenie was given the opportunity to Gracefully Bow Out. She spent the week in Castle Craig with her lady mother, the long-suffering Mrs. Darling (as it were)—poor Mrs. Darling never had a clue what any of her six children were actually doing, or when they were coming or going, and she was not best pleased at the black marks on her fine-boned daughter's Celtic white skin.

"Pirates," Queenie said. "I was bound to the mast by Captain Hook."

"When this dreadful war is over," said her mother, "I want to know Absolutely *Every Last Detail*."

"Absolutely *Every Last Detail* of my work falls under the Official Secrets Act, and I will be thrown into prison for the rest of my life if I ever tell you anything about it," Queenie told her mother. "So stop asking."

Ross, the youngest of the Glaswegian evacuees, overheard this conversation—it was just as well Queenie *hadn't* given her lady mother any details (careless talk costs lives, etc.)—but the official-looking, pretty wireless operator became rather a worshipped goddess among the Craig Castle Irregulars after that—*she had been held prisoner by pirates.*

(I love those wee laddies, I really do. Nits and all.)

During that week also, Queenie's darling elegant French nanny, her lady mother's constant companion, in a fit of maternal compassion began to knit Queenie a pullover. Being limited in materials, due to shortages and rationing, she used a gorgeous sunset-colored wool that she had unraveled from a suit tailored for her by Ormaie's most expensive modiste in 1912. I mention my sweater's advent here because I think of it as part of the endgame—as though my poor loving nanny is a sort of Mme. Defarge, knotting my fate inexorably into the stitches of this nobly field-tested woolen garment. It doesn't look much like military issue, but it has seen active service and has the bloodstains to prove it. Also it is warm and fashionable—at least, the memory of fashion clings to it. It is still warm.

At the end of my week of reflection I decided that, like my dubious ancestor Macbeth, I was in figurative blood stepped in so far that there wasn't much point in turning back; and also I *loved* being Eva Seiler. I loved the playacting and the pretence and the secrecy of it, and I flattered myself with my own importance. Occasionally I pulled Very Useful Information out of my "clients." Location of airfields. Aircraft types. Code. Things like that.

At any rate, after that April interview, everyone, including Eva, agreed that she needed a change of scene. Perhaps a few weeks on the Continent, where she could put her sangfroid and multiple languages and wireless operator's skills to much-needed use in Nazi-occupied France.

It seemed like a good idea at the time.

Do you know—you probably *do* know—that in enemy territory the life expectancy of a w/op, or W/T operator as they say in SOE, is only six weeks? That's the usual time it takes your direction-finding equipment to ferret out the location of a hidden radio set. The rest of a Resistance circuit, the web of contacts and couriers, skulks in shadows, squirreling away explosives and carrying messages that can't be trusted to a postman, moving every day, never meeting in the same place twice. At the hub of the wheel, still and vulnerable, the wireless operator sits amid a pile of equipment that is awkward to shift and difficult to conceal, snarled in a fixed web of stat and code, radiating noisy electric beacons that beckon your trackers like neon advertisements.

It is six weeks today since I landed here. I suppose that's quite a good innings for a wireless operator, though my success at staying alive for so long would carry more weight if I'd actually managed to set up a radio before I was caught. Now I really am living on borrowed time. Not much more to tell.

Still, Fräulein Engel will probably appreciate the closure of hearing about Maddie's operational flight to France. I suppose somebody *will* be court-martialed for that. I'm not sure who.

The Special Duties squadron leader was supposed to take me. The Moon Squadron was suffering a bit at the end of September—they'd had a fantastically successful summer, a dozen flights a month, twice as many agents dropped off and scores of refugees picked up—but injury and incident had winnowed their Lysander pilots down to four at this particular point in time, and one of those was so stricken with 'flu he couldn't stand up (they were all exhausted). You can see where this is going.

For me, the preparation took months—another parachute course, then an elaborate field exercise in which I had to scramble around a real city (an unfamiliar one, they sent me off to Birmingham to do it) leaving coded messages for contacts I'd never met and arranging clandestine pickups of dummy parcels. The chief danger is that a policeman will notice your suspicious activities and arrest you—in which case it is quite difficult convincing your own authorities that you're not working for the enemy.

Then there were specific arrangements to do with my own assignment—taking apart and putting together every one of those flipping radios a dozen times; making sure my clothes couldn't be traced back to England, ripping the labels out of all my underthings (you see why the pullover is so ideal a garment—wholly anonymous and made over from locally obtained materials). Learning yards and yards of code—you know (all too well) that the wireless code gets keyed to poems so that it is easier to remember, and I was rather hoping von

Linden would make his cipher breakers try to crack the "Tam o'Shanter" so I could laugh at them. But he is wise to me.

Then I had to undergo the nastiest sort of drills to make sure I had my story straight. They found it very difficult to simulate an interrogation for me. Most people find it disconcerting being woken in the middle of the night and dragged off for questioning, but I simply *could not* take it seriously. I knew the routine far too well. After about five minutes we would be wrestling over some detail of protocol or else something would send me into gales of laughter. In extremis they blindfolded me and held a loaded gun to the back of my head for nearly six hours—it was sinister and exhausting and I did go a bit wobbly eventually. (We all did. It wasn't fun.) But even so, I wasn't ever *afraid*. You *knew*—you knew you'd be all right in the end. There were a lot of people involved because they had to keep swapping over guards, and my C.O. refused to tell me who it had been, to protect them, you know? Two weeks later I presented him with a list of suspects that turned out to be 90 percent accurate. I'd made the narrow rodent eyes at *everybody* for a few days, and over the next week every single one of the men who had been in attendance that night bought me a drink. The women were harder to figure out, but I could have opened a black market corner shop with the chocolate and cigarettes they slipped me. Guilt is a marvelous weapon.

So, mentally prepared, there was then packing to do— cigarettes (for gifts and bribes), clothing coupons (forged and/or stolen), ration cards, two million francs in small notes (now confiscated—it truly makes me ill to think about it), pistol, compass, brain. And then just waiting for the moon. Actually I was very good at being summoned to action without any notice; I was used to that (also at learning poetry by heart)—but this business of waiting, waiting, waiting for the moon, nibbling at your cuticles and watching the moon nibbling at the sky, is very testing. You sit by the telephone all morning, leap out of your skin when it rings; then when it turns out there's too much fog over the Channel, or the German army has put a guard over the farmer who owns the field you're supposed to land in, you're let off again for the rest of the day. Then there's nothing to do except mooch about wondering if you can bear to sit in a smoke-filled cinema watching *The Life and Death of Colonel Blimp* for the sixth time, and if you will get in trouble if you do, because the Prime Minister disapproves of it and secretly you fancy Anton Walbrook as the noble German officer and you're pretty sure your C.O. knows it. Just as you have decided "Bother the Prime Minister!" and are looking forward to spending another dreamy afternoon with Anton Walbrook, the phone rings again and You Are Operational.

Have I got the right shoes on, you wonder frantically, and *bloody hell*, where did I leave my two million francs?

AN IRREGULAR FERRY FLIGHT

Maddie, lucky beast, did not have to endure any of this. Maddie just picked up her ferry chit as usual from the Oakway Operations hut, grinned at the "S" and the destination "RAF Buscot" because it meant she'd get to share a cup of tea with her best friend at some point in the next twenty-four hours, and walked out to the Puss Moth with her gas mask and her flight bag. *It was routine.* Incredible to think what an ordinary day it was for her, to begin with.

It was still light when we landed at RAF Special Duties. Moonrise was early, half past six or so, and because of Double Summer Time we had to wait for it to get dark. Jamie—call sign John—was flying out that night, and Michael. The call signs are all from *Peter Pan*, of course. This particular night's venture was called Operation Dogstar, which seems appropriate. "Second to the right, and then straight on till morning."

It's awful, telling it like this, isn't it? As though we didn't know the ending. As though it could have another ending. It's like watching Romeo drink poison. Every time you see it you get fooled into thinking his girlfriend might wake up and stop him. Every single time you see it you want to shout, "You stupid ass, just *wait* a minute," and she'll open her eyes! "Oi, *you*, you twat, open your eyes, wake up! *Don't die* this time!" But they always do.

OPERATION DOGSTAR

I wonder how many piles of paper like mine are lying around Europe, the only testament to our silenced voices, buried in filing cabinets and steamer trunks and cardboard boxes as we disappear—as we vanish into the night and the fog?

Assuming you don't incinerate all record of me when you're done with it, what I'd love to capture, to trap here for eternity in amber, is how exciting it was to come here. Me skipping across the concrete as I got out of the Puss Moth, through crisp October air smelling of leaf smoke and engine exhaust, thinking, France, France! Ormaie again, at last! The whole of Craig Castle had wept for Ormaie as the German army marched in three years ago—we have all been here before, visiting *la famille de ma grandmère*—now the elms are all cut down for firewood and barricades, the fountains are all dry except the one they use to water horses and put out fires, and the rose garden in memory of my great-uncle in the Place des Hirondelles has been dug up and the square is full of armored vehicles. When I got here there was a row of rotting dead men hanging from a balcony of the Hôtel de Ville, the town hall. The evil of daily life here is *indescribable*, and if this is civilization then it is beyond the capacity of my smallish brain to imagine the evil of a place like Natzweiler-Struthof.

You know, I speak German because I *love* German. What good was a degree in German literature going to do me? I was reading it because I *loved* it. *Deutschland, das Land der Dichter und Denker*, land of poets and thinkers. And now I will never even *see* Germany, unless they send me to Ravensbrück—I will never see Berlin, or Cologne, or Dresden—or the Black Forest, the Rhine Valley, the blue Danube. I hate you, Adolf Hitler, you selfish wee beastie of a man, keeping Germany all to yourself. YOU RUIN EVERYTHING

Bother. I did not mean to deviate like that. I want to remember—

How after supper, my admirer the police-sergeant-cook produced real coffee for us. How Jamie and Maddie lay on the hearthrug in front of the fire in the sitting room beneath the staring glass eyes of the stuffed foxes and partridges on the mantelpiece, Jamie's sleek blond head and Maddie's untidy black curls bent low together in conspiracy over Jamie's map, thoroughly against all regulations, discussing the route to Ormaie. How we all crowded around the radio to hear our own code announced on the BBC—*"Tous les enfants, sauf un, grandissent"*—the random message that told our reception committee in France whom to expect that night. It is the first line of *Peter Pan*. "All children, except one, grow up." Expect the usual lads with one exception—tonight there's one wee lassie coming along.

How we all sat shivering on deck chairs in The Cottage garden, watching the sun set.

How we all jumped when the telephone rang.

It was the squadron leader's wife. Peter—that is not his real name, Engel, you silly ass. Peter had met his wife for lunch, driven her to the railway station afterward, and almost immediately after dropping her off had been involved in a messy road accident in which he had broken half his ribs and been knocked completely unconscious for most of the afternoon. His wife had not heard about it earlier because she had been sitting on a train that had been three hours delayed after it was shunted onto a siding to give priority to a troops train. In any case, Peter would not be flying to France tonight.

I confess that it was my idea to find a substitute.

After the sergeant hung up, there was a lot of flap as every-body gasped in dismay and concern and disappointment. We had been tut-tutting from time to time all evening over Peter's late arrival, but it never occurred to *anyone* that he wouldn't turn up well ahead of takeoff. And now it was dark and the BBC announcement had been made and the reception committees in France were waiting and the Lysanders were out there with their long-range tanks full of fuel and their rear cockpits full of guns and radios. And bouncing on her flat heels, full of coffee and nerve and code, was Eva Seiler, Berlin's interpretive liaison with London, soon to insinuate herself into the German-speaking underworld of Ormaie.

"Maddie can fly the plane."

She has *presence*, Eva Seiler or whomever she thought she was that night, and people pay attention to her. They don't always agree with her, but she does command attention.

Jamie laughed. Jamie, sweet Jamie—the interpretive liai-son's loving toeless Pobble of a brother, laughed and said with force, "No."

"Why not?"

"Just—no! Never mind the breach of regulations, she's not even been checked out—"

"On a *Lysander?*" the liaison said scornfully.

"Night flying—"

"She does it without a radio or a map!"

"I don't fly without a map," Maddie corrected prudently, playing her cards close to her chest. "It's against the rules."

"Well, you don't have your destination or the obstacles marked most of the time, which is much the same thing."

"She's not flown to *France* at night," Jamie argued, and bit his lip.

"You made her fly to France," said his sister.

Jamie looked at Maddie. Michael, and the goddesslike Special Operations officer who was there to oversee Queenie's packing, and the RAF police sergeant, and the other agents who were flying out that night, watched with interest.

Jamie played his ace.

"There's no one to authorize the flight."

"Ring the Bloody Machiavellian English Intelligence Officer."

"He's got no Air Ministry authority."

ATA First Officer Brodatt made her move at last, and trumped him calmly.

"If it's a ferry flight," she said, "I can authorize it myself. Let me use the telephone."

And she rang her C.O. to let him know she had been asked to taxi one of her usual passengers from RAF Special Duties to an "Undisclosed Location." And he gave her permission to go.

He knows now.

Nacht und Nebel, night and fog. Eva Seiler is going to fry in hell. Oh—I wish I had some clue whether I have done the right thing. But I don't see how I can finish this story and keep Eva secret. I did promise to give him every last detail. And ultimately, I can't imagine that giving her identity away will change my fate much, whatever it is.

Because I'd written such a lot the day before yesterday it has taken a while for Hauptsturmführer von Linden to get caught up on the translation, and he and Engel (or somebody) must have kept going without me after I'd been locked up in my cell again last night. I have still not quite slept off the excesses of that day and was out cold at three a.m. or whenever it was that he came in—but woke instantly when the padlocks and bolts on my door began their official-sounding sequence of thuds and clicks, as it always fills me with the most curious mixture of wild hope and sick dread when they unlock my door. I have slept through air raids more than once, but when my door is unlocked I am instantly On My Guard.

I stood up. It is pointless backing against the wall, and I have stopped bothering about my hair. But the Wallace in me still makes me want to face the enemy on my feet.

It was von Linden of course—I almost want to say "as usual," as he often comes in now to chat briefly with me about German literature when he's finished work. I think it is the only self-indulgence of his day's strict routine—*Parzival* as a nightcap, to clear his mind of the blood that flecks the silver pips on his black collar patches. When he stands in my door and asks my opinion on Hegel or Schlegel, I dare not give him less than my full attention (though I have suggested he needs to take modern writers like Hesse and Mann more seriously. How those schoolboys of his, back in Berlin, would love *Narziß und Goldmund!*).

So, a visit not wholly unexpected, only last night it was not "as usual"—he was *alight*. Animation and color in his face, his hands locked behind his back so I could not see them shaking (perhaps also so I would not notice his ring—I am wise to such evasive tactics). He threw the door wide so my cell was lit by the blazing electric bulbs in the interrogation room and uttered in disbelief, "*Eva Seiler?*"

He had only just found out.

"You lie," he accused.

Why the hell would I lie about *that*? I'm Eva Seiler. Ha-ha, not really.

You know, I was *astonished* he had heard of me, that he seemed to know who Eva Seiler is. I'll bet it was that imbecilic Kurt Kiefer who spilled the beans on her, after he got back to Paris and blabbed about his conquests. I warned Intelligence he wasn't clever enough to be a double agent.

I suppose Eva *was* quite successful at extracting information the Jerries would rather not have leaked to the Brits, and perhaps she's even become one of many niggling thorns in the Führer's side. But I hadn't thought von Linden would know who I was talking about (I might have mentioned her sooner if I had). At any rate I didn't miss a beat—this is how I operate. This is what I am *so good at*. Give me a hint, *just one hint*, and I will fake it. It's the thin end of the wedge for you, me laddie.

I scraped my hair back from my face in the severe head-mistressy way they used to fix it, and holding it in place with

179

one hand, I straightened my shoulders and clicked my heels together. If you don't stand too close to someone who is taller than you, you can still affect to sneer down your nose at him. I said coldly, in German, "What *possible reason* could I have to *pretend* to be Berlin's interpretive liaison with London?"

"What proof? You have no valid papers," he said breathlessly. "You were caught with Margaret Brodatt's papers on you, but you are not Margaret Brodatt, so why should you be Eva Seiler?"

I don't think he knew whether he was talking to *me* or to *Eva* at this point. (He suffers a certain amount of sleep deprivation as well, due to the nature of his work.)

"Eva Seiler's papers are all forgeries in any case," I pointed out. "They wouldn't prove anything."

I paused—counted to three—and advanced on him. Two baby steps only, to make him feel advanced on. Still enough of a distance between us, a meter perhaps, that he could not make an advantage of his height. Then another step, to allow him the advantage. I let go of my hair and looked up at him, disheveled and feminine, all doe eyes and vulnerability. I asked in German, in a voice of wonder and hurt as though it had only just occurred to me, "What is your daughter's name?"

"Isolde," he answered softly, his guard down, and went *red as a beetroot.*

I had got him by the balls and he knew it. I fell about laughing, instantly myself again.

"I don't need papers!" I cried. "I don't need proof! I don't need electrified needles and ice water and battery acid and the threat of kerosene! All I do is ask a question, and you answer it! What more perfect proof than one lovely word out of you—*Isolde?* I'm a wireless operator!"

"Sit down," he commanded.

"What does Isolde think of your war work?" I asked.

He took the final step toward me, using his height. *"Down."*

He *is* intimidating, and I am *so tired* of being punished for my legion small acts of defiance. I sat down obediently, quivering, expecting violence (not that he has ever laid a finger on me himself). I pulled the eiderdown up around my neck, an illusion of armor.

"Isolde is innocent of my war work," he said. Then suddenly he sang softly:

"Isolde noch
Im Reich der Sonne
Im Tagesschimmer
Noch Isolde . . .
Sie zu Sehen,
Welch Verlangen!"

Isolde still in the realm of the sun, in the shimmering daylight still, Isolde—How I long to see her!

(It is Wagner, one of the dying Tristan's arias. I can't quite remember it all.)

He has a light, nasal tenor—*so beautiful.* It hurt worse than being slapped, being shown the irony of his life. And of mine, of mine—OF MINE—Isolde alive in the day and the sun while I suffocate in Night and Fog, the *unfairness* of it, the random unfairness of *everything,* of me being here and Isolde being in Switzerland, and Engel not getting any cognac and Jamie losing his toes. And Maddie, Oh lovely Maddie,

MADDIE

I pulled the eiderdown over my head, sobbing at his feet.

Then he stopped very abruptly. He bent down and uncovered my head gently, without touching me.

"Eva Seiler," he breathed. "You might have spared yourself a great deal of suffering if you had confessed this sooner."

"But I wouldn't have been able to write it all down if I'd done that," I wept. "So it was worth it."

"For me as well."

(I suppose Eva Seiler must be a huge catch! He thought he'd reeled in yet another brown trout, and it turns out he's got a thirty-pound salmon struggling to wrench itself off his barbed fishhook. Perhaps he is hoping for a promotion.)

"You have redeemed me." He straightened up and bowed his head courteously. Almost a salute. Finally he said good night politely, in French: *"Je vous souhaite une bonne nuit."*

And again I gratified him by gaping.

He slammed the door shut behind him.

He has been reading the Vercors—he has read *Le Silence de la Mer*, *The Silence of the Sea*—the French Resistance tract, *at my recommendation!* How else—?

He may get in trouble for it. He baffles me. I suppose it is mutual.

This time I know where I was, I know exactly where I left off. I know exactly where we were. Where Maddie was.

For the nth time, four different people checked over the ration books and parachutes and papers. They briefed Maddie, let her know whom she'd be collecting for the return trip, checked over the maps and the routes, gave her a call sign to use on the radio until she got to France ("Wendy," naturally). The police sergeant tried to give her a revolver. All the SD pilots carry pistols when they fly to France, he said, just in case. But she wouldn't take it.

"I'm not RAF," said Maddie. "I'm a civilian. It's a breach of international agreement to arm civilians."

So he gave her a *pen* instead—it's called an Eterpen, a truly wonderful thing, no messy ink to refill and it dries instantly.

He said they have ordered 30,000 of them for the RAF to use in the air (for navigation calculations) and a grateful RAF officer recently smuggled out of France had given one of the samples to Peter, who'd given it to the sergeant, who gave it to Maddie. The sergeant told her to pass it on to someone else when she had successfully completed her mission. He likes us very much.

Maddie was ridiculously pleased with her pen. (I did not appreciate then why it pleased her so much, the infinite supply of quick-drying ink, but I do now.) She also liked the idea of passing it on as a gift after a successful operation—a variation on the Aerodrome Drop-Off Principle. She confessed in a whisper to her passenger, "I wouldn't know what to do with a revolver anyway." Which was not entirely true, since on her second and third trips to Craig Castle, Jamie had taken her shooting and she had actually bagged not one but two pheasants with Queenie's 20 bore. But Maddie was—is? Was, all right, was. Maddie was a modest sort of person.

"Ready to do some practice landings?" Maddie asked her passenger casually, as though Ormaie were as ordinary a destination as Oakway. "They've lit the mock flares over at the training field. I've not often landed on the flare path at night, so we'll hop over there before we set sail."

"All right," her passenger agreed. It was impossible for either of them to be anything but elated—one of them on her way to France, the other flying the plane. Everything was loaded except Queenie—the sergeant offered her a hand up the ladder to the rear cockpit.

"Wait, wait!"

She threw herself at Maddie. Maddie was rather startled. For a moment they held on to each other like shipwreck survivors.

"Come on!" Maddie said. *"Vive la France!"*

An Allied Invasion of Two.

Maddie made three perfect daisy cutter landings on the flare path, and then her stomach began to nag at her about losing the moon just the way it sometimes nagged at her about losing the weather over the Pennines. She set her course for France.

Southampton's barrage balloons floated gleaming in the moonlight like the ghosts of elephants and hippos. Maddie crossed the silver Solent and the Isle of Wight. Then she was over the war-torn Channel. The drone of the engine mingled with her passenger humming over the intercom—"The Last Time I Saw Paris."

"You are far too jolly," Maddie scolded sternly. "Be serious!"

"We are told to smile *all the time*," Queenie said. "It's in the SOE instructor's handbook. People who are smiling and singing don't appear to be plotting a counterattack. If you go around looking worried, someone will start to wonder what you're worrying about."

Maddie did not answer, and after half an hour of flying over the serene, smooth, silver and black eternity of the English Channel, Queenie asked suddenly, "What *are* you worrying about?"

"It's cloudy over Caen," Maddie said, "and there's light in the clouds."

"What d'you mean, *light?*"

"Flickering light. Pinkish. Could be lightning. Could be gunfire. Could be a bomber squadron going up in flames. I'm going to change course a bit and go around it."

This was a lark. Light in the clouds, who cares? Let's change direction. We were *tourists*. Maddie's alternative route over the Normandy coast went straight over Mont St. Michel, the island citadel glorious in the moonlight, casting long moon shadows over the swelling tide in a bay that shone like spilt mercury. Searchlights swept the sky but missed the gray-bellied Lysander. Maddie set a new course for Angers.

"Less than an hour to go at this rate," Maddie told her passenger. "Are you still smiling?"

"Like an idiot."

After that—this is hard to believe, but it was a dull flight for some time after that. The French countryside was not as stunning by moonlight as the English Channel, and after a long time of staring into indistinguishable blackness, Queenie fell trustingly asleep, curled among the cardboard cases and baled wires on the floor of the rear cockpit with her head on her parachute. It was a bit like sleeping in the engine room of Ladderal Mill—noisy beyond belief but stupefyingly rhythmic. She had been keyed to fever pitch these past few weeks and it was well past midnight now.

She woke when her relaxed body was suddenly slammed against the back end of the fuselage along with all eleven crates. She was not hurt or even frightened, but she was hugely disoriented. Her subconscious mind held the reverberating echo of a hell of a bang, which had in fact been the thing that woke her rather than being tossed about. Bright orange light rimmed the windows of the rear cockpit. Just as she figured out that the Lysander was plunging earthward in a screaming dive, the increased gravity knocked her cold again. And when she woke up a second time, some moments later, it was dark and the engine was still throbbing reliably, and she was heaped uncomfortably among the tumbled cargo.

"*Can you hear me? Are you all right?*" came Maddie's frantic voice over the intercom. "Oh *bother*, there's another one—" And a lovely white ball of fire arched gracefully over the top of the Perspex canopy. It made no noise and lit the cockpit beautifully. *Limelight, limelight.* Maddie's night vision was instantly ruined again.

"Fly the plane, Maddie," she muttered to herself. "Fly the plane."

Think of her three years ago, a weeping jelly of fear under fire. Think of her now, guiding a wounded aircraft through the unfamiliar fire and darkness of a war zone. Her best friend, untangling herself in the back of the plane, shivered with dread and love. She knew that Maddie would land her safely or die trying.

Maddie was battling the control column as though it were alive. In the brief phosphoric flashes her taut wrists were white with exertion. She gasped with relief when she felt her passenger's small hand gripping her shoulder through the gap in the armor-plated bulkhead.

"What's going on?" Queenie asked.

"Dratted antiaircraft guns in Angers. The tail's been hit. I think it was flak, not a night fighter, or we'd be dead. We don't stand a chance against a Messerschmitt 110."

"I thought we were falling."

"That was me screaming downhill to put out the fire," Maddie said grimly. "You just dive as fast as you can till the wind blows it out. Like blowing out a candle! But the tailplane control's come disconnected or something. It's—"

She gritted her teeth. "We're on course. We're still in one piece. We lost a bit too much height in that dive, but all the dratted plane wants to do now is climb, so, well, that's not a problem. Only, if we go much higher the Jerries might be able to see us on their Radar. The plane's still flyable, just, *and* we've made such good time we're not even behind schedule. Only, I think you should know that it's going to be—um—a bit of a challenge for me to land. So you might have to do another parachute jump."

"What about *you?*"

"Well, I might too, I suppose."

Maddie had not ever practiced jumping out of a plane, but she *had* practiced landing broken planes more times than she could count—had, indeed, landed broken planes on plenty of occasions—and both girls knew that if it happened a thousand times Maddie would every time die with her hands on the flight controls rather than trust a blind plunge into darkness.

Especially as, like most shot-down British airmen, she spoke only the most basic schoolgirl French and had no clever forged identity to fall back on in Nazi-occupied France.

"I might drop you out and try to fly home," Maddie said casually, hopeful words spoken through clenched teeth.

"Let me help! Tell me something to do!"

"Look for the landing site. Less than half an hour to go. They'll flash at us when they hear us—Morse for *Q.* That's long-long-short-long."

The small hand did not let go.

"You'd better put your parachute on," Maddie reminded her passenger. "And make sure you've got all your gear."

There was a lot of crashing and cursing in the rear cockpit for a while. After a few minutes Maddie asked with a gasp of fearful laughter, "What are you *doing?*"

"Tying everything down. I'm responsible for this lot whether or not I see it again tomorrow morning. If we bounce I don't want to be strangled in electric wire. And if I have to jump out before you try to land, I jolly well don't want it trailing out after me and smacking me in the head."

Maddie said nothing. She was peering into the dark and flying the plane. Queenie gripped her shoulder again.

"Should be getting close," Maddie said at last. Her voice, faintly distorted over the crackling intercom, was neutral. There was nothing of either relief or fear in her tone. "Descending to 700 feet now, all right? Look for those flashes."

Those last fifteen minutes were the longest. Maddie's arms ached and her hands were numb. It was like holding back an avalanche. She hadn't looked at the map for the past half an hour and was navigating wholly by memory and the compass and the stars.

"Hurrah, we're in the right place!" she said suddenly. "See the confluence of those two rivers? We land right in between." She gave a shiver of excitement. The small, comforting hand gripping her shoulder suddenly let go.

"There."

Queenie pointed. How she'd spotted it through the page-sized gap in the bulkhead was a mystery, but she'd seen the signal, a little to the left of them. Clear and bright flashes in fixed series—Q for Queen, long, long, short, long.

"Is that right?" Queenie asked anxiously.

"Yes. Yes!"

They both gave spontaneous yells.

"I can't let go to give them the answer!" Maddie gasped. "Have you got an electric torch?"

"In my kit. Hang on—what's the letter to answer them?"

"*L* for Love. Dot-dash-dot-dot, short-long-short-short. You've got to get it right or they won't light up for us—"

"I'll get it right, silly," Queenie reminded her fondly. "I can flash Morse code in my sleep. Remember? I'm a wireless operator."

Hauptsturmführer von Linden says he has never known any educated person so foul-mouthed as I am. No doubt it was extraordinarily stupid of me to bring his daughter's name into the catfight we had last night. This morning I am to have my mouth swabbed with carbolic—not carbolic SOAP, like they do in school, but actual carbolic ACID—phenol—which is the same stuff they use for lethal injections at Natzweiler-Struthof (according to Engel, my ever-flowing source of Nazi minutiae). She has diluted it with alcohol—she wore gloves to do the mixing, as it is incredibly caustic. But she won't come near me with it because she knows I will battle her and it will go everywhere. Even with my arms tied behind me (which they aren't, obviously) I would have a good go at getting it everywhere. I am hoping the whole situation will evaporate if we postpone it long enough, and I think she is too.

The catfight started over the heartbreaking French girl (I think she is the only other female prisoner here), whom they have been stubbornly and persistently questioning day and night all week, and she, just as stubborn and persistent as they are, refuses to answer their questions. Last night she was weeping noisily for hours, in between shrieks of genuine heart-stopping agony—I have actually *torn out* chunks of my hair (it is that brittle) whilst trying to endure her shrieking. At some point deep in the middle of the night I broke—she did not, but I did.

I jumped up and began to scream at the top of my lungs (*en français pour que la résistante malheureuse puisse me comprendre*):

"*LIE! Lie to them*, you stupid cow! Say *anything*! Stop being such a damned martyr and *LIE*!"

And I started wrestling insanely with the iron stub where the porcelain door handle used to be (before I unscrewed it and threw it at Thibaut's head), which is pointless, because of course the door handle and its attendant hardware are purely decorative and all the bolts and bars are fixed to the outside.

"LIE! LIE TO THEM!"

Oh—I got a result I did not expect. Someone came and pulled open the locks so suddenly that I fell out the door, and they picked me up and held me blinking in the sudden bright lights, while I tried not to look at the wretched girl.

And there was von Linden, in civilian clothes, cool and smooth as a new frozen curling pond and sitting in a cloud of acrid smoke like Lucifer himself (no one smokes when he is around—I don't know and don't want to know what they were burning). He didn't speak, merely beckoned, and they brought me over to him and threw me to my knees.

He let me cower for a few minutes.

Then:

"You've advice for your fellow prisoner? I'm not sure she realizes you are addressing her. Tell her again."

I shook my head, not really understanding what the hell he was playing at *this* time.

"Go to her side, look in her face, speak to her. Speak clearly so we can all hear you."

I played along. I always play along. It is my weakness, the flaw in my armor.

I put my face alongside hers, as though we were whispering. So close it must have seemed intimate, but too close for us to actually look at each other. I swallowed, then repeated clearly, "Save yourself. Lie to them."

She is the one who used to whistle "Scotland the Brave"

when I first came here. She couldn't whistle last night—it's a wonder they thought she could even speak, after what they had done to her mouth. But she tried to spit at me anyway.

"She doesn't think a great deal of your advice," said von Linden. "Tell her again."

"*LIE!*" I yelled at her.

After a moment she managed to answer me. Hoarse and harsh, her voice grating with pain, so that everyone could hear her. "Lie to them?" she croaked. "Is that what you do?"

I stood trapped. Perhaps it was a trap he had laid for me on purpose. All was very quiet for a long time (probably not so long as it seemed), and finally von Linden directed with disinterest, "Answer her question."

That was when I lost my senses.

"You *fucking hypocrite*," I snarled at von Linden unwisely (he may not have known what the word meant in French, but still, it wasn't a clever thing to say). "Don't you ever lie? What the hell *do* you do? What do you tell your daughter? When she asks about your work, what *truth* does the lovely Isolde get out of *you?*"

He was white as paper. Calm, though.

"*Carbolic.*"

Everyone looked at him uncertainly.

"*She has the filthiest tongue of any woman in France. Burn her mouth clean.*"

I fought. They held me down while they argued about the correct dosage, because he hadn't made clear whether or not he actually wanted them to kill me with the stuff. The French girl closed her eyes and rested, taking advantage of the shift in attention away from her. They'd got out the bottles and the gloves—the room became a clinic suddenly. The truly frightening thing was that not one of them seemed to know what he was doing.

"Look at me!" I screeched. "*Look at me*, Amadeus von Linden, you sadistic hypocrite, and *watch this time*! You're not questioning me now, this isn't your work, I'm not an enemy agent spewing wireless code! I'm just a minging Scots slag screaming insults at your daughter! So enjoy yourself and watch! Think of Isolde! *Think of Isolde and watch!*"

He stopped them.

He couldn't do it.

I choked with relief, gasping.

"Tomorrow," he said. "After she's eaten. Fräulein Engel knows how to prepare the phenol."

"Coward! *Coward!*" I sobbed in hysterical fury. "Do it *now*! Do it *yourself!*"

"Get her out of here."

There was paper and pencil laid out for me as always this morning, and the drinking water waiting along with the phenol and alcohol, and Fräulein Engel is rapping her fingernails in impatience across the table as she always does while she waits for me to pass her something to read. She is waiting eagerly to see what I have written this morning, I know, as it has not been explained to her what I actually *did* last night to warrant such vicious punishment. Von Linden must be asleep (he may be inhuman, but he is not superhuman). Oh, God. There isn't much left for me to write. What is he expecting me to finish with? Isn't the end of the story rather obvious? I want to finish it, but I hate to think about it.

Miss E. has managed to scrounge some ice for my water. It will have melted by the time we get around to scouring out the filthiest mouth in France, but it was a nice thought.

Now we are back in the air again, suspended over the fields and rivers north of Ormaie and under a serene but not-quite-full moon at its splendid silver height, in a plane that can't be landed. The wireless operator flashes the correct signal to the ground and barely a minute later the flare path appears. It is perfectly familiar, three flickering points of light forming an upside-down L, just like the makeshift runway Maddie made her efficient practice landings on four hours ago in England.

Maddie circled once over the field. She didn't know how long the flare path would stay lit, and didn't want to waste the light. She began to descend in the oblong flight pattern she'd used earlier. Over her shoulder, through the opening in the bulkhead, her friend watched the faintly illuminated dial on the instrument panel that showed the altitude—they weren't losing much height.

"Can't *do* it," Maddie gasped, and the Lysander floated rapidly upward like a helium balloon. She hadn't even added power. "I just can't do it! Remember what I told you about the first Lysander I ever landed, how the handwheel for adjusting the tailplane was broken, and the ground crew thought I wouldn't be strong enough to hold the control column forward without trimming it? Only, I was able to set it neutral before I got in. Well, it's not neutral now, it's stuck in the climb—for the last *hour* it's taken every ounce of strength I have to stop us climbing—and I'm just not strong enough to hold it far enough forward that we can land. I keep dropping power and it doesn't make any difference. If I turn the engine off and try to dump the dratted thing down in a dead stall I think it'll *still* try to climb. And then it'll fall into a spin and kill us. If I could stall it, that is. It's impossible to stall a Lizzie."

Queenie didn't answer.

"Going 'round," Maddie grunted. "Going to have another go anyway, try a shallower descent. Still have quite a lot of fuel, don't really want to crash and go up in flames."

They'd soared up to two and a half thousand feet in the time it took Maddie to explain all this. She flexed her wrists and wrestled the control column forward again. "Bother. Drat. *Double drat*." ("Double drat" is the most fearsome oath Maddie ever swears.)

She was getting tired. She didn't manage to descend as far as she had the first time, and overshot the field. She turned back steeply, lost no height, and swore again as the airframe shuddered, automatic flaps clattering alarmingly as the plane tried to decide what speed it was flying.

"Perhaps not impossible to stall!" Maddie gasped. "Jolly well don't want to stall at five hundred feet or we're *dead*. Let me think..."

Queenie let her think, watching the altimeter. They were gaining height again.

"Climbing on purpose now," Maddie said grimly. "I'll take you up to 3000 feet. Don't want to go higher or I'll never get back down. You'll be able to jump safely."

That horrid trio of guards has just come to fetch me somewhere—Engel chatting with them in annoyed tones *just* beyond my range of hearing, outside the door. They did not appear to be gloved, so perhaps they are not here to administer the phenol. Please God. Oh *why* am I so coarse and thoughtless? Whatever it is now, I dread not being able to finish almost more than I dre

I have fifteen minutes.

The battered French girl and I were taken together down through the cellars and out to a little stone courtyard that must once have been the hotel's laundry. She proud & limping, her pretty bare feet hideous with open wounds and her white face swollen with bruising, ignoring me. We were tied to each other, wrist to wrist. In that small stone space open to the sky they have erected a guillotine. It is the usual way a woman spy is executed in Berlin.

We had to wait while they prepared this and that—threw open a gate to the lower lane to shock & entertain passers-by, hoisted the blade & ropes in place, etc. I don't know how the mechanics of it work. It had been used recently, blood still on the blade. We stood tied together mutely, and I thought, They will make me watch. They will kill her first and make me watch. Then they will kill me.

I knew she knew it too, but of course she would not look at me or speak to me, though the backs of our hands were touching.

Five minutes.

I told her my name. She did not answer.

They cut the cords that tied us together. They pulled her forward and I did watch—I did not look away from her face. It was all I could do.

She called out to me just before they pushed her into position on her knees there.

"My name is Marie."

I cannot believe I am still alive; I have been brought back here to this same table and made to pick up the pencil again. Only it is von Linden who sits across the table from me now, not E. or T. He is watching me, as I requested him to do.

When I rub my eyes, my hands come away from my face with Marie's blood still red and fresh on my knuckles.

I asked v.L. if I could write this down before I continue the day's work. He said I indulge too much in the detail of what happens to me here—an interesting record but not to the point. He's allowed only 15 min. for this—he's timing it.

I have 1 min. left. I wish I could have told more, done her justice, given her something more meaningful than my worthless name.

After my fiasco last night, I think they killed her for *no reason* other than to scare me into confessing that I have lied to them. It is my fault she is dead—one of my worst fears realized.

But I have not lied.

Von Linden says to me now: "Stop."

He leans back, watching me coolly. The phenol is still sitting there where Engel left it, but I do not think they are going to use it. I told him to watch me and he is watching.

"Write, little Scheherazade," he says. It is a command. "Tell of your last minutes in the air. Finish your tale."

Marie's blood stains my hands, figuratively and literally. I must finish now.

"You tell me when to go," Queenie said. "Tell me when you're ready."

"I will."

The small hand on Maddie's shoulder didn't let go, all through the climb. Maddie glanced down at the flare path far below, three pinpoints of light beckoning, welcoming, calling—and she made up her mind to try to land. But not with a passenger, not with anyone else's life in her hands—not with anyone she might fail.

"All right," Maddie said. "You'll be all right here. It's a bit windy, so keep your eye on the lights and try to land on the flare path! They're waiting for you. You know how to get out?"

Queenie squeezed Maddie's shoulder.

"Better do it quick," Maddie said. "Before the blooming plane goes any higher."

"Kiss me, Hardy," Queenie said.

Maddie gave a sobbed gasp of laughter. She bent her head to the cold hand on her shoulder and kissed it warmly. The small fingers brushed her cheek, gave her shoulder one last squeeze, and retreated through the bulkhead.

Maddie heard the rear canopy slide open. She felt the faintest dip in the aircraft's balance as the weight shifted. Then she flew alone.

You know Mary, Queen o' Scots, (whose grandmother, incidentally, was French, like mine; as was her mother)— Mary, Queen of Scots, had a little dog, a Skye terrier, that was devoted to her. Moments after Mary was beheaded, the people who were watching saw her skirts moving about and they thought her headless body was trying to get itself to its feet. But the movement turned out to be her dog, which she had carried to the block with her, hidden in her skirts. Mary Stuart is supposed to have faced her execution with grace and courage (she wore a scarlet chemise to suggest she was being martyred), but I don't think she could have been so brave if she had not secretly been holding tight to her Skye terrier, feeling his warm silky fur against her trembling skin.

I have been allowed to use the past three days to re-read all I've written and check it over. It makes sense and it's almost a good story.

Fräulein Engel will be disappointed, though, that it doesn't have a proper ending. I am sorry. She's seen the pictures, too; there's no point in making up something hopeful and defiant if I'm meant to be telling the truth. But be honest yourself, Anna Engel, wouldn't you rather Maddie hit the ground running, as the Yanks say, and made it safely back to England? Because that would be the happy ending, the right ending for a jolly girls' adventure story.

This pile of paper doesn't stack together very well—pages and pages of different widths and lengths and thicknesses. I like the flute music that I had to write on at the end. I was careful with that. Of course I have had to use both sides and write over the music, but I wrote very lightly in pencil between the notes, because someone may want to play it again someday. Not Esther Lévi, whose music it was, whose classically biblical Hebrew name is written neatly at the top of each sheet; I'm not stupid enough to think she'll ever see this music again, whoever she is. But perhaps someone else. When the bombing stops.

When the tide turns. And it will.

One thing I have noticed, reading over this story, which not even Hauptsturmführer von Linden has noticed, is that I have not put my own name down on anything I have written in the past three weeks. You all know my name but not, I think, my full name, so I am going to write it down in all its pretentious glory. I used to like to write my full name when I was small—as you will see, it was quite an accomplishment for a small person:

Julia Lindsay MacKenzie Wallace Beaufort-Stuart

That is what it says on my real papers, which you have not got. My name is a bit of a defiance against the Führer all on its own, a much more heroic name than I deserve, and I still enjoy writing it out, so I will write it again, the way I write it on my dance cards:

Lady Julia Lindsay MacKenzie Wallace Beaufort-Stuart

But I don't ever think of myself as Lady Julia. I think of myself as Julie.

I am not Scottie. I am not Eva. I am not Queenie. I have answered to all three, but I never introduce myself by those names. And how I have detested being "Flight Officer Beaufort-Stuart" these past seven weeks! That is what Hauptsturmführer von Linden usually calls me, *so* polite and formal—"Now, Flight Officer Beaufort-Stuart, you've been very cooperative today, so if you have had enough to drink, let's begin on the third set of codes. Please be accurate, Flight Officer Beaufort-Stuart, no one wants to have to ram this red hot poker through your eyeball. Could someone please sluice out Flight Officer Beaufort-Stuart's soiled panties before she is taken back to her room?"

So even though it is my name, I don't think of myself as Flight Officer Beaufort-Stuart, either, any more than I am Scheherazade, the other name he's given me.

I am Julie.

That is what my brothers call me, what Maddie called me always, and that is what I call myself. That is what I told Marie my name is.

Oh, God—if I stop writing now, they will take this paper away, all of it, the yellowed recipe cards and the prescription sheets and the embossed stationery from the Château de Bordeaux and the flute music, and I will be left with nothing but to wait for von Linden's judgment. Mary Stuart had her Skye terrier—what comfort will I take with me to my execution? What comfort for any of us—Marie, Maddie, the cabbage-stealing scullion, flute girl, the Jewish doctor, alone at the guillotine or in the air or in the suffocating freight wagons?

And why? *Why?*

All I have done is buy myself time, the time to write this. I haven't really told anyone anything of use. I've only told a story.

But I have told the truth. Isn't that ironic? They sent

me because I am so good at telling lies. But I have told the truth.

I have even remembered some electrifying famous last words which I have been saving up to finish with. They are Edith Cavell's, the British nurse who smuggled two hundred Allied soldiers out of Belgium in The Last Lot, the 1914–1918 war, and who was caught and shot for treason. Her very ugly monument stands not far from Trafalgar Square and I noticed it, not bombed but buried in sandbags, when I was last in London ("The Last Time I Saw London"). Some of her last words are carved on the statue's plinth.

"Patriotism is not enough—I must have no hatred or bitterness for anyone."

She has ALWAYS got a pigeon on her head, even under the sandbags, and I think the only reason she manages not to feel any hatred for those flying rats is because she has been dead for twenty-five years and doesn't know they're there.

I think her actual last words were "I am glad to die for my country." I can't say I honestly believe such sanctimonious twaddle. Kiss me, Hardy. The truth is, I like "Kiss me, Hardy" better. Those are fine last words. Nelson *meant* that when he said it. Edith Cavell was fooling herself. Nelson was being honest.

So am I.

I am finished now, so I will just sit here writing it again and again until I can no longer stay awake or someone discovers what I am doing and takes the pen away. I have told the truth.

I have told the truth. I have told the truth. I have told the truth. I have told the truth. I have told the truth. I have told the truth. I have told the truth. I have told the truth. I have told the truth. I have told the truth. I have told the truth.

I have told the truth. I have told the truth. I have told the truth. I have told the truth. I have told the truth. I have told the truth. I have told the truth. I have told the truth. I have told the truth. I have told the truth. I have told the truth. I have told the truth. I have told the truth. I have told

O.HaV.A. 1872 B. N° 4 CaB

SS-Sturmbannführer N. J. Ferber
Ormaie **⚡⚡**

30 November 1943

SS-Hauptsturmführer von Linden—

This is my final reminder to you that Flight Officer Beaufort-Stuart is a designated NN prisoner. She has been seen twice in your custody and I will be forced to take formal action against you if it happens again.

I recommend you send her at once to Natzweiler-Struthof as a specimen, with the order that she be executed by lethal injection after six weeks if she survives the experimentation.

If you show this devious little liar one atom's worth of compassion I will have you shot.

Heil Hitler!

s as if they were wool blankets or alcohol, es

e-and-water-filled early days of our friendship

m. I was so sure she'd landed safely. It has b

te anything, and there is a simple reason why

come to get me the first day, I suspected, a

sleeping—just like a holiday. The blanket has

d of the second day I was getting very hungry

absolute pitch dark. Then these pictures. They

stroyed rear cabin of Maddie's Lysander, but

uts from the pilot's cockpit. Oh Maddie Maddi

aceful moment of my holiday. Also, they have b

again. I was lying with my nose pressed to th

er—I'd been crying, and it is the only place I

ed her feet as they dragged her by (she has

is always barefoot). I would not have slept w

yway, but have I said before that my room is

for interviews, etc.? You would have to be s

even in a feather bed. The following morning a

into chains—chains!—and hauled me to a su

vas going to be dissected. No, it turned out to

kitchen of this desecrated hotel, which is wh

us gray cabbage soup (they do not bake brea

ead it is stale ends cast off from someplace e

man who scrubbed the pots, swept the floors

wn less moldy sawdust in its place, hauled woo

PART 2
KITTYHAWK

I have got Julie's identity papers.

I have got Julie's identity papers.

I have got Julie's identity papers.

DRAT DRAT DOUBLE DRAT AND BLAST

I HAVE GOT JULIE'S IDENTITY PAPERS

WHAT WILL SHE DO WITHOUT ID???

What will she do?

Just can't think when it happened. She checked her papers, I checked my papers, Sergeant Silvey checked both of us, that headmistressy Special Operations officer who was nannying her checked, everybody checked. Anyone could have muddled them.

Drat. Double drat. She must have mine.

This isn't a very good place to write things—will ruin my ATA Pilot's Note Book and I probably shouldn't make a record in any case, but it is the only thing I have to read or write on or do anything with until one of the Resistance circuit comes back. Can't believe I didn't check sooner. Two days have passed since we got here. I have looked and looked and I have got my ATA Authorization Card, but my license and National Registration card are gone, and in their place are Julie's ration coupons and forged *carte d'identité*—photograph doesn't really look like her, she's wearing her fair and scary Nazi spy face. Katharina Habicht. Can't think of her as Katharina at all, though she tried to make me call her Käthe all summer—had only just got used to thinking of her as Eva.

Not that my own papers or lack of make any difference to me as I AM NOT SUPPOSED TO BE IN FRANCE. But

Julie, who is supposed to be here, has NO IDENTITY. I have got her FORGED IDENTITY DOCUMENTS.

How—how? Like when Intelligence took my clothing coupons, but that was done on purpose. And I swore to be more careful.

I don't know what to do.

If I am caught writing this I will be in trouble, whoever catches me—German, French, British. Even American. I shouldn't write anything down. COURT-MARTIAL. But I have absolutely nothing else to do, and I have the most marvelous pen in the world—an Eterpen, it has a tiny ball bearing in the nib and is full of quick-drying printer's ink. The ink rolls over the ball. You can write with this pen at altitude and it does not smudge and the supply of ink lasts for a year. The RAF have ordered 30,000 of these pens from the exiled Hungarian newspaperman who invented them and I have got one of the samples, a gift from Sergeant Silvey, who is soft on lady pilots and small, fair double agents.

I know I shouldn't write but I've got to do something— something. That last ferry flight would have been an "S" chit, so that means I'll have to make a report. Also an Accident Report. Ugh. I will have to do it anyway. I'll work on that.

ACCIDENT NOTES

Crash landing in field Damask, near Ormaie, 11 Oct. 1943— Aircraft Lysander R 3892

Permission for flight obtained from C.O. and I had made 4 successful night landings, 3 on simulated flare path, immed. previous to departure. Flight over Channel w/out incident although deviated from planned course over Caen to avoid antiaircraft fire. New route took us from Mont. St. Michel to Angers, where the aircraft was shot at from the ground and the tailplane was hit. I took action to control fire but could not achieve level flight as tailplane control was completely gone, aircraft now trimmed for steep climb and barely maneuverable in descent

Now that I think about it, the tailplane adjustment cable must have snapped during the climb out from the dive—or I wouldn't have been able to dive.

That thought has given me chills, that has.

All right. Where were we? Stuck in the climb and also lacking some rudder control. Engine pressures/temps & fuel levels acceptable so continued to destination, which (w/passenger's assistance) I had no trouble in locating—however on arrival found descent v. difficult and was concerned about touchdown, and agreed passenger should bail out over airfield as she'd had appropriate training and was more likely to survive a parachute jump than a crash-landing with half-full fuel tanks and cargo of 500 pounds' Explosive 808 and detonating wire.

Had already attempted 2 circuits over field prior to passenger's departure and found it dead tiring so I stayed overhead for half an hour to burn off fuel before a final attempt to land. Flare path remained lit so I assumed and had to trust that I was still expected—possibly my passenger had come down safely and informed the reception committee about the damage to the aircraft. Maintaining level flight continued to prove challenging and eventually I attempted a descent.

Not sure how I actually managed to get the dratted thing down. Sheer obstinacy I expect. Rudder wouldn't let me sideslip, and even at low speed with flaps down and no power the blasted thing wanted to stick its nose up. Couldn't let go to put the landing light on, came down in the dark tail first and bounced straight back up again—wish I'd seen it from the ground—snapped off the whole tailplane and the poor Lizzie came to rest with the back of the fuselage stuck in soft ground at the very end of the field, near where the rivers meet, the whole aircraft pointing at the sky like a standing stone. Made me think of Dympna's Puss Moth crash back on Highdown Rise, only the other way up. I didn't know what had happened till afterward, as the control column thumped me in the stomach and knocked the wind out of me at the same time as the back of my head bashed against the armor plating of the bulkhead. Woke up hanging on my back in the cockpit staring at the stars and wondering how long before the Bang.

I'm not managing to make it sound like an accident report—bother. At least getting it down while I remember.

Had switched off ignition and fuel before landing as per Pilot's Notes and Standing Orders for forced landing, so all was quiet, a few creaks and groans but nothing else. Then three men of the reception committee, one of them English (an SOE agent, the organizer of this circuit, code name Paul), slid open the canopy and pulled me out of the cockpit upside down. All four of us landed on the ground in a big heap. These were my first words on French soil:

"Sorry, I'm sorry, I'm so sorry!"

Over and over, thinking of the unlucky pair of refugees who were supposed to be ferried back to England on my return trip. And for good measure I remembered to say in French: *"Je suis désolée!"* Oh, what a mess.

They helped me sit up and tried to get the mud off me. "This'll be our Verity," the SOE organizer Paul said in English.

"I'm not Verity!"

This was not helpful information, but it is what I burst out with.

Confusion and mayhem and a gun held to my head. Sorry to say the gun was far too much to cope with following my first ever reportable prang, in a plane I probably shouldn't have been flying, and I burst into tears.

"Not Verity! Who the hell are you?"

"Kittyhawk," I sobbed. "Code name Kittyhawk. First Officer, Air Transport Auxiliary."

"Kittyhawk! My God!" exclaimed the English agent. "You flew me to RAF Special Duties the night I came to France!" Paul explained me in French to his companions, then turned back to me and said, "We were expecting Peter!"

"He had a smashup in his motorcar this afternoon. I shouldn't—"

He covered my mouth with a big muddy hand, and commanded, "Don't say anything that could compromise you."

I started blubbing again.

"What happened?" he asked.

"Flak over Angers," I sobbed. This was my proper normal guns-and-bombs reaction, coming an hour and a half later than usual. "Set fire to the tail and disconnected the tailplane trim cable and I think one of the rudder cables too. Had to dive to put the fire out, knocked poor Ju—Verity—out cold in the back, then had to fight the plane so hard for the last leg that I couldn't look at the map—"

And more sob, sob, sob, dead embarrassing.

"*You were hit?*"

They were all astonished. Not because I'd been hit, I discovered later, but because I'd successfully managed not to go down in flames over Angers, and had safely delivered them their 500 pounds of Explosive 808. They have been painfully nice to me ever since, all of them. I don't really deserve it. There is only one reason I did not go down in flames over Angers, and that is because I knew I had Julie in the back. Would never have had the presence of mind to put that fire out if I hadn't been trying to save her life.

"Going to have to destroy your plane, I'm afraid," Paul said next.

Didn't know what he meant at first, as I thought I'd done a dead brilliant job of destroying it myself.

"Won't be able to use this field again," he said. "Pity. However—"

They'd shot a German sentry.

I really ought not to be writing this.

I don't care. I'll burn it later. Can't think straight unless I write it.

They'd shot a German sentry. He had come along on his bicycle at the wrong moment, while they were laying out the flare path. He'd stood for a while watching and, as it turned out, taking notes—when they spotted him he pedaled off as fast as he could go and they couldn't chase him on foot or get to their own bicycles in time to catch up with him, so the English agent shot him. Just like that. They were pleased to have bagged a bicycle but horrified that they had a body to dispose of.

The wrecked Lizzie, with living pilot, was a godsend. They would have had to destroy the plane anyway, to make it look like a crash rather than a planned landing. So they installed the dead patrolman in the pilot's cockpit dressed in my ATA tunic and slacks, believe it or not. They had to slit the trousers right down the side seams to get them on the poor chap and even then couldn't fasten them, he was so much wider than me. It all took a while and I didn't help much, sitting quite dazed on the edge of the field wearing only a camisole and panties under a borrowed sweater and overcoat. Mitraillette, who gave me her pullover, must have been freezing with only that frilly blouse under her coat. They also took my boots—I'm brokenhearted about my boots! But apart from my flight bag, all my British pilot's gear had to be destroyed, helmet and parachute and all. Even my gas mask. Won't miss that. All it ever did was take up space, dangling uselessly over my shoulder in its haversack like a wingless khaki albatross for the past four years. Don't think I ever put it on except for drills.

Wish I'd taken that typist's course now—could do with knowing shorthand. I have managed to fit this in 3 pages of my Pilot's Notes in the titchiest print ever. It's not a bad thing if it's impossible to read.

Getting the plane ready to blow to blazes took a long time—and a lot of running around in the moonlight. Suppose they're organized but I hadn't much clue what was going on and was neither useful nor necessary at this point. Was also developing a splitting headache, anxious about Julie, and wondering why they didn't just set the dratted plane on fire and get it over with. Turns out they had quite a lot of equipment they wanted to get rid of, in addition to the damning corpse—half a dozen useless wireless sets they'd stripped for parts, plus a couple of obsolete ones nobody wanted anymore—they sent someone to fetch them out of hiding, headed off on bicycles and returned with wheelbarrows. The barn they'd used to hide this stuff is where I am hiding now. The farmer who owns it threw in an old gramophone missing its horn and a broken typewriter in a cardboard suitcase, and a chick incubator full of bits of wire too short to connect to anything, to make it look like the plane had been carrying a full load of wireless sets! Mitraillette, the farmer's elder daughter who was the only other girl there besides me, was very jolly about filling the plane with rubbish.

"Onze radios!" she kept muttering to herself and giggling. *"Onze radios!"* Eleven wireless sets. It is a joke because it is so unlikely we would send eleven sets at once. Each set is linked to its operator, and each operator is equipped with distinct code and crystals and frequencies.

It will puzzle the Germans when they examine the wreckage.

The 500 pounds of Explosive 808 was dragged away on a horse-drawn wagon. It took time to find it all as a few of the boxes had fallen out of the damaged fuselage and the rear cockpit, which Julie had left open, of course. She'd done a jolly good job of tying most of the cargo down. It was all done by moonlight because nobody dared use any lights—there is an early curfew so everybody was growing extremely nervous—I'd landed after 1:00 a.m. and it took about an hour to organize the destruction of the Lizzie.

Can't say I feel entirely safe in the hands of the Resistance, but they are certainly resourceful. Once the radios and mock radios were piled up, and the dead German fixed in place, they simply opened the fuel tanks—of course the plane was nearly vertical and the fuel came pouring out—and used a bit of the explosive and detonating wire to light it. Easy peasy. It made a very jolly bonfire.

It must have been nearly 3 in the morning by the time we raced away from the field as Peter's Lysander went up in flames. Had to ride in one of the wheelbarrows as I now had neither trousers nor shoes—they hid me under the same sacking they'd used to hide the radios, stinking of onion and cows. Then handed me up a series of makeshift ladders into a loft above another loft in the barn where I am now. It is a hidden space just below the peak of the roof. Can just manage to sit up if I wedge myself right below the peak. I've not started feeling claustrophobic yet. I suppose I do spend most of my life strapped into tiny cramped spaces. There is plenty of room to stretch out if I lie down. Pretend it's the back of a Fox Moth—it's just as cold. Most awkward for washing and things, all water and soiled pans have to be handed up and down the ladders.

Can't think what else there is to tell about the crash. I've been clothed and fed and sheltered very generously considering they'll all be shot if I'm discovered. I'm a huge risk—a danger to myself and everyone around me, probably the only shot-down Allied airwoman outside Russia. I've seen the leaflets. Ten thousand francs reward for captured Allied flight crew or parachutists, "more under certain circumstances." "Certain circumstances" are bound to include a lass who can give the Luftwaffe a position fix on the RAF Moon Squadron.

And this terrifies me, and if I never tell anyone my real name perhaps no one will notice, but in addition to all that, *I am Jewish.* It is true that I went to a Church of England grammar school and our diet is not in the least bit kosher even in the holidays and Grandad is the only one of us who ever goes to synagogue. But I am still a Brodatt. I don't think Hitler will let me off for being godless.

Best not think about it.

I didn't think about anything for the first day and a half. Slept more than 24 hours, flat out, which is just as well because that was the day when the farm was simply crawling with German soldiers. The crash site was cordoned off for 2 days as they took photographs from every possible angle, including the air, and sifted through the wreckage. It's still cordoned off but apparently they have a hard time keeping out the usual vultures—small boys hunting for RAF souvenirs! A much more dangerous hobby in France than at home.

I am still unbelievably sore—not from the crash but from holding the dratted plane in level flight all during that final hour. Every muscle on fire all the way up my arms, right from fingertips to shoulders and even across my back. Feel like I've been wrestling tigers. Don't mind being able to rest, really. I never quite feel fully rested even on my days off. I could sleep for a week.

Starting to nod again now. Light comes in through slats netted over with chicken wire to keep out pigeons. The platform of this loft space is halfway up the slats—if you were suspicious and counted them, you would see more slats on the outside than on the inside. It's a clever hiding place, but not foolproof. Before I fall asleep again I am going to construct some place to hide these stupid notes. If anyone reads this, court-martial will be the least of my worries.

I wish Julie would turn up.

Spent all this afternoon (Thurs. 14 Oct) on the threshing floor of this barn learning to fire a Colt .32 revolver. What fun. Mitraillette and a few of her chums kept guard, Paul provided lessons and gun. The gun is part of his SOE kit, but he has got a bigger one, a Colt .38, from an arms drop, and they all think I need one as I have nothing else to hide behind—no papers and very little French. As far as Paul's concerned I'm just another SOE agent to be trained up quickly—not sure how this happened, but at any rate I am learning to be proficient in the SOE's "Double Tap" system. You fire twice, rapidly, each time you aim so you never have to take any prisoners. I am a decent shot. I think I would even find it quite a satisfying challenge if it weren't for the noise—and Paul's wandering hands. I remember him now, from that ferry flight in England. His hand on my thigh IN THE AIR. Ugh. Mitraillette says it is not just me, he does it to every woman under 40 who comes near enough for him to touch. Don't know how Julie puts up with such stuff, encourages it even, as part of her work. I suppose she's just bolder than me, in that as in everything.

Mitraillette, it turns out, is not the Resistance girl's real name. She laughed at my stupidity for thinking it was—it is her code name. She has told me both, as it is awkward her father shouting her real name just below my louvered window when she's supposed to come feed the hens—it is a poultry farm. I won't write down her real name. Mitraillette means "submachine gun." It suits her.

Maman—her mother—is from Alsace and the children all speak German fluently. There is a younger sister they call La Cadette—think it means "the little sister." The brother, the eldest, is a Gestapo officer—an actual Frenchman who has been made an underling in the Ormaie Gestapo headquarters. The family, including Maman, despise the boy's Nazi collaboration, but they fuss and cluck over him when he visits home. Apparently collaborators are so violently detested in Ormaie that anyone will shoot them, even ordinary citizens who have no connection to the Resistance, and he has to keep his head down. Etienne, I think he's called, his real name. He does not know it but he is quite safe. He is brilliant cover for his own family's Resistance entanglement and there are orders out to keep him alive.

Mitraillette spent a good two hours chatting with me last night, up here in the loft in the dark. Her English is as rubbish as my French, but though we persist in thoroughly mangling both languages, we understand each other pretty well. We were watching the road while they shifted some of the explosive—she has a wooden bird whistle for warning the people below if she sees headlamps coming down the hill. Since I arrived the explosive has been not-very-safely hidden under bales of hay on the floor of the barn. This building is easily 300 years old, probably more, timber-framed wattle-and-daub plaster like Wythenshawe Hall, and if anyone should drop a match or cigarette the whole place would go up like Vesuvius. There's no way I'd ever be able to get out. I try not to think about it.

I also try not to fret over Julie. Word is that the day before yesterday she met her first contact. I don't know where or who—my information is all thirdhand—but what a huge relief to know she landed safely! My understanding is that the reception committee who prepared the landing field is not connected to Julie's prearranged contacts in Ormaie—more accurately they are all different members of the same circuit. It is meant to work like a relay race with Julie as the baton, but she has missed out the first leg of the race, the connection at this end—probably due to coming down in the wrong place in the dark.

Must get in the habit of calling her Verity. Everyone else does. Her circuit is called Damask, after their most venerable member, who is 83 years old and a rose grower—they generally label circuits by some trade. I haven't been told the rose grower's name. No one goes by, or even knows, real names. I wouldn't want to give Julie's name away by accident.

Her assignment is so dead secret that her first contact wasn't told she and her goods had arrived until she'd told him herself, so although he was aware there had been a Lysander crash outside Ormaie, he hadn't known she'd survived until he met her—and when she spoke to him, neither one of them knew that the explosives landed safely as well. But word is spreading through the circuit that both ~~Julie~~ Verity *and* the explosives are here. Next stop the town hall. She is supposed to get access to the city archives and look up the original architect's drawings for the old hotel building that the Ormaie Gestapo use as their headquarters. She won't be able to do that till we sort out her ID, though.

We are puzzling over how to do it. Mitraillette is not allowed to speak directly to ~~Julie's~~ Verity's contact, so she has to find someone else to take the message. They keep their tasks and names very carefully separated. And we don't want to hand over Verity's "Katharina Habicht" papers to anyone but Verity, i.e. "Katharina" herself. Mitraillette is going to try to arrange for V to pick them up from one of the Resistance "*cachettes*," their secret letter boxes. That means we have to pass word along somehow.

219

I say "we" as though I were going to do something dramatic to help, other than sit here blowing on my fingers to keep them warm and hoping no one finds me!

The operation is to go ahead as planned—they've got the equipment, they've got Verity, the contacts are all in place. With a little care and planning it'll be the Ormaie Gestapo HQ that goes up like Vesuvius, and not this barn. If only Käthe Habicht weren't operating "behind enemy lines," as it were, with Kittyhawk's British identity papers!

I am beginning to think it was one of her less clever ideas to call herself Kitty Hawk in German. Terribly sweet, but not very practical. Though to be fair she wasn't expecting me to come along.

Have taken Paul's revolver apart and put it back together 7 times. It is not as interesting as a radial engine.

Another Lysander has come down.

Unbelievable but true. This one made it past the anti-aircraft guns and came in just as planned, easy peasy, about 70 miles north of here, on Mon. 18 Oct. Unfortunately the landing field had become a sea of mud because there has been nothing but rain, rain, rain for the past week, all over France I think. The reception committee at the field up there spent five hours trying to haul the plane out of the mud—they hitched a pair of *bulls* to it, as it was too muddy even to drive a tractor onto the field, but finally had to give up as it was about to get light. So they have destroyed another aircraft and there is another Special Duties pilot stuck here.

I say another, but of course I am not really Special Duties. There's some small comfort in not being the only one—mean and piggish of me, I know, but I can't help it.

There had been talk of trying to get me out of here on that plane. They were going to try to squeeze me in with the two people I was supposed to have airlifted back to England in the first place—I'd have had to sit on the floor, but SOE and ATA are rather frantic about me at home and want me out of here. It hasn't happened. Any number of things need to be arranged, then rearranged, then go wrong at the last minute. Every message to London has to be laboriously encoded and delivered on a bicycle to a hidden wireless set 10 miles from here. The message perhaps doesn't get sent straight away because someone has disturbed the leaf in the keyhole or the eyelash folded in the note left for the courier, and then they have to wait three days to make sure they are not being watched. The rain has been dreadful, with cloud at 1000 feet and visibility next to nothing in the river valleys where the mist hangs—no one could land here anyway. No field closer than Tours, 50 miles away, to replace the one I ruined.

They call a ruined field *brûlé*—burnt. Which mine is.

They will have to send a Hudson to collect us all, as there just isn't the room in a Lysander. And that will mean waiting for the mud to dry out.

Ugh! I have never been so damp and miserable for such a long time—it is like living in a tent with no light, no heat. They pile the goose feather quilts and sheepskin in with me, but the rain is constant—gray, heavy autumnal rain that stops you doing anything, even if you weren't trapped in a crawl space under the eaves. I have been down a few times—they try to give me a meal in the farmhouse each day to warm me up and break the monotony. Haven't written anything here for a week, as my fingers are starting to get chilblained—so dead cold always. I need those mittens I made out of the pattern book Gran gave me, with the flaps that flip back so you can use your fingers. *Essentials for the Forces*, that book was called. If I'd known *how essential* those mittens would be now, I'd never have taken them out of my flight bag—except to wear them. Not like the flipping gas mask.

I wish I was a writer—I wish I had the words to describe the rich mixture of fear and boredom that I have lived with for the past 10 days, and which putters on indefinitely ahead of me. It must be a little like being in prison. Waiting to be sentenced—not waiting for execution, as I'm not without hope. But the possibility that it will end in death is there. And real.

In the meantime my days are duller than a lifetime as a mill girl endlessly loading shuttles—nothing to do but suck on my cold fingers, like Jamie in the North Sea, and worry. I am not used to it. I am always doing, always at work on something. I don't know how to occupy my mind without my whole self being busy. The other girls at Maidsend all lay snoring or knitting or doing their nails when the rain was tipping it down in such grotty visibility no one could fly. Knitting was never enough. Got so bored with it, can't concentrate on anything bigger than socks or gloves. I always ended up scrounging bicycles to go exploring.

Remember the Bicycle Adventure when I told Julie all my fears—they seem so trivial now. The quick, sudden terror of exploding bombs is not the same as the never-ending, bone-sapping fear of discovery and capture. It never goes away. There isn't ever any relief, never the possibility of an All Clear siren. You always feel a little bit sick inside, knowing the worst might happen at any moment.

I said I was afraid of cold. It's true cold is uncomfortable but . . . not really something to be afraid of, is it? What are 10 things I am afraid of now?

1) FIRE.

Not cold or dark. There is still a great pile of Explosive 808 hidden under the hay bales on the floor of this barn. The smell is overwhelming sometimes. It's like marzipan. Just can't forget it's there. If a German sentry poked his nose in here I don't know how he'd not notice it.

It makes me dream I'm eternally rolling icing for fruit-cakes, believe it or not.

2) Bombs dropping on my gran and grandad. That hasn't changed.

3) Bombs dropping on Jamie. In fact I worry about Jamie a good deal more now that I've experienced a little of what he's up against.

4) New to this list: the Nazi concentration camps. Don't

know any of their names, don't know where they are—I suppose I haven't been paying attention. They were never very real. Grandad roaring about ominous stories in the *Guardian* didn't make them real. But knowing I may very likely end up in one is more frightening than any news story could ever be. If they catch me and they do not shoot me right away, they will slap a yellow star on me and ship me out to one of these dreadful places and no one will ever know what happened to me.

5) COURT-MARTIAL.

I'm trying to remember what else I told Julie I was afraid of. Most of those "fears" we talked about that first day, in the canteen, were just so stupid. Getting old! It embarrasses me to think about it. The things I told her on our bicycle adventure were better. Dogs. Hah—that reminds me.

6) Paul. I had to chase him out of here at gunpoint—it was of course his own gun, the one he gave me and taught me to use. Perhaps I was overly dramatic to pull the gun on him. But he had actually come up into my loft, on his own in broad daylight, without any of the family knowing he was here, which is dead alarming of itself. They are so careful about keeping track of who comes and goes, and they need to trust him. I suppose all he wanted was a kiss and a cuddle. He backed off looking deeply injured and left me feeling guilty and dirty and prudish all at once.

It frightened me terribly, more afterward when I thought about it than at the time. If he—or anyone—tried to force himself on me, I couldn't run away. I couldn't call for help. I'd have to endure it without a fight, and in silence, or risk giving myself up to the Nazis.

I lay awake in a funk nearly all night with Paul's dratted gun in my hand, my ear pressed to the trapdoor listening, expecting him to come back and try again under cover of darkness. As if he hasn't got better things to do under cover of darkness! Finally I fell asleep and dreamed there was a German soldier battering at the trapdoor. As he broke through I shot him in the face. Woke up gasping in horror—then fell asleep and had the same dream again and again, at least three times in a row. Every single time, I thought, That was a dream, earlier, but THIS TIME it's real.

When Mitraillette turned up to bring me my breakfast ration of bread and onions and their dreadful pretend coffee, I blurted out the whole sordid story. In English, of course. I finished by bursting into tears. She was sympathetic but confused. Not sure how much she understood and don't think there's anything she can do about it anyway.

"In English of course" leads me to Fear Number 7—being English. I think I told Julie I was afraid of getting my uniform wrong and people laughing at my accent, and I suppose in a sense I am still worried about these things—with better reason. My clothes! Mitraillette's don't fit me in the waist and hips. I have to wear a frock belonging to her mum—outmoded and severe, a thing no self-respecting girl of my generation would be caught dead in. Mitraillette's pullover does fit, and I have a many-times patched-over wool jacket that once belonged to her brother, but the combination of these warm outer garments and the dowdy frock looks dead weird. The outfit is completed with *wooden clogs*—just like Gran's gardener wears at home. There is no hope of better equipping me unless we use Julie's clothing coupons. I don't mind not being stylish, but I am obviously wearing an odd collection of cast-offs, and if I am seen, people will wonder.

And my "accent"! Well.

Mitraillette says she can tell by the WAY I WALK that I

am not from Ormaie. If I walked to the corner shop dressed in the height of fashion and didn't breathe a word to anyone, I would still betray myself and everyone around me. I am so afraid of letting them down.

Oh, yes, letting people down. Is this next lot fear or guilt? It feels like a lump of granite stuck in the gears of my brain and stripping them raw. Letting people down. A great circular list of failure and worry. What if I'm caught and give away the location of the RAF Moon Squadron? I've already let down every one of those Lysander pilots—who liked and encouraged me so much they were daft enough to let me take one of their planes to France. Special Operations Executive trusted me, too, not to mention the refugees I was supposed to pick up here. I'm a colossal failure as far as my own ATA ferry pool is concerned, done a bunk and AWOL indefinitely, and I dread betraying my hosts by accident—by being found on their property—or by being caught and giving them away under pressure. Don't really believe I could keep anything from the Gestapo if they got to work on me. Oh, help—here I am again, back to the location of the Moon Squadron and the Gestapo.

Everything leads to the Ormaie Gestapo. Well, they can be Fear Number 9. The Nazi secret police, something else it makes me sick to think about. I am fairly certain the Ormaie Gestapo HQ will be my first stop on my way to whatever prison I end up in.

Unless the Ormaie Gestapo HQ is blown to bits first. But that doesn't seem likely to happen any time soon. It is 10 days since we got here. Part of the reason I've not written since last week is because I don't want to put to paper what I am about to write, don't want to give any kind of reality to this ugly "perhaps." Also, if I'd let myself write this week I'd have just wasted half my paper listing possibilities and wondering.

It's been too long. It is torment, pure torment, waiting for news—for anything.

Julie has vanished.

It's true she made her first meeting—Tues. 12 Oct., the day after we got here, but then she simply disappeared as if she'd never been in France. Today's the 21st. She's been missing over a week.

I understand now why her mother plays Mrs. Darling and leaves the windows open in her children's bedrooms when they're away. As long as you can pretend they might come back, there's hope. I don't think there can be anything worse in the world than not knowing what's happened to your child—not ever knowing.

Here, it happens all the time. It happens all the time—people just disappear, entire families sometimes. No one ever hears of them again. They vanish. Shot-down pilots, of course, torpedoed sailors, of course, you expect that. But here in France it happens to ordinary people, too. The house next door just turns up empty one morning, or the post office clerk doesn't show up for work, or your friend or your teacher doesn't come to school. I suppose there was a time, a couple of years ago, when there was a chance they'd run away to Spain or Switzerland. And even now there is a narrow hope that Julie has gone to ground until some unknown danger passes. But more often than not the missing face has been sucked into the engines of the Nazi death machine, like an unlucky lapwing hitting the propeller of a Lancaster bomber—nothing left but feathers blowing away in the aircraft's wake, as if those warm wings and beating heart had never existed.

There is no public record of the arrests. They happen every day. Often people look the other way if there is a fight in the street, to avoid getting in trouble themselves.

Julie has vanished.

It shocks me to write it, to see it here in the margin of my ATA Pilot's Notes alongside "De Havilland Mosquito— Engine Failure After Take-Off." But it's true. She has vanished. She may already be dead.

I'm afraid I will be caught. I'm afraid Julie is dead. But of all the things I'm afraid of, there's nothing that frightens me so much as the likelihood—the near certainty—that Julie is a prisoner of the Ormaie Gestapo.

It made my spine crawl as I wrote it down and it makes me shiver again to read the words I just wrote.

Must stop. This ink is amazing, it really doesn't smear even when you cry on it.

Verity, Verity, must remember to call her Verity. Bother.

They can't move forward—no inside contacts yet. With Julie out of the picture, everything's stalled. She's supposed to be the central link in this operation, the informer, the German-speaking translator moving between the town hall and the Gestapo HQ. Mitraillette can't do it—she's local, too suspicious. Now the whole Damask Circuit is on edge, afraid that Julie's capture will betray them.

I mean, that Julie will betray them herself. By giving them away under pressure. The longer the silence the more certain it is that she's been caught.

Meanwhile, they're still trying to do something about me. It's been over two weeks—nothing's changed.

Had my photograph taken. It will be a while before the exposures are developed. Difficult setting me up with the trusted photographer, who's busy on many fronts. Most of the negotiating didn't involve me. Again, they've gone to a good deal of effort on my behalf—could tell how nervous Mitraillette's Maman was about having me and the photographer and Paul all gathered in her sitting room.

The idea is to do over Verity's false *carte d'identité* to turn Kittyhawk—I mean me—into Käthe, I mean Katharina Habicht. I would become the family's quiet and not-too-bright cousin from Alsace, whose parents have been bombed out and who has come here to be looked after and help with the farm. It's a risk for countless reasons, the worst being that there's always a possibility that if Julie has been caught, she may have already compromised the name. We've talked and talked about it—Mitraillette, Maman, and Papa, me as chief consultant and Paul as translator. If the Nazis have got Verity, we've to assume 1) they've also got Margaret Brodatt's pilot's license and National Registration card and already know MY real name, and 2) Julie's told them *her own* real name, because as an enlisted officer under the Geneva Convention that's what she's supposed to do and it's her best chance of being treated decently as a prisoner of war. We don't think she'll tell them the name on the forged Katharina Habicht *carte d'identité*. Paul doesn't think they're likely to ask, and even if they did, she could tell them *anything* and they wouldn't know the difference. She could make up a name—she would, too. Or perhaps give them Eva Seiler.

But the real reason she won't tell them Käthe Habicht's name is because she knows that if I landed safely, it is the only identity I have.

The photographer works "for the enemy," too. Proper British airmen flying over the European Continent carry a couple of photographs in their emergency kit, just in case they're shot down and need fake ID. But my photographs are being taken by an official Gestapo-employed French photographer! One of his other jobs is developing enlarged pictures of my crash—he brought some of the prints to show us. Impossible to describe the dual thrill and dread in watching him undo the string fastener of his cardboard folder, then slide free the glossy paper—paper destined for the desk of the Gestapo captain in Ormaie. Like feeling the buffet of the first shadow fingers of cool air touch your wings, as the storm cloud you've been trying to outrun begins to catch up with you. This is how close I am to the Ormaie Gestapo—the photographer could hand me over with the pictures.

He warned me in English, "Not nice to look at."

The most disturbing thing was knowing it was meant to

be me. That terrible charred corpse was wearing my clothes, bone and leather fused into the shattered cockpit in my place. ATA wings still tracing a pale outline on the sunken wreck of the breastbone. There was a blown-up detail of the ghostly wings, just the wings—you couldn't tell it was an ATA crest in particular.

I didn't like it. Why focus on the pilot's badge—just . . . Why?

"What is this for?" I asked. I could just about manage the French. "What will they do with these photographs?"

"There is an English airman being held in Ormaie," the photographer explained. "They want to show him these pictures, ask him questions about them."

They shot down a British bomber this week. In decent weather we get swarms of Allied aircraft flying over every night, and some in daylight, too. Think we've stopped bombing Italy since the Allied invasion last month, but now that Italy's declared war on Germany, things are really heating up. We're too far from Ormaie to hear the sirens unless the wind is in the right direction. But you can see the sky flashing when the gunners on the ground fire at the passing planes.

That was me holding tight to the close-up print of my burnt wings, trying to figure it out. It's the least horrific of the pictures of the fake pilot, but it's the one that disturbed me the most. Finally I looked up at Paul.

"What's a captured lad from a bomber crew going to know about a wrecked reconnaissance aircraft?"

He shrugged. "You tell me. You're the pilot."

The sheet of glossy paper shook in my hand.

I stopped that straight away. Fly the plane, Maddie.

"You think their captured English airman might be Verity?"

Paul shrugged again. "She's not an airman."

"Nor English," I added.

"But she's probably carrying your English pilot's license and National Registration card," Paul pointed out quietly. "There aren't any photographs on your British ID, right? You're a civilian. So even if they know your name they won't know what you look like. Tell me, Kittyhawk, how convincing do you think these pictures are? Would you recognize yourself? Would anyone else?"

That melted corpse was hardly even recognizable as a human being. But those ATA wings ... Oh, I don't want Julie to see these pictures and be told she's looking at me.

Because she knows the plane. There's no denying it's the same plane—the markings are still visible, R 3892. I just—can't think about this, Julie in prison, being made to look at these pictures.

I said to Paul, "Ask the photographer how long he can stall before he has to turn these in."

The photographer understood me without needing a translation.

"I wait," he said. "The Gestapo captain will wait. The pictures were not good when I made them, perhaps, not clear enough, and need to be made over again. It will take a long time. The Englishman must tell the captain of other things. He will not see the pictures of the pilot yet. We can give them these others to begin—"

He pulled more glossy sheets from the folder and held one out to me. It was the inside of the rear cockpit, loaded with the ashy remains of *"onze radios"*—eleven "wireless sets."

I gasped with laughter. Beastly of me, I know, but it is a BRILLIANT photograph—totally convincing. It is the best thing I have seen in the last two weeks. If they have got Julie and they show her that picture, it will be a gift. She will make up an operator and a destination for every single one of those phony radios, and the frequencies and code sets to go with it. She will lead them blind.

"*Oui, mais oui*, oh, yes!" I stuttered, a bit too hysterically, and everybody frowned at me. I handed both photos back—the one that will break Julie and the one that could save her. "Give them these."

"Good—" said the photographer, cool and neutral. "Good, it will make less trouble for me if some of the prints are produced on time." I am so—just dead humbled by the risks everybody takes, the double lives they all lead, how they shrug and go on working. "Now we take your picture, Mademoiselle Kittyhawk."

Maman made a fuss over me and tried to make my hair pretty. Hopeless. The photographer took three shots and began to laugh.

"Your smile is too big, mam'selle," he said. "In France, we do not like these identity cards. Your face must be—neutral, *oui*? Neutral. Like the Swiss!"

Then we all laughed, a bit nervously, and I think I ended up glaring. I do try to smile at everybody—it is one of the only things I know about being undercover in enemy-occupied territory. That and how to fire a revolver using the "Double Tap."

Can't begin to say how much I hate Paul.

The photographer had also brought me a pair of lined woolen climbing slacks belonging to his wife, good ones, well-made and not much used, which he gave to me after he put away his equipment. I was so surprised and grateful I started to blub again. The poor man took this the wrong way and apologized for not bringing a prettier dress! Maman descended on me, mopping my tears with her apron with one hand, showing how warm and thick the slacks are with the other. She worries about me a good deal.

Paul turned to the photographer and made a remark in a matey undertone, as though they were sharing a pint in a pub. But he said it in English so that I could understand it, and no one else would except the photographer.

"Kittyhawk won't mind trousers. What she's got between her legs she doesn't use anyway."

I hate him.

I know he is the organizer, the keystone of this Resistance circuit. I know my life depends on him. I know I can trust him to get me out of here. But I still hate him.

The photographer gave Paul an embarrassed chuckle—man to man, jolly saucy joke—and gave me a sideways glance to see if I got it—but of course I was blubbing away in Maman's large French farmhouse embrace and looked like I probably hadn't heard. And I pretended that I hadn't, because it was more important that I thank the photographer properly than that I tackle Paul.

HATE HIM.

After the photographer left I had to go have another target practice session with Paul. He STILL doesn't keep his hands to himself—even after being told off at gunpoint, even with Mitraillette watching—doesn't let them stray, but just leaves them on your arm or shoulder for much too long. He must know how much I'd like to blow his brains out with his own gun. But he obviously thrives on danger, and despite my violent dreams I don't really have it in me. Expect he knows that too.

The last weekend in every month Maman is permitted to kill a specially authorized chicken so she can produce Sunday dinner for half a dozen Gestapo officers. Because of Etienne being local, his family has to entertain his superiors pretty regularly, and of course the Nazis know the food is better on the farm than in town. I spent the whole three hours of their last visit gripping my Colt .32 so tightly that four days later my hand is still stiff. By squinting sideways through the slats in the barn wall I could just make out the bonnet of their gleaming Mercedes-Benz where they left it parked in the courtyard, and got a glimpse of the hem of the captain's long leather coat, which caught on the fender as they got back in.

It was La Cadette, the little sister, who told me about the visit. La Cadette is really called Amélie. Seems a bit daft not to write the family's names now, as the Nazis are so familiar with them anyway. But I've come to think of the Thibauts as simply Maman and Papa, and I can't think of Mitraillette as Gabrielle-Thérèse any more than I can think of Julie as Katharina. The family lets Amélie do most of the talking when the Nazis occupy their kitchen—she appears to have a head full of feathers but utterly charms the visitors with her fluent Alsatian German. Everybody likes her.

They try to make this monthly visit informal—everyone wearing civilian clothes, though they all defer to the Gestapo captain as if he were the King of England. Both Mitraillette and her sister agree he's dead scary—calm and soft-spoken—never says anything without consideration. About the same age as Papa Thibaut, the farmer. His subordinates all live in terror of him. The captain doesn't make favorites of anyone, but he likes talking to Amélie, and brings her a small gift every time he comes. This time it was a matchbook embossed with the crest of the hotel they've taken over for their offices—C d B, Château de Bordeaux. Amélie has passed it on to me. It's sweet of her but I'm not keen to set fire to anything in here!

They start with drinks. The men all stand about the kitchen sipping cognac, La Cadette serving, Mitraillette sitting awkwardly in a corner with the sullen German lass who gets dragged everywhere as the captain's secretary/valet/slave girl—she's also their driver. Doesn't take cognac with the men, as her hands are full holding the captain's file folder and gloves and hat during all the small talk.

Today the brother, Etienne, had a great big ugly lump on his forehead over his left eye—quite fresh, a purple bruise with a bloody dent in the center, still swollen. La Cadette was all over him with sympathy, Maman and Mitraillette a bit more restrained. They didn't dare ask how he got it—well, his little sister did dare, but he wouldn't tell her. He was also thoroughly embarrassed by the attention, the fuss being made in front of his boss and two colleagues and the other girl too.

So La Cadette turns to the captain and asks, "Does Etienne spend the whole working day scrapping with people? He might as well be back in school!"

"Your brother's very well-behaved," the captain answers. "But sometimes a vicious prisoner reminds us how dangerous a policeman's work can be."

"Is your work dangerous too?"

"No," he tells her blandly. "I have a desk job. All I do is talk to people."

"Vicious prisoners," she points out.

"That's why I have your brother to guard me."

At this point the slave-girl secretary sniggers very, very quietly behind her hand—pretending to clear her throat and making a sketchy wave at Etienne's bruised head—and she murmurs to Mitraillette beside her, "A woman did that."

"Did he deserve it?" Mitraillette whispers back.

The secretary shrugs.

It is HELL not knowing what has happened, or what is happening to Julie. More than three weeks now, already into November. Complete silence—she might as well be on the dark side of the moon. Incredible what slender threads you begin to hang your hopes on.

They don't interrogate many women in Ormaie—usually send them straight to prison in Paris, I think. I am sure my heart actually stopped for a second when I heard it, and again writing it down.

"A woman did that."

Don't know whether I'm disappointed or relieved—spent most of yesterday (Sun. 7 Nov.) trying to get out of France, and now I'm back here in the same old barn—exhausted but whizzing, I'm able to write because it's getting light already and Paul gave me a Benzedrine tablet last night to keep me going.

Glad to have these notes back. I left them here so as not to have them on me if I was caught during the 50 mile trek to the landing field. Of course as I've told myself a million times I shouldn't be making the blasted notes in the first place, but I think I'll take them with me next time. Felt a bit like I was pulling myself apart to leave them here, and it's a treasonable offense to lose my Pilot's Notes.

Rode in the boot of a small auto belonging to a chum of Papa Thibaut's, a Citroën Rosalie—4-cylinder engine, at least 10 years old, running—just—on a disgusting mix of coal tar and sugar-beet ethanol. Poor engine hates it—coughing and spluttering the whole way—suppose I'm lucky I didn't asphyxiate in the exhaust. Papa Thibaut has got a delivery van of his own for the farm, but it and his driver are so carefully regulated that they don't dare use them for Resistance activity. On yesterday's trip, a Sunday afternoon, there were no less than six checkpoints to get through, more than one every 10 miles. They don't always know where the checkpoints will be, and it was a good means to find out so we could avoid them on the way home after curfew. I was in the back with a wicker picnic hamper and also a couple of chickens—laying hens—which were legitimately being taken to another farm. The fuss made over the chickens at the checkpoints is not to be believed. Unlike me, they had their own papers.

Dead clever distraction, though. As soon as anyone opened the boot, which they did at half the checkpoints, the chickens began to carry on like—well, like chickens! The difficulty for me, curled at the back of the boot under empty feed sacks, was not in trying to avoid heart failure every time somebody looked in on us but in managing not to give myself away with hysterical laughter.

It took ages to get to the landing field—getting dark when we arrived, minus hens, which had been dropped off at their final destination. I had to wait in my hiding place for nearly an hour while the hen transaction was completed, but they saved a sandwich and a drop of cognac for me. Then on to the field, bit of an uphill slope but not too bad, unfortunately some high power cables in the approach that I didn't like the look of at all, and ultimately neither did the pilot who didn't land there—I'll get to that—

In addition to me and the hens, our carload included Papa Thibaut's friend the driver, Papa Thibaut for authenticity of chicken sales, Amélie and Mitraillette for authenticity of Sunday picnic, and Paul for general knowledge and execution of plan. Paul sat between the girls the whole way with Amélie purring on his shoulder. She is a wizard actress, La Cadette. Under the backseat they had hidden a couple of Stens—Mitraillette's namesake submachine gun—and a wireless set. The field was right up at the end of a dirt track, three wooden gates to open and shut on the way—"guards" of our own posted on each gate already. They'd all arrived on bicycles, hidden in the wayside shrubs now—a few of the riders had doubled up so that when the aircraft passengers left, there wouldn't be extra cycles to take back with them. The local "ground crew" set up our radio by attaching it to the poor Rosalie's battery and sticking the antenna up a tree that conveniently hid the car from the air, as well. Reception was all right at first, though as the wind picked up later it got more and more difficult to hear anything.

We crowded 'round the headset as the BBC came on air, two or three of us to an earphone—

—ICI LONDRES—

THIS IS LONDON! Such a thrill, no other word for it, THRILLING, to hear the BBC—just incredible. How amazing, *astonishing* it is that we have this technology, this link—all the hundreds of miles between us, field and forest and river and sea, all the guards and guns, bypassed in an eye blink. And then that moderate voice, speaking clear French that even I could understand, as though the chap were standing next to you, secretly telling you in your blacked-out European field that your rescue plane is On The Way!

Paul introduced all the lads of the reception committee— not by their real names, of course. You have to shake hands with *everyone*. Hard to remember them all after one meeting in the dark. There was a girl who was supposed to be picked up with us, a wireless operator, they were dead keen to get her back to England as she has apparently got half the Gestapo in Paris on her tail.

"Don't know what we'll do without you, Princess," Paul said, squeezing her around the waist.

"I'll come back," she said quietly. Not like Julie at all, really—shy and soft-spoken. Must be every bit as brave, though. Can't imagine what nerve these people must have.

Then Paul pointed out to me, "That young fellow just coming with the last bicycle is the other pilot, the one who got stuck in the mud west of here. You probably know each other?"

I looked up. It was Jamie, JAMIE BEAUFORT-STUART. Even in tossing shadows and under a waxing moon I knew him, and he saw me at the same time. He dropped his bicycle and we leaped for each other like kangaroos. He burst out, "MA—"

He nearly said my name. He caught himself and stammered a little, then smoothly cried out, *"MA CHÉRIE!"* and slung me over backward in a swooning Hollywood kiss.

We both came up gasping for air.

"Sorry, sorry!" he hissed in my ear. "First thing I thought of—didn't want to blow your cover, Kittyhawk! Won't do it again, I promise—"

Then we were both overcome with silliness, giggling like idiots. I kissed him back very quickly, so that he knew I didn't mind. He swooped me upright but kept one arm over my shoulder—they are all like that, those Beaufort-Stuarts, affectionate as puppies, dead casual about it. It's not British! Not English, anyway, but I don't think it's very Scottish, either. For a moment I saw Paul watching us, himself with one arm still clamped around the other girl's waist—then he turned away and said something to one of the landing team.

"Any word from our Verity?" Jamie asked suddenly.

I shook my head, didn't quite trust myself to answer.

"Bloody hell," he muttered.

"I'll tell you Paul's long shot—"

We went to sit in the car with Amélie, who had fallen blissfully asleep on the backseat. Mitraillette was perched on the bonnet with one of the Sten guns propped on her knees, keeping a good lookout as usual. It would be a couple of hours before the plane arrived—the reception committee were laying out the flare path—electric torches tied to sticks. Nothing for us to do but wait and watch till it was time to turn on the lights.

"The long shot?" Jamie prompted.

"There's a woman in Paris who announces a radio program aimed at the Yanks," I told Jamie. "Paul's asked her if she can interview the Ormaie Gestapo, perhaps include some propaganda supporting them in her show—let the American boys on the battleships know how unfeeling it is of us to use innocent girls as spies, and how well the Germans treat them when they catch them. The broadcaster's called Georgia Penn—"

"God, doesn't she announce that sickening 'No Place Like Home' for Third Reich Radio or whatever they call it? I thought she was a Nazi!"

"She's—" I couldn't think of the right word—except "double agent," which isn't what I meant, though I suppose that's what she really is. "She's not a courier, she doesn't carry messages— Who's the person a king sends ahead of his army and expects won't get killed?"

"A herald?"

"That's it exactly!" I should remember. It's the name of the American paper she used to work for.

"What's she going to do for us while she's pulling off this positive Nazi propaganda campaign in Ormaie?"

"Try to find Verity," I said softly.

That's what this woman does, this mad American broadcaster, though her wages get paid by the Nazi Minister of Propaganda in Berlin—she walks bold as brass into prisons and prison camps and finds people. Sometimes. Sometimes she's refused entry. Sometimes she's too late. Too often the people she's looking for just can't be found. But she tries. She gets let in as entertainment for the imprisoned soldiers, and comes out with information. And she hasn't been caught yet.

Dratted wind. Still howling all over France—a beautiful day otherwise, for once.

Well—the plane got there, finally, one of the Moon Squadron Lizzies—lovely familiar ducky fuselage and itty-bitty hawklike wings—would have been a tight fit with the three of us in the back, but we'd have made it, none of us very big—anyway, it didn't land. Gusts must have been 40 knots, blowing crosswind over the landing strip, pylons to tangle with in the approach, batteries dying on the electric torches we were using to light the flare path—finally Paul and Jamie and I had to stand there switching the lights off whenever the pilot climbed away, and back on as he started another circuit of the field. The chap circled overhead for three quarters of an hour and tried to come down half a dozen times before finally bottling out. Suppose it's a bit mean to say he "bottled out," anyone with half a brain would have done the same and I don't think I'd have stuck around as long as he did. The moon set about 4:00 a.m. today and it must have been down by the time he got back to England.

Jamie and I knew he wouldn't make it in. Still—I was desolated when he climbed away and headed back west. We stood watching, faces to the sky in the dark and fingers gripping the torch switches, only a few seconds, and then we couldn't see a thing of course—but we could hear the familiar engine throbbing for a minute or two as it faded into the distance.

Like the end of *The Wizard of Oz* when the balloon goes off without Dorothy. I didn't mean to, couldn't help it, let out an enormous babyish sob as we trudged back across the field. Just seem to howl at *anything.* When we reached the car Jamie took hold of the back of my head and pressed my face against his shoulder to shut me up.

"Shhh."

I did stop, out of shame mostly, because the hunted wireless girl was being so stoic about it.

Had to pack everything up and head back the way we'd all come—we refugees to our different hiding places, and now of course it was well past curfew and we didn't have the chickens to bluff with this time. Started bawling *again* when I had to say good-bye to Jamie.

"Now stop. You go back to Ormaie and look after Verity."

I know he is dead sick with worry about her too and was being brave to make me brave, so I nodded. He wiped my cheeks with his thumbs.

"Good girl. Buck up, Kittyhawk! Not like you to blub."

"Just feel so *useless*," I sobbed. "Hiding all day, everyone rushing around me risking their lives, waiting on me all the time, sharing food when they have to account for every missing crumb, can't even wash my own panties—and what'll happen when I do get home? They'll probably send me to prison anyway for hoodwinking my C.O., nicking an RAF plane and dumping it in France—"

"They will grill us all and we will all defend you. They've not stopped any of us flying—they're desperate for Moon pilots. You only did what you were told."

"I know what they'll say. Silly girl, no brains, too soft, can't trust a woman to do a man's work. They only let us fly operational aircraft when they get desperate. And they're always harder on us when we botch something." All true, and what I said next was true too, but a bit petty—"You even get to keep your BOOTS and mine are BURNT."

Jamie burst out laughing. "It's not because I'm a lad that they let me keep my boots," he said, with just as much outrage in his voice as I must have had in mine. "Only because I haven't any toes!"

That got a little choking laugh out of me at last.

Jamie kissed me lightly on the forehead. "You've got to look for Julie," he whispered. "You know she's counting on you."

Then he called out softly, "Oi, Paul! I want a word with you!" Jamie kept one arm lovingly around my waist—so like his sister. Paul came close to us in the dark.

"Used this field before?" Jamie demanded.

"For parachute drops."

"The pylons are always going to be a problem for landing, even without the crosswind. Listen, old chap, if you can risk taking Kittyhawk about in daylight a bit more, she's your best bet for field selection around Ormaie. She's a cracking good pilot-navigator and a reasonable mechanic too."

Paul was silent for a moment.

"Aircraft mechanic?" he asked finally.

"And motorbikes," I said.

Another moment of silence.

Then, casually, Paul asked, "Explosives?"

I hadn't even thought about it. But—well, why not? That's a brilliant thing to put my idle mind to work on: making a bomb.

"Not yet," I answered cautiously.

"Tough work for a slip of a lass—are you willing to risk it, Kittyhawk?"

I nodded like an eager puppy.

"Let's get those papers made for you and let you off the leash a bit while you wait for the next flight out." He turned back to Jamie, and spoke in that nudge-nudge-matey tone again as if I couldn't hear, as if I were deaf. "Bit of a dark horse, isn't she, our Kittyhawk? Thought she didn't like men. Ready to go like a stoat with you, though."

Jamie let go of me. "*Shut your mucky gob, man.*" He stepped close to our fearless leader in the dark, took hold of his jacket by the collar, and in a dead quiet voice that had gone dangerously Scots, threatened heatedly, "Talk like that again wi' these brave lassies listenin' an' Ah'll tear the filthy English tongue frae yer heid, *so Ah will*."

"All right, lad," Paul said calmly, gently shaking Jamie loose. "Back down. We're all a bit excited—"

What was left of Jamie's slim hand looked perilously small in Paul's firm grip, and Jamie in general is nowhere near as big as Paul—a bit like a ferret going after a Labrador. At this moment the air began to hum. Another plane was crabbing in as low as it could safely fly, two broad searchlight beams stretching and leaping toward the ground before and behind it.

Paul reacted first and pulled the wireless operator under the shrubs where the bicycles were hidden. The rest of us threw ourselves into the low ditch that was the field boundary. No part of last night seemed to last as long as those five minutes lying trapped and defenseless in frozen mud and dead grass, waiting for the Luftwaffe machine guns to drill us into the packed earth or pass us by.

Obviously, the plane passed by. It didn't linger over our field in particular, either—must have been on some kind of routine patrol—don't like to think what would have happened if it had done its flypast while we were loading up a Lysander.

It sobered everybody up.

We drove the refugees and anyone else who fitted back to within a mile or two of their safe house, 3 bicycles tied on the running boards and roof of the Rosalie, the motorcar absolutely jammed full with 3 of us in the front seat, 4 in the back, 2 in the boot, and me and the w/op riding on the rear bumper and hanging on to the roof like baby monkeys clinging to their mum—the idea being that if we were stopped, she and I would at least be able to jump down and make a run for it. No one else would stand a chance. It's marvelous, in a desperate kind of way, to opt for speed over subtlety—like screaming downhill to put out the fire when your aircraft's in flames.

Every time we came to a gate, the two of us jumped down to open and shut it and took flying leaps back onto the rear bumper as the Rosalie set off again.

"You're so fortunate to be in Damask," the wireless girl shouted at me as we clattered through the dark—no lights, not even those useless slitty blackout headlamps. Didn't need them with the moon nearly full, though. "Paul will take great care of you. And he'll do everything he can to find your missing agent—that will be a matter of pride for him. He's never lost any of his circuit before." Posh Southern English with a faint French accent. "My own circuit has collapsed—14 arrests made last week. Organizer, couriers, the lot—someone's leaking names. It's been sheer hell. I've been given to Paul for safekeeping—shame he's such a lech, but as long as you *know*—"

"I can't stand him!" I confessed.

"You have to ignore it. He doesn't mean any harm. Close your eyes and think of England!"

We both laughed. Suppose we were a bit high-keyed up with the Benzedrine, rattling through the French countryside in the moonlight, people we love and work with disappearing around us like burnt-out sparklers. Hard to imagine how dead we'd have been ourselves if we'd met anyone—felt alive and unbeatable.

Don't like to think of her being hunted. Hope she makes it out of France.

I am Katharina Habicht now. It's not nearly as frightening as I thought it would be—the change brings such tremendous improvements to daily living that the additional danger's nothing. Who cares? I couldn't become a bigger jangle of nerves than I already am.

I'm sleeping in Etienne's room now—"hiding in plain sight" taken to extremes. I've also nicked some of his stuff. We cleared out a drawer to make room for Käthe's under things and extra skirt—illegally scrounged with Julie's coupons. At the back of the drawer was a super Swiss pocketknife with a tin opener and screwdriver attachment, and this notebook—a school exercise jotter dated fifteen years ago. Etienne's written out a list of local birds on the first three pages. For a week in 1928 Etienne Thibaut decided he was going to be a nature enthusiast. Sort of thing you do when you're ten, about the age I took Gran's gramophone to bits.

The list of birds makes me sad. What changes a small boy from a bird-watcher into a Gestapo inquisitor?

No good place for me to hide things in this room—Etienne knows where all the hiding places are. Two loose floorboards and a niche beneath the windowsill and a hole in the plaster are all crammed with his Small Boy Stuff—he hasn't touched any of it for years, all of it dust-covered, but I'm sure he knows it's there. I am keeping this notebook and my Pilot's Notes IN the mattress—which I have slit with Etienne's own knife.

I have met him. Trial by fire for Käthe. Went cycling with Amélie and Mitraillette, my first sortie looking for landing fields—three girls on bicycles, you know, having a jolly afternoon out together, what could be more normal? My bicycle is the one that belonged to the sentry Paul shot when I landed here. It has been "remade." On our way back up the main road we met Etienne coming the other way, and of course he stopped to bait his sisters and find out who I am.

My evasive action consists of smiling like an idiot, hiding my face in my own shoulder as though I'm too shy to deserve to live, giggling a bit and mumbling. My French has not improved but they have taught me a few responses to greetings that I am allowed to give when I am directly addressed—then let Mitraillette and her *cadette* sister do the rest of the talking for me. "She's Mum's cousin's daughter from Alsace. Their house has been bombed and her mum's been killed. She's having a holiday with us till her dad finds a new place to live—she's a bit fragile at the moment, doesn't like to talk about it, you know?"

In an emergency they are supposed to say a code word, MAMAN, and speak directly to me in German. That's the signal for me to burst into noisy tears, which the girls will respond to with equally noisy comfort and cooing—all in German. This performance is designed to shock and embarrass whoever is pestering us so deeply that they will quickly give us back our papers, without looking at mine too closely, and run the other direction to get away from us.

We've practiced this routine and made rather a fine art of it. And every morning since I moved into the house, La Cadette—Amélie—comes and bounces on my bed crying out, "Wake up, Käthe, come and feed the chickens!" Suppose it's quite easy for them to remember my "name" as they've only ever known me as Kittyhawk anyway.

So—we met Etienne. And of course the *whole conversation* was carried on in German, because not only do they speak it at home with their mother, but as their cousin I'm expected to understand it too. Every ounce of strength in me was invested in listening for the code word mixed in among their talk, which might as well have been Glaswegian for all I could make out! My maidenly blushes were not phony—felt my face would catch fire with fear and embarrassment. I had to let the Thibaut girls do the hard work of covering for me, explaining me to their brother as a cousin he'd never heard of before.

But then Etienne and Amélie started scrapping, Amélie going whiter and whiter the more he talked—expect I did too, after a while—until I actually thought she was going to be sick, at which point Mitraillette snarled oaths at their turncoat brother and threatened to thump him. He went dead stiff, said something nasty to Mitraillette, and started off on his bicycle away from us. But then he stopped and turned and gave me a nod, dead polite and formal, before he cycled off.

When he was nowhere near in earshot anymore, Mitraillette burst out in English, "My brother is a SHIT." Don't know where she learned that word—not from me! "He is a SHIT." She said it again and switched to French, which was harder for me to understand but easier for her to swear in.

Etienne has been assisting at an interrogation. It is beginning to tell on him, and he took it out on Amélie, who had *again* poked fun at the fading bruise on his forehead. So he told her in hideous detail what would be done to her if she was a prisoner who refused to give answers when the Gestapo questioned her.

Can't get it out of my head now that it's in there.

I keep hearing it over and over in dribs and drabs from Amélie herself, who thinks I'm a good listener although I can't understand half of what she says. She's partly upset by the Gestapo captain's involvement, as she puts him on the same shelf in her brain as her priest or the head of her school—someone in authority, a bit distant, mostly kind to her, but above all someone who plays strictly by the rules. Someone who *lives* by rules.

And forcing pins under a person's toenails because they won't talk to you doesn't count as any rules that anyone has ever heard of.

"I don't believe they'd do that to a woman," Amélie told her brother as we stood in the road with our bicycles.

"The pins go in your breasts if you are a woman."

That was when Amélie gulped and went green, and when Mitraillette got angry.

"Shut your trap, Etienne, you donkey. You'll give the kids nightmares! God! Why the hell do you stay there if it's so horrible? Does it make you excited, watching people stick pins in a woman's breasts?"

That was when Etienne became cold and formal.

"I stay because it's my job. No, it's not exciting. No woman is attractive when you're pouring ice water over her head to revive her and she's managed to be sick in her own hair."

I tell Amélie not to think about it. Then I tell myself not to think about it. Then I tell myself I *must* think about it. It is REAL. It is happening NOW.

What Jamie said is giving me nightmares. If Julie is not already dead—if she is not already dead she is counting on me. She is calling me, whispering my name to herself in the dark. What can I do—I can scarcely sleep. I just go around in circles all night trying to think what I can do. WHAT can I do?

Have found a super field—rather far from here, though—cycling all day with M., Fri. 12 Nov. Incredible how difficult it is to find a decent landing field for the SOE. It's all so samey, farm after farm, shrines at every crossroad and a community bread oven in every village. The fields are so flat you could land anything anywhere. But there are never any good night-time landmarks or any kind of cover for a reception team. Must be lovely flying in peacetime.

I have been in France five weeks now.

My legs are stronger than they've ever been—cycled a good sixty miles twice this week, once to find the field and again two days later to take Paul to see it. He needs to get his w/op to send an RAF plane to take pictures for Moon Squadron approval. In between marathon bicycle rides I spend most of my time taking care of chickens, learning how to wire up small explosive devices, and trying hard not to suddenly scream my head off with nerves.

The broadcaster Georgia Penn has had a "no" from the head of the Gestapo in this region—a powerful and terrible man called Ferber, I think, the Ormaie captain's boss. Penn has let us know she plans to ignore his refusal and try again by going straight to the captain—she'll backdate her application, tie them up in their own red tape, right hand not knowing what the left hand is doing. An amazing woman but totally crackers, if you ask me—hope her own right hand knows what her left hand is doing.

Another Lysander pickup is planned for tomorrow night, Tues. 16 Nov., at the same pylon-infested field near Tours. Weather unpredictable but it's the last chance before we lose the November moon. I may go home with my munitions expertise untested.

No, I am still here. Dratted Rosalie.

Can't blame the poor car, I suppose, but don't like to blame the stupid, well-meaning driver.

Oh, I'm tired. Moonrise at ten p.m. last night so plane not due in till two in the morning—Paul came to collect me after curfew and we bicycled to meet the car, him cycling and me riding behind him standing on a bar wedged through the frame. Had to cling to him for dear life for five miles. Bet he loved that. The car was late meeting us—the driver had to avoid an unexpected patrol—Paul and I stood for half an hour shivering and stamping around in the drainage ditch where we hid the bicycle. Don't know when my toes have *ever* been so cold, standing in icy mud, mid-November, in wooden clogs—thought so much of Jamie floating in the North Sea. I was nearly crying by the time the car arrived.

There were only three of us along for this trip—dangerous in both directions, didn't want to drag Papa Thibaut into it. His friend who owns the motorcar set off at top speed, full out and going like the clappers, no lights as usual except the waning gibbous moon on the rise. The Rosalie really did not want to go like the clappers and performed its usual consumptive drama every time we came to an uphill slope, coughing and gasping like a dying Dickens heroine, and finally just stopped—engine still gasping a bit but the car just *stopped*. Simply could not move forward up the hill. Choke full out but cylinders firing pathetically as though we were trying to make the poor thing run on nothing but air.

"Your choke's not working," I said from the backseat.

Of course the driver didn't understand me, and I didn't know the French for choke, and neither did Paul—*Le starter*, it turns out, which is not the same as the starter that might turn on your English engine. Unbelievable confusion followed. Paul tried desperately to translate and the driver resisted taking advice from a Slip of a Lass or whatever the French is for Slip of a Lass, I'm sure the direct translation in any language is more or less "Featherbrain," as it's what I get called whenever I'm expected not to be able to do whatever it is—fly a plane, load a gun, make a bomb—fix a car—so we lost fifteen minutes arguing.

Finally, as it was dead obvious that the choke *wasn't* working, the driver jiggled it about violently enough that something finally slid back into place and after a few healthier-sounding coughs the Rosalie reluctantly set off again.

This whole routine was repeated detail for detail three more times. FOUR TIMES IN TOTAL. The car stopped, I said the choke wasn't working, Paul tried to translate without success, we all argued for fifteen minutes, Papa Thibaut's friend jiggled the choke lever for a while, and finally the Rosalie wheezed into life and trundled off again.

We had now lost an hour, a solid hour, and I was *fuming*. So was the French driver, who was tired of being shouted at in English by a Slip of a Lass younger than his own daughter. Every time we moved off again Paul would reach back and give my knee a reassuring squeeze, till finally I thumped him and told him to keep his mucky hands to himself, so that even when the car was moving, we were all growling at one another like tomcats.

I was no longer afraid of being caught by the Nazis or worried that we'd be too late for the Lysander pickup—both of which were more and more likely the longer we were on the road. I was just mad as a hornet because I *knew* what was wrong with the car and they wouldn't let me do anything about it.

When the car stopped for the fifth time I climbed over Paul and got out.

"Don't be an idiot, Kittyhawk," he said through his teeth.

"I will WALK to this airfield," I said. "I know the coordinates and I have a compass. I will WALK there and if I am too late to meet the plane I will WALK back to Ormaie, but if you EVER want me to get in this French car, EVER AGAIN, you are going to have to make that French moron who is driving it open up the engine cowling so I can fix the choke RIGHT NOW."

"My God, we haven't time for that—we're an hour and a half late already—"

"OPEN THE COWLING OR I WILL SHOOT IT OPEN."

I didn't mean that. But it was an inspired threat, mostly because it gave me the idea of leveling my Colt .32 at the driver's head and making him get out of the car.

He didn't even turn the ignition off—the engine was still gasping as we pried up the side panel of the bonnet with the tin opener on Etienne's Swiss knife. All was inky pitch black beneath it. The driver cursed and complained but Paul murmured reassuring words to him in French, as I couldn't be stopped now. Got one of them to hold an electric torch for me while the other made a tent with his jacket to hide the light. Oh—the screw that held the cable to the choke valve had come loose—probably with all that blasted jiggling—the flap that is supposed to close over the air feed to the carburetor wasn't closing properly, and all I had to do was tighten the screw with my wizard pocket screwdriver nicked from the Nazis.

I slammed the bonnet shut, leaned in the driver's door

and yanked the choke on, and the engine roared into life like a zooful of happy lions.

Then I climbed back into my maidenly spot in the backseat and didn't say anything else till we got to the field, half an hour after the plane had left. Most of the reception committee had left, too, only a couple of them still waiting for us to turn up in case something awful had happened to us.

I was too mad this time to think of Dorothy at the end of *The Wizard of Oz*. I gave the poor Rosalie such a kick in the front fender that I made a dent in it with my wooden clog. Everyone was shocked. Apparently I've got a reputation for being quiet and a bit weepy—in a word, they think I'm gormless.

Paul again, explaining: "They couldn't have waited—it's so late now it'll be daylight by the time they get back to England. They couldn't risk being caught over France in daylight."

Then I felt dead selfish and bossy and mean, and tried to apologize to Papa Thibaut's mate, in my rubbish French, for denting his fender.

"No, no, it is I who must thank you, mademoiselle"—says he, in French—"for you have mended my choke!" And he held the door open for me gallantly. No suggestion that he had wasted yet another night risking his life for an ungrateful foreigner who would never be able to repay him—the Aerodrome Drop-Off Principle taken to extremes.

"*Merci beaucoup, je suis désolée*—" Thank you so much, I'm sorry, I'm sorry—seems like I'm always saying "Thank you, I'm sorry."

One of the reception committee stuck his head into the car after me. "The Scottish airman said to give you these."

Jamie left me his boots.

True to my reputation for gormlessness I blubbed most of the way back to Ormaie. But at least my feet were warm.

Penn's found her. Georgia Penn's FOUND HER! Julie disappeared 13 Oct. and Penn talked to her yesterday, 19 Nov. NEARLY SIX WEEKS.

I don't recognize my emotions anymore. There's no such thing as plain joy or grief. It's horror and relief and panic and gratitude all jumbled together. Julie's alive–she's still in Ormaie–she's in one piece, in her usual battle gear, every elegant hair swept neatly into place two inches above her collar, she's even still managing to do her blooming nails somehow.

But she *is* a prisoner. They caught her almost immediately. She looked the wrong way before crossing the street. Typical Julie. Oh–I don't know whether to laugh or to cry. So fed up with crying all the time, but too upset to laugh. If she'd had the right ID on her when they first questioned her she might have got away with it. She didn't stand a chance without ID.

Miss Penn had asked if she could interview an English-speaker and they got to talk face-to-face, under guard, and Penn verified Julie by her code name. She wasn't told Julie's real name. Don't know what excuse they gave. Penn came away fairly well convinced the whole interview setup was a complete sham, and Julie herself was being kept on a tight rein somehow. Invisible, but there. I suppose Julie knew that if she stepped out of line they'd silence Penn too–I know Julie would never risk that. She didn't even go against orders and say her name. All information was passed in hints and code words. The captain and slave girl were both there, and one or two others, and they all sat around drinking cognac—except the slave girl, of course!—in the captain's dead-swanky office where Julie has been temporarily put to work as a translator. So in fact she's actually doing what she was sent here to do!

No name given, no military service or rank mentioned—she introduced herself to Penn as a wireless operator. She has told the Nazis she's a wireless operator. MADNESS—that's not why she's here and so now they've gone to a lot of effort to get code out of her—Penn hadn't any doubt they'd got code out of her, must be obsolete or invented, but definitely something they can try to work with. Penn thinks that's exactly why she told them she was a w/op—they call it W/T in SOE, wireless telegraphist: so she could give them code. It's more common for a girl in SOE to land in France as a courier, but if Julie had told them she was a courier they'd have grilled her about her circuit—obsolete code is safer to betray, I suppose, than real live people. And it's straight truth in terms of Julie's original training and her WAAF commission, and it goes along with the pictures they took at the crash site, which they've certainly shown her by now. As long as they're focused on her nonexistent wireless activities they won't ask her about Operation Blow-Up-the-Ormaie-Gestapo-HQ or whatever it's really called.

Penn was shown only a few of the administrative offices and an empty dorm room with four tidy beds in it—no contact with any other prisoners and no sign of the conditions they're kept in. Julie gave her some clues. She said

She

Julie was

—BLAST IT. Fly the plane, Maddie.

I WILL NOT CRY.

I got to talk to Miss Penn myself. Mitraillette and I met

her by a little pond in a posh residential area of Ormaie and sat on a bench winding yarn while we talked, one of us girls on each side of Miss Penn and a canvas bag in her lap full of worn-out woolly socks to be unraveled. She must have looked like our nanny. She's nearly a foot taller than either of us. She talked and we kept dipping into the bag for more yarn while we listened. Suddenly in the middle of her report, as I reached for another sock, Miss Penn took hold of my hand and held it tight. Just mine, not Mitraillette's. Don't know how she guessed that I was the one who'd take it hard. A bit of an interrogator herself, now that I think about it—same job as the rest of them, pulling sensational stories out of reluctant sources. They all do it differently, but it's the same job. And Julie, also an expert, made it easy, volunteering information that Penn didn't ask for.

"You feeling brave, Kittyhawk?" Penn said, holding my hand tightly.

I gave her a sort of grimace of a smile. "I suppose."

"There's no nice way to tell you this," Penn said, and her crisp, no-nonsense American voice was angry. We waited.

Penn told us quietly, "She's been tortured."

Couldn't answer for a minute. Couldn't do anything.

Probably seemed quite sullen—not surprised, really, but Penn was so frank it felt like being hit in the face. Finally I croaked stupidly, "Are you sure?"

"She showed me," Penn said. "She was pretty clear about it. Adjusted her scarf as soon as we'd shaken hands—gave me a good look. Ugly row of narrow triangular burns across her throat and collarbone, just beginning to heal. It looked like it had been done with a soldering iron. More of the same all along the insides of her wrists. She was very clever about showing me, cool as you please, no drama about it. She'd give her skirt a twitch as she crossed her legs, or let her sleeve ruck back as she took a cigarette, only moving when the captain was looking somewhere else. Ghastly bruises on her legs. But the marks are fading now, must have all been done two or three weeks ago. They've eased off on her. I don't know why—she's made some kind of deal with them, that's for sure, or she wouldn't still be here. You'd have thought by now Ormaie would have either got what they wanted out of her or given up."

"Made a deal with them!" I choked.

"Well, some of us manage to pull it off." Miss Penn gently guided my hand back to the bag of socks. Then she confessed, "Hard to tell what your friend thinks she's doing, though. She was—she was *focused*. She didn't expect to hear her own code name come up in the conversation and it shook her, but she didn't—you know, she didn't hint at rescue—I think she's still dead set on completing her assignment, and has reason to believe she can do it from inside." Miss Penn gave me a sideways glance. "Do you know what her assignment was?"

"No," I lied.

"Well," Miss Penn said, "here's what she told me. Maybe you can make something of it."

But I can't. I don't know what to do with any of it. It's like—it must be like paleontology. Trying to put a dinosaur together based on a few random bones and you don't even know if they're all from the same kind of animal.

I'll write down what Julie's given us, though—perhaps Paul will make sense of it—

1) The building the Gestapo use in Ormaie has got its own generator. Penn was complaining about power cuts, and how annoying it is not to be able to count on electricity when you work in radio, and Julie said, "Well, here we make it

ourselves." How like her to talk as if she'd become one of them. Like the time she took me to see *Colonel Blimp* and sat there weeping all through the scene where the imprisoned German officers are listening to Mendelssohn.

2) The fuse box is under the grand staircase. Miss Penn didn't say how our Julie managed to communicate that. Did also mention:

3) It is a known fact that the Nazis have a wireless office across the square from the Gestapo HQ, in the town hall, and according to Julie this must be because there is no regular broadcasting setup in the Château de Bordeaux building–Penn thinks because the walls are too thick for good reception, but I reckon the generator interferes with the reception more than the walls. This information was passed dead casually–SOE call radio work "arthritis," easy peasy. Can just imagine Julie. Studying her nails. "Fortunately I don't suffer from stiff joints. No one does here. How these Nazis would take advantage!"

4) Penn also found out a lot about the slave-girl secretary. Julie thinks she is about to have a crisis of conscience, which we might be able to take advantage of–suggests we watch her and make it easy for her to find a Resistance contact when she's ready.

It boggles me trying to think how Julie managed to communicate all this with the Gestapo captain *listening*. Apparently they were speaking English and the slave girl had to translate for the captain, so either she just didn't get it or she put up with it, which partly proves Julie's point. Julie calls her "the angel"–"*l'ange*"–dead embarrassing if you ask me. No wonder the poor girl keeps mum. It's masculine, too, in French, not just a plain noun like it is in English. It is a direct translation of her surname, Engel, from the German.

Sometimes Julie used to make me jealous–her cleverness, her ease with men, how posh she is–the grouse-shooting and the Swiss school and speaking three languages and being presented to the king in a blue silk ball gown—even her MBE after she caught those spies, like being knighted, and *especially* her term at Oxford—and I hate myself for ever having thought any of it was worth envying.

Now all I can think of is where she is and how much I love her. And I start to cry again.

I dreamed I was flying with Julie. I was taking her home, flying up to Scotland in Dympna's Puss Moth. We were heading up the coast along the North Sea, the sun hanging low in the west—sky and sea and sand all gold, gold light all around us. No barrage balloons or anything, just empty sky like in peacetime. But it wasn't peacetime, it was now, late November 1943, with the first snow on the Cheviot Hills in the west.

We were flying low over the long sands at Holy Island, and it was beautiful, but the plane kept trying to climb and I was fighting and fighting to keep it down. Just like the Lysander. Scared and worried and tired all at once, angry at the sky for being so beautiful when we were in danger of crashing. Then Julie, sitting alongside me, said, "Let me help."

In the dream the Puss Moth had side-by-side dual controls like a Tipsy, and Julie took hold of her own control column and gently pushed the nose forward, and suddenly we were flying the plane together.

All the pressure was gone. Nothing to be afraid of, nothing to battle against, just the two of us flying together, flying the plane together, side by side in the gold sky.

"Easy peasy," she said, and laughed, and it was.

Oh Julie, wouldn't I *know* if you were dead? Wouldn't I feel it happening, like a jolt of electricity to my heart?

Amélie has just seen an execution at the Château de Bordeaux. Château des Bourreaux is what everybody calls it now—Castle of Butchers. The kids here get Thursday off school instead of Saturday, and Amélie had gone into Ormaie with a couple of her chums to a cheap café they like, which happens to be at the end of the lower lane at the back of the Gestapo building. Amélie and her friends were sitting in the café window and noticed a crowd gathering in the lane— being kids they piled along to see what was going on—turns out those bastards had a guillotine rigged up in their rear courtyard and were executing people—

The kids *saw.* They didn't know what was going on or they'd have never gone to look, Amélie says, but they arrived just as it was happening and they saw it. SAW IT HAPPEN. She has been sobbing her heart out all evening, impossible to comfort her. They saw a girl killed and Amélie *recognized her* from her school, though the girl had been a few years ahead of Amélie and had already finished—what if it had been my old friend Beryl? Or Beryl's sister? Because that's what it's like, schoolmates being guillotined as spies. I didn't understand before—really didn't understand. Being a kid and worrying that a bomb might kill you is terrible. But being a kid and worrying that the police might cut your head off is something else entirely. I haven't words for it. Every fresh broken horror is something I just didn't understand until I came here.

When I was eight, before the Depression, we had a holiday in Paris—I remember bits of it, we took a boat trip on the Seine, and we saw the *Mona Lisa*. But the thing I remember most is how Grandad and I went to the top of the Eiffel Tower. We took the lift up but we walked the whole way down, and on the way we stopped at the first stage and we could see Gran standing in the park below, wearing a big new hat she'd bought that morning, and we waved at her—she looked so posh, all alone in the Champ de Mars, that you'd have never known she wasn't French herself. She took a picture of us and though we were so far away and tiny you can't see us in the picture, I know we are there. And I remember also there was a shop, way up there on the first stage, and Grandad bought me a tiny gold Eiffel Tower on a gold chain as a souvenir, and I still have it, back home in Stockport.

It wasn't so long ago. What is *happening* to us?

Maman Thibaut has been dosing Amélie with café au lait at the big kitchen table. Mitraillette and I taking turns holding her tight and exchanging horrified glances over her head. She won't stop talking. I only get every third word or so. Mitraillette whispers a rough translation—

"*Il y en avait une autre*—there was another. *Il y avaient deux filles*—there were two girls—*La Cadette et ses amies n'ont rien vu quand on a tué l'autre*—"

They didn't see the second girl executed. It was torment for *all* of us, dragging this information out of La Cadette. There were *two* girls brought there together, tied to each other. The second had to stand and watch as they butchered the first—so close, they made her stand *so close*, that Amélie said the blood spattered on her face. Then they closed the gates. Over the courtyard wall Amélie and her friends saw them raising the blade again and that was when they left.

The second girl was Julie. Certain of it. There can't be another petite blonde in a pullover the color of autumn leaves being held prisoner in the Ormaie Gestapo HQ. Amélie *saw her*.

But I don't believe they killed her, either. I just don't believe it. I keep thinking of those pictures of the pilot. They must have shown Julie those pictures by now, and perhaps she thinks I'm dead. But I'm not. And it's the same for her, I'm sure of it. It might look like she's dead, but she's not. They've got a reason to fake her death now, since Georgia Penn talked to her this week and they need to re-establish their supremacy or whatever—their control over what everybody knows or doesn't know. That captain/commander must be in trouble—he went behind his superior's back to let Penn in. Perhaps he's been told to kill Julie. But I think he's just as likely been told to stage her death, so she disappears again. Sharing cognac with her and sending her to the guillotine in the same week? I just don't believe it.

I WANT TO BLOW THAT PLACE APART.

Planes go over almost every night—there are some munitions factories working for the Germans and launch sites here in France that they are desperate to put out of action. They won't drop a bomb in the middle of Ormaie, not on purpose, for fear of hitting civilians. They have hit the railway junction here and had a go at the factories to the north of the city, though I don't think Ormaie carries on any significant manufacture apart from umbrellas. But the RAF won't bomb the middle of the city. It's why Julie was sent here, so we could get at it from the ground. Not many people here know the RAF is trying to avoid hitting them—no one feels safe.

The Americans dropped some bombs on Rouen in broad daylight. People panic when they hear the air raid sirens and dive for shelter just like we did back in the Manchester Blitz. But nothing ever hits the center of Ormaie.

Sometimes I wish it would—just one great big blast to wipe out the Castle of Butchers. I want that evil place to go up in flames. I want it so badly it *hurts*. Then I remember that Julie is still inside.

I don't believe she's dead, I don't believe any of their bluff and lies and bullying threats. I don't believe she's dead and I WON'T believe she's dead until I hear the shots MYSELF and see her fall.

Another Nazi Sunday dinner at the Thibauts', 28 Nov. Had to make myself scarce. Can just imagine La Cadette feeding them our line—"Käthe has got an *older man!* You would not believe how fast she works. It is a friend of Papa's driver. She met him when we were loading hens a couple of weeks ago. They go out together every Sunday. And some evenings too!"

And Maman, rolling her eyes, "It's not right, not right for such a young girl, he's twice her age. But what can I do to stop her? She's not my own—we work her hard and she gets no wages, so I have to give her Sunday afternoons—and she's of age. I just hope she's careful, doesn't get herself *in trouble....*"

"In trouble" with Paul, yeccchhh.

He and I bicycled off together to someone else's house to refine my bomb-making and gun-firing skills. It is such a relief to focus on some neutral thing—how much plastic explosive you need to blow up a car, how to wire up the switches, how to use a magnet to attach a detonator, how to hit a moving target with a pocket pistol—a borrowed one, as Käthe doesn't normally carry a gun since she would get arrested if she was caught with it. Thank you, Jamie and Julie Beaufort-Stuart, for the first few shooting lessons. Today's moving target was not an Me-109 or a pheasant but an empty tin on a stick, waved about by a very brave soul at the other end of the garden. The noise is hidden by the sound of a sawmill adjacent to the house. I don't know if they normally work on a Sunday afternoon or if the noise was laid on specially for us.

"It is a pity we cannot keep you, Kittyhawk," said the man whose house it was. "You were born to be a soldier."

Huh. Makes me quite puffed up with pride and yet fills me with scorn all at the same time—what rubbish! I wasn't born to be a soldier. There's a war on, so I'm delivering airplanes. But I don't go looking for adventure or excitement, and I jolly well don't go around picking fights with people. I like making things work. I *love* flying.

Have to remind myself I am still Maddie—haven't heard my own name for seven weeks. And my stunt double Käthe is going to be pushed to her limits in the next few days.

She—I—am supposed to deliver the message—invitation?—to Julie's recruit, the German slave-girl secretary, Engel. Why me? Because I'm not local and with luck I won't still be here after the next full moon. Engel doesn't know my face. Very few people do. But I hadn't ever seen her before today, so we arranged for me to get a good look at her before I have to approach her in the street tomorrow. Paul and I came back to the Thibauts' farm before the Nazi visitors left, and we waited—waited—waited for them to come out.

We'd closed the gate. So the Gestapo Mercedes had to stop, and Engel, who is their driver, had to get out to open the gate.

There was me, standing at the side of the road with my murdered man's bicycle, waiting well back from the Merc with my head down and wearing one of Maman Thibaut's motherly kerchiefs. There was Paul, feeling up the German girl bold as brass—I am sure no one gave me a second glance because *what* a performance he put on. He let the poor lass get the gate open about a foot or so, then put one of his big hands over hers, to help, right, but he managed to get his other hand spread across her bum as they pushed the gate open together. I think it is safe to say she now hates him as much as I do. She scurried back to the car clutching her coat and skirt tight around her legs, and Etienne was in the backseat laughing.

But all Paul's fooling about did give me a good look at her. She's tall, about my age, dark brown hair in a severe crimped bob, a bit old-fashioned. Astonishing pale green eyes. Not pretty but interesting—she'd probably be a knockout in a red cocktail dress, but looked dead frowny and drab in her sensible shoes and dust-colored overcoat.

Oh I sound like Julie. "I say, Nazi Slave Girl, you'd look *super* if you'd let me have a go at your eyebrows."

So Engel stormed back to the car and stalled it getting into gear—she was that angry. Started it up again right away though, pulled away smoothly—didn't even look at Paul as she drove off, left him to close the gate himself.

Don't think any of them noticed me. They were far too busy watching the Paul and Engel romantic comedy.

I got a look at the Gestapo captain too.

I know I was supposed to keep my head down. But I couldn't stop myself gaping a little. That is the man who interrogated Julie, the man who will order her execution—or who already has. I don't know what I expected, but he just looked like *anybody*—like the sort of chap who would come into the shop and buy a motorbike for his lad's sixteenth birthday—like your headmaster. But also—he looked like he was on his knees. Dog tired, absolutely haggard with it. He looked like he hadn't slept for a week. The pilots all looked like that in September of '40, during the worst days of the Battle of Britain—the vicar's lad looked like that, running out to his plane, the day he was killed.

I didn't know then—I mean, I didn't know earlier today, when I saw the captain's face and thought how tired and worried he seemed—but I know now that the Ormaie Gestapo is in uproar not only because of the captain having made the mistake about allowing Penn's interview, but also because they have been *burgled*. Mitraillette dragged this out of Slave-Girl Engel during the ritual cognac at the Thibauts'. A set of keys went missing for an hour early last week and then turned up again in the wrong place, and nobody can account for the time they were gone. Every single one of the staff has been grilled by the captain, and tomorrow the captain himself goes to be grilled by his commander, the dreadful Nikolaus Ferber.

If I were the captain I would clamp a muzzle on Engel—fairly certain she's not supposed to leak information like that. Well—if she won't come to us willingly, perhaps we can blackmail her—now's our chance—

And it's down to me to pull her in. Can't believe I told that intelligence officer I couldn't do this kind of work! Couldn't be more anxious than I am anyway—*so relieved* to be doing anything useful. Don't think I'll sleep much tonight, though. I keep thinking about what Theo said after my first Lysander ferry flight—"We might as well be operational—"

FLY THE PLANE, MADDIE

Horrid dream about guillotines. All in French, probably very bad French—never imagined I could dream in French! I was using Etienne's pocketknife to tighten up screws attaching a cable that lifted the blade, to make sure it would fall cleanly. Sickening—if it was a messy death it would all be my fault. I kept thinking, It works just like a choke—*C'est comme un starter*—

Aye right, miss, as Jock would say.

If I don't end up in that foul hotel courtyard with my head in a tin washtub it will be a blooming miracle.

I sat in Amélie's favorite café for an hour waiting for an old man whose name I don't know to tell me, *"L'ange descend en dix minutes—"* Ten minutes till the angel comes down. That meant Engel had gone to get the car out of the garage so she can take the Gestapo captain to meet his dreadful C.O. Then all I had to do was walk past the front of the hotel just as she was ushering him into the car, and hand her a lipstick with a slip of paper hidden in the sleeve, which tells her where we have arranged her own personal *cachette*—if she wants to make contact with the Resistance, she can leave a note in the kids' café, folded in a linen handkerchief that is wedged beneath a table leg to stop it rocking.

Of course, she can also set a trap for me now, since I will have to collect the note and she knows it.

You know what? If she's going to rat on me, she doesn't need to set a trap. If she's going to rat on me, I'm already dead.

When I caught up with her this afternoon I knelt quickly at her feet, as though she'd lost something, when really it was me planting it there. Then I stood up and held out the little shiny tube. I smiled like an idiot and spoke half a dozen of the two dozen words I know in German.

"*Verzeihung, aber Sie haben Ihren Lippenstift fallengelassen—*" Excuse me, you dropped your lipstick.

The captain was already inside the car and Engel hadn't opened her own door yet. He couldn't hear us. I wouldn't be able to understand anything she answered, so I was just supposed to smile sweetly and if she didn't take the lipstick I was supposed to say "*Es tut mir leid, daß es doch nicht Ihr Lippenstift war—*" I'm sorry, it wasn't your lipstick after all.

She looked down at the gold tube, frowning, then looked up at my bland, gormless grin.

She asked curiously, and in English, "Are you Maddie Brodatt?"

It's a good thing I was already smiling. I just sort of let the smile sit frozen on my face. Felt utterly false, as though I had on a mask—like I was wearing someone else's face. But I didn't stop smiling. I shook my head.

"Käthe Habicht," I said.

She nodded once—like a bow. She took the lipstick, opened the driver's door of the Mercedes, and climbed in.

"*Danke*, Käthe," she said before she shut the door. Thanks, Käthe. Dead casual. Informal and cheeky, as though I were a little girl.

As she drove away I remembered that Käthe isn't supposed to understand English.

Fly the plane.

I wish I could, I wish, I WISH I HAD CONTROL.

I'm not dead yet, and we've got Engel's answer. I collected it myself, getting quite confident about cycling into town, as Mitraillette always uses the same checkpoint—they know me now, and wave me through without bothering to check my papers. Engel's left us Julie's scarf. I didn't recognize it at first. It was lying under the table in the café, and the lad who sweeps the floors handed it to me. *"C'est à vous?"*—is this yours? I didn't know what it was, at first—a wad of dull gray cloth—but when I touched it I realized it was silk, so I took it, in case it was important. I knotted it around my neck, smiling my idiot's smile—*"Merci."* Thanks.

I sat there for ten more minutes, my stomach turning over with fear and excitement, forcing myself to finish a bowl of the most horrid phony coffee ever brewed so I wouldn't look suspicious leaving in a hurry.

Bicycled home like a demon, pulled the crumpled silk from around my neck, and spread it flat on my bed in Etienne's room. That's when I realized it was Julie's Parisian silk scarf—

I was only little when Dad died, but I remember how I used to open the drawer where he kept his ties, before Gran cleared them out, and take a big sniff. And the ties all smelled like Dad, still—like cherry tobacco and cologne and a whiff of motor oil. I loved the smell of those ties. It brought him back.

Julie's scarf doesn't smell like Julie anymore. I did stick my nose in it. It smells like carbolic soap. Like a school. Or a prison, I suppose. There's ink smeared all over one corner and the silk's all perished down the middle, as though she and Engel have been playing tug of war with it.

That chemical smell, sweet and tarry. Not like Julie at all. It reminded me that Penn told us Engel is a chemist.

I ran downstairs. "*Tu cherches Gabrielle-Thérèse*—you want my sister?" asked La Cadette, glancing up from her school-books at the kitchen table.

"*Oui—tout de suite—right now.* I need an iron—a hot iron—oh bother—" Frustration, I had no idea how to say it. Mimed iron-ing. That kid is so sharp—got it right away, tossed Maman's irons into the kitchen fire to hot up, pointed me to the iron-ing board, and ran for her sister.

Mitraillette and Amélie and I stood like the witches in *Macbeth* over the ironing board, holding our breath—I was so worried I'd ruin it, burn the scarf, but I didn't—and after a minute or so Engel's message began to appear in scratchy brown print among the gray paisley, in the corner opposite the ink stain.

You don't need to be trained by the Special Operations Executive to know how to use invisible ink. You don't even need to be a chemist. Beryl and I learned how to do it in Girl Guides. We used to write secret messages in milk. It's easy.

I don't know what Engel used, but she wrote in French, so I don't remember her exact words. She's either tipped us off or betrayed us. We won't know which till later tonight. Mitraillette has sent for Paul—they use his courier as the go-between—we don't actually know where he stays.

This evening there are 19 prisoners from Poitiers being transported to a concentration camp somewhere in the northeast of France. The bus will swing by Ormaie and pick up 5 more prisoners here. Julie will be with them.

If I make it like an accident report—

Don't think I can possibly make it sound like an accident report, but I've got to write something—I'll have to remember—there may be a trial. I don't bloody care if there is. I want to get it right while I remember.

Mitraillette tried to dose me with knockout drops again a few minutes ago—30 minutes to oblivion. But this time I'm wise to her and I want to write. Perhaps I'll take it after.

I think I will. When I'm finished I won't want to think anymore

INCIDENT REPORT

Attempted Sabotage of Poitou River Bridge on Tours-Poitiers Road, with intention of stopping German military bus carrying 24 French and Allied prisoners—Wed. 1 Dec. 1943

Well, we did stop them.

Made a great big hole in the bridge, too, that'll keep them deporting anybody via the railway station at Tours for a while

I HATE THEM
I HATE THEM

Must remember Paul—Paul, who I also hated.

He was marvelous. I have to say it. He planned it all on the fly, made it up as we went along. The carnage wasn't his fault. Mustered an army of a dozen men and two women in about an hour. We left all the bikes and the car hidden—it is the same Citroën Rosalie, I don't know how the man who owns it avoids being found out or at least having his car impounded, and I think he is too old for this kind of job anyway. We hid the car in a garage, believe it or not, belonging to a lovely and heroic old woman who lives by herself in a riverside villa on the Tours side of the Poitou. She is the rose-grower the circuit is named for. We left our car parked *behind* her car, which is conveniently a newer and bigger model Rosalie, so it looked like ours had been her previous car, and we hid it under a dust sheet as well. The bikes were hidden in her abandoned stables beneath twenty-year-old hay.

Then we borrowed her boats. One beautiful teak nineteenth-century rowboat and two chestnut Canadian canoes. Much too good for us. The bridge is upstream from the house—they've disrupted traffic here before, some time ago, and for a while the lady was under strict surveillance. Hope she won't be in too much trouble again now—though she seems to have got away with it this time. We were careful.

Godless as I am, I pray she's got away with it. It's like ripples in a pond, isn't it? It doesn't stop in one place.

Anyway, we loaded up our fireworks in the boats—don't think I can give details on the explosives, as I wasn't responsible and didn't pay attention, and we rowed up to the bridge in the dark. Took about an hour with muffled oars. You read about muffled oars in pirate stories—I'm sure there's a bit in *Peter Pan* where they use muffled oars. Perhaps it was *Swallows and Amazons*. English summer and the school holidays seem dead far away now. It was hard to see—the river was full of fog. But we made it. We wired up the bridge and waited.

What went wrong?

I don't know, I honestly don't know. It wasn't a trap. We weren't outnumbered, not at first. I suppose we were just playing for higher stakes than the Germans. Shouldn't we have guessed they'd be more ruthless than us? How *could* we guess? We were pretty ruthless.

What went wrong—perhaps it was just too dark, night and fog both. The fog was good as well as bad, because it hid us, but it was just so hard to see. There should have been a quarter moon, for what that's worth, but the sky was overcast, and we were blind until the prison bus turned up with its headlights blazing.

That bit went well—within a minute we had thoroughly disabled it. We were pretty well camouflaged in the riverbank scrub—a tangle of willow and alder and poplar full of mistletoe. Lots of tall withering weeds hiding us, and the fog did too. Our small explosion hurt no one except the bridge and the bus. The radiator grille got blown out, but the blast missed the headlights and the battery must have been OK, because there was enough light that Paul and the owner of the Rosalie somehow managed to put bullets through three of the tires.

The driver got out. Then a guard got out. They had electric torches—both men walked up and down the length of the bus inspecting the damage and cursing.

Paul picked them off like ducks at a funfair with his Sten submachine gun. While that was going on I was curled uselessly in a ball with my arms over my head and my teeth clenched, so I missed a bit of the action. Born to be a soldier, my foot. A raid is actually quite a lot like a battle. It is war. It's war in miniature, but it's still WAR.

Two other guards came out of the bus and fired random shots into the bushes at us in the dark. Mitraillette had to sit on me to stop me blowing our cover, I was in such a flap. Finally Paul gave me a clout over the head.

"Get a grip on yourself, Kittyhawk," he hissed. "We need you. You're a crack shot but no one's expecting you to kill anybody. Focus on tools, all right? They'll start trying to fix things in a moment. Try to disable their equipment."

I gulped and nodded. Don't know if he saw me nodding, but he shifted back to his own position beneath the gently rustling willow herb and hemlock alongside the Rosalie driver, and they bagged another guard.

The surviving guard leaped back into the bus. There was ominous silence—not a thing happened for a minute or two. Then the four remaining soldiers ushered every single one of the prisoners out of the bus and made them lie down side by side on their faces in the middle of the road. It was all done by the glancing light of electric torches and we didn't dare fire at anyone now, for fear of hitting one of ours.

Couldn't see any individual faces—couldn't tell anything about the captives, not their age or their sex or how they were dressed, but you could tell by the way they moved that some of them were scared and some were defiant, and some were chained together by their feet. The chained ones had a hard time getting down to the road, tripping each other up as they climbed off the bus. When everybody was lined up on their faces in the mud like sardines, one of the guards shot six of them in the head.

It happened SO FAST.

This dreadful man shouted at us in French. Mitraillette whispered all the English words she could come up with in my ear—"Revenge—two for one—their own dead. If we kill—"

"I know, I know," I whispered back. *Je sais.* For every one of them we murdered they would murder two of us. Disposable hostages.

Three guards kept their guns trained on the prisoners while the fourth set off on foot back down the road—to find a telephone, I think.

Then we waited. Stalemate. It was bitterly cold.

Paul and a couple of other men had a quick whispered council and decided to work their way beneath the bridge and try to attack the guards from behind. There really were only three guards left, plus the one who had gone for help—it seemed impossible we shouldn't be able to get the better of them.

But they had 18 hostages lying helpless and chained at their feet.

And one of their hostages was Julie.

Or perhaps, I worried then, perhaps she'd already been shot. Impossible to tell at first. But the guards set up a portable floodlight attached to the bus's battery, and got the prisoners spotlit, and you could see now that only a few of them were women, and that everybody looked half starved. And among them, right in the middle of them, was the one I was looking for—a mound of blond hair and a flame-colored pullover. Her arms were bound tightly behind her back, with wire it looked like, so she really was lying flat on her face more than the others, who were resting on their forearms. But she wasn't at the end of the row, she wasn't one of the six that had just been killed. She was breathing quietly, waiting. Shaking with cold like the rest of us.

And we waited, I think, for an hour.

The guards made sure they were hard to aim at. They kept moving and flashing their electric torches into our faces—or where they thought our faces were—occasionally blinding us. I discovered later that I'd bitten my thumbnails down to their bleeding nail beds waiting for Paul's planned assault from behind. It never came. The three German soldiers organized themselves so that they were always facing in different directions, and one of them always kept a gun trained on the prisoners. We just couldn't get to them. One of the women lying in the road began to weep—I think it was just because she was so cold—and when the man next to her tried to put his arm around her, a guard shot him in the hand.

That was when I realized that we weren't going to win this battle—that we could not win.

I think Mitraillette knew it then, too. She squeezed my shoulder lightly. She was also weeping. But silently.

The fourth guard came back and began to chat casually with his mates. We waited. It was not quiet anymore, because as well as the soldiers talking and the woman crying, the man with the hurt hand was groaning and gasping. But there wasn't much other noise—only the little noises of night on a riverbank, wind in the bare branches, the hollow rush of water beneath the damaged stone bridge.

Then Julie lifted her head and said something to the sol-diers that *made them laugh*. I think—I swear, we couldn't hear her, but I swear she was chatting them up. Or something like it. One of them came over and prodded her here and there with the end of his rifle, as though he were testing a piece of meat. Then he squatted down by her head and took her chin in his hand. He asked her a question.

She bit him.

He pushed her face down into the road, hard, and scram-bled to his feet, but as he lowered his rifle at her, one of the other guards laughed and stopped him.

"He says not to kill her," Mitraillette whispered. "If they kill her there will be no—fun."

"Is she crazy?" I hissed. "What the blazes did she bite him for? She'll get herself shot!"

"*Exactement*," Mitraillette agreed. "*C'est rapide*—fast. No Nazi fun."

The reinforcements arrived. Two military lorries with can-vas sides, with half a dozen armed guards in each. Even then we still weren't badly outnumbered. They began to unload sandbags and planks and managed to lever the bus up out of the hole it had landed in, reversed it, and laid planks over the damage so they could try to get the lorries across.

But then when they were ready to load the lorries, they got resistance. Not just from us. A few of their captives came to life—a handful of the men who weren't chained just ran for it, dived into the ditch at the opposite side of the road and, lucky for them, it turned out, ran straight into Paul and his men, who hustled them under the bridge and back to the boats by the river path. More shooting as a couple of soldiers went after them and Paul's men pounded the soldiers. Go for the equipment, Paul had ordered, and for a minute the gunfire was so fierce I knew two shots from my small revolver would go unnoticed. I aimed at the chains. The Double Tap, two quick shots at the same target. The chains I was aiming at burst apart like a toy balloon—could hardly believe my luck. And the two men I'd managed to free also ran.

When another man tried to run, the soldiers mowed him down like bank robbers in an American gangster film.

When the first men had fled, the guard Julie had attacked held her down with his heel dug into the back of her neck—he wasn't giving her a chance. She fought hard and got kicked for it by the one who had said not to kill her. So now, with a few of the hostages dead and a few loaded up in the lorries and a few escaped, there were only seven living people left lying on the ground—Julie, with the guard's boot against the back of her neck, and two other women. Two of the remaining men were chained ankle to ankle. And now the German corporal or whatever he was, the fellow in charge who had arrived with the reinforcements, decided to teach everyone a thorough lesson—us for trying to free their prisoners and the prisoners for wanting to be freed—

He picked on the men, mainly, the two who weren't

chained, and hauled them to their feet. And seeing that Julie was getting special treatment from the man who was holding her in place with his foot, he hauled her to her feet as well and pushed her over to stand next to the two other standing prisoners—one of them a sturdy workman and one a handsome lad my own age, both ragged and battered.

Julie was ragged too. She was still wearing exactly the clothes she'd had on when she parachuted into France, gray wool flannel skirt and Parisian chic pullover the burnt scarlet-orange of Chinese lanterns, with holes in the elbows now. Her hair shone brassy gold in the artificial light, falling loose and wild down her back. Her face was skin over bone. As though—as though she'd aged fifty years in eight weeks— gaunt, gray, frail. The dead spit of Jamie when I first met him in hospital. But thinner. She looked like a kid, a head shorter than the shortest of the men standing around her. Any of those soldiers could have picked her up and tossed her in the air.

Three prisoners in a line. The soldier in command gave an order, and the guard who'd been holding Julie down took aim at the younger of the captive men and with one bullet maimed him low between his legs.

The lad shrieked and collapsed and they fired at him again, first blowing apart one elbow and then the other, and they hauled him to his feet again, still shrieking, and made him walk to the lorry and climb in and they turned to the next man and fired on him low in the groin also.

Mitraillette and I both knelt wheezing with horror, side by side under cover of the undergrowth and darkness. Julie stood cowering, white as paper in the harsh glare of the flood-light, staring straight ahead of her at nothing. She was next. She knew it. We all knew it. But they weren't finished with their second victim yet.

When they shot him in one elbow and then again rapidly in the same place to shatter it, my not-very-reliable control just went and I burst into tears. I couldn't help it, something snapped, like when we went to help the gunner at Maidsend and found the dead boys. I burst into loud, gulping sobs, bawling like a baby.

Her face—Julie's face—her face suddenly lit up like a sunrise. Joy and relief and hope all there at once, and she was instantly lovely again, herself, *beautiful*. She heard me. Recognized my fear-of-gunfire blubbing. She didn't dare call out to me, didn't dare give me away, Ormaie's most desperate fugitive.

They fired at the second man again, destroying his other arm, and he fainted dead away. They had to drag him to the lorry.

Julie was next.

Suddenly she laughed wildly and gave a shaking yell, her voice high and desperate.

"KISS ME, HARDY! Kiss me, QUICK!"

Turned her face away from me to make it easier.

And I shot her.

I saw her body flinch—the blows knocked her head aside as though she'd been thumped in the face. Then she was gone.

Gone. One moment flying in green sunlight, then the sky suddenly gray and dark. Out like a candle. Here, then gone.

I'll just keep writing, shall I? Because that wasn't the end. It wasn't even a pause.

The officer pulled another woman up from the ground to take Julie's place. This doomed girl screamed at us in French: *"ALLEZ! ALLEZ!"* Go! Go! *"Résistance idiots sales, vous nous MASSACREZ TOUS!"*

FILTHY RESISTANCE IDIOTS, YOU'RE KILLING US ALL

I knew what she was saying even with my rubbish schoolgirl French. And she was right.

We ran. They fired at our backs and came after us. Paul and his men fired at THEIR backs, swarming over the bridge walls, and they turned to face this rear attack. Carnage. CARNAGE. Half of us, Paul with them, were torn to bits on the bridge. The rest of us made it back to the boats and set off down the river with the five fugitives we'd managed to save.

When we were away from the bank and someone else was rowing and there was nothing more for me to do, I bent over with my head on my knees, my heart in pieces. It is still in pieces. I think it will be in pieces forever.

Mitraillette gently unlocked my fingers from the Colt .32 and made me put it away. She whispered, *"C'était la Vérité?"* Was that Verity?

Or perhaps she just meant, Was that the truth? Was it true? Did any of it really happen? Were the last three hours *real*?

"Yes," I whispered back. *"Oui. C'était la vérité."*

———

Don't know how I kept going. You just do. You have to, so you do.

The original idea, when we hoped we'd have 24 extra people to move and hide, was to ferry them to the opposite bank where we'd divide them into smaller groups of 2 or 3. Then we were going to split up our own team to guide them cross-country toward various sheds and cow byres for the night before the more complicated task of smuggling them safely out of France across the Pyrenees or the English Channel. But now we only had 5 fugitives to hide and there were only 7 of us left so there was room for everybody to make a single trip back to the riverside villa. Mitraillette made the decision to keep us together. Don't think I'd ever noticed—so absorbed in my own fears and worries—but she was Paul's second-in-command.

Not sure we'd have pulled it off without her, either. We were all just *so dazed*. But she drove us like a demon. *"Vite! Vite!"* Quickly! Orders whispered sharp and quiet—boats hauled back onto their racks, oars put away, all of it carefully dried off with dust sheets, which we hid beneath the floorboards afterward. You can work in a daze. If someone gives you a mindless job to do you can do it automatically, even if your heart is in pieces. Mitraillette thought of everything—perhaps she's done it before? We brushed the oars and hulls lightly with handfuls of ancient straw from the stables, leaving a fine layer of dust over everything. The 5 men from the prison bus worked silently and willingly alongside us, anxious to help. The boathouse was perfect when we left—looked like it hadn't been used in years.

Then the Nazi search party arrived and we spent an hour lying in the mud along the riverbank, hiding in the bulrushes like Moses, waiting for them to leave. Could hear them chatting with the groundskeeper. He came back later to lock up the boathouse and give us the all-clear—such as it was—now there were Nazi guards posted on the front drive, so we'd not be getting the Rosalie out any time soon. But the grounds-keeper thought it would be safe for a couple of bicycles to leave by the river path on the opposite bank. Benzedrine handed out all 'round. Got one of the canoes out again and ferried two of the bikes, two of us, and two of the escaped prisoners over the river and saw them off into the fog.

At this point one of the remaining lads from the bus collapsed in a shivering heap and Mitraillette sort of stalled.

"Nous sommes faits," she said. We've had it.

We bedded down in the stables with the bicycles. Not the safest place in the world.

I wonder where that is right now—the safest place in the world? Even the neutral countries, Sweden and Switzerland, are surrounded. Ireland's stuck with being divided. They have to mark the neutral bit "IRELAND" in big letters made of whitewashed stones, hoping the Germans won't drop bombs there thinking it's the UK side of the northern border. I've seen it from the air. South America, perhaps.

We were all still wide awake when it grew light. I was sitting with my arms wrapped around my knees, side by side with one of the lads who'd escaped when I shot his chains apart. The men who'd been chained had to stay with us, because they had to get rid of the fetters on their ankles before they could go anywhere.

"How did they catch you? What did you do?" I asked, forgetting he was French. He answered me in English, though.

"Just what you did," he said bitterly. "Blew up a bridge and failed to stop the German army."

"Why didn't they just shoot you?"

He grinned. All his upper teeth had been savagely broken. "Why do you think, *gosse anglaise?*" English kid. "They cannot question you if they shoot you."

"How come only some of you were chained?"

"Only some of us are dangerous." He was still grinning. I suppose he had reason to be optimistic—he'd been given a second chance at life, at hope. A slim one, but better than he'd had twelve hours ago. "They chain you if they think you are dangerous. The girl whose arms were tied behind her, did you see her? She wasn't dangerous, she was a—*collaboratrice*." Collaborator. He spat into the disintegrating straw.

The shattered pieces of my heart went cold. I felt as if I'd swallowed shards of ice.

"Stop," I said. "*Tais-toi*. SHUT UP."

He didn't hear me, or didn't take me seriously, and carried on relentlessly: "Better off dead, that one. Did you see her, even lying in the road last night, sweet-talking the guards in German? Because her arms were bound, someone would have had to help her, on the way to wherever they were taking us—feed her, help her drink. She would have had to offer favors to the guards to get them to do it. None of us would have done it."

I am dangerous too, sometimes.

That morning I was an antipersonnel mine, a butterfly bomb, unexploded and ticking, and he touched the fuse.

I don't actually remember what happened. I don't remember attacking him. But the skin of my knuckles is torn where my fist connected with his broken teeth. Mitraillette says they thought I was going to try to dig his eyes out with my fingers.

I do remember three people holding me back, and I remember screaming at the boy, "You wouldn't have helped her EAT AND DRINK? SHE'D HAVE DONE IT FOR YOU!"

Then in panic, because I was making so much noise, they sat on me again. But as soon as they let me go I was back on top of him. "I FREED YOU! You would still be IN CHAINS and packed in a stinking freight wagon LIKE A COW by now if it wasn't for me! *You wouldn't have helped another prisoner EAT AND DRINK?*"

"Käthe, Käthe!" Mitraillette, weeping, tried to take my face between her hands to comfort me and shut me up. "Käthe, *arrête*—stop, stop! *Tu dois*—you must! Wait—*attends*—"

She held a tin cup of cold coffee laced with cognac up to my mouth—helped me. Helped me drink.

That was the first time she KO'd me. It takes thirty minutes for the drug to work. Suppose I'm lucky they didn't hit me over the head with a bicycle to speed it up.

When I woke up they made me go with the chauffeur up to the villa. I felt like hell warmed over, stupid and faintly sick and absolutely famished, and I think I probably wouldn't have cared if the old woman who lived there had turned me over to the police. ISN'T THAT WHAT HAPPENS WHEN YOU KILL YOUR BEST FRIEND?

But no, the chauffeur took me into a dark and elegant oak-paneled hall, and the woman came to meet me—she is one of those beautiful, porcelain-perfect people of the last century, with snow-white hair done up in exactly Julie's chignon—I noticed that. She took my hand without saying a thing and led me upstairs into a bathroom the size of a ballroom, where there was a dead-boiling bath drawn up and waiting, and she sort of pushed me into the room and left me there to get on with it.

I thought about putting Etienne's pocketknife to use by slitting my wrists, but it seemed rather unfair on the frail, heroic woman whose house it was, and also—ALSO I WANT REVENGE, BLAST IT

So I had a bath. Which, I confess, was heavenly. Dried

off in a huge fluffy towel obviously left for me, feeling sinful. And a bit unreal.

The old woman—I should say elderly, not old. She is a refined sort of person—she met me at the door when I came out. I was clean underneath, but my hill-walking trousers were caked with mud and my wet hair was standing on end and I felt shabby as a street urchin. Didn't seem to matter—once more she took me by the hand, and this time led me to a small parlor where she had a fire going, and a kettle on the hob. She made me sit down on the frayed silk of her eighteenth century settee while she made me a little supper, with bread and honey and coffee, and tiny yellow apples, and a boiled egg.

The tray went on a small marble-topped side table and she knocked the top of the egg off for me with a pretty silver spoon as though I were a baby and needed feeding. Then she dipped the spoon into the egg and the yolk came up golden like the sun popping out of a cloud bank. It made me think instantly of eating supper with the Craig Castle Irregulars the first time I went there. Then I realized that Julie and I had never been there at the same time and now we never would, and I bent over and began to cry.

The old woman, who didn't know who I was, and whose life was in danger just because she had me in her house, sat down beside me on the old settee and stroked my hair with thin, wrinkled hands, and I sobbed hopelessly in her arms for nearly an hour.

After a while she got up and said, "I will make another egg for you, three minutes only—how the English like it. This one is cold now."

She did another and she made me eat it while she ate the cold one herself.

When I left to go back to the stables she kissed me on

both cheeks and said, "We share a terrible burden, *chérie*. We are alike."

I am not sure what she meant.

I kissed her cheeks, too, and said, *"Merci, Madame. Merci mille fois."*

A thousand thanks is not really enough. But I haven't anything else to give her.

Her gardens are full of roses—sprawling, old tangled bushes, quite a few of them autumn-flowering damasks with their last flowers still nodding and drooping in the rain. The old woman is the one the circuit is named for. Mitraillette says that before the war the woman was quite a noted horticulturalist—the chauffeur/groundskeeper is in fact a skilled gardener—and she has bred and named a few of the roses herself. I hadn't noticed the roses when we arrived last night, or even walking up to the villa in daylight in a stupor, but I noticed them on my way back to the stables after my bath. The flowers are sodden and dying in the December rain, but the sturdy bushes are still alive, and will be beautiful someday in the spring, if the German army doesn't mow them down like the ones in the Ormaie town square. For no good reason they made me think of Paris, and ever since then I have had that song stuck in my head yet again.

None of the rest of us was given a bath or a hot soft-boiled egg, though cold hard-boiled ones were passed around. I think I was sent up to the house as a diversion while they were getting rid of the lad I'd tried to murder that morning and the other chained man. Anyway, I never saw them again. I don't know how they got their leg irons off, or where they went, or if they are safe. I hope so. I really do.

Everybody else left in stages over the next two days. Mitraillette says it is actually safer to travel by day than at night if you are a fugitive, since daytime is when people are out and about and there isn't any curfew—don't think I'd realized that, since I am always trying to get on a plane that arrives after midnight at some distant airfield.

She and I and the Rosalie owner were delivered home by the rose lady's chauffeur in her own car—we thought we ought to leave the old Rosalie there for a bit longer in case the Nazis come back to check on the garage again. The bridge still hasn't been fixed, and except for the German soldiers we killed, every one of the bodies is still lying there in the rain, with guards posted over them to keep anyone from trying to bury them. *Fifteen people* lying there. I haven't seen it. We couldn't drive that way anyway as the bridge was out. They'll have to clear the road when they get the bridge fixed, but I have a sick and certain feeling they will just pile everybody alongside the road to remind us not to try again. Julie, Oh lovely Julie,

JULIE

I am going to drink this stuff now and try to sleep again, but I should put down that I have a project to work on when I wake up—while Mitraillette and I were gone, a friend of Maman Thibaut's who runs a laundry service dropped off a bag of clean *German-made* chemises labeled "Käthe Habicht," and hidden underneath them was a huge pile of paper that I have to go through. I don't know what it is—haven't had the heart to look—but it must be from Engel again. Amélie peeked and discovered that the pages are numbered, so she's put them all in order for me, but it's in English and she couldn't read it. It's still hidden in the laundry bag beneath my "anonymously" donated new collection of underclothes. I jolly well don't feel like reading anything Engel has sent me anymore tonight, but tomorrow is Sunday and there will be croissants with the coffee and I expect it will still be raining.

It is not Engel's writing
   It is Julie's

I've not finished reading yet. I've scarcely started. It is *hundreds* of pages long, half of it on little bits of card. Maman Thibaut just keeps making me more coffee and the girls are keeping a good watch on the road and the back lane. I can't stop. I don't know if there's any urgency or not—Engel may need the papers back, as there is an official-looking number printed at the end in red ink, and a horrible execution order on Gestapo stationery attached by the evil Nikolaus Ferber. Not an order, I mean, only a recommendation—according to Engel's translation. But I think it was in the process of being carried out when we stopped the bus.

I can tell when Julie's been crying. Not just because she says so, but because the writing goes all smeary and the paper crinkles. Her tears, dried on these pages, are mixed up with mine making them wet again. I have cried so hard over this that I am beginning to feel stupid. They *did* show her those blasted pictures. And she *did* give them code—eleven sets of encoding poems, passwords, and frequencies. Eleven code sets—eleven dummy code sets, ONE FOR EACH OF OUR DUMMY WIRELESSES, one for each of the *"onze radios"* we planted in the wrecked Lysander. Those pictures were a gift. She could have told them *so much*, she knew SO MUCH, and all she gave them was fake code.

She never even told them my code name—though they must have wondered. She never told them Käthe Habicht's name, which might have given me away. She never told them ANYTHING

Names names names. How does she do it? Cattercup—
Stratfield—SWINLEY??? Newbery College? How does she *do*
it? She makes it sound like she is *so cut up* to be giving them
this information, and it's all just bumph out of her head.
She never told them ANYTHING. I don't think she's given
them the right name of any airfield in the whole of Britain,
except Maidsend and Buscot, which of course were where
she was stationed. They could have easily checked. It's all so
close to truth, and so glib—her aircraft identification is rather
good, considering what a fuss she makes about it. It makes
me think of the first day I met her, giving those directions
in German. So cool and crisp, such authority—suddenly she
really was a radio operator, a German radio operator, she was
so good at faking it. Or when I told her to be Jamie, how she
just suddenly turned into *Jamie*.

This confession of hers is rotten with error—I did my
Civil Air Guard training at Barton, not "Oakway," and the
fog line at so-called Oakway is electric, not gas. It wasn't
a Spitfire the first time I flew to Craig Castle, of course it
was a BEAUFORT, and she jolly well knew that! Though I
have ferried Spitfires to "Deeside." I suppose she truly didn't
want to draw attention to any real names. She calls the RAF
Maidsend Squadron Leader "Creighton," and she knows perfectly well his proper name is Leland North. Creighton is
the name of the Colonel in *Kim*. I know, because Julie made
me read it—partly, I am dead sure, as a warning about how
both of us were being fine-tuned for the war machine by that

Bloody Machiavellian Intelligence Officer whose real name she also knows perfectly well.

I don't at all remember the story about her grandmother's sister shooting her husband. Of course Julie would have had to fudge a lot of our conversations to keep the flow going, none of them run exactly as I remember. Mostly it's all there and I recognize it, only I don't think she ever told me that story. I have no memory of it at all.

It's eerie and unbearable. It's as though she's trying to tell me what she wanted me to do. But she couldn't have known what was going to happen, or even that I'd read this. She thought I was dead. So it must not have been aimed at me, but then—why tell it?

What's strange about the whole thing is that although it's riddled with nonsense, altogether it's *true*—Julie's told our story, mine and hers, our friendship, so truthfully. It is *us*. We even had the same dream at the same time. How could we have had the same dream at the same time? How can something so wonderful and mysterious be true? But it is.

And this, even more wonderful and mysterious, is also true: when I read it, when I read what Julie's written, she is instantly alive again, whole and undamaged. With her words in my mind while I'm reading, she is as real as I am. Gloriously daft, drop-dead charming, full of bookish nonsense and foul language, brave and generous. She's *right here*. Afraid and exhausted, alone, but *fighting*. Flying in silver moonlight in a plane that can't be landed, stuck in the climb—alive, alive, ALIVE.

C d B= Château de Bordeaux
H d V= Hôtel de Ville [town hall]
O.HdV.A. 1872 B. No. 4 CdB
O= Ormaie? perhaps A/Annals? Archives B/Box/Boîte
1872 - could be year, Archives 1872 box no 4

I SEE IT
ORMAIE TOWN HALL ARCHIVES 1872 BOX No. 4
CHÂTEAU DE BORDEAUX
We have them. WE HAVE GOT THEM.

✓ Our prison cells are only hotel bedrooms, but we
are guarded like royalty. And also, there are dogs.
✓ these cellars are empty because they are not secure
✓ There are a number of service lifts, dumbwaiters for
hauling trays upstairs in addition to the great big one for
loading crates and things from the main street

There's more—I know there's more—Engel's underlined all
the instructions in red—red's her color, Julie said. The pages
are numbered and dated in red too. Julie mentioned Engel
had to number the pages. They've created it between them,
Julia Beaufort-Stuart and Anna Engel, and they've given it to
me to use—the code's not in order, doesn't need to be. No
wonder she was so determined to finish it—
Ugh, there is SO MUCH PAPER HERE
here it is—

✓ there was an air raid and everybody scrambled to the shelters as usual ... for two hours

✓ "C d B" = Château de Bordeaux

✓ as with all the prisoners' rooms, my window has been boarded shut

✓ The Gestapo use the ground floor and two mezzanines for their own accommodation and offices

✓ "H d V" picked out in red = Hôtel de Ville

✓ through the cellars and out to a little stone courtyard [where there is] a gate to the lower lane

We can get in through the cellars, front and back. There is an entrance in the lower lane at the back and a loading lift through the street at the front. The cellars are not secure and they use the bedrooms as cells. During air raids the whole place is left unguarded apart from the dogs. We will have up to two hours. We can pull the fuses, disable the generator, and fill the dumbwaiters with Explosive 808 when we leave.

Julie put in the great-aunt story because she thought we might have to blow the place up with her inside. That there might be no other way. And she wanted us to do it anyway.

But we won't have to leave any of the prisoners inside. We can break into the rooms with crowbars and lockpicks and get everyone out. The official-looking numbers at the end in red ink are a CITY ARCHIVE REFERENCE. It will be the ARCHITECT'S DRAWINGS for the Château de Bordeaux. We will have a map of the building.

It is coming down. We are still a sensational team.

SOE LONDON-W/T MSG, DRAFT FOR
ENCODING
Regret report ~~your~~ organizer ~~code
name~~ Paul of Damask Circuit and Flt
Off~~icer~~ Julia Beaufort-Stuart both
killed in action 1 Dec 1943 STOP
request RAF operational flight w/in
France route overhead Ormaie this
full moon Sat 11 Dec to create
diversion enabling Operation Verity

La Cadette collected the drawings. It turns out *anyone* can go digging in the Ormaie Town Hall archives. It's like Nazi contempt for the Occupied country taken to extremes—as though they welcome the locals to come and ransack their own heritage so no one else need bother. You get searched when you enter the building, of course, but not on the way out, and they didn't even *look* at Amélie's ID—she said she was working on a project for school, easy peasy. She was supposed to say she was verifying a boundary of the Thibaut farm, but when she saw how easy it would be to get in and out, she made up a simpler story on the spot. She is *so sharp*.

It took her twenty minutes during her school dinner break, and she left the pages for me to collect so she wouldn't get caught carrying them around.

It was probably a mistake to tell her to leave them in Engel's *cachette*. I think of it as mine, but it's Engel's. Also, I think we are supposed to avoid using cafés. I wish I'd been trained for this. It didn't matter in the end, but oh how my stomach turned over when I walked in and found Engel sitting at the table.

I started to walk past to another table, smiling my stupid plastic smile—makes me feel like a zombie this week—but she beckoned abruptly.

"*Salut*, Käthe." She patted the chair next to hers. When I sat down she stubbed out her cigarette and lit another two and gave me one. Somehow it was the most heart-stopping thing I have ever done, touching my own lips with this cigarette that had touched Anna Engel's lips a second earlier. I feel like—I know her so intimately, after reading Julie's confession. She must feel the same way about me, though I don't suppose I scare her as much.

"*Et ton amie, ça va?*" she asked casually— How's your friend?

I looked away, swallowed, couldn't maintain the plastic smile. Took a drag on the cigarette and choked, haven't smoked for a while and never those French fags. After a minute or so she figured out that what I wasn't saying was not a happy ending.

She swore softly in French, a single violent word of disappointment. Then paused and asked, "*Elle est morte?*"

I nodded. Yes, she's dead.

"*Viens,*" Engel said, scraping back her chair. "*Allons. Viens marcher avec moi, j'ai des choses à te dire.*"

If she had been about to cart me off to prison, I don't think I could have refused— Come for a walk, I've got things to tell you? No choice.

I stood up again in Engel's cloud of smoke—hadn't even ordered anything, just as well as it always panics me to have to speak French to strangers. Engel patted the thick wad of paper folded next to her ashtray, reminding me. I picked it up and shoved it in my jacket pocket along with Käthe's ID.

It was midafternoon, streets not too busy, and Engel clicked into English almost right away—popping back into French only when we passed anybody. It's dead weird talking to her in English. She sounds like a Yank. Her accent is American and she's pretty fluent. Suppose Penn did tell me she'd been to university in Chicago.

We came around the corner of the back lane and into the Place des Hirondelles, the town hall square, full of armored vehicles and bored-looking sentries.

"I've got most of an hour," Engel said. "My dinner break. Not here, though."

I nodded and followed. She kept talking the whole time— we must have looked dead casual, a couple of chums having a walk and a smoke together. She doesn't wear a uniform—she's just an employee, she doesn't even have a rank. We walked across the cobbles in front of the town hall.

"She was crossing the street, right here, and she looked the wrong way." Engel blew out a fierce cloud of smoke. "What a stupid place to make a mistake like that, right in the middle of La Place des Hirondelles! There is *always* someone watching here—the town hall on one side and the Gestapo on the other."

"It was the Thibauts' van, wasn't it?" I said miserably. "The van that nearly hit her." A French van full of French chickens, that's what she'd said, in the first few pages she wrote.

"I don't know. The van was gone by the time I got here. I'm sure that driver didn't want to get tangled up in an arrest. All Ormaie looks the other way when there's a beating in the Place des Hirondelles—another Jew dragged out of hiding, or some idiot throwing manure at the office windows."

She glanced up at the offending windows—no dead bodies hanging there this week, thank goodness.

"She put up a hell of a fight, your friend," Engel said. "She bit a policeman. They got me to come and chloroform her, to knock her out, you know? There were four officers holding her down when I came running across the square with the chloroform, and she was still struggling. She tried to bite me, too. When the fumes finally overwhelmed her it was like watching a light go out—"

"I know. I know."

We were out of the square now. We turned to look at each other at exactly the same moment. Her eyes are amazing.

"We've turned this place into a real shit-hole," she said. "There were roses in that square when I was first sent here. Now it's nothing but mud and trucks. I think of her *every single time* I cross those cobbles, three times a day. I hate it." She looked away. "Come on. We can walk along the riverfront for about half a kilometer. Have you been?"

"No."

"It's still pretty."

She lit another cigarette. It was her third in about five minutes. Can't imagine how she manages to afford them all or even where she gets them—women are no longer allowed to buy cigarettes in Ormaie.

"I've chloroformed people before. It's something they expect of me, part of my job—I'm a chemist, I studied pharmaceuticals in America. But I've never despised myself so much as I did that day—she was so small and—"

She stumbled over her words and I had to bite the inside of my cheeks to keep from crying.

"So fierce, so *beautiful*, it was like breaking a hawk's wings, stopping up a clear spring with bricks—digging up roses to make a space to park your tank. Pointless and ugly. She was just—blazing with life and defiance one moment, then the next moment nothing but a senseless shell lying on her face in the gutter—"

"I KNOW," I whispered.

She glanced over at me curiously, frowning, sweeping my face with her sharp, pale eyes.

"Do you so?"

"She was my *best friend*," I said through my teeth.

Anna Engel nodded. "*Ja*, I know. Ach, you must hate me."

"No. No, I'm sorry. Tell me. Please."

"Here's the river," Anna said, and we crossed another street. There was a railing all along the riverbank and we stood leaning against it. Once there were elm trees lining both sides of the Poitou here—nothing but stumps now, because over the last three years they've all been cut down for firewood. But she was right—the row of historic houses on the opposite bank is still pretty.

Anna took a deep breath and spoke again.

"When she passed out I turned her over so I could check to see if she was armed, and she was clutching her balled-up silk scarf in her fist. She must have been clinging to it all through the battle, and when she lost consciousness her fingers went lax. I wasn't supposed to search her properly, that's someone else's job, but I wondered what she'd been protecting so doggedly in her closed fist—a suicide tablet, maybe—and I lifted the scarf out of her open hand—"

She held her own palm out against the railing, demonstrating.

"On her palm there was a smear of ink. On the scarf was the perfectly reversed imprint of an Ormaie Town Hall archive reference number. She'd written the number on her palm and tried to rub it out with the scarf when she was caught.

"I spat on the scarf—as though in contempt of her, you understand?—and wadded it into a ball, which I pressed back into her hand. But I rubbed the damp silk hard against her palm to blot out the numbers and closed her limp fingers around it, and all anyone ever found there was an ink-stained wad of cloth and *no one ever asked her about it* because she'd been filling out forms in the ration office just before she'd been caught, under the pretence of an errand for some made-up elderly grandmother, and her fingers were covered with ink anyway."

A flight of hopeful pigeons settled on the pavement

around our feet. I am always so amazed at the way they flare and touch down—never a bounce or a prang. No one teaches them, they do it instinctively. Flying rats, but how beautifully they touch down.

"How did you know what she wanted the number for?" I asked at last.

"She told me," Anna said.

"No."

"She told me. At the end, after she'd finished. She was writing nonsense. I took hold of her pen to stop her, and she let go without a fight. She was tired. We'd worn her down. She looked up at me without hope—there'd be no more excuses now, no more reprieves. Ferber's orders are all sup-posed to be cloaked in secrecy, but we both knew what he'd tell von Linden to do with her. Where they'd send her."

Anna hit the back of her hand lightly against the railing for emphasis and demonstrated with her cigarette, holding it as though it were a pen.

"In the palm of my own hand I wrote: 72 B4 CdB."

She took a drag on the cigarette-pen, steadying herself.

"She was the only one who could see it. Before the ink dried I closed my fingers and smeared the figures to an illeg-ible blur. I picked up the pages she'd finished with and shuffled them together.

"'That's *mine*,' she said.

"I knew she wasn't talking about the pile of loose paper and card I was stacking. She was talking about the archive ref-erence I'd written in my hand.

"'What use is it to you?' I asked.

"'No use,' she answered. 'Not anymore. But if I could ...'

"'What would you do with it?' I asked quietly. 'What should *I* do with it?'

"She narrowed her eyes like a cornered rat. 'Set fire to it

and blow this place to blazes. That would be the best thing to do with it.'

"I held her stack of paper tight against my chest. Her instructions. She looked up at me with that challenging, accusing squint, you know?

"'Anna the Avenging Angel,' she said, and then she laughed at me. She *laughed*. She said, 'Well, it's your problem now.'"

Anna threw her finished cigarette into the Poitou and lit another.

"You should go home, Käthe," she said suddenly. "This English girl who sells motorbikes to Jews, this Maddie Brodatt—she'll get you in trouble. You should go home to Alsace tomorrow, if you can, and let Maddie take her own chances."

Get Käthe out of the picture before anything happens—that makes sense. It'll be far safer for the Thibauts. Although I hate to go back into hiding. Tomorrow night I'll be back in the barn loft, and it's even colder there now than it was in October.

"What about you?" I asked.

"I'm going back to Berlin. I applied for a transfer weeks ago, when we started interrogating her and that pathetic French kid. *God*." She shuddered, smoking furiously. "What shitty jobs they give me. Ravensbrück and Ormaie. At least when I used to requisition pharmaceuticals for Natzweiler I didn't have to see what they did with them. Anyway, I'm only here till Christmas now."

"You might be safer here. We're bombing Berlin," I said. "We've been bombing it for nearly two weeks."

"*Ja*, I know," she said. "We listen to the BBC too. The Berlin Blitz. Well, we probably deserve it."

"I don't think anyone deserves it, really."

She turned suddenly and gave me a hard look with those pale, glass-green eyes. "Except the Castle of Butchers, right?"

"What do *you* think?" I challenged angrily.

She shrugged and turned to head back to the Place des Hirondelles. She was out of time.

You know who she reminded me of—this is crazy. She reminded me of Eva Seiler.

Not of Julie normally, not really, but of Julie when she was angry. Made me think of her telling me the story of her mock interrogation under SOE training, in flat violation of the Official Secrets Act—the only time I can ever remember her chain smoking the way Engel does, and swearing like a dockworker. *"And six hours later I knew I couldn't take it anymore, but I was just* damned *if I'd give in and say my name. So I pretended to faint and they all panicked and went running for a doctor. Bloody fucking bastards."*

Engel and I didn't say much on the way back. She offered me another cigarette, and I had a moment of rebellion.

"You never gave any to Julie."

"Never gave any to Julie!" Engel gave an astonished bark of laughter. "I damn well gave her half my salary in cigarettes, greedy little Scottish savage! She nearly bankrupted me. Smoked her way through all five years of your pilot's career!"

"She never said! She never even hinted! Not once!"

"What do you think would have happened to her," Engel said coolly, "if she had written this down? What would have happened to me?"

She held out the offered cigarette.

I took it.

We walked quietly for a while—two chums having a smoke together. Aye, right, miss.

"How did you get Julie's story?" I asked suddenly.

"Von Linden's landlady did it for me. He had it at the

desk in his room and while he was out she dropped the whole thing into a bag of linens to be washed. Told him she'd used it to light the kitchen fire—it *does* look like a pile of rubbish, all those damned recipe cards and the scratched-out forms."

"He *believed* that?" I asked, astonished.

She shrugged. "No choice. She'll suffer for it—milk and eggs cut to a limited supply strictly for her lodgers—the whole family under curfew in their own house, so they can't sit up in the evening, bedtime straight after supper. She has to do all last night's dishes in the morning before she makes breakfast for the guests. The children have all been strapped."

"Oh NO!" I burst out.

"They've got off lightly. The children could have been taken away. Or the woman sent to prison. But von Linden's a bit soft on children."

I'd left my bicycle in a street leading to the square. Just as I was taking hold of the handlebars, Anna put her hand over mine. She pressed something heavy and cold and thin into my palm.

It is a key.

"They asked me to bring some soap to scrub her up with when she had that interview," Anna said. "Something scented and pretty. I had some I'd gotten in America, you know how you save things sometimes, and I managed to make a print in it of the key for the service door at the back. This is a new one. I think you have everything you need now."

I squeezed her hand fiercely.

"*Danke*, Anna."

"Take care, Käthe."

At that moment, as though she'd called him up by saying his name, Amadeus von Linden himself turned the corner of the street, walking toward the Place des Hirondelles.

"*Guten Tag*, Fräulein Engel," he said cordially, and she

dropped her cigarette and crushed it out with her foot and straightened her back and her coat collar all in a rush of practiced panic. I dropped my cigarette too—seemed the right thing to do. She said something to him about me—she linked arms with me quickly, as though we were old chums, and I heard her say Käthe's name, and the Thibauts'. Introducing me, probably. He held out his hand.

I stood there absolutely frozen for about five seconds.

"Hauptsturmführer von Linden," Anna prompted gravely.

I put the key in my coat pocket with the architect's drawings and my forged ID.

"Hauptsturmführer von Linden," I repeated, and shook hands with him, smiling like a lunatic.

I've never had a "mortal enemy." I've never known what it meant, even. Something out of Sherlock Holmes and Shakespeare. How can my whole being, my whole life up to this point, be matched to one man in deadly combat?

He stood gazing through me, distracted by his own colossal problems. It never occurred to him that I could tell him the secret coordinates of the Moon Squadron's airfield, or give him the names of half a dozen Resistance operatives here in his own city, or that I was planning to send his entire administration up in flames in five days. It never occurred to him I was in every way his enemy, his opponent, I am *everything* he is battling against, I am British and Jewish, in the ATA I am a woman doing a man's work at a man's rate of pay, and my work is to deliver the aircraft that will destroy his regime. It never occurred to him that I knew he'd watched and made notes while my best friend sat tied to a chair in her underwear having holes burnt in her wrists and throat, that I knew he'd commanded it, that I *knew* that in spite of his own misgivings he'd followed orders like a coward and shipped her off to be used as an experimental lab rat until her heart collapsed—it never occurred to him that now he was looking at his master, at the one person in all the world who held his fate right between her palms—me, in patched hand-me-downs and untrimmed hair and idiot smile—and that my hatred for him is pure and black and unforgiving. And that I don't believe in God, but if I did, *if I did*, it would be the God of Moses, angry and demanding and OUT FOR REVENGE, and

It doesn't matter whether I feel sorry for him or not. It was Julie's job and now it's mine.

He said something polite to me, his drawn face neutral. I glanced at Anna, who nodded once.

"*Ja, mein Hauptsturmführer,*" I said through clenched teeth. Anna gave me a sharp kick in the ankle and leaped in to make an excuse on my behalf. I put my hand in my pocket and felt the crackle of thick paper seventy years old, and the new key weighing heavy in the seam of the threadbare woven wool.

They nodded to me and walked on together. Poor Anna. I liked her very much.

Käthe's gone back to Alsace and I'm waiting for the moon again—everything in place and we've had confirmation of a bomber flypast planned for Sat. night—whether or not Op. Verity is successful they're sending a Lysander for me, at the field I found, on Sunday or Monday—all of it weather permitting and, of course, assuming we can collect the Rosalie. Jolly difficult to sleep and when I do I just have nightmares about flying burning planes with faulty chokes, being forced to cut Julie's throat with Etienne's pocketknife, etc. If I wake up yelling three times a night there's not much point in trying to hide. I am flying alone.

Burning burning burning burning—

Behead me or hang me
That will never fear me
I'll burn Auchindoon
Ere my life leave me

Ormaie is still on fire in my head. But I am in England. I am back in England.

You know—perhaps I will be court-martialed. Perhaps I will be tried for murder and hanged. But all I feel is *relief—* relief—as though I've been underwater and breathing through a straw for the last two months, and now I have my head in the air again. Gulping in long, sweet lungfuls of it, cold damp December air, smelling of petrol and coal smoke and freedom.

The irony is, I'm not free. I am under house arrest here in The Cottage at the Moon Squadron aerodrome. I am locked in my usual bedroom, the one I used to share with Julie, and I have a guard beneath my window, too. Don't care—feels like freedom. If they hang me they will do it cleanly, break my neck instantly, and I will deserve it. They won't make me betray anyone. They won't make me watch it happening to anyone else. They won't incinerate my body and turn it into soap. They'll make sure Grandad knows what happened.

Julie's Bloody Machiavellian Intelligence Officer has been sent for so he can interview me. I trust he will do it without resorting to a soldering iron and ice water and pins.

Cups of tea, perhaps. I dread my interrogation for a number of reasons, but I'm not afraid of it.

Can't believe how safe I feel here. Don't care if I *am* a prisoner. Just feel *so safe*.

INCIDENT REPORT № 2

Successful sabotage and destruction of Gestapo Headquarters, Château de Bordeaux Building, Ormaie, France—11 Dec. 1943

My reports are so rubbish.

I know the Allied Forces are planning a proper invasion of Occupied Europe with tanks and planes and gliders full of commandos, but when I think of France being liberated I picture an avenging army arriving on bicycles. That is how we all came into Ormaie on Saturday night, all of us from different directions, all with our baskets and panniers crammed with homemade bombs. The sirens didn't go till after curfew and we all did a *lot* of nervous skulking—I bet there was an explosive bicycle behind every single newspaper kiosk in Ormaie—I myself lay underneath a lorry for at least two hours with one of Mitraillette's mates. Thank goodness for Jamie's boots.

We had to blow the back gate open—bit of a risk, but there was no one about once the air raid was under way, and of course we had the key to let ourselves in after that. It was the blasted *dogs* I was dreading coming face-to-face with more than anything else. Poor old dogs, not really their fault. I needn't have worried, as Mitraillette was merciless.

I feel like I should write in objective detail. But there's not much to report. We were fast and efficient, we knew exactly where to go—we operated in teams of 2 or 3 and each team had its own specific section and assignment—shoot the dogs, unlock the doors, corral the prisoners, unload the bombs.

Get the hell out. I'd say we were in and out in half an hour. Certainly no more than three quarters of an hour—not too many prisoners to release, as it's not technically a prison—17 in all. No women. But—

I did this on purpose, I assigned myself and my partner to free whoever was in Julie's cell. I hadn't really thought about what it would mean to have to walk through that interrogation room it is attached to—

Thankfully there was no one there, but *oh*—I can hardly bear to think about it. *How it stank.* It makes me retch just remembering. We walked in and it hit us in the face and for a moment I couldn't do anything except gasp and try not to be sick, and the French lad with me staggered a bit and grabbed me to support himself. Of course we were operating by the light of electric torches, so we couldn't really see anything— dim outlines of institutional furniture, steel chairs and tables and a couple of cabinets, nothing obviously sinister, but *oh*, it was the most sick-making, hellish stench I've ever breathed— like a full privy but also ammonia and rotten meat and burnt hair and vomit and—no, it was *indescribable* and it's making me want to throw up again writing about it. It wasn't till afterward that I even thought about Julie having to live with that smell for eight weeks—no wonder they scrubbed her up before letting her meet Penn—anyway we didn't think about *anything* but getting out of there as fast as we could without suffocating. Pulled our coats up over our noses and got to work on the door of Julie's cell, and we dragged its bewildered inhabitant out with us through that horrible room and into the corridor.

The man we'd rescued didn't understand when we talked to him in French. He turned out to be *Jamaican*—a rear gunner in the RAF, shot down last week—perhaps they'd been hoping to get Allied invasion plans out of him? He's in good shape, they hadn't got to work on him yet, and though he'd barely eaten for a week he managed to carry out a lad whose knees had been broken—

He is a lovely man, the Jamaican, and he is here. Well, I don't think he's here in The Cottage, I think he's been sent off to the proper RAF aerodrome, but I mean that he flew back to England with me. Hid with me, too, in the Thibauts' barn. He is from Kingston and has three kiddies, all girls. He followed me at a trot down the grand staircase of that dreadful, ruined hotel, with the silent, suffering boy whose legs were broken clinging to his back—me with an electric torch in one hand and Paul's Colt .32 in the other, navigating by a memorized map as usual.

We all met to count up everyone in the courtyard where the guillotine is. Last one out turned the generator back on— we had attached a timer to it. Once it was on we had twenty minutes. A couple of Lancasters were still circling overhead, daring the searchlights, and the night was noisy with half-hearted flak—a lot of the antiaircraft guns are manned by local lads, conscripted to beef up the Occupation army, and their hearts aren't really in it when they fire at Allied planes. Twenty minutes to get out of the Place des Hirondelles, and perhaps another hour to get into hiding before the all-clear.

Had to find someone close by to take the injured kid, Mitraillette managed that, and the rest of us scarpered on bicycles and on foot. My Jamaican rear gunner and I took a tortuous route over a series of garden walls to avoid the checkpoint on the road. But we were outside Ormaie and cycling tandem, me standing on the bar at the back and him pedaling because he was so much heavier than me, when the explosion came.

It gave us such a shock we toppled over. We didn't feel it—we were just startled witless by the bang. For a couple of minutes I sat in the road laughing like a maniac, full moon and fire lighting everything, and then my rescued rear gunner very gently made me get back on the bicycle and we set off again with Ormaie at our backs.

"Which way, Miss Kittyhawk?"

"Left at the fork. Just call me Kittyhawk."

"Is that your name?"

"No."

"Oh," he said. "You are not French, either."

"No, I'm English."

"What you doing in France, Kittyhawk?"

"Same as you—I'm a shot-down airman."

"You are pulling my leg!"

"I am not. I am a First Officer with the Air Transport Auxiliary. And I bet no one believes you, either, when you tell them you're a rear gunner in the Royal Air Force."

"You're right about that, gal," he said with feeling. "It's a white man's world."

I held on tight around his waist, and hoped he wasn't as much of a lech as Paul or I would have to shoot him, too, when we were stuck in the Thibauts' barn together by ourselves.

"What's troubling you, Kittyhawk?" he asked softly. "What's making you cry so hard? Good riddance to that place."

I was hanging on and leaning on his shoulder now, sobbing into his back. "They had my best friend in there—you were in her cell. She was there for two months."

He pedaled silently, digesting this. At last he said, "She die there?"

"No," I said. "Not there. But she's dead now anyway."

Suddenly I could feel through his jacket that he was crying too, shaking a little with silent, muffled sobs, just like me.

"My best mate's dead too," he said softly. "He was our pilot. Flew that plane into the ground—kept it flying straight and level so the rest of us could bail out after we were hit."

Oh—only now that I am writing it down, only now I see that's exactly what I did, too.

Funny—it seemed the most heroic thing in the world when he told me about his friend, dead amazing that anyone could be that brave and selfless. But I didn't feel heroic when I did it—just too scared to jump.

We rode through the moonlight with the flames of Ormaie behind us, and neither one of us stopped crying until we put the bicycle away.

We slept back-to-back in that tiny loft space in the old half-timbered barn for two nights—well, one and a half nights, really—played 21 for hours with a deck of dreadful obscene playing cards I'd nicked from one of Etienne Thibaut's hidey-holes. On Monday, yesterday, last night I mean, we got collected by the rose lady's chauffeur and taken to collect the Rosalie for our trip to the pickup airfield.

This was the third time the Thibauts all hugged and kissed me good-bye—Amélie creating a fuss, Maman trying to make a present of a dozen silver spoons—I just *couldn't*! And Mitraillette with tears in her eyes, first I've ever seen her choked up like that over something that didn't involve blood.

She didn't come with us this time. I hope—

I wish I knew how to pray for them all. I just wish I knew.

The Rosalie was waiting for us in the driveway of the big house on the Poitou riverbank. It was still light when we got there, so as not to get the chauffeur in trouble, and while they were putting the other car away the old woman with the white hair like Julie's took me by the hand, just as she'd done that first terrible day after, and led me without a word through her cold garden.

Down along the river was a pile of roses, a *huge* pile of damask roses, the autumn-flowering ones. She'd cut every single rose left in her garden and piled them there.

"They let us bury everyone at last," she told me. "Most are up there by the bridge. But I was so angry about those poor girls, those two lovely young girls left lying there in the dirt for four days with the rats and the crows at them! It's not right. It is not *natural*. So when we buried the others I had the men bring the girls here—"

Julie is buried in her great-aunt's rose garden, wrapped in her grandmother's first Communion veil, and covered in a mound of damask roses.

Of course that is the name of her circuit, too—Damask.

I still don't know her great-aunt's name. How is that possible? I knew it was her all suddenly, it just came to me in a flash—when she said that she'd used the veils that she and her sister had worn at their first Communion, I remembered that Julie's grandmother was from Ormaie, and then I remembered the great-aunt story, and what she'd said to me about sharing a terrible burden, and it all clicked and I knew who she was.

But I didn't tell her—I didn't have the heart to tell her. She didn't seem to know it was Julie—of course Katharina Habicht would have kept her real identity hidden to avoid compromising anyone. I suppose I should have said something. But I just *couldn't do it*.

Now I am in tears *again*.

Have heard a car pull up, so they may be sending for me soon, but I want to finish telling about getting out of France—which will probably also make me cry—what's new?

Even started off blubbing just listening to the radio message that let us know they were going to pick me up that night: "After a while, all children tell the truth"—in French it's "*Assez bientôt, tous les enfants disent la vérité.*" I am sure they stuck the word *vérité* in there on purpose, but they couldn't have known it would make me think of the last page Julie wrote—*I have told the truth*, over and over.

The whole routine is so familiar now, like a recurring dream. Dark field, flashing lights, Lysander wings against the moon. Except it gets *colder* each time. No mud this time, despite last week's rain—ground's all frozen solid. Dead smooth landing, the plane didn't go 'round even once—I like to think this is partly down to *my* excellent field selection—made the trade-off of goods and passengers in just under fifteen minutes. *That's how it should be done.*

My Jamaican rear gunner had already climbed on board, and I had one hand on the ladder to follow him up when the pilot yelled down at me, "OI, KITTYHAWK! You going to fly us out of here?"

Who else but Jamie Beaufort-Stuart—just—who else?

"Come on, swap seats with me," he shouted. "You flew yourself here, you can fly yourself home."

Can't believe he made the offer and I can't believe I took him up on it—all so wrong. Should have been retested after the crash-landing, at least.

"But you didn't want me to fly OUT in the first place!" I bawled.

"I was worried about you being in France, not worried about your flying! Bad enough one of you was going, without losing you BOTH. Anyway, if we get fired on you're better at crash-landings than I am—"

"Court-martial, they'll court-martial both of us—"

"What tosh, you're a CIVILIAN! You've not been in danger of court-martial since you left the WAAFs in 1941. The worst the ATA can do is dismiss you, and they'll do that anyway if they're going to do it. COME UP!"

The engine was idling. He had the parking brake on and there was just about room for us to change places once he'd hopped up onto the edge of the cockpit—didn't even have to adjust the seat as we are exactly the same height. He gave me his flying helmet.

I couldn't bear it. I told him.

"I killed her. I shot her."

"*What?*"

"It was me. I shot Julie."

For a moment it seemed like there was nothing else that mattered or had any meaning in the whole world. All there was in the world was me in the pilot's seat of that Lysander and Jamie perched on the edge of the cockpit with his hand on the sliding canopy, no noise but the idle roar of the engine, no light anywhere but the three small runway flares and the moon glinting against the dials. Finally Jamie asked a brief question.

"Did you mean to?"

"Yes. She asked me to—I couldn't—*couldn't* let her down."

After another long Lysander moment, Jamie said abruptly, "Now don't start weeping, Kittyhawk! Court-martial or not, you have to fly the plane now, because I don't trust myself quite, not after that confession." He managed to unwedge himself from the edge of the cockpit and swung lightly from the wing strut to the access ladder at the back. I watched him climb into the rear cockpit and after a moment heard him introducing himself to my Jamaican friend.

FLY THE PLANE, MADDIE

I slid the canopy shut and began to run through the familiar preflight checks.

Then just as I started to put power on, this hand on my shoulder.

Just like that—nothing said. He just put his hand through the bulkhead, exactly as she'd done, and squeezed my shoulder. He has very strong fingers.

And he kept his hand there the whole way home, even when he was reading the map and giving me headings.

So I am not flying alone now after all.

I am running out of paper. This notebook of Etienne's is nearly full. I have an idea what to do with all of it, though.

With that in mind I don't think I'll put down the Machiavellian Intelligence Officer's name. Didn't Julie say he introduced himself with a number at her interview? He introduced himself as himself this afternoon. Awkward to write about it without using a name, though. John Balliol, perhaps, that's a good ironic name, the miserable Scottish king William Wallace lost his life defending. Sir John Balliol. I'm getting good at this. Perhaps I should join the Special Operations Executive after all.

Oh, Maddie-lass, NOT IN A MILLION YEARS.

My interview with Sir John Balliol had to be in the debriefing room—I suppose they do briefings there as well as debriefings, but that's what everybody calls it. It had to be there, didn't it, because it had to be done properly. Sergeant Silvey took me down. I know Silvey is soft on me, he always has been, and I think he is brokenhearted over Julie, but he was dead stiff and formal escorting me to my interview—awkward, you know? He didn't like to be doing it. He didn't like it that I was locked in, either. Argued about it with the squadron leader. Doesn't matter—it's all down to protocol in the end, and the bottom line is that I shouldn't have taken that plane to France in the first place.

So I got marched down to the debriefing room under guard, and as I walked in I was suddenly shamefully aware of what a ragamuffin I am *always*—like a Glaswegian evacuee!—still wearing the French photographer's wife's climbing trousers and Etienne Thibaut's threadbare jacket and Jamie's boots, the same clothes I've been wearing for the past week and a good deal of the past two months and, by the way, the same clothes that I was wearing when I blew the Ormaie city center to blazes. No feminine wiles to fall back on—I stepped into the whitewashed stone room with my heart going berserk against my ribs like a detonating engine. The room was exactly as it had been the first time he met me there nearly two years ago—two hard chairs pulled close to the electric heater, pot of tea under a cozy on the desk. It didn't smell like the interrogation room in Ormaie, but it was impossible not to think of it.

"I'm afraid this may take some time," Balliol said apologetically, holding out his hand to me. "I trust you managed to get some sleep last night?"

He didn't have his specs on. That must be what caught me out—he just looked like anybody. Then the way he offered his hand to me. I was instantly in Ormaie again, in the cobbled street with the new key and the old plans in my pocket and my heart full of hatred and bloody-mindedness—and I shook his hand and answered through my teeth, *"Ja, mein Hauptsturmführer."*

He looked quite startled and I am sure I went red as a tomato. OH MADDIE WHAT A WAY TO BEGIN.

"Sorry—sorry!" I gasped. *"Je suis désolée—"* Unbelievable, I am still trying to speak French to people.

"Not quite out of the trenches yet, are we?" he remarked softly. With light fingertips against my back he guided me to one of the chairs. "Tea, Silvey," he directed, and Sergeant Silvey quietly served up and let himself out.

Balliol's glasses were lying on the desk. He put them on and perched against the edge of the desk holding his teacup in its saucer, and his hands were so steady I had to put my own cup on the floor—couldn't have bone china rattling in my lap while he stood there pinning me down with those huge magnified eyes. Crikey—Julie quite fancied him. Can't imagine why. He scares me to *death*.

"What are you afraid of, Maddie?" he asked quietly. None of this "Flight Officer Beaufort-Stuart" nonsense.

I am not going to say it again. There is no one else I need say it to. This was the last time—

"I killed Julie. Verity, I mean. I shot her myself."

He put his own cup down on the desk with a clatter and stared at me. *"I beg your pardon?"*

"I'm afraid of being tried for murder."

I looked away from him, at the drain in the floor. This was the place where the German spy tried to strangle Eva Seiler. I shivered, actually shivered, when I realized that. I have never seen such hideous bruises in my entire life, not before or since. Julie *was* tortured in this room.

When I looked back at Balliol he was still leaning against the desk, his shoulders slumped, spectacles pushed back on his head, pinching his nose between his fingers as though he had a migraine.

"I'm afraid of hanging," I added miserably.

"*Great Scott*, girl," he snapped, and jammed the specs back down over his eyes. "You'll have to tell me what happened. I confess you have—startled me, but as I'm not wearing my judge's wig at the moment, let's have it."

"They were transporting her in a bus full of prisoners to one of their concentration camps and we tried to stop it—"

He interrupted plaintively, "Must it be the murder first? Go back a bit." He peered at me with an anxious frown. "*Mea culpa*, forgive me. Unfortunate choice of words. You didn't say it *was* murder, did you? Only, you're worried others might see it that way.... Possibly a mistake, or an accident. Well, out with it, my child. Start from the beginning, when you landed in France."

I told him everything—well, almost everything. There is one thing I didn't tell him about, and that is this big stack of paper I have been humping around in my flight bag—everything Julie's written, everything I've written, all her scraps of hotel stationery and sheet music and my Pilot's Notes and Etienne's exercise book—I didn't tell him there's a written record.

I'm amazed at what a smooth liar I've become. Or, not a liar exactly—I didn't lie to him. The story I gave him isn't like a pullover full of holes, dropped stitches that will easily unravel when you start to poke at them. More like—slip one, knit one, pass slipped stitch over. Between Penn and Engel there was enough information that I didn't need to mention I'd got Julie's written confession up in my bedroom. Because I'm jolly well not turning it over to some filing clerk in London. It is *mine*.

And my own notes—well, I need them so I can make a proper report for the Accident Committee.

It *did* take a long time, the telling. Sergeant Silvey brought us another pot of tea and then another. At the end Balliol assured me quietly, "You won't hang."

"But I'm responsible."

"No more than I." He looked away. "Tortured and sent off to be used as a lab specimen—dear God. That lovely, clever girl. I may as well—I am *wretched*. No, you'll not hang."

He drew a long, shaking breath. "'Killed in action' was what the first wire told us, and 'killed in action' the verdict shall remain," he said firmly. "She *was* killed in action by this account, and given the number of people who died under fire that night I don't think we need give out details of who shot whom. Your story shall not leave this building. You've not told anyone here what happened, have you?"

"I told her brother," I said. "And anyway, you bug this room. People listen through the shutters to the kitchen. It'll have to come out."

He gazed at me thoughtfully, shaking his head.

"Is there anything about us you *don't* know, Kittyhawk? We'll keep your secrets and you keep ours. 'Careless talk costs lives.'"

In France it really does. It's not as funny as it sounds.

"Look, Maddie, let's break for half an hour—I'm afraid there are a beastly lot of details I'm meant to grill you about, which we've not even touched on yet, and I feel I've rather lost my composure."

He pulled out a dotted silk handkerchief, turned aside again, and wiped his nose. When he faced me once more he gave me a hand to raise me to my feet. "Also, I think you need a nap."

What did Julie say about me—I am trained to react positively to orders from people in authority. I went back to my room and fell soundly asleep for twenty minutes, and dreamed Julie was teaching me to foxtrot in the kitchen at Craig Castle. Of course she did teach me to foxtrot, though it was at one of the Maidsend hops and not in the kitchen at Craig Castle, but the dream was *so real* that when I woke up I couldn't at first figure out where I was. And then it was like being kicked in the head with desolation all over again.

Except now instead of "The Last Time I Saw Paris" I have got "Dream a Little Dream of Me" stuck playing in my mind over and over, which is what the band was playing when we were dancing at Maidsend. I don't mind at all, as I am *so sick* of "The Last Time I Saw Paris." If I ever hear either tune being played in some public place I am sure I will immediately start to howl.

So then Balliol and I had another session and it got a bit more technical, me having to remember names and numbers I didn't know I knew—code names for every single Resistance agent I'd been introduced to, Balliol tallying them against notes in a little calfskin notebook of his own, and the location of any arms or supplies or *cachettes* I knew about. There was a moment where I was bent over with my elbows on my knees, and I was pulling at my hair until the roots hurt, trying to come up with accurate map coordinates for the Thibauts' barn and the rose woman's garage. It dawned on me I'd been sitting there tearing my hair like that for the past twenty minutes, and suddenly I got mad.

I raised my head with a jerk and asked furiously, "*Why?* Why do you *care* whether I can come up with the coordinates out of my head? I can *make up coordinates* the way Julie made up code! Give me a map and I'll point it out, you don't *need* me to do this! What do you *really* want, you bloody Machiavellian BASTARD?"

He was silent for a minute.

"I've been asked to test you a bit," he confessed at last. "Turn up the heat, see how you respond. I'm not honestly sure what to do with you. The Air Ministry wants to take away your license and the Special Operations Executive wants to recommend you for a George Medal. They'd like you to stay with them."

NOT IN A MILLION YEARS.

But, but. My success as an unofficial agent for the SOE will cancel out my flight to France as an unofficial pilot for the RAF. I won't get a medal, and I jolly well don't want or deserve one, but I won't lose my license, either—I mean, you could say I've already lost it myself, but they'll reissue it. They won't take it away. They won't even take away my job. *Oh—* now this really is good reason to blub, tears of relief. They will let me fly again. I will have to go up before the Accident Committee, but that will just be about the actual accident—as if I were one of the Moon Squadron itself, pranging my own plane. I won't be charged with anything else.

And the Air Transport Auxiliary will be ferrying planes to France, come the invasion. Not long now—spring. I will go back. I know I will go back.

I am exhausted. Except my nap and for a couple of hours after we landed I haven't slept since Sunday night, and it's Tuesday evening now. One more thing, though, before bed—

Balliol has given me a copy of a message they have just received and decoded from the Damask W/T operator.

```
REPORT HEAVY ALLIED BOMBARDMENT
OVERHEAD ORMAIE NIGHT OF SAT 11
DEC AM SUN 12 DEC SUCCESSFUL OP
DESTROYING CDB AKA GESTAPO REGIONAL
HQ NO KNOWN ARRESTS ALL WELL SVP
PASS MSG TO KITTYHAWK SAY ISOLDES
FATHER IS FOUND SHOT THROUGH HEAD
BELIEVED SUICIDE
```

"Who is Isolde's father?" Balliol asked when he gave it to me.

"The Gestapo officer who—who questioned Verity. And sentenced her."

"Suicide," Balliol said softly. "Another wretched man."

"Another wretched girl," I corrected.

Those ripples in the pond again—it just doesn't stop in one place. All those lives that have touched mine so briefly—most of them I don't even know their real names, like Julie's great-aunt and the driver of the Rosalie. And some of them I don't know anything other than their names, like Benjamin Zylberberg, the Jewish doctor, and Esther Lévi, whose flute music Julie was given to write on. And some of them I met briefly and liked and won't ever see again, like the vicar's son who flew Spitfires and Anna Engel and the Jamaican gunner.

And then there is Isolde von Linden, at school in Switzerland, who doesn't know yet that her father has just shot himself.

Isolde still in the realm of the sun, in the shimmering daylight still, Isolde—

I have kept the matchbook that her father gave Amélie.

I've had a bath and borrowed a pair of pajamas from the pretty First Aid Nursing Yeomanry driver who never says anything. Goodness knows what she thinks of me. I am not locked in or guarded anymore. Someone is going to fly me back to Manchester tomorrow. Tonight—tonight I will sleep in this room one more time, in this bed where Julie cried herself to sleep in my arms eight months ago.

I'm going to keep her gray silk scarf. But I want Jamie to take this notebook, and my pilot's notes, and Julie's confession, and give them all to Esmé Beaufort-Stuart, because it is only right that Julie's lady mother should be told. If she wants to know, I think it is her right to know. Absolutely *Every Last Detail.*

I am back in England. I can go back to work. I haven't got the words to say how stunned and grateful I am that I have been allowed to keep my license.

But a part of me lies buried in lace and roses on a riverbank in France—a part of me is broken off forever. A part of me will always be unflyable, stuck in the climb.

Lady Beaufort-Stuart
Craig Castle
Castle Craig
Aberdeenshire

26 Dec. 1943

My darling Maddie,

Jamie has delivered your "letters"—both yours and Julie's, and I have read them. They will stay here, and be safe—the Official Secrets Act is of little consequence in a house that absorbs secrets like damp. A few more recipe cards and prescription forms tossed in amongst the teeming contents of our two libraries will surely go unnoticed.

I want to tell you what Jamie said to me as he gave me these pages:

"Maddie did the right thing."

I say so too.

Please come to see me, Maddie darling, as soon as they let you. The wee lads are all distraught with the news and you will do them good. Perhaps they will do you good, as well. They are my only consolation at the moment, and I have been fearfully busy trying to make it a "happy" Christmas for them. Ross and Jock have now lost both parents in the bombing, so perhaps I shall keep them when the war is over.

I should like to "keep" you, too, if you will let me—I mean, in my heart and as my only daughter's best friend. It would be like losing two daughters if you were to leave us now.

Please come back soon. The window is always open.

> Fly safely.
> Yr. loving,
> Esmé

P.S. Thank you for the Eterpen. It is most extraordinary—not a single word of this letter has blotted. No one will ever know how many tears I shed whilst writing it!

I do mean fly safely. And I do mean come back.

Author's Debriefing

As someone has already said, "My reports are so rubbish." I am legally bound to write this afterword, as I am legally bound to ensure that this book is not in breach of the Official Secrets Acts. This is meant to be a historical note, and it *pains* me to admit that *Code Name Verity* is fiction—that Julia Beaufort-Stuart and Maddie Brodatt are not actually real people, merely products of my adventure-obsessed brain.

But I'll try. This book started off rather simply as a portrait of an Air Transport Auxiliary pilot. Being a woman and a pilot myself, I wanted to explore the possibilities that would have been open to me during the Second World War. I'd already written a war story about a girl pilot ("Something Worth Doing" in *Firebirds Soaring*, edited by Sharyn November), but I wanted to write something longer and more accurately detailed and, above all, more plausible.

I started with research, hoping to get plot ideas, and read *The Forgotten Pilots* by Lettice Curtis. This is the definitive history of the Air Transport Auxiliary, and it's written by a woman, so it felt right and natural for my ATA pilot to be a girl. But the ATA story careened out of control when (by accident, while making dinner) I stumbled on the framework for

Code Name Verity and added in a Special Operations Executive agent.

More reading ensued—okay, I could have a pilot AND a spy, and they'd both be girls. And it would still be plausible. Because there *were* women doing these jobs. There weren't many of them. But they were real. They worked and suffered and fought just as hard as any man. Many of them died.

Bear in mind that despite my somewhat exhaustive quest for historical accuracy, this book is not meant to be a good history but rather *a good story*. So there is one major leap of fictional faith the reader has to grant me, and that is Maddie's flight to France. Women ATA pilots were not allowed to fly to Europe until well after the invasion of Normandy, when German-occupied territory was safely back in Allied hands. (When Maddie is called the "only shot-down Allied air-woman outside Russia," it is a reference to Russian women who were actually combat pilots during the war.) I worked very hard to construct a believable chain of events leading up to Maddie's Lysander trip to France—her trump card is really my trump card, the fact that she can authorize her own flight.

The other thing I did make up (like a certain unreliable narrator) is all the proper nouns. Most of them, anyway. My reasoning is that it is an easy way to avoid historical incongruities. For example, Oakway is a very thinly disguised Ringway (now Manchester Airport); but unlike Oakway, Ringway had no squadron on site in the winter of 1940. Maidsend is a composite of many Kentish airfields. The French city of Ormaie doesn't exist, but it's loosely based on Poitiers.

Early in my research I also planned to say here that I'd made up the specific jobs of SOE interrogator and SOE taxi pilot. But it turns out that there was an American ATA pilot, Betty Lussier, who more or less did both jobs herself at separate times during the war (though she worked for the

OSS, the Americans, not the SOE). Every time I find out the life story of another woman who was a wartime pilot or Resistance agent, I think, *You couldn't make these people up.*

I would love to go through my book page by page and document where Absolutely Every Last Detail comes from—how I found out that you can use kerosene to thin ink, or that school nurses used pen nibs to do blood tests, or where I first discovered a Jewish prescription form. Obviously I *can't* do it for Absolutely Every Last Detail, but since paper and ink are the fabric of this novel, let's talk about the BALL-POINT PEN! It was going to be very difficult to keep all my fictional writers supplied in ink, and it would be convenient to give them ballpoints. So I thought I ought to check to make sure ballpoint pens existed in 1943.

It turns out they did, but only just. The ballpoint pen was invented by László Bíró, a Hungarian journalist who fled to Argentina to escape the German occupation of Europe. In 1943 he licensed his invention to the RAF, and the first ballpoint pens were manufactured in Reading, England, by the Miles aircraft manufacturer, to supply pilots with a lasting ink supply! I had to use a sample pen in *Code Name Verity*—ballpoints weren't on the market yet. But it was *plausible*. That's all I ask—that my details be plausible. And I *love* that the ballpoint pen was first manufactured for the RAF. Who knew?

There's a real story, like this one, behind just about every detail or episode in the book. I think it was in one of Terry Deary's *Horrible History* books that I learned about the SOE agent who was caught looking the wrong way before crossing a French street. I myself nearly got killed once making the same mistake. I've also spent a couple of backbreaking afternoons clearing rocks from a runway. Even the breakdowns of the Lysander and the Citroën Rosalie are based in reality. The Green Man is a real pub, if you can find it. I didn't even make up the name of that one. But it's called something else now.

I know there must be mistakes and inaccuracies sprinkled throughout the book, but for these I beg a little poetic licence. Some of them are conscious, some are not. The code name "Verity" of the title is the most obvious to me. As far as I know, female SOE agents in France all had French girl's names as code names, and Verity is an English name. But it translates well as *vérité*—the French word for *truth*—and some of the code names for wireless operators are so random ("nurse," for example), that I've decided to stick with it. Another good example is the use of the term *Nacht und Nebel*, which refers to the Nazi policy of making certain political prisoners vanish as though into "night and fog." The term was so secret that it's highly unlikely Julie would have ever heard it. However, prisoners at the Ravensbrück concentration camp knew they were designated "NN," and by the end of 1944 they knew what it meant, too. Nelson's last words, also, are a subject of some considerable debate. But whatever he actually *said*, Hardy *did* kiss him. Where I fail in accuracy, I hope I make up for it in plausibility.

There are many people who helped to make this book complete and perfect, and they all deserve tremendous thanks. Among the unsung heroes are an enlisted trio of "cultural" and language advisers, Scottish, French, and German: Iona O'Connor, Marie-Christine Graham, and Katja Kasri, who threw themselves into their requested jobs with the enthusiasm of wartime volunteers. My husband, Tim Gatland, was my technical and flight adviser (as always); and Terry Charman of the Imperial War Museum of London vetted the manuscript for historical accuracy. Jonathan Habicht of The Shuttleworth Collection allowed me to get up close and personal with a Lysander and an Anson. Tori Tyrrell and Miriam

Roberts were indispensable first readers, and Tori actually suggested the section titles, which, obvious though they are, eluded me at first. My daughter, Sara, suggested some of the more harrowing plot twists. The book would not exist if not for the lovely Sharyn November, Senior Editor at Viking Children's Books, who originally asked me to write it; and under the orchestration of my agent, Ginger Clark, the editorial teams led by Stella Paskins at Egmont UK, Catherine Onder at Disney • Hyperion Books, and Amy Black at Doubleday Canada coaxed *Code Name Verity* into its finished form.

I also feel that I should discreetly thank a score of unnamed people whose lives are woven into mine and who have influenced me over the years: friends, family, teachers and colleagues—German, French, Polish, American, Japanese, Scottish, English—Jew and Christian—who during the global conflict of the Second World War were variously Resistance fighters, camouflage unit artists, RAF fighter pilots and USAF transport pilots, child evacuees, prisoners in American as well as German concentration camps, refugees in hiding, Hitler Youths, WAACs, soldiers and prisoners of war. LEST WE FORGET.

A Brief Bibliography

(not including road atlases, escape maps, pilots' notes, lists of RAF slang, etc.)

Air Transport Auxiliary

Books:

Curtis, Lettice. *The Forgotten Pilots: A Story of the Air Transport Auxiliary 1939–45*. Olney, UK: Nelson & Saunders, 1985. First published in 1971 by Go To Foulis.

Du Cros, Rosemary. *ATA Girl: Memoirs of a Wartime Ferry Pilot*. London: Frederick Muller, 1983.

Lussier, Betty. *Intrepid Woman: Betty Lussier's Secret War, 1942–1945*. Annapolis, Md.: Naval Institute Press, 2010.

Whittell, Giles. *Spitfire Women of World War II*. London: HarperPress, 2007.

Film:

Ferry Pilot. London: Trustees of the Imperial War Museum, 2004 (Crown Film Unit, 1941).

Museum Exhibit:

Grandma Flew Spitfires: The Air Transport Auxiliary
Exhibition and Study Centre, Maidenhead Heritage
Centre, 18 Park Street, Maidenhead, Berkshire.
http://www.atamuseum.org

Special Operations Executive

Books:

Binney, Marcus. *The Women Who Lived for Danger: The
Women Agents of SOE in the Second World War*. London:
Hodder & Stoughton, 2002.

Escott, Beryl E. *Mission Improbable: A Salute to the RAF
Women of SOE in Wartime France*. Sparkford, UK:
Patrick Stephens, 1991.

Helm, Sarah. *A Life in Secrets: The Story of Vera Atkins and the
Lost Agents of SOE*. London: Little, Brown, 2005.

SOE Secret Operations Manual. Boulder, Colo.: Paladin Press,
1993.

Verity, Hugh. *We Landed by Moonlight: Secret RAF Landings in
France 1940–1944*. London: Ian Allan, 1978.

Film:

Now It Can Be Told. London: Imperial War Museum, 2007
(RAF Film Production Unit, 1946).

Women's Auxiliary Air Force

Arnold, Gwen. *Radar Days: Wartime Memoir of a WAAF RDF
Operator*. West Sussex, UK: Woodfield Publishing, 2000.

Escott, Beryl E. *The WAAF*. Shire Publications, 2001.

France During the German Occupation

Caskie, Donald. *The Tartan Pimpernel*. Edinburgh: Berlinn, 2006 (First published in 1960 by Fontana.)

Knaggs, Bill. *The Easy Trip: The Loss of 106 Squadron Lancaster LL 975 Pommeréval 24/25th June 1944*. Perth, Scotland: Perth & Kinross Libraries, 2001.

Némirovsky, Irène. *Suite Française*. London: Vintage Books, 2007.

Maddie's Mittens

http://www.vam.ac.uk/images/image/13026-popup.html
(From *Essentials for the Forces*, scanned by the Victoria and Albert Museum, London, under "1940s Patterns to Knit" at http://www.vam.ac.uk/images/image/13069-popup.html)

ELIZABETH WEIN was born in New York City, grew up abroad, and now lives in Scotland with her husband and two children. She is an avid flyer of small planes and also holds a PhD in folklore from the University of Pennsylvania. Visit her at www.elizabethwein.com.